Scared Silent

PRAISE FOR THE TONY VALENTI THRILLERS

* *A House on Liberty Street* *

Turner hits the mark in a spellbinding, page-turning thriller featuring a worthy underdog hero and prose that tugs at the heartstrings. The author has a great sense of plot and timing. **IndieReader 4.5 Star Review**

Neil Turner unravels an ever-deepening drama that exposes the lengths one man will go to protect his family in *A House on Liberty Street*, a suspenseful and heartfelt thriller. Tapping into evocative themes of family, fatherhood, and second chances, this is a fast-paced read with a clever protagonist ducking and dodging in a classic pursuit of justice. The story-telling is casual but compelling, with memorable characters, intriguing dynamics, and an unpredictable case for readers to piece together. ...there are also touching moments of paternal wisdom and honesty that shine... *A House on Liberty Street* is a neatly penned thriller that will keep readers guessing to the very end. **Self-Publishing Review**

** Plane in the Lake **

Neil Turner's latest Tony Valenti thriller, *Plane in the Lake*, pits the no-nonsense lawyer and his fiery partner against entrenched power in this classic Chicago crime story. Lawyers and liars go hand in hand in the pearly offices of the city's underworld, as a well-to-do family's desperate attempt to cover up the truth behind their daughter's death spirals into something much more. As Valenti is faced with saving not only his firm but his family too, Turner skillfully wields an incisive pen that takes on the seemingly untouchable upper classes and shady crime families. With his trademark breezy style reminiscent of Dennis Lehane, Turner has produced another devourable thriller. **Self-Publishing Review ★★★★½**

Plane in the Lake is a satisfying blend of tense thriller and whodunit that calls into question and ultimately strengthens Tony Valenti's bonds with friends, family, and peers. The novel works on many different levels to involve readers in a puzzle that remains murky up to its surprise conclusion. It's a fine story that will keep readers (whether newcomers or prior fans of Tony's gritty streetwise style) thoroughly engrossed to the end. **D. Donovan, Senior Reviewer, Midwest Book Review**

** A Case of Betrayal **

In his third powerful Tony Valenti Thriller, *A Case of Betrayal*, author Neil Turner puts his charming and brilliant defense attorney back into the fray, where his loyalties to old friends will be tested against his passion for justice. Diving into tough subjects - from the deeply rooted racism in America to the struggles of single fatherhood - this installment stands out from other thrillers; there is real heart in this prose, as well as nuanced character development that keeps the read continually engaging. Packed with suspense, and a page turner from the start. **Self-Publishing Review ★★★★½**

** A Time for Reckoning **

"A character-driven thriller that fearlessly reveals the dark corners of human nature – misogyny, greed, violence, power, and control. Driven by strong dialogue, unpredictable twists, and more than a dash of colloquial country charm, this savagely honest novel is a stellar addition to the *Toni Valenti Thriller* series." Self-Publishing Review, ★★★★½

** Scared Silent **

"A brutal and gritty novel of survival on the merciless streets of Chicago, *Scared Silent* is a gut-wrenching ride. Given the national spotlight being recently turned towards the desperate plight of the poor, this gripping story is not only expertly penned, but also timely and fearless." **Self-Publishing Review, ★★★★★**

Scared Silent

Neil Turner

First Edition
Published by Neil Turner Books, Canada 2022

Published by Neil Turner Books 2022

Cover design by David Prendergast

Library and Archives Canada ISBN 978-1-7781279-0-8 Trade paperback

Library and Archives Canada ISBN 978-1-7781279-1-5 ePub edition

❀ Created with Vellum

PART I

1

October 20th

"Chill, dude," Spike says with a sneer. "This guy's an easy mark."

Fifteen-year-old Denzel Payton shoots Spike a sidelong look and offers up a nonchalant shrug. "I'm down with this, man."

But he isn't. He's frightened of what they're here to do; certain he's going to regret coming. He buries his hands deeper into his hoodie as they round a corner and run smack into an unseasonably chilly late-October wind. The homeless camp known as Tent Town is several blocks ahead, huddling in the shadows of a railroad viaduct on the fringes of the Southwest Chicago suburb of Cedar Heights. A gathering mist mixes with campfire smoke, picking up rays of moonlight filtering through the trees that tower above the little park. Denzel eyes the ramshackle collection of lean-tos thrown together with whatever flotsam and jetsam the impoverished residents of Tent Town were able to cobble together. A handful of tents dot the encampment.

"What's this guy's story?" Denzel asks Spike.

"Some dumbass whose granny died and left him a little bread. Dope's been flashing cash around. In a place like Tent Town, that's like an invitation to share, y'know?" Spike tucks his face deeper within the folds of his oversize hoodie. Condensation puffs out of the darkness with each word. "So we comin' for our little bit of the treasure, Denz," he adds with an easy laugh. "Hell, ever see the little girl in the Charlie Brown cartoons what says, 'I just want my fair share'? That be me."

Denzel feels a barb of regret as his thoughts turn to his own recently deceased grandmother. It doesn't seem right to steal what someone's gram left them, but he can't dwell on that kind of stuff. When Grams died of COVID, Denzel was left out in the streets on his own. Spike is all he has now—Denzel has to do whatever it takes to remain in the man's orbit.

"How do you know about this guy?" Denzel asks as they cover the final block to Tent Town.

"I get around, man. Hell, I told you a smart operator don't shit in his own sandbox, right? Only fools mess with the cutthroat motherfuckers in the city. The crowd out here is pretty mellow. Better eats in their food kitchen, too," he adds with a grin.

Spike seems to know all the angles. He hasn't answered Denzel's question, though.

"How do you know about this guy's deal?" Denzel asks again.

Spike doesn't answer. He shoots Denzel a side-eyed scowl instead. The stare sends a chill through Denzel. The man is supposedly called Spike because he once nailed someone to one of Chicago's elevated L tracks with a train coming. Probably bullshit, but it's the only name Denzel is allowed to use when referring to him. Their relationship is complicated.

Spike pokes Denzel's shoulder. "If you hafta know, I score some weed from this guy now and again. He supposedly gets a little military pension or something. Everyone out here gets a little piece of the action."

"He just gives stuff away?"

"I know, right?" Spike says with a dark chuckle. "So we just coming for our fair share. Harry might need a little persuading today if he really got himself a nice stash."

"A stash of what?"

"Just told you he come into a little bread, Denz. Listen up when I tell you shit!"

Denzel ducks his head. "Sorry, man."

"Anyway, the dumb shit bought hisself a nice tent, some new tech—Apple stuff, they say."

"Cool."

Spike gives an eye roll. "And then he waves it around. Dumb, dumb, dumb. Musta got more than just his ass blowed up in the army."

"He's a vet?"

"Sure. Got hisself all fucked up in one of them Arab sandpits."

"Guy's a *disabled* vet? Don't know how I feel about taking shit from one of them."

Spike clamps a hand on Denzel's shoulder, slows to a stop, and fixes his hard eyes on Denzel's. "Don't forget your place, Denz. You my yeah guy. *I* tell you what to think, boy!"

"Okay."

"This cracker's got money. Man, don't they *all* got money, no matter how fucked up they get? No reason we shouldn't get our cut, so stop with the bleeding-heart bullshit. You gonna come away with some nice new threads, maybe a pair of shoes, plus a little weed and some cash for a decent meal. Y'all got a problem with that?"

Denzel wants to say that he does if the stuff comes from what a disabled vet's gram left him, but it won't do to challenge Spike. "Nah, I'm down with it."

Spike smiles and claps Denzel on the shoulder. "That's right, my man. Let's do this."

Denzel falls in beside Spike as he marches into Tent Town and heads straight to a two-person tent. Light glows inside.

Spike stops outside the tent flap. "Hey, Harry. Y'all got company, my man."

A head pops out of the opening. Long, stringy blond hair frames an emaciated face of indeterminate age. Harry grins unconvincingly, revealing a mouthful of crooked teeth with a pronounced gap between the top incisors. He pulls a pair of AirPods out of his ears. "Hey, Spike."

"How's my man? I hear you come into some cash. Good for you."

Harry frowns. "Yeah, my granny passed and left me a few bucks. Picked up a couple things to remember her by. Losing her was a real bitch, man."

Denzel recognizes the pain in the tight skin around Harry's eyes when he mentions his gram. Knocking over this guy feels all wrong.

"Got some weed for us?" Spike asks.

"Got a little."

"Me and my man Denz here could sure use some." The edge in Spike's voice signals that this isn't really a request.

"Yeah, sure. Why not? I can give you guys a couple of joints."

"Coupla joints? That's it?"

"Other folks around here enjoy a smoke now and then."

Spike's smile vanishes. "I hear you scored yourself a bunch of C-notes, my man. Maybe more."

"It isn't much," Harry says warily. "I like to spread some joy around here."

Spike kneels to get in Harry's face. "Starting with me,

right? We ain't gonna hang around here all night, so we'll have our share now. We'll take some cash too." Spike nods his head back at Denzel. "My boy could use a Hamilton or two to get hisself a nice meal."

Harry's eyes rise to Denzel's. "You hungry, man? Don't got a home?"

"Nah. Lost my gram too, y'know?"

Harry nods sympathetically. "Sure, kid. I got a few bucks you can have. Hold on a sec." He ducks back into the tent.

Spike leans in after him. "Shee-it, man. Y'all got some sweet shit in here, brother."

Harry's voice is muffled. "Picked up a thing or two."

"New phone, huh? Sweet."

"Yeah."

Spike lets out a low whistle. "Whoo-ee. That's a righteous roll of Benjamins, dude."

"A bit, yeah," Harry says nervously. "Been ordering a little pizza and Chinese for my friends."

Spike snorts derisively and eases deeper into the tent until only his feet are outside. Denzel takes a step backward and glances around at a handful of faces staring back at him.

"Your cash ain't gonna go far if you be doing shit like that," Spike says from inside the tent. "Hell, folks do okay at the soup kitchen out here. They don't need no pizza or Chinese."

"Hey, man!" Harry exclaims. "What the hell are you doing? Give that back!"

"Gave you a chance to share nice. Looks like you ain't fixing to do so."

Fear creeps into Harry's voice. "Relax, man. I'll give you—"

A sharp crack cuts off Harry's response. The weight of something sagging against the side of the tent causes it to billow outward, threatening to take the whole thing down.

"Teach you to fuck with old Spike," Denzel's partner

mutters as sounds of rummaging spill out of the tent. Then Spike's head and torso pop out. He holds a baseball bat out handle first. "Got my hands full in here, Denz. Hold this for a minute."

Denzel takes the bat and stares mutely as Spike ducks back inside.

"Give me the bat and take this," Spike says when he reappears a moment later and thrusts a Chicago Bears jacket at Denzel. A pair of Converse sneakers follow. Denzel takes the offerings uncertainly; Harry was wearing the jacket—maybe the sneakers, as well.

Denzel edges closer, squats, and peers inside the tent beyond Spike. Harry is lying on his side, silent and still. The baseball bat lies across his legs. Spike is rifling through his pockets, from which he produces a white cell phone, which he immediately stuffs into his hoodie. He picks up the AirPods and pockets them too.

"What the hell?" Denzel whispers as he realizes what just happened.

"Shut the fuck up," Spike hisses as he pilfers more of Harry's belongings, including a roll of cash. Then he upends a backpack and shakes its contents onto the floor. He plucks up a couple of baggies that appear to be weed and stuffs them into his pants pocket.

Denzel's eyes settle on the inert form of Harry, who doesn't appear to be breathing. A rivulet of blood snakes down the side of his face beneath a patch of hair that glistens red. Denzel's stomach lurches as he continues to gawk. *Is he dead?* Denzel backs away from the tent, settles on his haunches, and meets the gaze of a destitute woman who edges closer with fury in her eyes. Her anger and courage seem to put a little backbone into a couple of men who follow in her wake.

Spike emerges and grins up at Denzel. "Time to go, my man," he says as he stands, claps a hand on Denzel's shoulder, and spins him away from the tent. He works his hoodie around his face with the other. "Put the coat on, dude. Look sharp!"

Denzel shrugs into the jacket, then ties the laces of the Converse sneakers together and slings the shoes over his shoulder.

Spike's head turns toward the woman and men who are inching closer. He freezes them in place with a menacing "Stop right fucking there." Once they do, Spike turns back to Denzel and tugs on his sleeve. "C'mon, man. Time to get the fuck outa here."

Denzel takes a final look at Harry's neighbors. He wants to apologize. He wants to dial the clock back ten minutes and change history. He wants to cry.

Spike wraps a hand around his arm. "This ain't no time to freeze, boy. Move!"

Denzel is too frightened to do anything other than allow himself to be dragged away. With Spike's hand locked on his arm, Denzel follows in a trance as Spike begins to jog back the way they came.

Denzel's stomach continues to lurch as he stumbles along, overwhelmed by the unexpected enormity and ugliness of what he's just been party to. Grams would have had his ass for getting mixed up in this. He makes it a block away from Tent Town before he yanks his arm free of Spike and veers into the entrance to an alley. He drops to his knees and begins to puke his guts out.

"Aw, shit, dude!" Spike exclaims in disgust. "Hurry the fuck up, man—and don't mess up that new jacket I scored for you."

Denzel barely hears him as his gut reaches down to his toes to dredge up everything he's eaten in the last week. Spike's heavy hand grabs the back of Denzel's jacket collar and yanks him upright.

"Shit!" Spike mutters while Denzel spits out bits of food. "What the fuck now?"

Denzel's gaze tracks Spike's wide eyes to where a cop car has turned onto the street a couple of blocks away. He's startled when Spike spins him so they're face-to-face, then reaches into the Bears jacket to stuff the bags of weed into the inside pockets. He peels a few bills off the roll of cash and tucks them into Denzel's front pants pocket. "Just making sure you get your fair share in case we hafta split up, dude."

"Yeah, sure," Denzel mutters.

Spike leans in close, his hard eyes locked on Denzel's, his voice a threatening growl. "Don't you dare give me up. You might do a little time in juvie if you get busted and keep your mouth shut. They'll throw away the fucking key if I get locked up. You give me up and you're a dead man. Understand?"

The police car stops, the doors open, and a pair of cops emerge. They take a few steps forward with their hands resting on their guns. Denzel is watching them when Spike slams his open palms into the boy's chest, sending him reeling backward.

"What the fuck, man?" Spike shouts. He backs away from Denzel, with his hands thrust out as if to protect himself. "Stay away from me! You didn't need to beat that poor bastard. I think you mighta killed him!"

Denzel stands in mute shock, trying to suck air back into his lungs. Spike's blow has winded him.

The cops pause, their hands nervously fingering their weapons. Spike takes another step away from Denzel and points at him. "Crazy nigger mighta just killed a dude to score a little weed," he shouts at the cops. "Watch yourself!" he adds as he sprints into the alley, leaving Denzel standing between Spike's escape route and the cops, who, guns now in hand, draw down on Denzel.

"Don't move! Hands up where I can see them. *Now!*"

2

It's a cold early January morning when my intercom comes to life at the legal juggernaut known as Brooks and Valenti—a colossus with all of two lawyers. Joan Brooks is calling from reception.

"Mr. Valenti, sir?"

That's me. Tony Valenti, law firm partner. "Yes, ma'am. What can I do for you?"

"Miss Brooks would like to see you in her office," comes the reply, sounding for all the world as if I'm being summoned to the boss's office—or the school principal's office—for remedial discipline.

"Please inform Miss Brooks that I'll be along presently."

"Make it snappy!" my partner, Penelope Brooks, calls out through the open door of her office. It's all of ten feet from my own.

"You two!" Joan says in supposed exasperation. We have a running gag that Joan, who happens to be Penelope's mother, is waging a long-suffering campaign to bring some measure of proper law firm decorum to our little operation—lawyers to little people and lost causes. It's one of the many things that makes working here a lot more fun than I ever had as a high-flying corporate attorney before that career crashed and burned in a spectacular flameout a few years ago.

I happily close the file of the dreary wrongful dismissal suit I've been staring at with glazed eyes for the past few minutes, then get to my feet and stretch my arms high until the knot in my lower back pops. Even with me standing six feet five, my arms don't come close to reaching the twelve-foot ceiling. Brooks and Valenti is housed in a recently renovated office suite on the second floor of a heritage building in downtown Cedar Heights. I run my hands through my wavy black hair. How wavy? One of the wits on my high school volleyball team christened me Brillo top. Enough said. I glance at a dark-blue pinstripe suit jacket hanging on the back of my door. Nah. My shirtsleeves are rolled up, my necktie is pulled down. We're reasonably casual around here. Well, I am, anyway. If Joan had her way, I'd choke on the knot from my neckties all day, my suit jacket would never come off, and my shirt cuffs would be stapled to my wrists.

"What's up?" I ask my partner as I darken her door. She's dressed in a gray business suit, blue blouse, and black pumps.

Penelope, like her mother, is a wholesome daughter of rural Kansas, both of them five-foot dynamos with hearts the size of the vast prairies. She looks up from under the bangs of her shoulder-length light-brown hair and smiles as she lifts the edge of some paperwork resting in the middle of the hunter-green blotter on her desk. "This just came in, Tony. Kind of urgent."

I step into her office and drop into one of the two chrome-and-fabric visitor chairs that sit in front of her hickory desk. "What is it?"

"We caught another case from the county." Penelope registered us to participate in a pilot program in which the chronically underfunded, understaffed public defender's office is permitted to farm out a small percentage of its workload to qualified private attorneys who agree to do the work on a cost-plus basis. The "plus" part of the equation seems to be measured in decimal points. Not surprisingly, private firms haven't been beating a path to the public defender's door looking for cases they can lose money on, but a number of publicly minded firms and individual lawyers have stepped up to the plate. We're publicly minded. We also eat a lot of mac and cheese.

I cock an eyebrow at Penelope. "Another charity case already?"

"They must like our work, partner."

"They must," I grumble. We just wrapped up a losing effort in a domestic violence case the county sent our way. Given the evidence, our client deserved to lose, so I wasn't unhappy with the verdict. I have some history being on the wrong end of domestic violence. We're all better off with these miscreants off the streets. "What's this one about?"

"All I have is a summary. The full file will follow if we accept the case."

I roll my eyes. "*If* we accept the case, and we're expected to decide without knowing the details. They'll stuff it down our throats if we don't play ball anyway."

She smiles. "Such a cynical partner I have."

I return her smile. "And I've got Susy Sunshine for a partner. Or maybe I should just call you Pollyanna."

She laughs lightly. "That's us. Brooks and Valenti, just like milk and cookies."

"Milk and cookies?"

"They go together well," she says affectionately. "Just like us."

She's right about that. Penelope is a brilliant strategist—a master of all things lawyerly, with the exception of standing in front of a judge or jury to argue a case. I, on the other hand, operate on instinct in a courtroom—the actor delivering the lines Penelope feeds me.

"So tell me what little we know about this case before things get downright sappy in here," I suggest.

She frowns. "Murder case."

"What the hell?" The county rarely farms out murder files. The cases are time-consuming and expensive to defend. The public defender's office generally keeps them in-house for just that reason.

"It's a juvie case," Penelope continues. "The murder took place on the evening of October twentieth. Sounds pretty cut-and-dried, so maybe they figured it wouldn't eat up too much of our time."

"Just feed the kid to the wolves," I say sourly.

"It comes with another twist. The PD office was handling it, but the attorney working the case died unexpectedly. They don't have enough extra bodies to pick up all her files, and this one is on a tight schedule."

"How hard can it be to get a continuance for a change of counsel under those circumstances?" I grumble. It's a routine procedure when a lawyer steps aside in a case and new counsel has to get up to speed.

Penelope's brow furrows. "I know, right? For reasons unexplained, the judge is eager to get the case into court. There's a hearing in two weeks."

"That's quick."

She nods.

"So the public defender is in a pickle and punted."

"I'd say that about sums it up. What do you say?"

One of my best friends is a public defender in Cook County, so I know exactly how crushing their workloads are, what an outstanding group of people they are, and how thankless their important work is. How can I say no?

"I guess we pitch in," I reply with a decided lack of enthusiasm.

"You could at least pretend to be excited."

"I'm willing to help. Don't expect me to break into a Snoopy dance about it."

She winks. "So noted. No dancing in the courtroom required. Mind you, I'd like to see this Valenti Snoopy dance I keep hearing about."

"Yeah, well, it's cute when Snoopy does it. Three-left-feet Valenti? Not so much."

That gets a chuckle. "I still want to see it."

"Don't hold your breath. We have a hearing in two weeks about who knows what in a murder case we know squat about. Nothing about this sounds good."

3

We receive the file for the murder case from the public defender's office the next afternoon. As I feared, nothing but bad news. Fifteen-year-old Denzel Payton is charged with murdering a homeless man to steal a small quantity of marijuana and a couple hundred dollars in cash. He was also carrying a stash of heroin—more than the average user would have on them. The Cook County state's attorney's office is hellbent on sending the case into adult court, so our first order of business is to keep Denzel in the juvie system. The difference between the two is stark. Juvie seeks to give kids a chance to turn their lives around so they can live productive lives. The adult system is all about punishment—tossing criminals into an unforgiving prison system for as long as they can keep them there. Preferably permanently.

The following morning finds me sitting in a small interview room at the juvie detention center on South Hamilton Avenue, waiting to meet our new client. I pull up the feature my friend, Pat O'Toole, a reporter with the *Chicago Tribune,* wrote about Harry Hood: *Beloved Homeless Veteran Slain in*

Senseless Theft. It's clear that the killing outraged Pat. I don't imagine she's too thrilled that we're defending his alleged killer. This isn't the first time she's written about Harry. She did a glowing feature on him a year ago. I read that story as well.

Harry Hood had come home from Iraq, damaged for life, yet with his enormous heart intact. In Pat's original feature, which was part of a series on the homeless, Harry admitted to being disillusioned with America's wars and the people who happily sent kids to fight them. He lamented how the government then cast the soldiers aside when they returned home missing limbs, burdened with memories that didn't let them sleep, and/or so emotionally wounded that they were unable to function. Harry said, "I couldn't rejoin this society and support the crap the US gets into around the world, you know? We go off to war thinking we're the good guys, but we're not, we're just another set of mercenaries sent to kill and plunder. Think of it, man! Kids being sent off to die and be maimed so rich bastards can line their pockets."

After talking about life in Tent Town, Harry took Pat around to meet some of his neighbors. "See? These folks aren't a bunch of losers. They're salt of the earth, man. A lot of us are fed up and choose to turn our backs on this effing society. We get by. We support each other. We don't hurt anyone. People have no right to look down their noses at us."

Pat then spent time with some of Harry's neighbors. The words of a middle-aged woman were typical: "He helps us all out, y'know. He gets a little VA pension and spreads it around, makes sure everyone is warm and gets a nice meal now and then. He's a saint, far as we're concerned."

Denzel is finally ushered into the room. My first impression of him isn't favorable. He's a gangly Black kid standing five foot ten or thereabouts with a bit of an Afro thing happening with his hair. Nothing wrong with any of that; it's the surly sneer radiating an attitude a mile wide that puts me off.

I paste a professional smile on my face. "I'm Tony Valenti, Mr. Payton. I've been appointed to represent you in this matter."

He gives me a sour look. "Better hope you make out better than my last lawyer, dude."

The offhand crack takes me aback. Is he making light of his deceased lawyer? Or was that a veiled threat? "Excuse me?"

The kid's eyes snap back to mine. "I hope you don't end up dead like her. Got a problem with that?"

I let it go and tap the file. "Do you understand the charges against you?"

"I ain't no dummy."

"I didn't suggest you are. You've been charged with murder. Do you understand the nuances behind the charges?"

"Sure. Miss Tyson explained it all to me."

I take it as a positive that he refers to his first attorney respectfully. "So I trust you're aware of the evidence against you?"

"The bat with my fingerprints, the dope, and the cash with the victim's fingerprints. DNA too."

"Pretty damning stuff, and let's not forget the heroin."

"Spike stuffed it in my pocket," he protests angrily. "I don't mess with that shit."

"And yet the cops found it on you. Tough to argue that away. Tell me how things went down, Denzel."

"Cops got it all figured out, don't they? I'm sure they'll tell you about it."

I tap the file folder again. "Their story is right here. There's always more than one version of every story. What's your side of this one?"

Denzel leans back in his seat, crosses his arms, and studies me. "Wrong place, wrong time, I guess. Got fucked over good."

"Explain."

His eyes flash. "Ain't no one wants to hear it, man."

I lean in and lock my gaze on his. "I do, Denzel. In fact, I *need* to. If you don't want to end up having your ass used by a bunch of big, mean men in prison, you better start talking to me. I'm the only thing standing between you and prison rape."

Fear passes over his face as my words register.

"That's right," I say. "You go into the adult system and your days of juvie day camp are over. They'll toss you in with the general prison population. That's a tough crowd."

The bravado returns. "I can look out for myself."

"All one-hundred forty or one-hundred fifty pounds of you in a jail filled with iron-pumping predators looking for an easy hole to pound? Sure you can."

He glares at the affront to his pride.

"Look, Denzel, I'm not mocking you. I just want you to understand the stakes. You've got one hope in life right now, and that's keeping this thing in the juvie system. Are you going to help us make that happen or am I wasting my time here?"

He stares back sullenly, apparently determined to play tough guy.

"You mentioned someone named Spike was with you. Who is he?"

Silence.

"That's enough crap," I announce, stuffing his file into my briefcase.

His eyes grow wide. "What are you doing?"

I get to my feet and snap the briefcase closed. "I have better things to do than sit here while you show me how tough you are. I'll go work with someone who *wants* my help."

I catch a tremor in his leg out the corner of my eye.

He finally looks like a scared fifteen-year-old kid in a pile of trouble. "What do you want from me?"

I ease back onto my seat but don't reopen the briefcase. "Tell me what happened in Tent Town. All of it. Then explain exactly how you got screwed over."

I sit back and listen to his story, stopping him every so often to clarify, add detail, and describe every visual he can recall. I need to see, hear, and taste every moment of those fateful few minutes. I want to experience it through his senses. Maybe there's a telling point I haven't heard. He seems to believe his version of the story; either that or he's an unusually skilled liar. In the end, I'm not sure what to think. Given the facts as the cops relate them, his tale doesn't add up.

"Who is this Spike character?" I ask. "All the cops saw was some guy running away from you. You didn't even give them a proper name for him. Either you come clean on who he is, or you don't have a prayer of beating the charges."

Denzel sinks deeper into his seat. "I can't give him up. He'll kill me if I do."

"Do you see Spike in here?"

He shakes his head.

"That's right. You're here all by yourself. If I were you, I'd be a little less concerned about protecting Spike."

"That's because you don't know him. Don't be talking about stuff you don't know nothing about."

The fear in his eyes and the quivering voice are real. Maybe Spike is too?

"Anyway, fuck it," he says as he shuts down. "If you don't believe me, just get outa here."

"There are a thousand holes in your story, Denzel. The prosecution will shred it as it stands now. Help me fill the holes and you'll have a fighting chance. *We'll* have a fighting chance."

Denzel raps his knuckles on the door to summon a guard. "I ain't got dick in the way of a chance, man. Never did."

"Denzel," I say as he stands up.

"I'm screwed. Might as well be done with it."

"Done with what?" I ask as the door opens.

"My shitty life."

4

"This shouldn't take long," Penelope says as she pours us both a cup from the office coffee machine. It's the first day of Martin Luther King Jr. weekend, and we have until Tuesday to decide if we want to take on Denzel Payton's case.

"Got big plans for the weekend?"

"Wedding planning with Mom." Penelope and her partner, Becky Seguin, plan to marry in a civil ceremony this spring. She gives me a sad smile. "Mom always dreamed of an elaborate church wedding in Kansas with my father marching me down the aisle to my future husband."

Well, that plan is DOA. There isn't a prospective husband and Penelope's father died three years ago. "Don't beat yourself up over it, partner. Things are what they are."

"I know. Still, I hate to trample on Mom's dreams."

"She'll come around."

"It's not like that, Tony. Mom's been great. It just makes me a little sad."

Coffees in hand, we wander into the conference room and plop ourselves down in adjacent seats.

Penelope leans back in her seat and crosses her legs. "You met our new client yesterday afternoon. Tell me about him."

"What do you know about the victim?"

"Pretty much just what I read in the file. Such a shame."

"Exactly. Harry Hood was a fine human being. Denzel is a surly little bugger, chip on his shoulder the size of a house. I didn't warm up to him, Penelope. The heroin bothers me. I can't work up much sympathy."

Her eyes widen. "Tell me about him."

So I do. His crappy attitude. His unlikely story of how Harry Hood's murder went down. "He claims he's just an unlucky kid who was in the wrong place at the wrong time."

"He *is* a kid, Tony. Probably a scared one."

I nod wearily. "I know. But here's the thing. He went to Tent Town that night. Even if his story that some other mysterious dude killed Harry is true, Denzel was still in on it. He went willingly."

Penelope's eyes narrow. "You don't feel you can represent Denzel?"

"I don't want to. I know he needs and deserves a lawyer. I just can't get fired up about being that guy."

Penelope rests a hand on my arm. "This kid must be a real piece of work. I've never seen you back away from a challenge."

I shrug.

She arches her eyebrows. "And yet."

"I know. We owe a down-and-out Black kid the best defense we can offer. But heroin, Penelope. I can't get past that. The kid was arrested with enough heroin to be a dealer. Representing a dealer goes against our ethos."

"True, but let's remember that the original public defender was skeptical about the heroin. What if Denzel really was set up, Tony? Who's going to find out if not us?"

I think for a long minute, my almost visceral distaste of Denzel at war with my conscience and the decency of my partner—who is, yet again, right. I sigh. "I guess I should put a little of that investigator course knowledge to work, huh?"

Brooks and Valenti's chronically shallow pockets sometime handcuff us, especially when it comes to hiring investigators to search for exculpatory evidence. We had help last year from a couple of ex-cops named Jake Plummer and Max Maxwell, but Jake has gone back to police work and Max is wintering in Florida. We've since veered uncomfortably close to driving a couple of cases over a cliff for want of investigative help. My attempts to plug the gap were, to put it mildly, inadequate, so I took a private investigator's course.

Penelope smiles. "First good idea you've had this morning."

"Maybe I can find out what really went down that night, one way or the other."

"Sounds like a plan, partner. *If* you promise to keep out of trouble."

I have an aptitude for stirring up nests of vipers. If Spike is real, history suggests I'll stumble across him in the worst possible way.

We sit quietly and sip coffee while I ponder everything I know about Denzel's case. With my mind finally focusing on what needs to be done as opposed to being angry about how unfair Harry Hood's death was, anomalies in what I've seen and heard spring to mind. A plan begins to form. "I can start at the scene. Maybe someone in Tent Town can tell me what happened."

"They might not be overly enthusiastic about helping the lawyers of the kid they think murdered their friend."

"Probably not," I agree. "Still worth a try. Maybe someone there can corroborate Denzel's version of events."

"We also need to track down people who can tell us more about Denzel," Penelope says. "We could use a few character witnesses."

"I'll reach out to Mike for suggestions." Mike being my

buddy Mike Williams, a public defender in Cook County. I dig out my cell phone and get Mike's voicemail. "If you ever return to work, give me a call, pal."

Penelope arches an eyebrow. "If he ever returns to work?"

"He's on vacation *again*. Jamaica this time."

"Mike works harder than anyone I know. What's this about constant vacationing?"

"Seems he has a girlfriend," I reply with a grin and a wink.

After a beat, an enormous smile lights up Penelope's face. "Aretha Jackson?"

"Yup." Aretha was a witness in a murder trial in which Mike lent us a hand. He and Aretha hit it off.

Penelope claps her hands in delight. "That's great. I love that girl."

We spend a minute talking about Mike and Aretha before we turn back to work—in a roundabout way.

"Ever read Michael Connelly's Harry Bosch books?" Penelope asks.

I shake my head. I'm not a big reader. I do, however, recall watching a show on a streaming service about a detective named Bosch. "Did they turn it into a TV show?"

She nods, then wags a disapproving finger. "I'll grant that they did a pretty good job with the TV show, but always read the book, partner."

She sounds just like Pat O'Toole on this topic. They're two of the smarter people I know, so maybe there's something to this reading business.

"Anyway," Penelope continues, "as Bosch says, 'Everyone counts, or no one counts.'"

I turn that over in my mind. "I like that. Kinda fits our little practice, doesn't it?"

She smiles. "I hadn't thought of it that way, but yes it does. Of course, Bosch is talking about victims of crime, but I think we can stretch its meaning to include outgunned defendants."

"Especially Black ones."

"Exactly." She cocks an eyebrow. "Does anyone come to mind?"

I pause for a moment, knowing just the name she wants to hear. "Denzel Payton."

She nods.

"So I have my marching orders?" I ask.

She points at the door and winks. "After taking a day or two off."

As if I have time for that. Murder trials are full-court presses, and I'm going to have to squeeze this one into an already busy schedule. Not to mention running a single-father household. Speaking of which, big happenings at the Valenti house in a couple of hours. I pack up and hurry home, hoping my latest bright idea isn't a disaster in the making.

5

Deano, our sixteen-year-old gray Labrador retriever who had once been our black lab, turns away from me in disgust after I empty a pan of browned Swedish meatballs into the slow cooker and step to the sink to wash my hands. He's been glued to my knee for the past thirty minutes, patiently awaiting his portion, which never came. He collapses onto his doggy bed, lets out a world-weary sigh, and casts a final look of contempt at me before he rolls over and turns his back—just in case I haven't yet picked up on his displeasure.

"Think he wanted one?" my sixteen-year-old daughter, Brittany, asks with a laugh as she watches. She's a slender five-foot, six-inch tall teenager with more than a hint of her mother's striking beauty. Much to my chagrin, boys have also noticed that she's growing into an attractive young woman.

I'm about to answer when the doorbell rings. I glance at my watch as Brittany takes off like a shot to welcome our guests—2:30 p.m. On time, right to the minute. I dry my hands and follow.

"It's them!" Brittany calls out in excitement.

"Think missing out on a meatball was bad?" I ask Deano

as I pass. "You're about to have your world rocked, old friend."

He replies with a disinterested yawn as Brittany opens the front door.

Milwaukee PD K-9 officer Tammy Whitworth stands on the other side of the screen door. A gorgeous German shepherd sits at her knee, ears perked straight up as she peers at us through the glass. Whitworth smiles and gives the dog a reassuring scratch behind the ear as Brittany swings the door open. The dog, her pink tongue lolling out the side of her mouth, looks up at her handler for direction.

"Come in," I say from behind Brittany.

Whitworth greets and shakes hands with us, then glances down at the dog. "Come on, Dolly."

The shepherd bounces to her feet, walks inside, and immediately sits down beside Whitworth. We've been through this meet-and-greet routine a couple of times now, so I know the drill. I squat and extend a hand toward Dolly, who wags her tail and stretches her snout to give me a sniff. Brittany gets down on her knees and follows suit, then hugs the dog, who happily leans into the contact.

Dolly straightens up, ears swiveling forward as she looks beyond Brittany. We follow her gaze to where Deano has lumbered into the kitchen doorway, his eyes fixed on the intruder. Dolly sniffs the air warily. She and Deano have met once before without incident, but Dolly is now on Deano's turf.

Dolly takes a few tentative steps forward until she's nose-to-nose with Deano. Brittany drapes an arm over the dog's shoulder and leans close to Deano. "It's all cool, big guy. Relax."

Deano gives her hand a quick lick, shoots a curious look at Dolly, then sags to the floor. His eyes remain on Dolly, as if to ask, *When are you leaving?*

"Coffee?" I ask Whitworth, then wink and add, "Doughnut?"

She has the good grace to laugh. "Got me pegged, do you?"

I start toward the kitchen, waving Whitworth after me.

"Love the house," she says.

"Thanks. My father's handiwork." Our home is a typical post-war Chicago-style brick bungalow on the outside, but Papa put his considerable carpentry talents to work inside. The kitchen is a wonderland of alder cabinetry and trim. The countertop features dozens of individually laid one-inch pastel colored ceramic squares; the floor boasts sixteen-inch ceramic tile. The rest of the house also showcases Papa's woodworking prowess.

Whitworth settles into one of the chairs surrounding our maple kitchen table. "Have you decided where Dolly is going to sleep?"

There has been some debate about this. Deano has a sumptuous bed beside mine, which is where he's slept for sixteen years, although my mother and father occupied the bedroom for most of that time. Mama passed two years ago; Papa has been in Italy for more than a year now, soaking up the old country and catching up with his sister and her family in his native land. Brittany and I have been here going on two years.

"I was thinking initially that I'd have her camp out with Deano and me," I reply to Whitworth's question. "Brittany had other plans."

I reach into a brand-new ceramic cookie jar at the end of the kitchen counter, holding Dolly's alert gaze as I pluck a Milk-Bone from its depths and show it to her. Her tail sets to wagging and her tongue darts out in anticipation of a treat, yet she reluctantly holds her position beside her handler, straining against her instinct to hurry over.

The dog shoots Whitworth a sideways glance, but this is

my show. When I utter the magic word "Release," Dolly trots over. She parks her butt tight in front of me when I lift my hand, palm up, in the *sit* command she's been taught. I bend over and give her a vigorous rub behind the ears and then offer her the treat in my open palm. "Good girl!"

Deano lumbers in from the front hall with Brittany in his wake. He heads straight to where Dolly is cleaning up the Milk-Bone crumbs, sniffs, then turns an accusatory look on me.

Whitworth chuckles as she watches. "Show Dolly around while I bring her things in."

I pocket another Milk-Bone, order Deano to stay, and lead Dolly off to explore. She glues herself to my side as I lead her downstairs to Brittany's basement hideaway and on into the back storage and laundry area. On our way back, she sniffs around our guitars and amplifiers with a curious expression. Brittany and I are a couple of months into jamming together, which has turned out to be a blast. I played a little back in the dark ages; Brittany picked guitar up a few years ago in Atlanta. She's a darned sight better than I am at this point, but I'm getting back into the groove.

"We'll find out what you think of live rock and roll soon enough," I tell Dolly as she noses around.

Whitworth appears at the top of the stairs. "Bring her up, Tony."

Dolly bounds up the stairs with her tail wagging furiously. When I reach the kitchen, Whitworth hands me a shiny new Nylabone.

"Parting gift," she says with a wistful smile. "Better that it comes from you."

I feel a pang of empathy for the cop. She's clearly pained at the prospect of her imminent separation from Dolly. I imagine the dog will have a hard time of it, as well, but she doesn't know what's coming, so she happily takes her new toy and settles on the floor to start mangling it.

"I put Dolly's bed and blanket in Brittany's room," Whitworth says.

My daughter, who is sprawled on the floor with Deano, smiles up at me. "This is gonna be so cool."

I smile back. Having the seemingly docile former K-9 mutt sleeping beside Brittany every night will offer me a level of comfort. After all, the primary reason we decided to bring a police-trained dog into our home was for protection. It's been a couple of tumultuous, nerve-racking years since we moved back to Cedar Heights. Dolly is here to protect Brittany if any additional mayhem is unleashed on our Liberty Street home. Watching Dolly happily gnawing away on her bone, I find it hard to imagine her taking down a bad guy. Let's hope she's never put to the test.

6

Three days later, Mike Williams looks at my ragged ass as I huff and puff at the merciful end of our regular Tuesday hoops outing at the Cedar Heights RecPlex. He's taken me down five games to none. That runs his streak to—oh, I don't know, maybe a thousand to zero? We're both big men at six-and-a-half-feet tall, both athletic—I was an NCAA Division I volleyball final MVP—but only one of us was born with a basketball gene. It wasn't me. While I have spent the past hour close to asphyxiating myself trying to keep up with Mike on the court, he's been happily telling me about his idyllic week at a resort in Negril, Jamaica with his girlfriend, Aretha Jackson. I'm eager to discuss Denzel's case, but we have a firm rule that work talk is off-limits on the court, so we're still talking basketball as we put the ball away and head for the showers.

"We've been at this for what, two years now?" he asks.

I wheeze out a "Yes."

He chuckles. "You're getting a little better. Hell, you made it into double digits *twice* today."

"But you got to twenty-one every game."

"True enough, but your game is coming along. I may have to brush up on my D."

"Ha ha," I reply, but his comment is a little encouraging. Unbeknownst to Mike, I've been playing pickup hoops and have enlisted the help of a local high school hot shot to give me pointers. I'm out a couple of hundred bucks so far, but if Mike's noticing improvement, we'll call that money well spent. After two or three lifetimes of intensive training, I may someday steal a game from Mike.

Ten minutes later, after showering and dressing, we arrive in the cafeteria. We order our usual post-match Danish and coffee, then settle on little orange plastic chairs at a diminutive yellow plastic table. It feels like being seated in a grade school classroom.

Mike settles back to study me. "I hear you caught the Denzel Payton case."

Penelope and I have decided it's a go. I nod.

"How's it going?"

I tell him about my misgivings. "I'm struggling to get past the kid's crappy attitude. Not the easiest client to work with."

"You know what happened to Marcie Tyson, right?"

Tyson was Denzel's first attorney. I nod. "Murdered."

Mike's lips straighten in anger. "That's right. Marcie was the nicest human being you'd ever want to meet. Have you looked at her case notes?"

I nod. "He seems to have worked well enough with her."

"Not surprising. Let me tell you a thing or two about Marcie. She was one hell of a lawyer, maybe the most tenacious I've ever seen. She was an even better person. We all care about the folks we represent—you know that—but Marcie cared more than anyone. She worked harder than the rest of us. She was tougher too."

"I'm sorry."

"Thanks. Marcie got close to every one of her clients—way

too close. It broke her heart every time she lost a case. Every time. Yet she kept befriending her defendants. Know why?"

I shake my head no.

"Because she thought she fought harder for them if she let herself care. Most of us don't have the guts to go through that kind of hell time after time after time. Marcie never mailed it in. Not once."

"Sounds like a heckuva lawyer."

"Marcie liked Denzel, Tony. She was a little sweet on the kid, matter of fact. Not romantically or anything, of course. She thought he was a scared kid who'd been dealt a shitty hand in life and had fallen in with a bad crowd."

"That's pretty much how Denzel sees things."

Mike frowns. "You ain't buying the story?"

"Not really. The kid was caught with a healthy stash of heroin."

"I see where you're coming from with that, but all may not be as it seems."

"What do you know about it?" I ask.

"Only that Marcie wasn't sold on the police line. I wish I'd taken the time to talk about it with her in more depth, but I was up to my ass in other cases."

"I can't get past the idea that he was mixed up with heroin. He was part of a plan to rob and murder a homeless vet."

"I hear you, but Marcie saw something there, Tony. Besides, this kid is Brittany's age, man. We can't be throwing fifteen-year-olds out with the trash, which is exactly what will happen if they kick his ass out of juvie. He doesn't belong in the adult system. No kid does."

That pulls me up short. Sure, I know Denzel's age, but the juxtaposition with my daughter underscores how tragic it is to throw away kids that age.

Mike tears an angry bite out of his Danish, chews, swallows, and leans across the table. "Here's another thing about this case. Marcie was a little nervous before she was murdered, and she sure wasn't scared about Denzel coming after her."

"She was scared about *this* case?"

"Yeah. She was pushing hard to figure out who Denzel was with that night. She asked all of us to put out whatever feelers we could in the community. I think that got her killed."

I swallow hard. I'm about to don my investigator hat and do the same thing. "Did she unearth any leads?"

"Don't know." His expression hardens. "Let me tell you how Marcie died. It'll give you a sense of what kind of bastard Denzel may have gotten mixed up with. The son of a bitch slit Marcie's throat in her own bed with her son asleep in the next room, then left her for the boy to find in the morning. Reminds me of how Marsha was filleted."

The reference to Marsha chills me. Marsha Williams, the ex-wife of Mike's younger brother, was the victim of a particularly vicious stabbing last year.

"Anyway, let's make happy talk for a minute," Mike says. "What's this I hear about you and Brittany recruiting Sara into a band of some sort?"

Sara is Mike's little sister.

"News to me. I didn't know Sara played, and I sure haven't heard anything about Britts being on a recruiting binge."

"Well, it seems she is, my friend. When are you folks planning to drop a tune or two?"

"About the same time I whip your tail on a basketball court."

"Nothing imminent, huh?"

We share a laugh at that, chat family for a few minutes, then reluctantly call it a morning and head outside to go to work.

Mike pauses beside my car before I get in. "Watch your ass

out there, Tony. I don't want to lose another friend to whoever killed Marcie."

I'd be lying if I said the thought hasn't begun to weigh on my mind.

7

The next evening, I park my Porsche Panamera in a surface lot adjacent to the small public park known to locals as Tent Town. I've timed my visit for the same time of night Harry Hood was murdered. My hope is that some of the people who were here then might be around tonight. I look in dismay at the ramshackle lean-tos and tents, then pull my Gore-Tex winter coat closer around myself to fend off the bitter north wind that has brought a polar vortex to Chicago. If we truly live in the richest country in history—blah, blah, blah—how is it that so many Americans huddle in places like this from sea to shining sea?

All is quiet as I approach the first few hovels. Whoever is here tonight is no doubt hunkered down in whatever pockets of warmth they can find.

"Hello?" I call out.

"Fuck off," a woman responds from within a lean-to thrown together with plywood and corrugated plastic.

I don't answer as I walk deeper into the encampment, calling out unanswered hellos as I go. A head finally pops out of a tent on the far side of an empty space between other dwellings, and I find myself being examined by a Latino man of indeterminate age.

"Hey," he says in a voice neither welcoming nor threatening.

I extend a hand in greeting. "Hi. My name is Tony Valenti."

A slow smile softens the harsh angles of his face as he takes my hand and shakes it firmly. "I'm known around here as Toe."

"Toe? As in the digit on your foot?"

"Yeah."

"I bet your mother never called you that."

"Oh, she called me all sorts of names," he replies with a chuckle. "But not that. I heard a lot of *chico malo*."

"Which means?"

"Bad or naughty boy, pretty much."

"My mother was Italian," I say, seeking to bond on the immigrant theme. Probably a dumb move—he's likely every bit as American as I am. "It was *cattivo* for me."

He chuckles. "So, we are the bad boys of Tent Town!"

I nod and cock an eyebrow. "Why Toe?"

"I left a couple in Iraq when we were over there making the world safe for capitalists. Some dick started calling me Toe after that."

"And it stuck."

He nods.

"Sorry."

"No biggie, man. The rest of me got back in one piece. Not everyone did." He looks me up and down. "Dude like you ain't looking for a spot to pitch a tent. Why are you here?"

"Just hoping to talk to a few people." I hook a thumb at the empty spot next to his tent. "Looks like you might have a vacancy, though."

My attempt at humor falls flat. Toe's eyes drift to the

empty patch of snow, then back to me as a pained expression pinches his face.

I follow his gaze. "Harry Hood's spot?"

He nods sadly. "Yeah. We left his space empty as a kind of memorial. Everyone here misses the crap out of Harry. Sucks big-time, but we're trying to move on, y'know?"

I cringe. "Actually, Toe, I came to speak with anyone who was here the night Harry was murdered."

He eases his body away from me without moving his feet —more of a lean, really—as his expression hardens into distrust. "You a cop?"

"Lawyer."

The narrowing of his eyes suggests I've uttered an occupation at least as bad. "You're down here beating the bushes for someone to support your bullshit case against that boy?"

"Actually, I'm one of the lawyers representing Denzel—the kid in question."

"You're his lawyer, huh?"

I nod. "Why did you say it's a bullshit case?"

He gives me a long look, then opens the flap of his tent and steps inside.

Guess I asked the wrong question. I'm turning to go when Toe's head pops back out of the tent. "Get your tail in here, Mr. Lawyer. If I'm gonna tell you that story, I ain't gonna freeze my balls off doing so."

He's caught me by surprise. When I hesitate, he gives me a questioning look. "Too good to step into a homeless man's tent?"

"Not at all." I duck inside and look around.

"It's a little cozy in here," Toe says. "The tent keeps the wind out for the most part."

That it does. A couple of emergency candles sit in the middle of a floor that appears to be the type of wrestling mat you'd find in a school gymnasium. Between the candles and body heat, the tent is warm enough to be comfortable. Not luxurious by any stretch, but it beats sleeping on the ground. A ratty army-surplus sleeping bag is rolled up in the back corner.

Toe points at it with a gap-toothed smile. "Guest chair for lawyers and other eminent visitors."

I pull it over and sit down. "Thanks."

He settles cross-legged on the floor mat. "Uh huh." That's Chicago-speak for *you're welcome.*

"Been following the case?" I ask.

"We hear a thing or two now and again. No cable news around here."

Blessing or curse? I wonder. "You mentioned a bullshit case."

He nods.

I dig into my coat pocket, produce a Hershey chocolate bar, and toss it to him.

He frowns as he catches it. "What the hell?"

I realize my error immediately, so I try to explain. "My friend Pat suggested I bring a few snacks to hand out. Says she never goes to a homeless camp empty-handed. Just a little gesture to lend a hand."

"Yeah?" he asks suspiciously. "Who's this friend of yours?"

"Pat O'Toole, a reporter at the *Tribune*."

The suspicion melts from Toe's face, replaced by a smile and a chuckle. "Didn't see that coming."

I don't know how to respond, so I don't.

"First I ever heard of Pat consorting with a lawyer," he adds.

"Well, most everyone collects an unsavory friend or two that their mother doesn't approve of, right?"

"True story," he says as he peels the wrapper off the chocolate bar, breaks off a square, and pops it into his mouth.

"So," I say, "the bull—"

His hand shoots up to stop me as he closes his eyes and

savors the chocolate with a faraway smile. His eyes open again after he swallows a good thirty seconds later. "That's a little bit of heaven, man. How'd you know Hershey is my bar?"

I chuckle. "Dumb luck."

"My good luck!" he replies happily as he pops another square of chocolate into his mouth and relishes it for the better part of a minute. Then he carefully folds the bar back into its wrapper and tucks it away in an outside pocket of a duffel bag. "Gonna spread that pleasure around. Folks miss the treats Harry used to pass around now and then."

I smile. Toe is a good guy.

"You're not real talkative for a lawyer," he says.

"Mama taught me that I'd learn a lot more listening than I was likely to teach myself by running my mouth."

He laughs. "When did you start taking that advice?"

"A lot later than I should have."

"That makes two of us, Mr. Lawyer. Anyway, if you're in a listening mood, I have a story you might be interested in."

"Harry?"

"Yeah. Now, being right up front here, I gotta tell you that I didn't see what happened that night."

Damn. I've been imagining Toe on the witness stand telling the jury that Denzel didn't do it. My host is a likable type and is clearly no fan of the cops or prosecutors.

"But I heard all about it from people who saw it go down," he continues.

"Anyone I can talk to tonight?"

"No. Some folks made tracks right after it happened—didn't want nothing to do with the cops. A few others who were scared of the bastard who wasted Harry split. There are still a couple of people here who saw it all."

"Cool."

"Don't know if they'll wanna talk with you. They're at shelters tonight. Too cold out here if you don't have a tent and a few candles. I'm lucky. Get a few dollars from my VA disability pension every month. Most other folks here don't got shit. Poor Di hasn't had anywhere to hide from the cold since Harry's been gone."

"Di?"

"Lovely little lady," Toe answers with affection. "She and Harry were a little sweet on each other. Shared his tent from time to time—especially on nights like this."

"She was his girlfriend?"

"Things here don't really work that way. Jealousy and shit like that are poison. Plus we're all loners in one way or another. Lots of love floating around Tent Town, just not that way."

"Got it. This Di saw it all that night?"

"Yeah, her and an old Native guy named Horace. They saw as much as there was to see, anyway. Mind you, I suspect Horace will be moving along soon. He's been bitching about what a mistake it was to stay in Chicago for the winter. He usually winters in Phoenix."

"I wish."

"You and me both, brother," Toe agrees with a grin. "Especially tonight!"

I think about sunshine and palm trees for a minute, then get back to business. "Tell me what they told you about that night."

He thinks on that for a moment, then says, "Probably best if you get it straight from them, but I'll tell you this much. That Denzel kid was just a spectator. Horace and Di told that to the cops. They didn't wanna hear it—not the detectives, at any rate. They ain't about to listen to a couple of homeless folks, right? Like we ain't got no eyes or ears."

I'm not inclined to argue the point after what I've seen of some cops. Not all of them, of course, but more than enough.

"The guy who killed Harry is bad news," Toe continues. "Scary, scary dude."

"You know who did it?" This could be huge.

"Know him to see him. Don't know his name, though. He came around to shake down Harry from time to time."

"What can you tell me about this guy?"

"Like I say, real scary bastard. Black dude. Tall. Muscular. Not steroid huge but solid enough. Never seen his face very well, but we all know who he is when he comes around."

I'm confused. How do they know if they've never seen his face? "You can't tell me what he looks like?"

"Afraid not, Mr. Lawyer. Horace and Di looked at some mug shots the cops brought around, but mostly all we've ever seen is eyes in the shadows of a hoodie. Anyway, typical badass dude, wears his pants down around his knees, big hoodie and all—you've seen the type."

I nod. Gangbanger.

"Unlaced high-tops. Always comes at night, face hidden in that hoodie. Always went straight to Harry's tent, got whatever he was after and split. Didn't talk to anyone else. We gave him a wide berth, y'know?"

I can imagine. "What did Harry have to say about him?"

"Nothing, man. Told us we were better off not knowing. Said we should just stay out of his way."

"Maybe someone from Harry's past?"

Toe thinks on that for a minute. "Harry never said anything like that, but the guy sure seemed to know when to come shake Harry down, so who knows?"

Interesting.

"Di said something kinda weird after it happened."

"Which was?" I ask.

"Di reads a lot. She's got a library card and all. Anyway, you know Lord of the Rings and Harry Potter and all that?"

"A bit," I reply with a smile. I never expected to have a literary discussion in a homeless camp.

"A bit, huh? Me too," Toe says with a self-conscious grin. "Di called him the Ringwraith guy or Mr. Dementor. You know, like Voldemort's servants in Harry Potter or those dicks who worked for Sauron in The Lord of the Rings. Di says this guy leaves a chill in the air like those monsters do. 'Oozes evil.' Soon as she said that, I knew what she was talking about."

Just hearing it unnerves me. This is the guy I need to hunt down? "I need to talk to Di."

"I doubt she'll want to. She avoided the cops too. Doesn't wanna get involved."

"Why not?"

"Ain't gonna bring Harry back, is it?"

"True, but it could bring the cops down on the real killer."

Toe cocks an eyebrow. "Or it might bring the real killer down on Di."

8

"What are you doing here?" Denzel asks me two days later when he walks into the attorney-client room at the juvie center.

"I'm still your lawyer."

"Why? You don't believe me. How do I get rid of you?"

"Ask the judge, I suppose. My guess is he or she will say no."

"That ain't right," Denzel mutters. "Man ought to be able to pick his own lawyer!"

"You can if you've got the money to pay one."

"That's crap."

I sit down. "I can't argue that point."

He fixes a sullen stare on me for a long moment, then sighs and sits across from me. "What do you want?"

"To talk. Seems that some folks in Tent Town saw what happened."

"How do you know?"

"I've been there asking around."

He eyes me suspiciously. "Why?"

"Because I'm your lawyer."

"What do these folks say?"

"You were in the wrong place at the wrong time."

He slams an open hand on the table. "Didn't I tell you?"

"You did."

"See?"

"What I see is that *you* put yourself there, Denzel."

He sags in his seat, crosses his arms, and stares at the wall above my head.

"Did Spike drag you there?" I ask sharply.

"Wasn't like I had a choice."

"No? Explain that to me." When he doesn't reply, I lean in. "Look at me, Denzel."

He does, but grudgingly.

"If you don't want to explain that, then explain the heroin the cops found in your pocket. I have no time for people who deal drugs—especially the hard stuff. I told my partner that we shouldn't have taken this case because of the drug connection."

"I don't know anything about that shit, man!" Denzel shouts in righteous indignation.

"So you say, which is the only reason I'm here. But now that I am and you're copping an attitude with me, I wonder if I should be. If you don't want to start all over again with a new lawyer—assuming you can even find one this late in the game—you're going to have to convince me that you've never dealt heroin. Or any other street drugs, for that matter."

"How the hell can I do that?" he asks in exasperation, then squares up and pastes his badass face back in place. "That is, if I want to bother."

"You're going to do that by looking me right in the eye and answering a couple of questions."

He doesn't reply, but he doesn't look away either.

"I've been doing this a long time, Denzel. I've gotten pretty good at telling when someone is lying to me. I don't like it."

"Whatever, man. Ask your questions."

"How did that bag of heroin end up in your pocket?"

"I told the cops. I told everyone who would listen! You gotta know what I said. Why are you asking again?"

I lean closer. "Because you haven't told *me* to my face."

He surprises me by folding his arms in front of himself so that we're nose to nose across the table. "First time I saw that heroin was when the cop took it out of my pocket. Spike musta put it there."

"Who is this Spike? I need his real name."

Fear widens Denzel's eyes. "Don't really know who he is."

I decide not to press. The kid is scared to death. "Where did Spike get the heroin?"

"Don't know. We made a couple of stops that night on the way to Tent Town. He musta picked it up at one of them."

It has the ring of truth, or at lease plausibility. He's batting two for two on the honesty scoreboard so far, but he needs to go three for three or I'm out of here. I keep my eyes fixed on his for a long moment. "Have you ever dealt drugs, Denzel? Heroin or anything else?"

His eyes smolder. "Never. Never did. Never will."

Whatever lies behind the vehemence of the answer is convincing. Family history? I'll circle back to this later. "Does Spike ever deal when you're out with him?"

Denzel sinks back in his seat and locks his hands behind his head. His eyes never leave mine. "Could be. If so, never in front of me, but yeah, he probably has. He leaves me outside to wait a lot of the time."

"You're not involved in *any* way?"

"C'mon, man. No!"

"I believe you."

"That's *such* a relief."

I let the sarcasm go. "You hate the stuff, don't you?"

He nods.

"Well, I feel the same way. I detest hard drugs, so I despise the scum who peddle them—just like you do. Something put that fire in your belly. Why do you hate it so much?"

The frightened fifteen-year-old resurfaces. "Just family stuff."

"Where is your father?"

His eyes widen a bit. The topic seems to spook him for some reason.

"Why isn't he coming around to help you?" I ask.

"Don't see him no more."

"Why not?"

"Just don't," he mutters. "He hasn't been in my life for years. He came around a few times after Gram passed, just to give me a few bucks and check in, but we don't hang or nothing."

I don't get that. It bothers me to be apart from Brittany for the length of a workday.

"Why is that?" I ask.

"Nothing I can… that I'm gonna talk to you about."

"Fair enough." Cracks are appearing in his tough-guy façade, which I can now see *is* a façade. Still, there's something in the way he avoids talking about his father, almost as if it's related to his fear of Spike. Maybe dear old dad knows Spike? That's a prospect worth checking out.

"We good?" Denzel asks after a beat.

"We good," I reply in a voice that mimics his as best I can manage.

The corner of his mouth twitches. Is that the beginnings of a smile? Does this kid still have a sense of humor buried somewhere beneath all the anguish and hurt? I hope so—he's going to need it.

9

On Monday afternoon, I arrive home from work and am barely into the house when Pat O'Toole pulls up in her Hyundai Sonata. Brittany is in the passenger seat. They're coming from Brittany's volleyball match at Hyde Park College Preparatory School. This is fast becoming a tradition —Pat taking Brittany to her games, cheering her on, and then staying for dinner after they get home. They fell into the pattern a few months ago while I was involved in my latest dustup with criminals and other ne'er-do-wells.

Pat sent me a note earlier this afternoon to say she had some Denzel Payton family news to share. If she has news, it should be interesting. She's an award-winning local reporter with access to sources I can only dream of. "And I want to meet the new pooch!" she concluded.

I greet them at the front door.

Brittany busses me on the cheek. "Hey, Pops!"

"Hi, Britts. Hi, Pat." I disarm the security system, then look at my daughter and cock an eyebrow. "So? Volleyball?"

She replies with an exaggerated thumbs-down gesture.

"Through no fault of Brittany's," Pat pipes up with a wink before she gives me a quick hug.

Dolly is studying the new arrival, who is shrugging out of a green, knee-length winter coat that makes her slender frame look ten sizes larger than it really is. Pat smiles at us as she peels off a pair of scarlet mittens and unwraps a lengthy matching scarf from around her neck, then shakes out her shoulder length red hair. She's been a friend since high school.

"So you're the new girl," she says as she squats to address Dolly at eye level. "You're beautiful!"

The tip of Dolly's pink tongue sticks out an inch or so as she stares back into Pat's sea-green eyes. Her twitching tail signals approval. Pat slowly extends a hand into the space between them and holds it still, allowing Dolly to make the next move. The dog sniffs for a second, then pulls back with a look of curiosity.

Pat glances up at us. "I was painting before we went to the game. She probably smells the mineral spirits I cleaned up with. Can you imagine the smell of that dialed up a hundred or more times?"

Pat is a pretty good artist. One of her paintings hangs above our fireplace.

Brittany pulls a face. "Yuck!"

Deano saunters over to shoulder Dolly aside so he can get the affection to which he deigns himself entitled. He's spent a lot of time lately with Pat, who has been dog sitting, Brittany sitting, and just hanging out with us. She was a godsend nursing us through our recent traumas. I don't know where we'd be if she hadn't been there for us.

Brittany gets down on all fours, takes Dolly's face in her hands to plant a noisy smooch on the tip of the dog's nose, and breaks into song. "Hello, Dolly! You're looking swell, Dolly! Who's a good girl?"

"I don't recall that last line," Pat says with a chuckle.

"Oh, I'm not just a guitar wizard," my daughter says. "Killer song lyricist too!"

After the doggy greetings are complete, I head for my bedroom to change out of my suit and tie. Brittany has already disappeared down the hall to dump her backpack in her room. When I come back out, she and Pat are in her bedroom with Dolly, who is sitting and watching Puckerface make the rounds of the goldfish bowl. The fish is a source of endless fascination for Dolly. She edges closer and cautiously lifts her snout to give the bowl a sniff.

Brittany giggles as she watches. "Dolly loves her new roomie."

"You or Puckerface?" Pat asks.

"Both of us!"

I smile and head for the kitchen to prepare dinner. When they arrive five minutes later, I'm digging leftover Chinese out of the fridge, plates out of the cabinets, and silverware out of a drawer. As always, I ordered way too much food yesterday. I'm Mr. Indecisive with a Chinese food menu in hand. Rather than choose between the many tantalizing options, I simply order one of everything that appeals to me in the moment. We generally have enough for at least three meals. As a bonus, my orders always qualify for a bonus entrée or extra order of rice. That's just smart shopping, right?

I look at my daughter and point at the cabinet that houses our glassware. "You're in charge of beverages."

While the microwave heats up dinner, I hear all the details of today's volleyball match. It was close.

"If Shelly Abraham wasn't off lounging on a beach in Tortola, we would've won," Brittany claims.

Kicking back on a sunny Caribbean island while Chicago temperatures flirt with absolute zero sounds heavenly.

"Be happy for Shelly," I say.

Brittany rests a hip against the counter and gives me a long look, which morphs into a cocky grin. "I might be able to if I wasn't filled with envy because *my* father never takes *me* to the beach for a week in the middle of winter."

"She has a point, Valenti," Pat says.

Yeah. Well. "Maybe if we can wrap this case up quickly."

Brittany ventures a hopeful smile. "Really?"

"Possible, if not likely," I reply. "We'll see how things shake out at work over the next couple of weeks."

Pat looks a little surprised. "That soon?"

"The transfer hearing is coming up next week. The judge only gave us ten days when we asked for a continuance. There will probably be a lull in the action after that."

"A lull as in fun in the sun?" Brittany asks in surprise.

Now that the idea of a quick jaunt south is on the table, I'm warming up to the idea—no pun intended. "Unless something else at Brooks and Valenti absolutely needs my immediate attention, yeah, maybe we can do that."

We settle at the table with three steaming plates of food and dig in.

I pause in the process of forking up a chicken ball and look at Pat. "Denzel's family report?"

"I checked out his father, Darnel Wix. He's the ultimate bad-news dad."

"How so?"

"Actually, let's start with the mother, who gave birth to Denzel when she was sixteen and Wix was twenty-seven. Drug addict, busted for possession six times, prostitution a couple of times, died when Denzel was three."

"Poor kid," Brittany says.

"Leaving Denzel in the loving care of his daddy," I mutter.

"Yeah," Pat says. "Father to a kid he didn't want from a woman he didn't much want except to screw. Wix is a career criminal, maybe a gang guy, maybe not—the jury seems to be out on that—but he's got a criminal record the length of my arm. It runs the gamut from breaking and entering; robbery—armed and not; dealing dope; assault with and without a weapon; and bank robbery. The detective I spoke with says there's also a few murders he's suspected of being involved in but was never charged with. Including Denzel's mother."

"How come he's not locked up?" I ask.

"Pleading down to misdemeanors, early-release programs, the usual. But here's the thing—he had some darned good lawyering on the more serious charges."

"How good?" I ask.

"The kind of lawyers who skate on the dark side. Organized crime and the like."

"How can he afford that?"

Pat gives me a pointed look. "He probably can't, which means he's mixed up with some seriously bad folks. Tread carefully."

"Yeah," Brittany says.

"Wix has kept his nose clean the past few years," Pat continues. "Either that or he's learned how not to get caught. One source told us he's connected with a Russian syndicate, running drugs and maybe underage girls, which would explain the recent dearth of arrests. Those people spread around enough cash to keep the law looking the other way, hire the best lawyers, bribe a judge or two or three, and keep more than a few prosecutors from being overly curious about what they're up to. Long story short, they're able to run their operations with very little disruption from the law. That makes it possible for operators like Darnel Wix to function with impunity."

"That's wrong!" Brittany exclaims angrily.

I shoot her a sideways smirk. "Ya think?"

She isn't amused and looks away with her scowl intact. "So, Denzel's been on the street for twelve years?"

Pat shakes her head. "Luckily, Denzel had a grandmother who took him in and raised him right. Unluckily, COVID took her last year."

"How do you know so much about this?" Brittany asks Pat.

I'm interested in the answer as well. I knew some but certainly not all of it.

"I had a nice chat with Denzel's aunt on his mother's side," Pat replies before her eyes cut to mine. "Pretty sad story, Valenti. Wouldn't hurt for you to speak with the family to get all the details. I've only given you the view from forty thousand feet."

I shrug. "I tried. Nobody would speak with me."

A smile plays on Pat's lips. "That was before you stopped hating on Denzel."

"I didn't hate on him!"

"That isn't how Denzel saws things, Valenti. That upset a few people in his circle. The good news is that the aunt is willing to talk to you."

"Guess I managed to mend that fence a bit, huh?"

"Guess so. I'll text her contact info. You'd best call and get with them before you step in the poo again with Denzel. The clock is probably ticking on that," she adds with a wink.

"I'll call tonight."

10

Thank God for Uber. While I don't approve of the business model gig economy companies have ginned up, most Uber drivers don't know the city like regular cabbies do. I made calls to six different cab companies asking for a ride here without a single taker. The poor schmuck behind the wheel of my Uber ride looks ready to wet his pants as we ease to a stop in front of the address his GPS has delivered us to. I have an itch to scratch, and this is where I expect to find some answers. After Pat left last evening and Brittany headed off to bed, I spent four hours putting my budding investigative chops to work tracking down Darnel Wix. He should be here in this old, three-story, red-brick walk-up building. It's coated in at least a century's worth of city grime and pockmarked with what look to be scars left by bullets flying about the neighborhood. Lovely.

I lean forward from the backseat and slide a twenty to the Uber driver and, just for giggles, ask, "Want to wait around for me?"

His panicked eyes meet mine in the rearview mirror as he folds the bill into his shirt pocket. "No, sir. So sorry. I have another fare."

"No worries." I take a deep breath, summon some courage—or maybe it's nerve—and step out of the car, which rockets away almost before my shoes hit the crumbling asphalt. I look up and down a street littered with trash, boarded-up window frames, and shattered windows awaiting their plywood replacements. The stench of garbage, marijuana, and who knows what all hangs in the frigid air.

My eyes settle on the front stoop, where a couple of stringy Black teenagers—if they're even that old yet—stand guard, freezing their skinny butts off in baggy jeans, laceless high-top sneakers, and T-shirts under windbreakers. Tough guys. But the guns tucked into the waistbands of their sagging pants are real enough—every bit as real as the Glock resting in a shoulder holster beneath my left armpit. Staring into the vacant eyes of these kids and feeling the weight of more eyes from the surrounding buildings disabuses me of any misconception that I can handle things here by simply waving my Glock around if things go sideways.

"Whatcha doin' here?" the taller of the porch sentinels asks. A mist of freezing condensation shoots out through his blueing lips when he speaks.

"Looking for Darnel Wix."

"Who says he's around here?"

I shrug. "Doesn't matter to you. Tell him I'm here."

The kid doesn't seem sure how to handle my blowing past his veneer of gatekeeper authority. He settles on anger, steps down to the sidewalk, draws himself to his full five foot or whatever height he is, and rests his hand on the butt of his pistol. This probably isn't the right time to caution the kid about the dangers of blowing off his junk before puberty and a chance to put it to its proper use.

I peel back the lapel of my sport coat just enough to show him the Glock. "Yeah, I've got one too," I say when his eyes widen. "And guess what? I've used it a few times, and I'm still here to talk about it. The guys I was up against? They're not."

"Who the hell you be?"

"You know who Denzel Payton is?"

"Who the hell that be?"

"Mr. Wix's son. I'm his lawyer."

He screws up his face in confusion. "Mr. Wix got a boy? First I hear of it."

"Probably never came up." This kid almost certainly has no idea about just how much he doesn't know.

"So, he got a kid. He in trouble?"

That's why he has a lawyer. "Sure is. I'm trying to help him."

"No bullshit, man?"

"None."

Having been put in the position of having to think, the kid freezes. I start to feel a little sorry for him. "Just let Mr. Wix know I'd like to speak with him about Denzel. He'll see me or he won't."

The boy shoots a sideways glance at his fellow doorman, who shrugs.

"Well, get on inside and tell Mr. Wix he got company," the taller kid barks, seemingly relieved to have a way to exercise a little authority.

"Thanks," I say after the junior underling scurries inside.

"Uh-huh." The kid returns to his perch on the top step, where he stands a few inches taller than me.

"So," I say conversationally after a beat. "Tough getting a cab around here?"

The kid smirks. "Think you gonna hafta git your friend back here to pick you up, dude."

I smile and nod.

His smile broadens. "You probably be walkin', though. That cat be in a hurry to haul ass outa here."

A nasty-looking bit of middle-aged punk bursts through the door before I can reply. "What this be about, cracker?"

I assume this is the charming Darnel Wix. I stand my ground as he bounds down the steps two at a time to get in my face. His black gymnasium-logoed muscle shirt displays a wiry torso with well-defined, ropy muscles running down his arms.

"Mr. Wix, I assume?" I ask politely.

"Who's asking?"

"Tony Valenti. I'm one of the lawyers assigned to defend Denzel."

"Defend him from what?"

Really? This guy doesn't even check in often enough to know about the pickle his boy has landed in? "Murder and drug charges, Mr. Wix."

"That shit from a few months back?"

I nod.

"Thought that shit be over by now."

"They're trying to move it into adult court."

He looks away, blows out a long breath, and shakes his head. "Bastards be ruining another Black boy."

I don't mention that a little parental guidance might have helped steer his son clear of ruination. His blazing gaze remains fixed somewhere far away, perhaps while he ponders that same question. I hope so. Wix clearly has his own baggage to drag behind him, but it would be nice if he put in a little effort to lighten Denzel's load.

After a moment of him staring off into nothing, I grow impatient. "Do you know anything about a guy named Spike?"

"Spike? Who the hell is that?"

"Just a name I picked up along the way. Might have something to do with Denzel's predicament."

Wix's eyes narrow dangerously. "He tell you that?"

Whoa! *Back off, Valenti.* I'm not supposed to know Spike's name. I paste what I hope is a confused expression on my face. "Did who tell me? Denzel?"

"Yeah. Ain't that who we be talkin' about?"

"Denzel didn't mention anything about this Spike character. I got that from a cop."

The news seems to alarm Wix. I file that away, then steer the conversation elsewhere. "I'm hoping you can talk to me a bit about Denzel, Mr. Wix. Maybe you can help keep him in the juvie system."

"How the hell you figure I gonna do that?"

"If the court sees family taking an interest in the boy and his future, sometimes it builds sympathy in a judge."

He laughs bitterly. "Oh, yeah. Like some lily-white judge is gonna look at me and my rap sheet and turn the kid over to me. No way I be gettin' involved in any court shit."

Part of the reason I'm here is that I can't imagine the father of a fifteen-year-old standing aside while his kid is in jeopardy. "Denzel is your son, for God's sake. He needs your help!"

"Lemme tell you something, man. I don't know who Denzel's real daddy be. I be banging Sissy when she find out she be pregnant, but I weren't the only man getting into her pants, know what I'm saying? Anyway, she be kinda my old lady, so I got saddled with the boy. Kid needs a home, right?"

Maybe I judged this guy too harshly. "Did you get a DNA test to make sure he's yours?"

"Shit, man, that weren't even a thing then, leastways nothing we poor folk did. Like I say, could be any one of a few homeys I runned with—they all had a piece of Sissy, know what I mean?"

"Do you still run with that crowd?"

"One or two of 'em, yeah. Anyway, it don't matter who, I s'pose."

"Maybe the real father would get more involved with Denzel, spend some quality time with him—give him a chance to get his life back to where it was when he lived with his grandmother."

"What chance that boy got in this fuckin' world, huh?" Wix snaps back in a voice that oozes as much anguish as anger.

"Not as much chance as he should have, but at least I'm trying to help."

Wix's expression darkens, and his lips peel back into a snarl. He gets right up in my face. "You sayin' I ain't?"

I don't reply. Why bother? We both know the answer.

He steps back and gives me a contemptuous once-over. "Crackers like you—all dressed up in shiny threads and livin' high off the sweat of brothers and sisters—you don't know shit about how life is for the Black man. Not a fuckin' thing. Now, git your ass outa here and don't show that snowball face of yours here again."

With that, he turns and stomps back inside. The door guards close ranks at the top of the steps, signaling that I'll have to go through them if I want to follow. I almost laugh at the display of pre-pubescent machismo.

The taller kid smirks at me. "Y'all gonna call your Uber ride, homey?"

I point west. "L station that way?"

"Could be," the junior doorman replies in a bid to match his compadre's insolence.

His buddy offers me a miniscule nod, so I turn and walk away.

Oh, and that itch I wanted to scratch? Maybe Wix really does know Spike.

11

It's Thursday of the same week, the day Penelope and I typically have our weekly partner meeting over lunch at the Sandwich Emporium, a quaint sandwich shop housed in a 1920s-era bungalow a few blocks away from our office. It's minus twenty degrees outside and we're walking. Why? Because my partner is a lunatic.

"It's bracing!" she exclaims when we step outside and I immediately start complaining about the cold. "I love it!"

I don't get it; she's an otherwise sensible person. We often use this walk and sometimes part of our lunch hour to catch up on small talk. Somehow, in an office with only three people and offices ten feet apart, we seldom find time for chitchat.

"How's Dolly?" she asks. She's met the new mutt once and was charmed. Aren't we all?

"Settling in. When I woke Britts up for school this morning, Dolly's bed was empty. Didn't even look slept in."

Penelope pulls a face. "You can't tell if a dog's bed has been slept in!"

"Dolly and Britts were curled up together on the bed. Sure looked like the mutt had been there all night."

"That poor dog's sure in for a rough go of it at her new home."

"Oh yeah."

"Let's talk about work," Penelope says. "Denzel's hearing is barreling down the track at us. How's that coming along?"

"Too slowly." I haven't had a chance to bring her fully up to speed on my meeting with Denzel last Friday. I do now. I follow that up with the story of my Tuesday visit with Darnel Wix.

She stops and turns to me, eyes wide with alarm and, perhaps, a touch of anger. "You went by yourself?"

I nod.

She gears up to say more, then reconsiders and quickly covers the final ten feet to the door of the Sandwich Emporium, leaving me to trail in her wake. I follow her inside. A force of nature greets us, effortlessly blowing aside any storm clouds that may have followed us in.

"Miss Brooks! Tony-*san*!" Maiko Campbell exclaims. She's wearing a smile as wide as the sun, and possibly brighter.

"Maiko!" we reply in unison.

The weekly ritual then plays out. Maiko and her husband throw together some of the most ridiculous sounding sandwich creations imaginable every day and, somehow, they always work. Today's daily special is written in garish orange chalk in Maiko's inimitable cursive handwriting.

"The Elvis BELT?" I ask with a smile. The explanation is often the best part of the game. "We'll take two."

"You're gonna love it!" Maiko says while shaking her hips in a hilarious imitation of the King of Rock 'n' Roll.

"What's in it?" Penelope asks while I pay.

"You know what an Elvis sandwich is?"

My partner shakes her head.

"The traditional Elvis sandwich is peanut butter, banana, and crisp bacon—and the bacon must be very crisp!"

"And what makes it a BELT?" I ask.

Maiko beams at me. "Add lettuce and tomato. Get it? Elvis wore those big belts, right?"

I laugh. The logic, twisted as it is, falls into place.

Maiko hands me my change and makes a show of lifting a lip in a little Elvis sneer. "You'll be shaking your bums after you eat these."

We make our way back to our private table for two, a wobbly little thing wedged into an alcove leading to the emergency exit.

"There's also good news on the Denzel front," I announce once we're seated, then relate Pat's news that Denzel's family is willing to speak with us.

"You called?"

"I'm having a hard time connecting with these folks. Denzel too, at times, although that's getting better. The aunt took a few days to get back with me."

"They'll succumb to all that Valenti charm sooner or later. How did the call with the aunt go?"

"I'm going for a visit this evening."

"That's good, right?"

"You'd think so. This *has* to work, Penelope. We have no time or room for error. The transfer hearing is a week from today."

She looks away thoughtfully, then turns her gaze back to me. "You're up to the challenge, partner. You always are."

I give her a wry smile as Maiko bustles over with our sandwiches.

"You two are looking very serious today," she says as she slides paper plates piled high with our Elvis BELTs onto the table. A pair of sweating water glasses follow.

Sweat in this weather? Go figure.

Penelope looks up at Maiko. "Weighty matters on our minds today."

Maiko's smile dims to the wattage of two or three football stadiums at night. "There is nothing a good sandwich won't put in a better light. Eat! Enjoy! Then you'll feel better and your troubles won't seem so big."

Penelope smiles. "Good advice!"

Maiko winks and hurries away to serve more Elvis BELTs.

Penelope watches her go. "God, how I love that woman!"

"Me too." I pull my plate closer and reach for my sandwich.

Penelope slaps my hand away. "Napkins!"

Ah, yes. My partner has made it her mission to protect my clothing from all manner of foodstuffs. Sadly, I need the assistance. My dry cleaner undoubtedly disapproves of her efforts, but my bank account loves her for it.

I drape napkins all over myself before we dig in, then ponder my dilemma for tonight. I can't afford to blow this. I'm damaged goods already. I set my sandwich down about halfway through, take a drink of water, and settle back in my seat to study Penelope.

She watches me watching her until she swallows. "What's going through that devious mind of yours, partner?"

"I want you to come with me tonight."

She sets her chin in her palm and thinks for a long minute. "This isn't like you, Tony."

True enough. I recently went into the jaws of hell all by my lonesome to confront Wix. I decide to wait her out.

"Losing your mojo?" she teases.

I neither smile nor make a return crack. She may have a point.

Her smile melts away. "What time?"

"Seven."

"Where?"

"I'll pick you up at quarter to."

She nods. We plan our visit while we finish lunch. The sandwiches turn out to be okay, but no lips are curling and no bums are shaking by the time we finish. Nor does either of us break out singing "You Ain't Nothing but a Hound Dog" or "Jailhouse Rock."

We somehow make it back to the office without frostbite.

"Let's hope this works out," Penelope says six hours later as we pull up outside a well-kept bungalow in the suburb of Berwyn.

"It will," I assure her with a smile. "Everyone falls instantly in love with you Kansas gals and immediately spills their guts."

"Since when?"

"Since always! Seriously, though, I think bringing in a fresh face is the right move. I've had some rough moments with Denzel. There may be some lingering resentment or doubt where I'm concerned."

Thelma Payton greets us at the front door with a generous smile. "Get on in here out of that cold! Brrr." She closes the door firmly behind us and holds out her hands for our coats. After she hangs them on a freestanding wooden coat rack, she presents a hand to me.

"I'm Thelma. You must be Tony."

I shake her hand and venture a smile. "I am. You don't say that like it's a totally bad thing."

She smiles back, then turns to Penelope and shakes her hand. "And you are?"

"Penelope Brooks. I'm Tony's law partner."

Thelma beams. "Our Denzel has *two* lawyers working for him! Ain't that something."

Penelope makes a show of sniffing the air. "Something smells heavenly."

"Brownies fresh out of the oven. Just in case you folks showed up hungry. Come on in the kitchen."

We dutifully follow Thelma into a sparkling kitchen,

where a tray of brownies sits on a cooling rack on the stovetop. She fills three mugs with coffee, places brownies on plates, and sets it all down in front of a trio of chairs.

I'm thinking things are off to a great start until I feel something rubbing up against my leg and look down. *Cat!* They *know* when you don't want them around, especially if you're allergic. Or, in my case, both. Penelope notices and turns to our host.

"Thelma, Tony's allergic as heck to cats."

Thelma leans down to look. The cat is wrapped around my calf. She reaches a hand to nudge it away from me. "Now shoo with you, Mr. Boots! Go on. Git!"

Penelope laughs. "Mr. Boots?"

Thelma smiles. "You folks are probably too young to recall those Puss'n Boots cat food commercials from way back. Our kids named Mr. Boots after the kitty in those commercials."

"Was that its name?" I ask. "I don't remember it that way."

"Who knows?" Thelma says with a laugh. "I wasn't about to argue. It made them happy."

Penelope nods in agreement. "In Kansas, we call that common sense."

"How old is Mr. Boots?" I ask.

"She must be going on sixteen, seventeen, by now."

"She?" I ask with a chuckle. "The kids named a girl cat *Mr*. Boots?"

Thelma shrugs. "What do little kids know about the sexes?"

"Oh, plenty these days!" Penelope answers.

Thelma frowns. I frown. *We* have kids. Parents find it harder to find humor in little kids knowing all about the human birds and the bees in grade school.

"So," Thelma says after taking a bite of brownie, savoring it, and chasing it with a slug of coffee. Time for business.

"Thanks for seeing us," I say. "I didn't get off to a great start with Denzel."

She gives me an appraising look. "So we heard."

"What changed?" I ask.

"To make me agree to speak with you?"

I nod.

"Pat O'Toole vouched for you. That and a chat I had with Denzel. Seems he wasn't as respectful to you as he shoulda been."

Pat again. Is there anyone she doesn't know? She seems to be opening doors for me all over.

Penelope jumps in. "Tony can be a little crusty."

Thelma's bemused eyes shift to my partner. "Might of heard something like that."

"In his defense," Penelope continues, "Denzel *was* there when Harry Hood was murdered, and the police found heroin when they took him into custody. Heroin is a red line for us."

Thelma's eyes shift to me. "Can't say as I blame you on either count, Mr. Valenti. What changed your mind?"

"Actually, that still troubles me, but he's also a scared fifteen-year-old kid with a story that explains at least some of it away. But he went willingly to Tent Town with ill intent, even if he wasn't the guy who took a baseball bat to Harry."

Thelma hears me out thoughtfully. "So let's talk about how that came to be."

"Okay." I settle back to listen.

"Denzel was saved from being a latchkey kid after his mama died by his granny on his father's side. She kept him on the straight and narrow. Makes a soul wonder how Denzel went so wrong so fast after she passed."

"And yet," Penelope says.

Thelma sighs. "He's pretty much on his own now, rudderless, with nobody he feels obligated to do well for—certainly not that worthless lowlife Darnel Wix."

"Why weren't you involved in his life?" I ask.

"His granny was saintly in many ways but she didn't truck with our side of the family, what with Sissy and all."

"Sissy was Denzel's mother?" Penelope asks.

"That's right. Denzel's granny doubted any family that raised the likes of Sissy could be trusted with a child."

"Seems harsh," I say.

"Well, it holds a grain of truth," Thelma says ruefully.

"But Darnel Wix," I counter. "People in glass houses and all."

"Ain't no mama sees her own child through a clear lens, Mr. Valenti. Any kids of your own?"

"Yeah," I answer with a grin. "A little angel, in fact."

"There you go," she says with a wink. "'Course, we saw a little of Denzel here and there. He was curious about his mama's kin, so he came around now and then without telling his granny. After she passed, we tried to reel him in when we saw he seemed to be headed in a bad direction—offered him a room here."

"He didn't accept?" Penelope asks.

Thelma shakes her head sadly. "That's right."

"Why not?" I ask.

"Don't rightly know. Part of it seemed to be a holdover of his granny's distrust of our side of the family."

"But he needed a place to stay," Penelope argues.

"That's right. When I said exactly that, Denzel claimed his daddy was helping him out some."

Darnel Wix again? "My understanding is that this Spike character took Denzel under his wing."

Thelma frowns. "I've heard that name a time or two."

"Do you know him?" I ask hopefully.

She shakes her head no. "No idea who he might be."

"Could Spike be Denzel's father?" Penelope asks.

"My goodness," Thelma says in surprise. Then she falls

silent while she turns the idea over in her mind. "Ain't never heard Denzel refer to his daddy as Spike."

We chat for a few more minutes without learning anything else relevant to our case. Next week's hearing to transfer Denzel's case to adult court is looming large. That's where our focus needs to be. We'll have plenty of time to worry about Denzel's family matters after that.

12

"Let's hope she has some useful information for us," I say to Penelope after lunch the following day. We're about to meet with investigator Rana Asadi from the public defender's office. She's been working Denzel's case from the beginning. As part of the pilot project this case falls under, they're making the investigator available to us.

"I'm sure she will," Penelope says. "What do you think of putting Thelma Payton on the stand next week?"

We both spent the morning in court on other cases and spent the drive home last night discussing them, so we haven't yet had a chance to discuss our visit with Thelma.

"I really like her. She'll make a good witness. I'm not sure I want to tip our hand about all our witnesses this early, though."

Penelope nods thoughtfully. "True, but our immediate goal is to keep Denzel in the juvenile system."

"I know. Let's see what else we have to use next week and decide if we need Thelma's story then."

"Fair enough."

We fall silent and think about the case until we hear voices in the lobby. When the visitor informs Joan that she's from the public defender's office, we walk out to introduce ourselves.

I've asked Mike Williams about Rana Asadi. Interesting story. Her family came to the United States from Iran in the late 1970s, fleeing both the shah's security services and the religious fanatics who were about to overthrow him. Mike says she's grateful for the opportunities available here but is growing increasingly apprehensive of our country's slide toward authoritarianism. "All *isms* unnerve her," Mike concluded. Amen.

Rana's appearance is average in almost every respect: height, weight, shoulder-length black hair, unprepossessing dark slacks, and an unremarkable powder-blue blouse. The exception is her black eyes, which brim with alert intelligence. Penelope waves Rana into the conference room ahead of us. The investigator is lugging a large, wheeled briefcase behind her. Surely her files for Denzel's case don't fill the entire thing? It's Friday afternoon, and I'm suddenly having visions of being buried in paperwork for the entire weekend. We settle around the table and chat for a minute while Joan delivers coffee for me, chai tea for Penelope, and a bottled water for Rana.

"So," Penelope says after Joan leaves.

Rana leans down, opens the briefcase, and pulls out a couple of thick file folders held closed by thick rubber bands. She sets them on the table. "Where would you like to start?"

"Why don't you lay out things in whatever order makes sense to you?" Penelope suggests.

Rana smiles. "Ah, some respect for your investigator's brain. I like that."

"You come highly recommended by Mike Williams," I say.

"Mike's a good guy." She snaps her fingers. "I knew I'd heard your name. You worked with him on his brother's case, didn't you?"

I nod again. Bobblehead Valenti.

"You guys kicked butt," she says with a satisfied grin as she peels the rubber bands away from the file folders.

"Yes, they did," Penelope agrees. "Now let's figure out how to do that in this case."

Rana frowns. "This is a tough one. The state has a lot of ammunition to throw at Denzel."

Penelope meets Rana's concern with a tight smile. "Tell us what we have to counter that."

Rana's eyes pass between Penelope and me. "Let's start with next week's transfer hearing. What's your strategy?"

"Still working it out," I reply. "We need people to stand up for Denzel's character."

Rana nods. "We have a few of those."

"Tell us about them."

She does. She's gotten around, having spoken to a few teachers, some of Denzel's grandmother's friends and neighbors, even the pastor of the church she attended for four decades. Their statements echo what Thelma Payton told us last night: Denzel is a good kid whose world started to fall apart the day he buried his grandmother.

"I'm not an attorney, but this doesn't paint a picture of a chronically recidivist kid who can't be rehabilitated," Rana concludes. "In my humble opinion, that's your strongest argument to keep this case in the juvie system. Denzel doesn't have a lengthy juvenile record the state can point to that suggests otherwise."

"That's how we see things," Penelope says. "We just need enough evidence of it to convince a judge."

I weigh in. "You're welcome to make suggestions, Rana. You've been doing this a long time. I don't doubt for a minute that you have valuable insights to offer."

Penelope nods. Rana smiles. I smile. Maybe we should get Joan in here to snap a photo of Denzel's happy defense team.

Rana taps one of the file folders. "All the interview transcripts are in here. These are copies for you to keep."

I slide the folder in front of me but leave it closed. We can read through the material later. I want to pick Rana's brain while we can. "Of all these folks, who do you think will be best in front of a judge next week?"

"Pastor, high school vice principal, Little League baseball coach," Rana replies without hesitation. "All polished, all passionate about this kid, and they've all known him for years—the vice principal was at Denzel's middle school. They moved to high school in the same year."

"What about Thelma Payton?" Penelope asks.

"Who's she?"

Penelope explains.

"That damned Wix," Rana says angrily. "When I asked him if there was any other family, he told me, 'Nobody worth mentioning.' He wouldn't give me a single name. That man is bad news."

"I've had the pleasure of a visit with him," I say dryly.

"How much do you know about him?"

"Not much. Hothead."

"Aging punk," Rana says dismissively. "Petty thug, though he seems to have graduated from the petty gang stuff he's been around most of his life. He may have gotten mixed up with some of the big boys."

"Such as?" I ask.

"Foreign types. I don't have anything solid, just suspicions."

"Great," I mutter. "You're the second person I've heard mention that."

"Who else?" Rana asks.

I tell her about my relationship with Pat.

She nods. "You might want to put Wix on the stand to show the judge what Denzel has managed to overcome since his mother passed."

"Not the worst idea," Penelope agrees.

"Have you read through Marcie's notes?" Rana asks. "She believed in Denzel."

"She had a lot more empathy for him than I did, at least initially," I say.

Rana pulls a surprised face. "Why is that?"

I explain about the attitude I encountered on my first visit, note the heroin angle, and finish up with my concerns about Denzel being in Tent Town with Spike that night.

She hears me out. "There's no way to explain away the fact that he was there with a bad man, but if I were the prosecutor, I'd tread carefully around the heroin angle."

"Why?" I ask.

"The cops found it in Denzel's pocket, true, but the jacket belonged to Harry Hood, and Denzel's fingerprints weren't on the baggie."

"Whose are?" Penelope asks.

"Nobody's."

Penelope lifts an eyebrow in surprise. "Gloves?"

"Denzel claims he wasn't wearing any. He says Spike was."

"Can we prove Denzel wasn't wearing gloves?" I ask.

Rana shakes her head. "There weren't any on the inventory of his belongings when the cops took him in, but the prosecution will argue that he could've ditched them."

"Probably so," Penelope agrees. "But his prints are on the bat, which suggests he wasn't wearing gloves."

"True," I grumble.

Penelope may not have spent much time working criminal cases with me, but she's smart enough to run circles around most of us much of the time. Working an entire case with her is going to be interesting.

"How do we handle the Spike issue next week?" I ask. "All we have to suggest that the guy even exists—let alone that he killed Harry Hood—is Denzel's word."

"Plus the ghost the responding cops saw him with," Rana adds.

"But even there, all the cops can tell us is that someone was with Denzel when they arrived on the scene," I counter. "Someone who accused Denzel of the assault and ran away from him. There's diddly-squat to prove they arrived together or visited Harry Hood's tent together."

Rana blows out an exasperated sigh. "True."

"I don't think we should go there during the transfer hearing," Penelope says. "Let's focus on the character issues. Let's convince the judge that Denzel deserves the chance at rehabilitation the juvie system is designed to give a kid his age."

I hold up a cautionary hand. "Not so quickly. The third pillar of our argument to keep Denzel in juvie is that he will be an at-risk inmate in the general prison population. Spike threatened Denzel, and Denzel believes Spike has the reach to get to him in prison. We want the judge to take that threat seriously."

"But will she?" Penelope asks.

For Denzel's sake, I hope she does.

13

I was right to fear spending the weekend lost in an avalanche of paperwork. In addition to Rana's case files, I ventured down a few investigative avenues that her work suggested might be fruitful. I came away with a handful of ideas to explore, but nothing likely to keep Denzel out of the adult system at this week's transfer hearing. It's now eight o'clock Sunday evening, and I'm back at Tent Town for a third consecutive night. With the departure of the polar vortex, I'm hoping to find the elusive Di back from the homeless shelter. Time is running out on us to develop more than a character defense for Denzel on Thursday.

"Well, well, if it ain't my pal Mr. Lawyer," Toe says with a smile when I walk up and find him sitting on a battered old lawn chair outside his tent. He stands, ducks inside, and emerges with a bathing suit dangling from his fingertips. "Think I might go for a dip in the lake now that it's warming up."

I smile, blow out a breath, and point at the condensation floating away from my lips. "It's not exactly balmy out here, Toe."

He chuckles and tosses the bathing suit back into the tent.

"You're a persistent cuss, Mr. Lawyer, I'll give you that. That Denzel kid is in good hands."

"Thanks, but we're still spinning our wheels."

"You might be in luck tonight. Di came back today."

"Finally! Where can I find her?"

"Not so quick. She's not keen on talking to you."

"But she might. Where is she?"

Toe points to the lawn chair. "Have a seat. I'll go talk to Di and see if I can coax her into having a chat with you. She sure won't if you go barging into her space."

I study Toe for a moment, then nod and sit down. "Be persuasive."

The gap-toothed grin returns. "Oh, I can be mighty persuasive. Back soon."

I pull out my phone and check email. Nothing of interest other than a note from my father asking if Brittany is still going to join him in Italy for spring break. I reply: *That's the plan, Papa.*

Speaking of Brittany, she sent a text: *If you can see your way clear to spending an evening at home with your lonely daughter, band practice tomorrow night at 7 PM sharp!*

I smile. *It's a date.*

Then I read through the local news for a few minutes. Nothing of interest. Where is Toe? I stifle the urge to go looking for him and Di, then lean back in the lawn chair to wait. A crescent moon hangs high in the night sky, surrounded by a handful of stars that burn brightly enough to punch through Chicago's light pollution. I count a couple dozen before I hear muffled voices approaching. It's Toe and a woman I assume to be Di. She's dressed in puffy beige winter boots, black leggings, a bulky white winter coat, gloves, and a kelly-green ski cap with flaps pulled down to her chin. A scarf hides her face, leaving only a slit for her eyes. She studies me wordlessly.

I offer what I hope is a disarming smile as Toe gently takes her elbow and speaks to her softly. I don't hear what he says, but it seems to work. With a curt nod, she shuffles closer. Her eyes are alert and wary when I get to my feet and tower over her as I extend a hand. "Tony Valenti. Pleased to meet you."

She backs up a step without touching my hand. "I'm Di."

"Thanks for agreeing to help."

Her eyes widen in alarm as they cut to Toe. "Help?"

"Tony just means telling him what you saw."

Her eyes turn back to me. "I think this is a mistake. I know your type. White men of a certain age. Not to be trusted."

The verbal assault is launched in a gentle voice that bespeaks an articulate, if hopelessly biased, mind. How do I reply?

"Hemingway, Weinstein, the list goes on and on."

She isn't going to tell me a thing. Maybe she'll speak with Penelope.

Di takes another half step away, eyes glued to the ground at her feet. "I can't get involved in this, but just so you know, the kid didn't kill Harry."

"Who did?"

She holds her hands up and backs farther away. "That all I have to say. I shouldn't have even told you that."

"Will you talk to my partner?" I ask in desperation. "She's a woman."

Di snorts. "A woman under your thumb? I won't contribute to her abuse by playing your games."

With that, she turns and marches away.

Toe meets my gaze. "Sorry, man."

"Should I send Penelope?"

"That's your partner?"

I nod.

He shrugs. "Why not?"

14

On the afternoon of February 2nd, the day before Denzel's transfer hearing, I nervously pace around the desk in my office while I wait for Penelope to return from Tent Town. Toe called late this morning to tell us that Di was willing to speak with my partner, after all. Of course, we received the same summons on Monday, but when Penelope arrived, Di was a no-show. Will she keep today's appointment? Penelope's been gone well over two hours—because she's having a long heart-to-heart with Di, or because something has gone wrong? I've had a hard time keeping my phone in my pocket instead of calling to check; Penelope told me not to call or text. She worried that it might spook Di, who certainly seems skittish. I've picked my keys up a few times, on the verge of driving over to Tent Town to investigate. I've put them down every time. So far.

I've killed time by burning through a bag of Vitner's chips and a Hershey's bar while reading and rereading our witness testimony. What we have won't be enough. Yes, we're going to have some upstanding people telling the judge that Denzel is a fine young man. Then the prosecutors will play up the senseless injustice of Harry Hood's murder, the drug and robbery angle, and whatever else they can conjure up to tug on the judge's heartstrings and/or hunger for vengeance. I've convinced myself that our only chance is to trot Di into court to repeat her story that Denzel did not kill Harry Hood. Everything the prosecution has is supposition. If we can produce eyewitness testimony to contradict their version of events, it may be enough to prompt the judge to keep the case in juvenile court.

Aside from planting a seed of doubt about the strength of the evidence against Denzel, I'll argue that with the real killer on the loose, the threats to silence Denzel are credible, and that placing him into adult jail will expose him to attack. Juvie is safer for him. Not that he'll be entirely safe there, but a lot more people meet their sticky end in jail or prison than they do in juvie. Yup, I'm clutching at straws.

Joan surprises me by poking her head into my office with a look of concern. "Have you heard from her?"

"I was hoping you had. Should we call?"

"Better not. She warned me not to. Made me promise not to, actually."

"Me too." The worry weighing Joan down concerns me. It's out of character for a woman who seems to take everything life can throw at her in stride. She finds a ray of sunshine somewhere in most any circumstance—a gift she passed along to her daughter.

"You know how people like to jaw with Penelope," I say in as light a voice as I can muster. "Di's probably talking her ear off."

Joan rewards my effort with a wan smile before she returns to reception. I drop into my chair, brace my elbows on my desk, and set my head in my hands. I need to do something constructive. We're less than twenty-four hours from the start of the hearing. I reach for the phone to make a couple of calls I expect will be a waste of time. The first is to Cedar Heights chief of police Jake Plummer. I've known Jake for a couple of years now, going back to when he was a homicide detective. He's a good guy.

"What can I do for you?" he asks after we exchange greetings.

I really shouldn't be calling him to discuss a case that involves his department, so I fumble for a reply that doesn't involve Denzel's case. Calling Jake was a mistake.

"Does this involve the Payton case?" he asks with a hint of impatience.

"It did, but I thought better of it."

"Good call."

"It's just..."

"You can't help yourself when you're convinced you're on the right side of a case, can you?"

"I'm worried sick about that kid winding up in jail, Jake."

He doesn't reply.

"I'm sorry—" I begin before he cuts me off.

"Truth be told, I'm not crazy about this either. Nothing good ever seems to come from throwing kids in with the general prison population."

"Can you do anything?"

"Like what? Wave my imaginary police chief magic wand to keep young Mr. Payton in juvie? I'm afraid not."

"I think this Spike guy is for real."

Jake falls silent for a long moment. I can hear him breathing. "Could be," he finally says. "The name has come up a time or two in other cases, but we don't have a thing on the guy. Tell your kid to keep his wits about him wherever he ends up. And now it's time to end this call."

"Okay. Thanks, Jake."

"Chief Plummer to you," he says with a smile in his voice, probably to let me know he's not overly upset with me for calling.

My next call is to Rana Asadi. She would have called if she had anything new, but maybe she's close to shaking something loose. It takes less than thirty seconds to discover that she's not. I've just hung up when I hear Penelope walk into the lobby. I hurry out in time to see her finish hanging up her coat and turn to face us. Her slumped shoulders and dejected expression tell the tale.

"No-show again?" I ask.

She nods. "I hoped she'd have a change of heart. I hung around as long as I could."

"What did Toe have to say?"

Her eyes meet mine. If anything, she looks even more distressed. "He told me Spike came around Monday afternoon. It spooked the heck out of Di. She doesn't want to be seen speaking with us."

"Much as I hate to admit it, that's probably the smart move."

"So how do we bring her in?" Joan asks, surprising us by weighing in. She seldom does.

Penelope frowns. "Best guess? We never see her again."

Ever, or during the next twenty-four hours? Which, so far as Denzel's transfer hearing is concerned, is the same thing. Denzel is going to be in the Cook County Jail by this time tomorrow unless we can manufacture a miracle before ten o'clock tomorrow morning.

15

Aside from the fact that we're about to lock horns with a prosecutor determined to flush a fifteen-year-old kid down the drain of the criminal "justice" system, the juvenile courtroom setup is familiar: judge's bench, prosecution table across the well to its right, defense table to the left, public seating behind them. Penelope and I settle behind our table and organize our files. I cast a look across the aisle when two young prosecutors arrive. I'm struck by the contrast in their demeanors. A tall, blond quarterback type is giving off a tsunami of alpha dog vibes. His mousy companion probably served on an obscure committee. He's all but invisible here, as well. Alpha dog turns an unnerving predatory smile on us—and I'm seldom impressed by these lawyerly displays of testosterone. To riff on an old cliché, I feel as if we've brought a knife to a gunfight—and a butter knife, at that. I nod at him curtly, then make a show of getting organized. Why does the guy intimidate me? Maybe it's no more than us being the only thing standing between Denzel having a chance to salvage his life and being thrown to the wolves?

A bailiff brings Denzel in. The poor kid looks terrified. He's deposited in the seat on the far end of our table, putting

Penelope between us. Having her at his side should be a comfort. We exchange terse greetings. Denzel, perhaps picking up on a feeling of hopelessness emanating from me, adopts a dejected expression. It deepens after Penelope informs him that Di stiffed us again. I remember Denzel's eyes widening in excitement when I first told him about her.

"You know," he said at the time, "most of what went down is a blur, but I remember her—especially her eyes. Man, the look she gave me—pure hatred."

Yeah, well, he's not going to have to worry about looking into those eyes again anytime soon.

"Any chance she'll show?" he asks Penelope.

"Very slim. Toe will try to drag her here if he sees her."

Slim doesn't begin to capture the slender odds of that happening.

Judge Saunders enters, the hearing is called to order, and thoughts of Di and miracles are parked outside the courtroom doors under the heading *Fairy Tale Endings.*

The proceedings begin with the prosecution's opening statement, delivered by alpha lawyer, who is named something or other Gilbert. I start to wonder if the rules of juvenile court are different than in grown-up court, because Gilbert blatantly crosses the line into argument again and again in his opening statement, which is generally a no-no. We all toy with that line in opening statements, but this is way over the line. Penelope finally makes an entirely valid objection pointing this out, a rarity during opening statements. The judge, who is proving to be something of a nasty witch masquerading in the guise of a kindly old grandmotherly type, slaps Penelope down, so my partner scowls and sits on her hands while Gilbert runs roughshod over the rules.

"This is how we treat our youth in Cook County?" Penelope whispers incredulously from behind her hand.

"I guess so," I reply, bitterly recalling a proclamation I read on the state's attorney's website that celebrated their apparently fictional commitment to rehabilitating youth or some such BS. Right.

Penelope and I have decided to share courtroom defense duties. She stands to present our opening statement. Speaking in a courtroom isn't her strong suit, but she's determined to overcome the stage fright that has haunted her in the past. She's certainly smart enough to handle trial duty, and I'm convinced that her earnestness and winning personality have the potential to sway any judge or jury. She simply needs to be the person we see outside the courtroom.

"Denzel Payton is a young man with a commendable history of responsible behavior as he's matured," she begins. "The court will hear from several adults who will attest to his many admirable qualities and accomplishments. Denzel's world was turned upside down when his beloved grandmother fell ill and died after contracting COVID-19. As the court learned in Denzel's detention hearing last fall, in the absence of responsible parents, Denzel's grandmother took him into her home when he was age three and did a superlative job raising him to be a respectful and responsible young man. Suddenly on his own after her tragic death, he lacked responsible adult supervision or even a pillow to lay his head on. Perhaps not surprisingly, Denzel fell under the influence of his miscreant father and his associates. On the evening of October twentieth, Denzel accompanied one of these men to the homeless camp known as Tent Town, where the man proceeded to rob and murder Harry Hood. He then fled, after setting Denzel up to take the fall for the crime. We will present evidence demonstrating that Denzel was not the individual most responsible for the events that evening. Thank you."

"Perfect," I say to Penelope when she sits down.

She gives me a relieved smile and whispers, "I did it!"

Denzel looks a little bemused but gives Penelope a little fist bump.

Then Gilbert begins his case, beginning with one of the arresting officers, who tells us that he's a cop, went to the academy, blah, blah, blah. Then it gets interesting, with the prosecutor and judge soon showing their colors. After soliciting testimony about how the cop and his partner happened upon Denzel and an unknown individual at the mouth to the alley, Gilbert steps to within a few feet of his witness.

"Now, you couldn't be sure if these two individuals were together or had just encountered each other in the street, correct?"

"That's right."

"But it's most likely they'd just run into one another when you first saw them, correct?"

I'm on my feet instantly. "Objection! Leading the witness, Your Honor."

The judge's eyes flicker my way. "Overruled."

"Your Honor, that is a textbook example of a leading question," I argue. Which is, of course, against every trial rule when questioning your own witness.

Saunders glares down at me. "Do *not* presume to lecture me on the law ever again, Counselor. Do I make myself clear?"

Oh yeah. Another judge with a God complex. I nod and sit down.

"Answer me!" Saunders demands.

"Crystal clear, *Your Honor,*" I mutter.

Gilbert smiles at me, then turns back to his witness. "The defendant then initiated an altercation with this other individual, didn't he?"

I reluctantly rise again and say in exasperation. "Leading the witness, Your Honor. Again."

The judge slams her gavel down with a sharp crack. What is this, a temper tantrum?

"Overruled, Mr. Valenti. Do not raise that objection again."

I'm flabbergasted. What did I ever do to this shrew? When I don't immediately respond, she leans over the bench and levels a finger at me. "Do you understand?"

Sure, I do. You're an evil witch in a black robe. "Yes," I reply tersely. I can't bring myself to append *Your Honor* to the reply.

And so it goes as the first cop's partner, a detective, and the medical examiner are led by the nose through a litany of leading questions and half-baked assertions not supported by any solid evidence. We cross-examine the witnesses, but it's clear Saunders isn't particularly interested as we try to back them off some of the most damning allegations. The fix is clearly in. Why?

The prosecution calls a former neighbor of Denzel's who is willing to allege that he "went bad" after the death of his grandmother. Denzel leans close to Penelope.

"This is gonna sound conceited, but this girl was sweet on me. I wasn't sweet on her, and she didn't like it. She's been bad-mouthing me ever since, even when Grams was alive."

Penelope lights into the young lady on cross. "Now, Miss Jones, isn't it true that you told the police back in October that Denzel pretty much dropped off the face of the earth after his grandmother died?'"

"Spo'se so."

"Yet you just told us that he 'went bad' in the months following his grandmother's untimely passing. You claim this frightened you."

"That's right."

"If you didn't have any contact with Denzel, how can that be true?" Penelope asks sharply.

"Just is. That's all."

"But you just told us that you didn't speak with Denzel during that period, did not in fact even see him. It's one or the other. I'd appreciate hearing the truth."

"Objection!" Gilbert thunders indignantly. "Asked and answered. Badgering the witness!"

"She didn't answer my question," Penelope retorts, earning herself a wrathful glare from the bench.

"The court responds to objections, Counselor," Saunders snaps.

So overrule the bogus objection and let's get on with things, I think impatiently. Penelope's taking this girl apart.

"The objection is sustained," the judge intones.

Penelope looks incredulous, opens her mouth to argue, then snaps it shut and takes a moment to rein in her temper. She turns an icy stare on Saunders. "No further questions, Your Honor." Then Penelope loses her shit. "No point if you're not going to compel witnesses to answer legitimate questions."

Uh-oh.

Instead of exploding in another temper tantrum, Saunders almost smirks when she announces, "You've just earned yourself a contempt citation, Counselor. We'll have a hearing about that at the end of today's proceedings."

I place a calming hand on Penelope's quivering forearm and tug her back down into her seat before she digs herself any deeper into the judge's shit pit by delivering the tongue-lashing the witch deserves.

Gilbert rests his case, making sure to turn a smug, gloating expression on us before he sits down.

"This guy is probably auditioning to get to *The Show,* or whatever prosecutors think of as the jump from juvie court to big-boy court," I mutter.

"We'll take our lunch recess now before I hear from the defense," Judge Saunders announces. "Be back at one o'clock."

"We're screwed, aren't we?" Denzel asks as the judge gets to her feet.

I don't argue the point. We all experienced the last couple of hours. A three-year-old could guess where this is headed.

Penelope, of course, rests a reassuring hand on Denzel's arm. "We get our turn after lunch."

"*If* the judge even bothers to let you talk, Miss Brooks."

Penelope smiles and pats his arm. "She *has* to."

She also has to be impartial, follow the rules, and allow both parties to argue evidence—none of which she's done to this point. I keep the thought to myself.

I place a desperation call to Rana during the recess.

"How did the morning go?" she asks.

"I thought this would be an actual hearing," I reply sourly. "It's turning out to be more like a grand jury proceeding—a foregone conclusion. Kangaroo court comes to mind."

"Who's the judge?"

"Saunders."

Rana groans. "Denzel is off to adult court, then."

"How can she get away with her BS?"

"She's a judge," Rana replies matter-of-factly. "Good friend of the chief judge as well."

"I'm surprised you didn't just tell me that she's Timothy Walker's wife." Walker is the state's attorney for Cook County.

"Aunt," Rana mutters.

"Jesus."

"No relation," Rana says with a resigned chuckle. "Although He wouldn't have any more clout in Cook County than the chief judge and Walker together."

"Thanks for the pep talk, Rana. Anything new for us?"

"No."

We end the call. I somehow refrain from taking the stairs to the roof and jumping off.

After lunch, we call our first witness, Kayla Tompkins, the vice-principal of Denzel's high school.

"Tell us about your experience with Denzel Payton," I ask after she's sworn in.

"He's a great kid. Never ran with any of the bad crowds. We always found him to be respectful of his teachers, coaches, support staff, and the other students."

"How were his grades?" I ask, knowing he was pretty much a straight-A student, except in math, where his grade fell to B.

"He always received good grades. Mostly As right across the board."

"Is there anything else you'd like to share with us about Denzel?"

Tompkins smiles warmly at her former student. "Absolutely! Denzel was a leader at school. He took it upon himself to tutor other students, then recruited other high-performing students to do so. The school administration was so impressed that we built a program around what Denzel began, one that still thrives within our school community."

Tompkins has delivered a powerful testament on behalf of Denzel. I thank her.

"Do you have anything for this witness?" Saunders asks Gilbert.

"Won't take but a minute," he replies as he gets to his feet and casts an almost bored look at Vice-Principal Tompkins. "When did you last see Denzel Payton at your school?"

Tompkins stiffens. "Shortly after his grandmother passed away."

"Last year?"

"Yes."

"So, Payton has been a truant for over a calendar year at this point, correct?"

"Yes, but we all know—"

Gilbert cuts her off tersely. "Just answer the question, Miss Tompkins."

"I'm sorry, but you need to understand that—"

"That's enough," Saunders snaps at the witness. "Simply answer yes or no unless Mr. Gilbert invites you to elaborate. Is that clear?"

By all rights, Penelope or I should come to the aid of our witness. Both Gilbert and Saunders are out of line with their callous treatment of the vice-principal, but intervening would be pointless and might very well prompt them to treat her even more shabbily.

"So," Gilbert says dismissively, "you have absolutely zero knowledge of who Denzel Payton has become over the course of the past twelve months, do you?"

Tompkins appears as if she wants to gamely battle on in defense of Denzel, but the twin glares of Gilbert and Saunders discourage her from trying. Her shoulders slump. "I suppose not."

"Is that a no?"

Tompkins's eye bore into the prosecutor. "No."

"Thank you," he says sarcastically as he turns away. "No further questions, Your Honor."

Our next witness is Denzel's Little League baseball coach, who smiles widely at Denzel while he speaks.

"Denzel is a great kid," he says, echoing Vice-Principal Tompkins's assessment. "Hard worker. Terrific teammate. Always showed up early and stayed late—helped out with clinics and practices for the younger players."

Anticipating Gilbert's cross-examination, I try to defuse what I know is coming. "Tell us, Coach, even if Denzel hit a rough patch, can you imagine him harming another human being?"

"Absolutely not. I saw Denzel endure a lot and never witnessed him lose his cool. That's pretty impressive for a young man his age—especially one who endured the heartache and challenges he faced growing up."

"Thank you for coming today, Coach," I conclude.

Gilbert all but bounces out of his seat. "Did Denzel play ball for you last year?"

"No," the coach replies.

"Is he registered to play this season?"

"No."

"So, *Coach,* you haven't seen Denzel at a baseball field for close to two years?"

"No, but I've seen him a—"

"That's a no?" Gilbert snaps. "Just yes or no."

"I guess not."

"You have no idea what Payton may or may not be capable of now that he's become a street thug, do you?"

"Objection!" I shout as I get to my feet, glaring at Gilbert as I do. "Prejudicial characterization of our client. No foundation." I'm tempted to add that the prosecutor is a son of a bitch, but hold my tongue.

"Sustained," Saunders says, all but causing me to fall over dead. Of course, without a jury, none of this theater matters, unless someone files an appeal.

The pastor of Denzel's grandmother's church is up next. He tells us about Denzel singing in the church choir, how he and his gram lent a hand around the church before and after mass almost every week, how Denzel was a leader in church youth programs, and how he was a faithful volunteer whenever the church needed help. "Just a devout, delightful member of our church community."

"Have you seen Denzel since his grandmother's funeral?" Gilbert asks to open his cross-examination.

"Yes," the pastor replies.

The answer seems to surprise Gilbert. "When?"

"I can't give you dates." The pastor has already picked up on—or been forewarned about—Gilbert's game plan. Perhaps a celestial whisper in his ear?

"Recently?"

"Depends on how you define recent, Mr. Gilbert."

Gilbert's eyes narrow. Mere holy men don't challenge Alpha Lawyer! "One year or more ago?"

"No, I don't think it's been that long."

"Six months?"

"Hmmm. Probably not that long."

"Where did you last see Denzel?"

"Oh, just around the neighborhood. Can't say exactly where."

"Has he attended church since his grandmother died?"

"Couple of times."

I doubt Gilbert has any clue, but I suspect he's probably calculated that the pastor isn't going to tell a flat-out lie. "Immediately after the funeral, right?"

"I think that's fair to say."

The answer seems to embolden Gilbert. "The truth is that you have no idea what depths Denzel Payton has descended to over the past year or more, do you?"

The pastor's eyes harden as he stares back at the prosecutor. "In all honesty, Mr. Gilbert, I don't know the answer to your question, but I can't imagine the Denzel Payton I know would ever do the things you've accused him of."

Gilbert gives the witness a sardonic smile. "So your answer to my question is no."

"As I just said—"

"Yes or no?"

"No." If this particular holy man had the power to assign souls to Heaven of Hell, it's abundantly clear from his expression that prosecutor Gilbert's afterlife would be a very warm one, indeed.

"We have no more witnesses, Your Honor," I reluctantly inform the judge after the pastor is excused.

"Does the defense rest?"

"We do."

"Fifteen-minute recess," she says. "Then we'll wrap this up."

"Why doesn't she just pack me off to adult court right now instead of wasting any more time," Denzel says after the judge retires. "This whole thing is a joke."

Out of the mouths of babes.

"Wrapping up" begins with Penelope's impassioned plea for clemency. "Denzel is a good kid who was dealt an extremely cruel hand by fate. Look at his history, Your Honor, as told by responsible, respected adult members of his community who came here today to bear witness to the goodness of Denzel. This boy deserves the chance to be rehabilitated in the juvenile system. Pushing him into the adult justice system will be a one-way ticket to ruin. Did he do wrong? Of course he did, but what he's guilty of is exhibiting poor judgement at age fifteen. Who among us didn't at that age? In his grief and abandonment, Denzel turned for support to someone he shouldn't have turned to. That led him to Tent Town that evening. Assault wasn't on the agenda, much less murder, at least not so far as Denzel knew. That it did fills Denzel with remorse, Your Honor."

I've been watching Saunders carefully while Penelope has been speaking. I'm surprised to see a hint of humanity on the judge's face as Penelope makes the case for giving Denzel a chance at a decent future. Is she getting through? Does Saunders have the capacity to see past her former prosecutorial biases and find compassion for a kid who's made mistakes?

Penelope pauses for a drink of water, then stands behind Denzel and rests her hands on his shoulders. "What does it say about us as a society if, when a young person makes a mistake—however big the mistake may turn out to be—we simply cast his life away? That is exactly what the state seeks to do today, whether or not Mr. Gilbert sees things that way. There's an old saw we all know, Your Honour: Two wrongs don't make a right. Please don't multiply Denzel's error in judgment into a second wrong. Thank you."

"Thank you, Counselor," Saunders says as Penelope sits down.

My partner has delivered a masterful, concise closing argument. "Great job! Didn't I say you could do it?"

She smiles. "It did go pretty well, didn't it? I think Saunders was listening."

"Of course she was. You were great."

"Thanks, Tony. I've been watching and learning. You're a pretty good teacher."

I smile. I'm happy for her. The sky's the limit now that she's got her courtroom legs under her again.

"Two wrongs don't make a right," Gilbert scoffs as he gets to his feet to deliver his closing. "Said as if a hardened teenage killer is just a little kid in need of a motherly admonishment to keep his hand out of the cookie jar. A disabled veteran of America's armed forces is dead!" he snaps with an angry glare at Penelope. "Murdered for a few dollars and a little dope. Murdered by a thug! Denzel Payton is anything *but* an innocent child, Your Honor!"

Gilbert pauses and walks back to his table, as if to gather himself in the face of such evil. "There is no question that this case belongs in adult court, Your Honor. Harry Hood was murdered in the commission of a crime, the theft of drugs, a little cash, some electronics—the defendant even took the coat off Harry's back!" Gilbert pauses and turns a baleful stare on Denzel. "Yes, Your Honor, this young man—this *saintly* young boy, if we're to believe a parade of character witnesses who haven't seen Payton in a year or more—stole the clothes right off the body of a man he'd just beaten to death with a baseball bat. Was he once a good kid? Perhaps he was, but he isn't a good boy any longer. Is it a shame this boy went bad? Yes, it is, but the fact is that Payton *did* go bad—very bad indeed. The man sitting in this courtroom is most assuredly not the child who was described by adults who knew him a lifetime ago."

I'm once again watching Saunders as she listens. She may have been impressed with Penelope's argument, but she's all in on this tirade.

Gilbert pauses for a drink of water, then pivots to the murder case itself. "Allow me to touch briefly upon this lurid fantasy that Payton wasn't Harry Hood's killer. There is no evidence—*none*—that this imaginary person Miss Brooks talks about even exists. There is zero physical evidence suggesting anyone other than the defendant was in Harry Hood's tent that night. Only the claim of a troubled man who was detained only yards from the scene of the crime, caught with the dead man's belongings in his pockets. Payton's fingerprints were on the murder weapon. Let's not buy into any of Miss Brooks's fairy tales about an imaginary killer. Denzel Payton most assuredly committed this crime."

Gilbert ruefully shakes his head. "Finally, Your Honor, I'll speak to the defense plea to spare this poor boy the horror of being incarcerated among his own kind: murderers, liars, thieves, and drug dealers. To hear Miss Brooks tell it, being in prison may harm this impressionable young child. How so? Might he learn about drugs? Thievery? Violence? How to kill someone? *Please.* What about the kids in our juvenile facilities—the kids who still have a chance at redemption? Why should we throw a predator like Payton in with them? Don't *they* deserve better from us? Don't we have a responsibility to protect them from this monster?"

I grudgingly admit that Gilbert is delivering a powerful closing. He walks a step closer to the bench and gazes up intently. "Your Honor, please do the right thing and allow the state to prosecute Mr. Payton in the forum designed to try and punish violent offenders who have proven themselves to be a danger to good law and order. Thank you."

Saunders doesn't bother with the pretext of taking a recess. "The court finds that the prosecution has successfully carried a burden of proof sufficient to transfer this case to the adult courts of Cook County. Thank you. Court is dismissed."

"Oh my God, what have I done?" Penelope asks disconsolately after the bailiffs take Denzel away. "I should have let you make our opening and closing arguments, Tony. I flopped."

I wrap an arm around her shoulders. "You were magnificent. Saunders was hell-bent on sending this to adult court. Nothing was going to affect the outcome."

"Why? What does that woman have against Denzel, for God's sake?"

"It wasn't personal, Penelope. This is our criminal court system. It's all about winning. All about vengeance."

"Where does it end?"

I shrug. "We just have to keep fighting the good fight. After watching a travesty like this, you realize what a miracle it is when we win one."

Penelope pulls away. A determined look enters her eyes. "We'll win in adult court, partner. We will."

16

I'm still licking my wounds two days later on Saturday evening when the doorbell rings. Dolly's head snaps around and her ears perk up. Deano shifts his eyes enough to look toward the door, then rolls over on his side.

"That should be Pat," I say as I turn and start walking toward the front door. Brittany follows. Dolly trots along behind us.

Pat hugs me, hugs Brittany, hugs Dolly, and hugs Deano when he eventually lumbers out to greet one of his favorite people. Once the lovefest ends, we settle around the kitchen table with a bowl of Vitner's potato chips and a cup of hot chocolate each. Dolly follows Deano's lead, sitting attentively at my side. I'm the most likely source of dropped crumbs.

"I suppose I should say that I'm sorry you lost in court yesterday," Pat says.

"We'll get another shot at it in grown-up court," I reply gamely.

"I can't work up any sympathy for your client, fifteen years old or not."

"I get it. I read the articles you wrote about Harry. I was struck by his bitterness about being sent off to war."

"Harry's bitterness about that, maybe a good bit of it, led to his estrangement from his father, Congressman Bobby Lowry. Are you familiar with the good congressman?"

"Not really."

"Look up asshat in the dictionary. There should be a picture of him."

I chuckle. "So, it speaks well of Harry that he estranged himself."

"It does."

"Why the different last names?"

"Harry switched to his mother's maiden name after he came home from Iraq."

"I bet Dad liked that."

"Trouble was brewing between them before Iraq, but the congressman was a big cheerleader for going to war. That didn't sit well with Harry."

I redirect the conversation, albeit not exactly in a pleasant direction. "How are things going with your mother?"

Mrs. O'Toole is in a precipitous slide into the murky depths of Alzheimer's, which came hard on the heels of her husband's sudden passing. It's been a hellish time for the tight-knit O'Toole clan. Pat and her siblings are platooning care shifts to keep their mother in the Cedar Heights home she's lived in for forty-some years. Where Pat has found the time and emotional reserves to also babysit us is beyond me.

"Mom has good days and bad," Pat replies. "Heck, she has good hours followed by bad hours—you just never quite know what to expect. It breaks our hearts to be losing her a little more every week."

Tears well up in Brittany's eyes. "It sounds so horrible."

Pat takes Brittany's hand in hers. "Well, she's still with us, kiddo, which is something. It's not all bad. I've learned to cherish and celebrate the better moments."

"Things went well in Hawaii?" I ask. The O'Toole children took their mother on one last trip to Maui, where their parents had spent many a happy vacation in years past, with and without the kids.

Pat smiles. "It went pretty well. I'm not sure how much it registered with Mom, but I noticed her looking around with a smile now and then. Maybe she remembers more than we think. I hope so."

We talk about Hawaii for several more minutes. Then the doorbell rings. I go to the door and find Cedar Heights chief of police Jake Plummer waiting.

"Here to meet the new addition to the family," he announces after we exchange greetings.

I wave him inside. Dolly, who has come to investigate, peers intently at Jake.

"It's okay," I tell her with a wink at Jake. "Just an old cop, well past his prime."

Dolly wags her tail and moves in.

Brittany is standing in the doorway with a hip resting on the frame. "I wonder if cops have a distinct smell."

"Oh yeah," I reply. "Doughnuts and burnt coffee."

Jake shoots me an exasperated side-eye, then smiles and ruffles the lustrous fur surrounding Dolly's neck. "I suppose these people are feeding you boring doggy treats, aren't they? You know who has the good stuff, don't you?"

Put that way—Milk Bones or doughnuts—I can see why a mutt might prefer cops to the rest of us.

Jake's eyes lift beyond Dolly to where Deano is flopped on his bed. Deano offers the new arrival a half-hearted tail wag in greeting.

"And hello to you, you old slug!" Jake exclaims as he walks over to give Deano the Fearsome Watchdog a quick scratch on the crown of his head, which gets Jake a couple more tail wags.

I pour Jake a cup of coffee while he and Pat exchange hellos and whatnot. Then we all settle around the kitchen table. Dolly wanders over to watch and listen, then flops on the floor beside me with a Deano-worthy sigh. I'm inordinately touched when she shifts to lay her head on my foot. Funny how animals can make us happy with a simple show of affection. Then again, it may simply be that I was the last person to give her a Milk-Bone.

After a bit of small talk, I get up and walk to the refrigerator with Dolly at my heels. "Burger time, folks. You gonna stay for a couple, Jake?"

He looks at me like I'm crazy. "In this weather?"

"It's above freezing."

"Barely!"

"It isn't even snowing."

"First time this week," he grumbles. Such a snow crybaby.

"I bought a little tent thing and set it up outside the back door," I say. "Put in a heater and everything. Mind you, the grill heats things up in a hurry."

He smiles. "You do make a decent burger. Don't mind if I do."

Deano snaps upright at the word *burger*. By the time I pull the platter of patties out of the fridge, he's shouldering Dolly aside to take up his rightful place in line as they follow me out the back door. Deano is showing Dolly who's the alpha dog around 47 Liberty Street—at least where food is involved.

Jake follows us outside and promptly pronounces me insane for cooking outdoors "in the dead of winter."

"Toughen up, Chief."

"I wish I was in Aruba," he grumbles.

I grin. "Speaking of which, I'm taking Britts to St. Maarten in a few weeks."

"Bully for you. No time off for the chief of police."

"Aww."

He shoots me the bird. "I'm going back inside before I get frostbite."

"Wussy."

"How much do you know about police dogs?" Brittany is

asking Jake when me and the dogs troop back into the kitchen twenty minutes later with fully cooked burgers. Brittany has everything out on the table: cheese slices, tomato and onion, condiments, a side of baked beans. She's also whipped up a basket of fries in the air cooker.

"A little," Jake replies. "Why?"

"Dolly's a dumb name for a dog. I want to change it."

"Why would you want to do that?" Jake asks. "As I understand the story, her original handler was an incurable Dolly Parton fan. That's not so bad, is it?"

"I get the idea of naming a dog after an admirable person, but it isn't exactly going to frighten off bad guys, is it?"

Jake chuckles as he fixes a burger. "You know the story of why Milwaukee PD retired Dolly, right?"

"Sorta," Brittany replies. "Her partner died on duty, right?"

"That's right. He had a massive heart attack and dropped dead when he and Dolly chased down some punks and got into a bit of a scuffle."

"They killed him?"

"Not unless you hold them responsible for causing his heart attack."

She immediately goes over to the dog and gives her a big hug while Jake continues.

"Dolly never got over it. She wasn't a problem or anything, but she lost her edge. She didn't chase after bad guys quite the same way. Tammy Whitworth told me that Dolly tended to hang back a bit, keeping a close eye on her partner instead of going hell-bent after whoever they were trying to chase down."

"Afraid her partner would drop dead again if they caught up?" Brittany asks.

"That's exactly the problem Milwaukee K-9 suspected. Dolly also became a little more aggressive once they did catch bad dudes. Probably trying to ensure that her partner didn't have to enter the fray."

"And drop dead," I muse.

Jake nods. "That's how Tammy figured things. They didn't want Dolly to hurt anyone, and they felt she was getting a little too stressed in chase situations."

Brittany's brow furrows. "Any danger of her attacking the wrong people?"

"Hell, no. As you can see, she's as sweet as can be," Jake says with a chuckle as he looks at Dolly. She's snuggled up against Brittany and seems curious about the repeated use of her name, which she's been trained to listen for as the prelude to a command. She's probably a little bewildered that no commands have followed a single mention of her name.

"In fact," Jake continues, "Dolly is almost too friendly for a police pooch."

"I'm sure she's plenty aggressive when called upon," I say hopefully.

Jake's eyes cut to mine. "A little hyperaggressiveness might be just the ticket if you keep attracting bad actors to your happy little home."

"Let's hope it never comes to that."

"Amen, brother." He pops a fry into his mouth. "Tough day in court yesterday."

"It was."

"When does it go to trial?"

"Looks like the end of June."

"Where is Denzel now?"

"Still in juvie. We petitioned to keep him there until we go to trial. Anything to keep him out of Cook County."

"I'll bet Walker didn't like that."

I don't much care what the Cook County state's attorney thinks. "Screw Timothy Walker."

"If only it were that simple." Jake mutters. "When will you know?"

"The hearing is on Monday morning."

"Good luck with it. That meat grinder is no place for a kid."

We studiously avoid further mention of the hearing or trial while we finish dinner.

Jake excuses himself after coffee. "The missus is waiting."

Pat and I step out of my house after Jake departs, leaving a grumpy Brittany behind with a mountain of homework. We're taking Deano and Dolly out for their evening constitutional around Independence Park. I lock the door and drop the house key into the right pocket of my coat, where it joins a quartet of dog poop baggies. A pair of leather gloves are already jammed into my other coat pocket. The temperature is dropping fast, heralding the arrival of another polar vortex that will discourage humans and canines from braving the elements. Yet another of the once-in-a-hundred-years weather events that seem to be growing commonplace.

"Can you handle them both yourself?" Pat asks as I gather the leash loops into my right hand.

"Sure. Deano's too lazy to pull on the leash nowadays, and Dolly is too well trained."

"That wasn't a half-bad dinner, Valenti."

"It was a great dinner." I'm secure in my mastery of burgers on the grill.

She gathers her fingertips together, touches them to her lips, and blows a kiss away from her mouth. "Exquisite!"

"Now you're just making fun of me."

"Not at all, Chubby. Without a word of a lie, you're the burger maestro."

"Again with Chubby, huh? I thought we were over that."

She grins. "With how much you hate it, Valenti? No way!"

We reach the end of our front walkway and turn right on the sidewalk as we set out for Independence Park at the end of the block. Liberty Street is a couple of lengthy well-treed blocks long. With the streetlights reflecting off the snow and the trees leafless, our way is well lit.

A young, laughing couple jog down a driveway a couple of houses ahead of us, towing a pair of toddlers behind them on red snow disks. The kids squeal in delight. Pat and I chuckle as the family turns onto the sidewalk ahead of us and starts to pull away.

"That's the Priolo's old place, isn't it?" Pat asks. The Priolo family was a fixture on Liberty Street for many years before the parents moved away a couple of years ago after becoming empty nesters. Other neighborhood fixtures have also moved away or, sadly, passed away.

"Yup," I reply. "Nice to see some young families moving into the neighborhood."

"About time."

We reminisce a bit about growing up in Cedar Heights as we stroll along, the dogs marking our progress in snowbanks and on trees. When we reach the park, we follow a trail of well-packed snow around the perimeter. The village has taken a few tentative steps to begin undoing years of neglecting Independence Park, but there's a long way to go. At least the sorry state of the almost bald playing fields is hidden beneath the snow, and the rusting play structures have been taken down.

"Plenty of sled tracks and little footprints here," Pat observes with approval.

I nod, watching as a fresh set is laid down by the family ahead of us. The parents are walking hand in hand. The kids race ahead, veering into the middle of the park, laughing and shouting as they fall and plow through snowbanks.

"Not in the face!" the mother shouts when a snowball fight breaks out.

The kids ignore Mom until she repeats the command with an edge in her voice.

"Yes, Mommy," they call back.

Dolly is watching with interest. I suspect she wants to join the fun. Deano pays no attention whatsoever, then lumbers out of line and begins circling. And circling. And circling. He eventually locates the right spot and squats to make a poop deposit. When I pull out a baggie, Pat reaches for the leashes.

"I'll hold the mutts while you clean up."

I smile and extend the poop bag to her. "How about I keep the dogs and you pick up after Deano?"

She snatches the leashes out of my hand. "Not happening, Valenti."

I mock pout before bending down to clean up, shooting Deano a nasty sideways glance as I do. "You should look a lot thinner after this," I say as I dig out a second baggie. He ignores me.

"This is why one gets a small dog," Pat says as she watches.

I make a show of struggling under the weight of the bags as I straighten up. "So noted."

"I'll keep the dogs," she announces when I return to the trail. "You look pretty weighted down."

"Deal." I motion ahead at the young couple. "Maybe they'll lend me one of those snow disks to transport Deano's goodies home."

"I'd like to see you work up the nerve to ask."

As if. We walk along in companiable silence, watching the antics of the kids frolicking in the snow. I recall doing the same with my brother and sister—both now deceased—years ago. Dolly lets out a little whine as she watches.

By the time we've rounded the far end of the park and circled back toward Liberty Street, the young family is at the newly installed chain link fence surrounding the derelict swimming pool where Pat and I spent the summers of our youth. The pool house has been demolished and the debris hauled away as part of interim Cedar Heights mayor Alvin Smith's efforts to rehabilitate the place. The hookers and druggies have been run off, which is a good start. I imagine the next challenge will be finding enough funding to restore Independence Park to its former glory.

The kids are peering through the fence as we approach. Mom and Dad, as well. The parents turn to us and we exchange *Good evenings*.

"Porsche?" the man asks me.

"My name's actually Tony," I say, extending my non-poop bag hand.

"Derek," he replies. "Love your wheels."

"Thanks."

"I'm the guy with the Honda Odyssey."

"Oh stop," his wife says with an eye roll at Pat. "Best people mover around."

"Right," Derek mutters.

She turns to Pat. "I'm Maggie."

"Pat O'Toole."

"I love your dogs!"

Pat points at me. "His dogs. If they soil your yard and you're looking for the right person to complain to, he's your man."

The kids are staring wide-eyed at the dogs, albeit with a trace of apprehension. The dogs are almost as big as they are. The children look to their mother for direction. She turns a questioning look on me.

I kneel in front of the kids. "You want to meet the dogs?"

They silently nod with big eyes.

I give a gentle tug on Dolly's leash. "Dolly, come."

She doesn't need to be told twice after I unclip the leash from her collar, but has the sensitivity to ease into the kids' space so as not to frighten them. Two little hands reach out to touch the dog's back, the tentativeness soon replaced by laughter and wide, happy smiles when Dolly nuzzles them. Deano suffers to have the kids give him a little attention, standing aloof with a lengthy sigh while the kids pet him.

Quickly ascertaining which is the fun dog, the kids turn their full attention on Dolly, and the trio are soon at play. Dolly starts to race in circles around the children, dodging in and out of their reach, first with her head down and butt pointing up at the moon with her tail wagging furiously, then rolling in the snow with them. Deano sits down to watch.

When I turn back to Derek and Maggie, she tilts her head toward the pool. "Our realtor told us that the village plans to have all of this rehabilitated and open in the spring. The kids are going to love it!"

And you believed it? I hold my tongue rather than burst her bubble. I don't want to be revealed as Downer Valenti within minutes of meeting these folks. "Mayor Smith has it on his radar."

Maggie's smile falters. "It's not a sure thing?"

"I don't think so," Pat says.

Maggie's eyes cut to Derek. "That bitch!"

He shrugs. "You can't trust half of what some realtors say."

I think he's being overly generous.

Pat reaches out to touch Maggie's sleeve. "Mayor Smith is committed to seeing this through. Probably not this year, but soon, we hope."

We chat for another minute or two before I announce that I still have a couple of hours of work to do.

"What line of work are you in?" Derek asks.

"Lawyer."

Pat pokes a thumb into her own chest. "Journalist. Now you know our deep, dark occupational secrets."

Maggie laughs, then points at her husband. "Derek's a cop."

I wave a hand around the group to encompass all of us. "All the public's favorite people in one place!"

We share a laugh over that, everyone tells everyone else

how nice it was to meet, we separate Dolly and the kids, and then we head home.

"Nice people," Pat says as we walk away.

"They are. Shame those kids don't have the park we grew up with, isn't it?"

Pat nods thoughtfully. "We should do something about it."

"We?"

She turns an enigmatic smile on me. The wheels in her head are turning for the rest of the walk home.

I suspect I'm going to be doing more than preparing for Denzel's trial over the next few months.

17

Brittany and I meet Pat for lunch at Portillo's the following weekend. Pat meets my gaze after we sit down with our meals. "I've been thinking about Independence Park since we met Maggie and Derek."

"What about it?" Brittany asks.

"It really needs a makeover. Me and Chubby here were talking about it last week, as in 'What can we do to kick-start that?'"

We were? Independence Park isn't a subject I'm comfortable with around Brittany. The dead body of her boyfriend, Bobby Harland, was discovered in the park's dilapidated pool house sixteen months ago. She's on the road to healing from that wound, but she still hurts. She avoids that corner of the park when we take the dogs walking there, even though Mayor Smith had the remains of the pool house bulldozed and hauled away last summer. I'm acutely aware of the thousand-yard stare in my daughter's eyes every time her gaze strays that way.

"So. Any ideas?" Pat asks me.

When I hesitate, Brittany turns to me and rests a hand on

my arm. "It's okay to stop pretending that corner of the park doesn't exist."

I nod uncertainly. "Okay."

"You know what?" she asks.

"What?"

"The day I see that place all fixed up with a sparkling pool filled with little kids screaming and laughing and playing, it won't remind me anymore about how ugly and desolate it looked back when, well… you know. It breaks my heart to imagine Bobby in that hell hole."

"Makes sense," Pat says softly as she reaches to squeeze Brittany's hand. Then she meets my gaze. "Let's make it happen."

My daughter's depiction of how she wants Independence Park to be stirs memories of my childhood years, when that was exactly how our summers at the pool were spent. An image of my late sister, Amy, frolicking in the pool at fifteen and cannoning into the water off the low diving board, pops unbidden into my mind. Yes, that's exactly how things should be.

"Big job," I say.

"I'll tell you who will have some ideas," Pat says. "Reverend Jakes."

I smile at the mention of the pastor of New Calvary Church in Lawndale. He's a community organizer par excellence. His effort to make over the West Side neighborhood has yielded remarkable results. Pat and I pitch in to help at least one afternoon every month. "He probably would. The key will be funding, and lots of it."

Pat already has her cell phone in hand. "Reverend!" she says happily when he answers. They exchange greetings and chat for a minute before Pat's eyes meet mine. "I'm with Tony. Can I put you on speaker?"

"Of course," I hear even before Pat activates the speakerphone.

"Hey, Reverend," I say.

I can hear his toothy, open smile in his reply. "How ya doing, Tony?"

"Fine, thanks. You?"

"The good Lord is smiling on me today, Brother Valenti."

"Glad to hear it."

Pat cuts in. "We're thinking it's time to fix up Independence Park."

"It sure is," Jakes agrees. "Gonna need yourselves some serious cash to make that happen."

"That's why we're calling," Pat says. "Any ideas about how to get the ball rolling?"

"I might have an idea or two. How about I get some of my folks together and see what we can do. Cheap labor never hurt no one."

I've been thinking about how much effort Jakes and his flock pour into the ongoing effort to rehabilitate Lawndale. It's important work, and a tough, unremitting slog. If Lawndale can help itself, so can we. "Thanks for the offer, Reverend, but you folks have more than enough on your plate. I'm going to get this done with our neighbors here in Cedar Heights."

Pat's eyes cut to me in surprise before a smile steals across her face.

"Whoo-ee!" Jakes exclaims. "Love that community spirit, Tony. That's the way to do it."

"Thanks," I say with an answering chuckle. It's impossible to do anything *but* smile and laugh in the face of Alvin Jakes's irrepressible joy with life.

"Course, I'm happy to chat anytime," he adds.

"I may call from time to time to pick your brain."

"Pick away as often as you like."

We say our goodbyes. As Pat and I bask in the afterglow of committing ourselves to doing good works, the face of another teenager swims into focus. Maybe if Denzel Payton had been able to hang out in a place like Independence Park used to be and will be again, things in his life might have played out differently.

If it's in any way within my power, I resolve to see that he has a chance to enjoy this place after we're done fixing it up.

18

After a short wait at the Cedar Heights Village Hall just before noon the following Tuesday, I'm shown into the office of the mayor. Alvin Smith, a tall Black man, rises to meet me. He's dressed in a deep-blue suit, a blinding-white shirt, and his signature fire-engine-red necktie. A full head of tightly cropped graying hair betrays middle age. He's an impressive man. I'm a fan—even if he is a politician. The feeling seems to be mutual—even though I'm a lawyer. We first crossed paths when I was fighting a developer intent on turning Liberty Street and Independence Park into a shopping center and condos. Smith's support was crucial to saving our home. The battle led to the downfall of the mayor at the time, who was forced from office in disgrace. Smith was appointed to finish out the crook's term.

He comes around his desk with his hand extended. "Tony!"

"Mr. Mayor."

"I hope you don't mind eating in? Busy day here."

"The hellish life of a civil servant, huh?"

"What can I say? Being mayor isn't all smooching baby

cheeks and kissing grown-up ass. Let's get sandwiches next door and bring them back here."

"Truly a man of the people," I quip.

He chuckles. "Won't hurt me to be seen with Tony Valenti in an election year."

I roll my eyes. "Right."

Smith seems to be a regular at the sandwich shop. The owners are friendly with him and not at all surprised to see him on their premises. Quite a few folks I assume to be regular customers nod and say hi, as if it's a common occurrence to dine with the mayor. Smith returns the greetings in the same familiar manner.

"What's good?" I ask as we study the menu.

"Everything."

"Is the egg salad safe?"

He cuts his eyes to mine. "Absolutely, and shame on you for asking."

He orders pastrami on rye and I ask for an egg salad on white bread. We make small talk while we wait on our order, then return to his office and settle at a modest conference table to eat.

I make a point of looking around. "I heard this office was enormous."

"Once upon a time. I had a little work done after I moved in."

"How so?"

"The reception area you came in through used to be part of this office." He hooks a thumb at a door cut into the rear wall. "There used to be a private dining room for Mayor Brown through there. We replaced it with a lounge where staff can take a break or eat lunch."

Alvin Smith hasn't changed his spots one bit since he assumed office. I hope the people of Cedar Heights have the good sense to vote him back into office this fall.

"So," he says. "You wanted to discuss Independence Park."

I bite into my sandwich, predictably managing to squeeze a glop of mushy egg out the opposite end of the sandwich. I wipe up the egg mess, then tell him about the visit Pat and I made to the park on the evening we met Derek, Maggie, and their kids. "Those kids deserve better."

"Amen."

"I appreciate what you and Chief Plummer have done to clean up the park."

"Should have been done years ago."

"What's your game plan moving forward?"

"Ultimately, to make it what it once was."

I smile. "Glad to hear it. When can we expect the village to get more work done?"

He sets his sandwich down and frowns. "Now there's the rub, Tony. Funding. That's the major impediment to getting things done."

"I've never understood how we got to this point, Mr. Mayor. We used to be able to build stuff forty or fifty years ago. Why can't we accomplish a thing these days?"

"We spend millions of dollars on consultants and accountants, none of whom seem to know how to actually get things done."

I nod. It's all too familiar to me. "Plenty of people skimming off the top to fund careers that sprang up over the past few decades. They talk a good game but don't seem to do much more than shuffle paperwork and move numbers around on spreadsheets."

The mayor nods. "By the time they're done, we seem to be skimping on dollars to get things built. Public funds need to be put to work for public use, not as a slush fund for connected developers. BS like the boondoggle we stopped on your street a couple of years back. Mayor Brown liked to give his developer friends public funds to build with, then didn't even tax the resulting little Taj Mahals. That's gonna change."

"Already has."

"Some. If I get reelected this fall, we'll put a stop to it."

"How?"

"We're not gonna have enough time for that over lunch. How's that for a politician's answer?" When I roll my eyes, he grins. "Don't worry. That topic will be front and center in my campaign. Speaking of which, are you still planning to lend a hand?"

"Yup. Looking forward to it."

He beams, then chews on his sandwich for a beat. "Let's set up lunch or breakfast in a month or so to chat about it."

I push my plate aside after I polish off my sandwich, then tell Smith about our ideas to rehab Independence Park. "We're looking to start by getting the pool replaced."

"Is that so?"

"Yeah, but we're struggling with a plan to raise enough money. Can you help?"

He thinks on that for a minute. "I might be able to round up a little funding. How much do you need?"

"Probably around fifty thousand. We're planning to fundraise, but that's a pretty steep hit."

"I'll see what I can rustle up," he says after he takes a final bite of his sandwich. "Maybe we can pitch in a few grand. I wish I could do more."

"Every little bit helps."

He winks. "Get me reelected and I'll find more."

"I can see the campaign posters now, Mr. Mayor: *Vote for Mayor Smith and win a park!*"

"I have no doubt that your neighbors will rally to your side."

"We'll see about that."

"You have more influence than you think, Tony."

"Ha! I can't even get a sixteen-year-old to do what I want.

Besides, I don't know half my neighbors, and I'll guarantee they don't know me."

"You're wrong there, my friend. I have faith that you and Pat will work things out. The village will get on board as best we can."

"Thanks."

He takes a sip of coffee. "I saw where things didn't go well for you with the kid you're defending for Harry Hood's murder."

"No, they didn't."

"My money is on you and Penelope. Haven't seen you lose a case yet."

"Then you haven't been paying attention. We've lost a few."

"None that matter."

He's got a point. Mind you, this one *does* matter, and things aren't looking good.

"How's the boy doing?"

I frown. "He was transferred to Cook County Jail over the weekend. We're worried about how that will go."

"Tough crowd in there. How's he handling it?"

"We'll find out this afternoon."

19

Thelma Payton calls in a panic an hour later, only minutes before Penelope and I plan to leave the office to visit Denzel.

"You need to get him out of there, Mr. Valenti! They beat him up. He has a couple of black eyes and his lip is split wide open. The poor child is wild with fear. They're gonna kill him in there!"

My thoughts immediately turn to Judge Saunders. Didn't we tell the stupid bitch this would happen?

"The guards don't care," Thelma continues. "I begged them to keep him safe. A couple of them laughed!"

I gather up my car keys. "We're on our way."

"They wouldn't let me stay," Thelma says indignantly. "Nobody would say if he's seen a doctor. What kind of people run that place?"

Animals. "We'll find out what we can, speak with Denzel, and I'll call you afterward."

Penelope and I arrive at the Cook County Jail at California and Twenty-Sixth twenty minutes later. We park and hurry inside. It's as dreary a place as I've ever been. I get a sense of foreboding every time it comes into view, and this afternoon is no different. If despair has a smell, this place reeks of it—a mix of sweat and fear, overlaid with unbridled testosterone that has no constructive outlet. With some ten thousand inmates—many of them hardened criminals—it's no place for a kid even younger than my daughter.

We wait twenty-five minutes before a guard finally brings Denzel into an attorney-client room. He's limping, his face is bruised and swollen, and his eyes are filled with rage.

"How could you let this happen to me?" he shouts.

There's no point telling him we did everything we could to keep him out of this place.

"Who did this to you?" Penelope asks.

"How in hell would I know? Couple of big guys saying, 'Welcome to the big house.'"

"Why?"

He gives her a look of disbelief. "How am I supposed to know? Maybe because I'm new here."

Penelope's eyes are brimming with tears. "I'm so sorry, Denzel."

It's an indication of his rage that he doesn't soften at all; he likes Penelope and has always treated her with kid gloves, even when he's upset.

He turns his rage on me. "This is how it's gonna be every day?"

"Not if we can help it."

"What are you gonna do?"

What *am* I going to do? Denzel needs to be separated from the general population. I'll start with the jerks running this place. Maybe threaten a lawsuit. Plead with the prosecutors to intervene. Go hat in hand to Judge Saunders. "We're on this. There has to be a way to keep you safe."

"We *will* keep you safe," Penelope says with steel in her voice.

She's as good as her word. First to feel her wrath are the Cook County Sheriff's Department underlings who run the jail, then the sheriff himself. State's attorney Timothy Walker gets an earful, as well. At Penelope's urging, Pat writes a scathing indictment of the jail and sheriff in the *Trib*, making a point of placing the primary blame for the situation on Judge Saunders's callous decision to send Denzel to the Cook County Jail in the first place. The article ends with a final shot at Saunders: "How disconnected from reality is a judge who thinks it's okay to send a fifteen-year-old boy into a jail with thousands of adult criminals?"

They get the results they're after. Denzel is transferred to a lonely cell, where he is isolated from the general jail population. But Timothy Walker and his aunt, Judge Saunders, clearly resent being publicly called onto the carpet by a lowly defense attorney and her reporter friend. I suspect this isn't over. We'll have to keep an eye on what's happening at Cook County Jail—and that's no mean feat. It's not as if the warden and his people are going to go out of their way to protect Denzel or to keep us posted about what's going on within the walls of the jail.

PART II

20

Penelope returns to the office from her honeymoon on May 2nd. It's been three months since Judge Saunders transferred Denzel's case to adult court and we're now less than two months away from trial. As is customary in murder cases, there's been a considerable lull in the action while the police investigation continues and we lawyers scheme and jockey for position. I've only seen Denzel four times since he was attacked. He wanted nothing to do with me for weeks, but eventually realized we were doing what we could to keep him safe.

We haven't forgotten about him; there just hasn't been much for Penelope and me to discuss with him while we await his trial. Rana has continued to investigate whenever there is something to look into, but she's busy with a mountain of cases. I've spent many hours trying to hunt down Di and Spike without success.

Penelope and I have been busy with other cases as well. Brooks and Valenti business has been picking up steadily over the past year. We've brought more family law into our mix of cases: wills, estates, real estate—steady work that keeps money coming in. We're busy enough that we've offered Sara Williams an intern position for the summer months. Sara, the younger sister of my friend, public defender Mike Williams, is finishing her third year of law school at Northwestern. She'll help with routine filings, pleadings, and other grunt work.

We carry our coffee cups into the conference room to catch up. Penelope and her partner, Becky Seguin, were married in a civil ceremony three weeks ago. It was well attended by both families and select guests, including me, Brittany, and Pat O'Toole. The newlyweds immediately departed to New Zealand—a hiking and climbing mecca for a couple who inexplicably enjoy that sort of thing.

Penelope explained their choice of destination before they left: "Becky's an incurable fantasy novel buff. New Zealand has been on her radar since she saw the first Lord of the Rings movie."

We settle into our usual seats. "Was New Zealand everything you hoped it would be?" I ask.

"Everything I hoped and feared. I think we traced every footstep Bilbo and Gandalf and the gang took in those movies." Penelope lifts a foot, slips it out of her shoe, and wiggles her toes. "I keep expecting to see my feet stretch and sprout hair."

I give her a blank look.

"Hobbit feet, partner!"

Ah. Now I get it.

"It was actually a lot of fun." She holds a finger up to her lips. "Don't ever let Becky know I said so."

"Got it."

Penelope regales me with honeymoon tales for a few more minutes, then dons her serious lawyer face. "So. To work."

I bring her up to speed. "Discovery has been arriving steadily from the state, and I've been told we should receive a substantial new dump this week. I scheduled a meeting with Rana Asadi next week to bring her up to speed on discovery and find out if she's made any progress. We should probably plow through all the discovery before we meet with Rana."

"Mom told me there's been a change of lead prosecutor," Penelope says. "What's the story there?"

"Not really sure. He resigned abruptly for some reason. I won't miss the smarmy SOB."

"Maybe he was caught up in misconduct of some sort."

I snort. "I doubt he would get in trouble for that. He's the type of dodgy prosecutor that goes far with Timothy Walker sitting in the state's attorney's office."

"How cynical of you."

"With plenty of reason."

"True. Do you have the name of the new prosecutor?"

I steal a peek at my phone and the email I received from her Friday afternoon. The tone was surprisingly cordial. "Judy Edwards."

Penelope's eyes widen and she claps her hands together, yet another of her endearing little quirks. Maybe it's a thing in Kansas. "Really?"

"I take it you know her?"

"We went to law school together. Now we're both practicing in Chicago. Small world."

I paste a stern look on my face. "No socializing with your pal Judy for the duration of Denzel's case. Fraternizing with the enemy and all that."

"We don't see much of each other, actually. Now and again at bar events, that sort of thing. I really like Judy and I think the feeling is mutual. We always say we should get together more often when we run into each other, but…"

"Life gets in the way."

"I guess so. We're all so darned busy!"

Which begs an examination of modern life's priorities. What have things come to when we're too busy to spend time with friends? I toss my philosopher's cap aside and get back to business. "The early signals from Judy are positive.

Discovery is arriving without us having to raise a stink to get it."

"Judy will play fair, Tony."

"Cedar Heights PD will also play this straight."

"Yup! Chief Plummer has certainly established a new tone over there."

He has. This is a refreshing change from the BS I've experienced in past cases involving the Cook County state's attorney's office and the Cedar Heights cops: delayed discovery, buried evidence, lying detectives, and all manner of prosecutorial misconduct.

"Is Judy from Kansas?" I ask.

"Sure is."

"Well, that explains plenty. You straight shooters from Kansas are pure as the driven snow."

"Thanks, Cliché Man."

"Kansas girls. Gotta love 'em."

"We're very lovable."

I chuckle. "We could spend hours citing your many virtues, but we have work to do."

"Right," Penelope says with a wan smile. She pulls a file folder off the top of the pile of discovery material and flips it open. "I assume you've been looking all this over as it came in?"

"Hell no. I've been drinking and golfing and chasing skirts for two weeks."

"You don't even golf," she says with a roll of her eyes. "You *have* looked at this stuff, right?"

"Of course I have. It won't hurt to have another look before we meet Rana."

"She's coming Tuesday?"

I nod, then recap my investigative efforts. Relaying the results takes all of thirty or forty seconds.

"Tough sledding, partner?"

"Afraid so."

"I'll go through everything this week and over the weekend. Let's meet Monday to discuss it." Penelope tucks the paperwork back into its file folder and tosses her pen on top, then pushes her chair back and crosses her legs. "So what's been happening in your world, partner? We haven't talked in weeks!"

"All is well. Brittany finished her volleyball season."

"How did it turn out?"

"Not well. They didn't make it out of their section qualifier. Brittany was pretty bummed. She's going out for track this spring, which she hasn't done since we left Atlanta. I'm glad. Keeping busy seems to help."

Penelope frowns. "How's she doing, Tony? Still moving forward?"

My partner is referring to the loss of Brittany's boyfriend almost two years ago—not a particularly long time where grief is concerned.

"Near as I can tell, she's doing okay. I hope she is—who really knows how someone else is dealing with grief?"

"Anything new in her life I should know about?"

"I don't think so. She returned from St. Maarten with a new tan worthy of a before and after commercial for the Caribbean. She's anxious for summer to arrive before it fades. Otherwise, nothing much happening that I know of."

Penelope laughs. "I wish that was the extent of my problems!"

"I hear you."

"Hmm. What else is happening away from work?"

I fill her in on my and Pat's nascent plans to tackle a makeover of Independence Park.

"Brittany mentioned the park project and told me that her daddy plans to build her a swimming pool. I had no idea the plans were so grand!"

I look up in surprise. "When did she tell you that?"

"We chatted for a minute when she called this morning."

"She said I'm building her a pool, huh?"

"Yup. Not *thinking about* doing so, partner. Doing it."

I laugh and shake my head. "I guess everything is decided."

Penelope's eyes twinkle. "Gonna be able to keep that promise, Dad?"

"I hope so. I'm jazzed by the idea of tackling the park project. The idea of having a life outside the office is growing on me."

"Budding rock star, would-be real estate developer—however will the little old Brooks and Valenti law firm fit into your grand plans?"

I shoot her a sideways smile. "Our little law firm is exactly what makes a full life possible. You're not getting rid of me that easily."

"Darn. I'll have to come up with a 'shed Valenti' plan B."

"You say the nicest things."

She smiles. "Tell me more. What's next?"

"A community meeting to find out how committed the neighbors really are."

"Good luck." She reaches out and rests her fingers on top of the file folders. "I better dig into whatever has piled up while I was off hobnobbing with wizards and dwarfs and whatnot. When did you last speak with Denzel?'

"A couple of weeks ago."

"How was he?"

"Hanging in. Still in isolation."

"Sounds lonely," she says sadly.

"But safe."

"I suppose, but can you imagine that at fifteen?"

I think of my daughter and try to imagine her bereft of friends and family. "No, I can't."

"We should probably make a point of visiting weekly, just to check in and keep him up to date on how things are developing."

I nod. "And to beat our heads against the wall some more by asking him to give up Spike."

"That would be nice. It's the oddest thing that Denzel is so determined to protect this man."

"No secret," I reply. "It's called fear."

"I wonder what it's going to take to prompt him to talk?"

"Maybe he'll come around when he sees us getting our tails kicked at trial."

Her frown deepens. "It might be too late by that point."

"Exactly my concern."

21

The denizens of Cedar Heights, at least those few of us crazy enough to have signed up to restore Independence Park, are gathered in the community room at the village hall. The space also serves as the council chamber and is often configured as a gymnasium. Banks of fluorescent lights alternate with white acoustic ceiling tiles high overhead, which, coupled with the eggshell-white walls, makes for a somewhat harsh institutional setting. But hey, it's functional. And free!

We've circled a bunch of chrome-and-fabric chairs to lend the meeting an informal air. The atmosphere is considerably more congenial than it was the last time I was in this room two years ago for the culmination of my battle to save Liberty Street and Independence Park from the village and its developers. Now, we've returned to spearhead an effort to return the park to what it should be: a gathering place for the families that live nearby.

Personally, I'm on a mission. I have been ever since Brittany's declaration that happy families frolicking in the park would help put the lurking ghost of Bobby Harland behind her. Couple that with the memory of the Donahue kids peering through the fence at the wrecked swimming pool and I'm determined to see this through.

The crowd is a mix of familiar and new faces. Our next-door neighbors of fifty years, Mr. and Mrs. Vaccaro, are here with their daughter, Sandy, and her husband, Phil Russo. Another of the original Liberty Street homeowners, Mr. Rosetti, who moved to Florida, is here with his niece and her husband, whom he sold his home to when he left for the sunny south. Neighborhood fixtures Mr. and Mrs. LaSusa are also in attendance. No surprise there; Mrs. L. has been the neighborhood gossip going on forever. Maggie and Derek are also here, sans children. Pat has come, of course, along with her sister and brother and their spouses. Brittany is seated with them. Independence Park has meant a lot to many people over the years. We're all anxious to resurrect it for a new generation of children. Another dozen or more people constitute the new faces, many of who I've seen around the neighborhood but haven't yet met. That's about to change.

Pat had the inspired idea to collect photos of people making childhood memories in Independence Park over the years, plenty of which depict happy families filling the park. They're a hit. People are looking them over with smiles on their faces—smiles of remembrance for those of us with a long history here, smiles of anticipation for those eager to add their own family memories to the collection.

"Hello, and welcome," I say when the clock strikes seven.

A chorus of hellos comes back to me, accompanied by plenty of warm smiles.

"My hope is that we'll leave here as a somewhat organized mob with a concrete plan to get our Independence Park show on the road," I begin. "I've spoken with Mayor Smith and have taken the liberty of contacting a few potential pool suppliers to get a sense of what this might cost. We'll chat about that and try to reach consensus on the way forward. Sound fair?"

Lots of nodding heads. Still plenty of smiles. So far, so good.

"I realize that many of you barely know me. I grew up on Liberty Street and have a bucketful of happy Independence Park memories. I moved back a couple of years ago, not long after my mother passed away. She would have loved to see us here tonight—she often lamented what had become of our neighborhood park. My father, who is spending most of his time in Italy these days, was thrilled to hear about what we hope to do. He's offered to do whatever carpentry work is needed. That's my story."

I pause for a sip of water, then set the plastic bottle back on the floor at my feet.

"Mayor Smith is on board with this. The village has already cleaned things up considerably, and the mayor will work with us to obtain additional funding going forward. That said, funding will be tight this fiscal year, so it's up to us to get the ball rolling."

"Why?" one of the newcomers asks tartly. She appears to be in her late twenties or early thirties. A toddler is perched on her lap.

"Why do we need to get things rolling?" I ask.

"Yes. We pay taxes. Why aren't services like parks and swimming pools provided?"

Man, am I glad not to be a politician. "Well, ma'am, we do receive village services: police, fire, roads, etc. I suppose there isn't money for everything."

"I have a child. I expect the village to provide basic childhood amenities. Our realtor told us that Mayor Smith had personally assured her we would have a new pool this summer. All I see out there is a hole in the ground." Her cheeks redden and her voice rises as she turns to me. "Instead of sending you in here to ask *us* to foot the bill, the mayor should keep his promises."

Maybe we should put the realtors in charge; they seem to have all the answers.

Maggie, seated a few chairs to the speaker's right, turns in her seat to look the woman in the face. "Do you think your realtor speaks for the mayor? Our realtor spun us the same tripe, but at least she didn't claim to be a close friend of the mayor."

"I have no idea why you are attacking me! *I'm* not the person who lied to us. The mayor did!" She points at me. "So did his mouthpiece here."

Maggie looks up at the ceiling—perhaps for divine guidance—then glances at me with pity before she locks eyes with her new nemesis. "What's your name?"

"Ainsley Cotton."

"Well, Ainsley Cotton, I believe you owe Mr. Valenti an apology. He isn't here to be a political punching bag because you're displeased with the lies your realtor told you. He's here volunteering his time to improve our neighborhood. Why are *you* here?"

My gaze shifts to Derek, who has his head down in an effort to mask a grin. He's probably seen this before. Actually, he's probably been on the receiving end a time or two.

Ainsley Cotton, now a picture of highly aggrieved indignation, glares at Maggie, huffs, gets to her feet, and stalks out.

Maggie looks around and shrugs her shoulders. "I say we charge her admission if she shows up wanting to use our pool."

Several people laugh out loud, a few chuckle quietly, others simply smile. Nobody takes exception to how Maggie handled the situation.

Maggie settles back in her seat, crosses her legs, sets her hands primly in her lap, and meets my gaze with a smile playing on her lips. "Over to you, Tony."

I smile at her, then look around the circle. "We can't afford to do everything at once, so let's try to reach consensus on what to tackle first."

Heads nod.

"My initial thoughts are a pool, play structures, and playing fields. Am I missing anything?"

Pat shoots an arm into the air.

"Miss O'Toole?"

"What about a pool house, *Mister* Valenti?"

"This pool house," Mrs. Vaccaro says. "Will it be like before? Change rooms and a shower outside?"

"That's exactly the sort of thing we need to discuss tonight," I reply.

"How much do we have to spend?" asks Mr. Rosetti, the retired banker.

"That will depend on how our fundraising goes," I reply. "How about we take a straw vote—nothing binding—just to get a feel for our priorities?"

"Good idea," Mrs. LaSusa says. Several others agree.

"Do we start with the pool?" I ask. "Show of hands."

Seventeen hands go up. My last count of attendees was twenty-seven. Less Ainsley Cotton, of course. "That's a solid majority for starting with the pool. Let's vote on everything else and see if we can put the projects in order."

Heads nod again.

"Play structures?" I ask.

Seven hands rise.

"Playing fields?"

Three votes.

"I think it's safe to say we're on board for the pool first, but I'm a little uncertain where the pool house fits in. Do we do it as part of the initial pool project or leave it until everything is done?"

"Part and parcel of the pool project," Pat suggests.

I look around. "Votes to do the pool and pool house as a single project."

Thirteen hands go up.

"Doing the play structures before the pool house?"

Thirteen votes.

I smile. "A tie! How do we want to break ties?"

A mountain of a man on the far side of the circle stands. "I voted for the pool house. I'll arm wrestle someone from the play structure contingent to break the tie."

Everyone has a laugh as Mountain Man sits down.

"Let's park that for now," I suggest. "It's pool first by my count. How about we focus on that for now, at least until we have a better sense of how much the other projects will cost? We can revisit priorities then."

If you don't count a frown or two from play structure proponents, everyone seems agreeable.

"I mentioned speaking with a couple of swimming pool contractors," I continue. "The existing pool is both good and bad news. Excavating costs will be minimal if we rebuild to the same size, but breaking up and hauling away the old pool is going to cost us a fair penny."

"What were you quoted to remove the old pool?" Mountain Man asks.

"Eight to ten thousand dollars."

He laughs. "BS. I'm a contractor. I'll take care of it. My time will be free, but I'll have equipment and staff costs to cover." He pauses to think for a moment. "I can do it for a couple of grand if I get some volunteer help to tidy up the pit when we're done."

Four or five people, including me, offer to pitch in.

I smile gratefully. "The initial swimming pool quotes included decking and landscaping, and it wasn't cheap. The pool costs averaged thirty-seven thousand dollars and the extras ran at least an additional twenty K in each case, so I went to our local home improvement store and spoke with the manager. He's willing to sell us decking material at cost, up to ten thousand dollars. If we supply our own labor, that should get the job done. Bottom line? The pool will cost us somewhere around forty thousand."

"That much?" Mrs. LaSusa exclaims in horror.

"You mean that little," Derek counters as he turns to Mrs. L. "We costed out a backyard in-ground pool last summer that's half the size of the park pool. Sixty grand!"

Mrs. L's eyes widen. "My goodness me!" Then she smiles sheepishly. "I guess it's not 1965 any longer."

"No it isn't, Francine," Mr. Vaccaro says with a chuckle.

"Where do we get fifty thousand dollars?" I ask.

"Fundraising," one of the newer Liberty Street residents says. "I have four kids, all in sports and school, so I know all about fundraising. I can help organize that."

I beam at her. I hate fundraising, but I'll do my part if someone tells me what to do, where to be, and when to be there to do it.

"I'm a pastor," a young man I've barely noticed says. "I know a thing or two about passing a hat around for donations. I'll go hat in hand to visit some of our local businesses and see what I can scare up."

Maggie winks at our holy man. "Be sure to wear your collar and lay plenty of guilt on them."

"You know it!"

This is going to be a fun bunch to work with.

Maggie looks around the group. "My folks had a little restaurant in Podunk, Iowa. Let's add a concession stand and some picnic tables to the pool house—make the park a destination."

"What will that cost?" Pat asks.

"A few thousand to get up and running. My family will operate it."

Derek turns a shocked look on his wife. "We will?"

My thoughts turn to memories of the Good Humor man arriving at Independence Park and being overwhelmed by hordes of kids. The guy probably made a fortune. Maybe

Maggie's idea could be a little cash cow for us? "Let's keep that in the backs of our minds."

Mountain Man's wife speaks up. "How about making the pool house big enough to serve as a community center? Somewhere for birthday parties and stuff?"

"Jesus, Tammy!" her husband blurts. "That would cost a fortune!"

"Just a thought," she says, nonplussed at his reaction.

To my horror, I can see a few other mothers turning the idea over in their minds with evident approval. Before anyone can suggest a full-blown day spa or something, I ask Pat to lay out the sign-up sheets she and Brittany prepared in advance of the meeting. While they set the pages in a row on the front edge of the stage, each with a pen, I issue instructions.

"Please give us name and contact info—email or phone—and tick any boxes you're interested in helping with. I'll be in touch fairly soon. We'll put together a few committees to spread the work around. Sound good?"

Apparently, it does. There's a lot of work ahead, but I'm jazzed to be getting started.

But first, Denzel.

22

The following morning, a Friday, I'm sitting in an attorney-client room at the Cook County Jail, waiting for a guard to bring Denzel. We've committed to a weekly visit from me, Penelope, or both of us, so I'm here to do a little hand-holding and to bring Denzel up to speed on our trial preparations, such as they are. If nothing else, it should break up a little of the monotony of jail life and lend some emotional support to the frightened fifteen-year-old man-child trapped in this hellhole.

So far, it seems to have been the right decision. Denzel has been engaged during our initial visits and seems to be in reasonably good spirits. Maybe being in jail with a roof over his head and three squares a day—while not getting beaten up—doesn't seem so bad after having been out on the street for several months.

So I'm startled by the haunted look in his eyes when a guard lets him into the room. He's literally shaking inside a pair of orange jailhouse rompers.

"What's wrong?" I ask as he sits down.

"A guy showed up outside my cell a little while ago. An inmate. He told me they know you're looking for Spike and pressing me to give him up. He gave me a message—said it came straight from Spike. Scared the hell out of me."

I'm excited at the prospect of getting my hands on something Spike touched. Maybe we can get prints. "Where is it?"

Denzel looks confused for a moment, then points a finger at his temple. "It's up here, Mr. Valenti. The message was, like, verbal."

Crap. "Tell me exactly what the guy said. Word for word, if you can."

"To keep my mouth shut. He said that if he can get to me, anyone can."

"Anything else?"

He slumps back in his seat. "Yeah. Told me to get a plea deal done quick. No more looking for Spike. You're making him nervous."

Meaning that maybe I'm getting close. If so, I don't know which of the rocks I've peeked under leads to Spike. Damn it.

"How does Spike know what we talk about in here, Mr. Valenti? You told me our talks are private."

Good question. Is there a leak? It wouldn't be the first time.

"You and Miss Brooks gotta do this plea bargain thing or I'm dead!"

I hold my hands out in a calming gesture. "Let's think this through, Denzel. Consider all the possibilities before we do anything. Spike may *not* have an avenue to eavesdrop on us. Maybe he's just getting nervous and is blowing smoke to frighten you into doing something that's against your interest."

"Getting shanked in here is against my interest."

He has a point. Still. "A plea deal means you admit to killing Harry Hood." I wave a hand to encompass the room we're in. "If you think this place is bad—and it is—you're going to find out what misery really is if you're sent to prison for murder. It's even rougher than this place. And if you plead guilty, there's no chance of walking free."

"Doesn't seem like I have much chance of that anyway, does it?"

"We're just getting discovery now, Denzel. I admit that it doesn't look great at the moment—not without Spike or Di—but we're working hard. There *are* holes in the case against you. It's definitely not hopeless."

His nostrils flare and his eyes narrow, then he exhales and collapses back into his chair.

"You okay?" I ask.

"This whole scene sucks big-time. I've been thinking about the folks who stood up for me at the transfer hearing. Pastor, Coach, Miss Tompkins. It was great to hear them say such nice things about me. Do you know what?"

"What?"

"They were right. I *was* that good kid before Grams went and died. Since I've been in here, Aunt Thelma has been around offering to take me in when I get out. She really cares," he adds with a touch of wonder.

"She does."

"Grams didn't let Mom's family come around. She said they were all bad folks. I think Grams was wrong. Anyway, then there's you and Miss Brooks trying to help."

"All true."

"So sometimes I think that maybe things aren't completely hopeless."

"That's right, Denzel. They aren't."

"Yeah," he says bitterly. "Then this guy comes along today with a wakeup call, reminding me that things *are* hopeless. Now what?"

I take a minute to think. Is the threat real? Maybe, but maybe not. Can Spike reach into an isolation cell to get at Denzel? I doubt it. Sending some flunky down the hall to make a threat is one thing, acting on it is another. "Could the guy from this morning have gotten to you if he had tried?"

"You mean, like with a knife or something?"

"Right."

Denzel ponders the question. "Not unless he had a gun or a spear. No way he reaches me otherwise."

Unless he gets a key...

I keep that thought to myself. "So, maybe it's an empty threat, Denzel. Spike can send someone to deliver a warning, but he can't follow through on the threat."

"Maybe. Maybe not."

"I think you're probably safe in isolation."

"What if they move me into a regular cell?"

"We can't let that happen."

"*Can* you keep it from happening, Mr. Valenti?"

"We can try, Denzel, and the new prosecutor is helping. I can't promise more than that."

He gets up to pace, which goes on for a full minute before he sits down again. "Okay, we'll try it your way, but we gotta stop talking about Spike in here, and you gotta promise to stop trying to find him."

I don't reply. We need to find Spike if we hope to have any chance at trial. If I agree to Denzel's demand, we lose. Simple as that. He won't survive long in prison, plea deal or no plea deal.

"Well?" Denzel asks impatiently.

"Let me think on it, discuss it with Penelope."

"What's to think on? It's A or B."

"Maybe there's a plan C we don't see yet."

He locks his hands behind his head and fixes a stare on me. "One week."

"One week?"

"If there's no plan C by next Friday, we do the plea deal."

I sigh. Just like home, bossed around by a teenager. "Okay, one week. Now let's get to the reason I came by this morning.

I have a few questions about the discovery material that you might be able to help with."

"Okay. Shoot."

"The cops claim they collected your DNA from inside Harry's tent."

"I didn't go in the tent!"

"Did anything you touched go into the tent?"

He thinks on that, then shakes his head emphatically. "Just the bat."

"The bat seems like an unlikely source for DNA. It sounds like they got the sample from Harry Hood's body."

A panicked look crosses his face. "What does that mean, though? If they got my DNA off the dead guy, I'm screwed, right?"

"It just doesn't make sense to me. We'll have our own expert look it over."

"Okay, but DNA is like science, right? Solid. Can't be a mistake."

"You're wrong there, Denzel. The cops and government want us to believe that story so potential jurors go into court convinced of it, but it's not true."

"It isn't?" he asks in surprise. "DNA is BS?"

"Not BS, but it's not quite the slam dunk they make it out to be. Not always. We'll see what our people say and go from there."

"What else is in this discovery stuff?"

"More like what isn't. Your fingerprints aren't on the marijuana or heroin baggies the cops took out of your pockets. Same story with the cash."

"Because Spike planted all that shit on me!"

"The lack of prints is a problem for the prosecution. It fits your story."

"What else?" he asks with a hint of excitement.

"That's all we've got at the moment."

"Shit," he mutters, shoulders slumping as the morsel of hope is snatched away.

"But we're still investigating."

The exasperated look he gives me mirrors the way I feel about the state of our case, but I'm not about to throw in the towel.

"One week today," Denzel reminds me as a guard leads him out.

I glance at my watch. Today is Friday, May 6th. Nothing good can come from making Friday the 13th a pivotal date, can it?

23

I pull into my designated partner parking spot in the alley behind the offices of Brooks and Valenti, Lawyers Who Park Alongside Dumpsters. I'm in a surprisingly upbeat mood despite my just concluded jailhouse meeting with Denzel. Maybe it's the weather. It's a lovely spring morning: temperature in the midsixties, the sun hanging in a cloudless blue sky, and the mildest hint of a breeze blowing in off Lake Michigan. I pluck my suit jacket out of the back seat—shirt-sleeve weather, good riddance polar vortex!—and head upstairs.

The frightened look on Joan Brooks's face when I walk into the office jolts me out of my weather-induced bliss. Joan's mascara is mussed.

"What's wrong?" I ask as I hurry across the lobby to touch her arm.

She tilts her head toward the open door of my partner's office. "You need to talk to Penelope."

My eyes flicker to the full coffeepot; I could use a cup. I walk straight to my partner's office instead, pausing to set my briefcase just inside my office. Penelope is seated behind her desk, chin cupped in her palm, finger tapping the tip of her nose—the Penelope thinking pose. She's staring vacantly out the window, however, which doesn't fit. My partner doesn't do vacant.

She doesn't seem to notice my arrival, so I rap lightly on the doorframe. "Good morning, partner."

Her eyes swing to me. "Where have you been? It's after ten o'clock."

"Visiting Denzel."

"Oh, right. I forgot."

I walk over to her desk and deposit myself in one of the visitor chairs. "What's going on? Joan looks like she's seen a ghost."

Penelope dips her chin, takes a deep breath, then looks back up at me. "Someone was waiting at my car when I left home this morning."

"Who?"

"No idea. He was wearing a ski mask."

An icicle of fear tickles my stomach.

"'I'm here to deliver a message, Miss Brooks,'" Penelope continues in a flat voice. "'You and your partner need to stop looking for Spike. If Denzel doesn't work out a plea deal soon, people are going to get hurt.'" Penelope squeezes her eyes shut and grimaces. "'Or worse.'" Then she opens her eyes and stares at me. "That's what he said, Tony."

"Jesus," I mutter as Penelope's shoulders slump. She drops her face into her hands with an involuntary shudder. I reach across the desk and squeeze her forearm. "Are you okay?"

Her head snaps up. Her tear-streaked face wears a look of disbelief. "Am I okay? Does it look like I'm okay?"

I'm taken aback by the uncharacteristic outburst, but don't react. She's scared. Asking if she was okay was probably the dumbest question I could have asked.

She forces a smile through her tears when I rip a handful of tissues out of the box on her desk and offer them to her. "Sorry I snapped at you."

I wave it aside. "No worries."

"You're the partner that's supposed to deal with the goons," she says after blowing her nose. "That man scared the heck out of me. I can't imagine how you face down people like that. How do you do it?"

"By accident," I reply drily.

A little laugh escapes her as she dabs at the corners of her eyes, sniffs a final time, then settles back in her seat and crosses her legs. "Oh, and about the plea deal. My visitor claimed they have a source inside the state's attorney's office who will know about any deals that are on the table."

"But is that true?"

She sighs. "Can we afford not to believe it?"

Good question. Two warnings on the same morning, delivered miles apart. How real is the threat? While I have doubts about Spike's ability to get to Denzel in jail, there's no question that Penelope—and Becky, and Joan, and me, and Brittany—are far more vulnerable. I reluctantly tell Penelope that Denzel was also threatened this morning.

Instead of reacting with additional distress, my partner's expression hardens in anger. "They're trying to intimidate us, Tony."

I venture a half smile. "Talk about stating the obvious, partner. That ticks you off?"

"Darn tootin', as we say in Kansas," she replies with the ghost of a smile. And just like that, my partner is back in the saddle.

"What do you want to do about this?" I ask.

"How is Denzel handling it?"

"Not well. He's giving us a week to get traction on a defense case. If we don't, he wants to cop to a plea deal."

"No way. He's fifteen, Tony. He can't make this type of decision."

I decide not to argue that he's the client. Change of subject. "Did you have a chance to get through all of the discovery over the weekend?"

She nods. "I was encouraged that Denzel's prints weren't on the drugs or the cash. Then I saw the DNA sample from the tent. That neatly plugs the hole in the prosecution's case, doesn't it?"

"Very convenient," I say with a heavy dose of sarcasm.

"Could just be dumb luck. I know you've run into some pretty egregious prosecutorial misconduct, partner, but I don't think Judy Edwards would pull a stunt like that."

"I can't see it coming from Cedar Heights PD under Jake Plummer, either."

We spend a minute trying to convince ourselves that there's still room for a little optimism before Joan appears in the doorway, an 8½-by-11 manila envelope in hand.

"Everything okay in here?" she asks with a pointed look at her daughter.

We both nod.

Joan places the envelope on Penelope's desk. "From the state's attorney's office."

"Thanks, Mom," Penelope says as her mother turns to go. Then she pulls the envelope to herself, picks up a Kansas Jayhawks letter opener, and neatly slices the envelope open. A thin sheaf of paperwork is inside.

"More discovery?" I ask as she slides it out.

She scans the papers with a developing frown that morphs to anger by the time she finishes, then flings the offending document across the desk to me.

"Statement of Jose Hernandez," I read in the heading of a witness statement. The key element of the statement, if we're to believe Mr. Hernandez, is that Denzel told him during his first night in jail that he "bashed in the head of the homeless twerp when he wouldn't hand over a little dope and cash."

"Ah yes. The jailhouse snitch gambit," I mutter as I slam the paperwork down on the desk.

"I can't believe this!" Penelope exclaims.

"The BS statement or the fact that your friend Judy would stoop to this?"

"Both," Penelope replies before exhaling a lengthy, frustrated sigh. She pulls the paperwork back in front of herself to reread it. "What the heck do we do with this?"

"Discredit it. We ask Rana to find out everything there is to know about Mr. Hernandez. Then we impeach the lying SOB on the stand."

"I wonder what he was offered to lie," Penelope mutters.

I settle back in my seat and stare out the window while I think. "They seem to have a strong case, right?"

"So?"

"Why resort to a jailhouse snitch?"

"Good question, partner. Maybe *they* don't think the case is a slam dunk?"

I slap a palm on the desk while a smile forms on my face. "Exactly what I'm thinking. We need to figure out why they feel that way. Where's the potential Achilles' heel of their case that they're worried about?"

Penelope returns my smile, then points at the mountain of discovery material sitting on her credenza. "Somewhere in there."

"Time to roll up our sleeves."

She frowns. "I'm so disappointed in Judy."

I give her a sympathetic look. "Guess you don't know her as well as you thought."

She nods sadly.

Then I reconsider. "Maybe this isn't Judy's doing. It has the stink of Timothy Walker all over it." Cook County's state's attorney is as unsavory a lawyer as I've ever had the misfortune to meet. There's no depth to which the smarmy SOB won't stoop to win a case.

The thought perks Penelope up a bit. It has the opposite effect on me. If Walker has decided to take a personal interest in Denzel's case, the forces arraigned against us have increased by a factor of at least ten.

24

"Where are you?" Pat asks after I accept her incoming call the following Monday afternoon.

"On my way to Brittany's track practice." Aside from playing supportive track-and-field dad, I'm on edge after Friday's threats, so I'm keeping closer tabs on my daughter while trying not to be obvious about it.

"Can I come by to watch?" Pat asks.

"Of course."

"And maybe hang out and have dinner with you?"

"Of course," I repeat.

"Thanks. See you soon."

I replay the call in my head, vaguely uneasy because of something in the tone of Pat's voice. Almost needy. Totally not Pat.

My thoughts turn to Denzel's case as I park and walk across Hyde Park College Preparatory School's expansive athletic fields, warily eyeballing the sky as I go. It's a cool, dreary spring afternoon—low overcast, a fine mist hanging in the air threatening more in the way of precipitation, and a chilly wind raising goose-bumps on my exposed arms. It's a good day for a jacket. Unfortunately, mine are hanging uselessly in the front closet of our Liberty Street home. Guess I should remember to check my weather app every morning.

I spent a good chunk of the weekend fruitlessly hunting through discovery in search of whatever flaw in the state's case prompted the prosecution to resort to a jailhouse snitch. Perhaps our investigator, Rana, will have some insight to offer when we meet with her tomorrow.

I skirt a field full of girls playing soccer, then angle toward a quarter-mile oval with plenty of activity on the running track and enclosed infield. Brittany is somewhere in that crowd. I gaze out on the facilities in wonder. I think back to the old track at St. Aloysius High School, where tufts of grass and weeds sprouted from the running surface. My, but times change, or maybe this is simply the difference between what everyday kids get at public school and what's on offer for the offspring of the wealthy. Brittany is somewhere between the two worlds, the daughter of a wealthy mother and a father who scrapes by at a fledgling legal firm that represents the people who clean the houses and maintain the yards of rich kids.

I spot Brittany practicing in the starting blocks on the track and stop to watch. She made the sprint team, running 100 and 200 meters. Her best time in the 100 is fourteen seconds flat; good, but not outstanding. Her friend Ashley Williams—Mike's niece—is a superstar sprinter who consistently runs the same distance in the mid-twelve-second range. "Now, that's freaking fast!" Brittany marveled after watching Ashley tear up the track.

Another of the parents coughing up exorbitant tuition sidles over to stand beside me. "Which one is yours?"

I shoot him a sideways glance. He's a corporate type, judging by the false bonhomie in his voice, immaculate grooming, and Gucci loafers.

"Sprinter," I reply with a vague wave in Brittany's direction.

He doesn't seem overly interested. He points at a girl racing down a short running track and launching herself over the long-jump pit before landing in a spray of while silicone sand. "My Melody is a long jumper."

"Nice," I say with feigned interest.

He nods. "What kind of work are you in?" Always straight to career queries with this type.

"Attorney."

"Corporate law?"

"Once upon a time. General practice now, although I seem to be stumbling into a lot of criminal defense cases these days."

His eyes cut to mine. "Criminal defense?"

I nod. He eases away. Good riddance.

Brittany is impressively focused as she works on her starts under the watchful eye of a coach. I've never been much of a runner of any sort, so any improvement taking place escapes me, but I'm proud of how diligently my daughter tackles whatever she sets her mind to.

"Hey," Pat says, touching my arm when she steps up beside me several minutes later.

"Hey yourself." I turn to her. A pair of oversize sunglasses incongruously hide half her face. Maybe she thinks the sun is about to burst through the clouds at any moment? "Everything okay?"

"Mom died."

The reply, delivered flatly, smacks me right in the face. I immediately flash back to the phone call I received from my father two years ago when my mother died. I pull Pat into a hug. "I'm so sorry."

She clings to me and buries her face in my shoulder. "Jesus, it hurts so much, Tony."

I rub her back. "I know. Whatever I can do, ask."

She turns her face up to mine with a corner of her mouth

ticking up in the hint of a smile. "I already did. Thanks for letting me hang with you guys this evening."

"When?" I ask a minute later.

"Yesterday afternoon."

"How's the family taking it?" The O'Tooles are an uncommonly tight-knit family. Always have been. Now they've lost both parents in a matter of months.

"Not well," Pat replies. "I love them all to bits, but I need a break from funeral planning and the like. Mom mapped it all out for us—I'm not sure why we're obsessing about adding little flourishes."

"Funerals are for the living. We all want to feel as if we're doing at least a little something to honor the people we love."

She lays her head on my shoulder. "Now I feel like a bitch for saying that."

"Don't. You feel what you feel when something like this happens. There really isn't any right or wrong way to deal with it."

She reaches up to give me a tighter hug. "Every once in a while, you sound like a wise man instead of a wiseacre."

"That may be the nicest thing you've said to me this year."

"You're exactly where I need to be right now. Thank you."

"Anytime, Pat. You know that."

"I do."

We stay that way for a long minute before Pat disengages, leaving a hand resting lightly on my arm. "Where's our girl?"

I look to the starting blocks. No Brittany, so I gaze around the track until I spot her in a group of six doing wind sprints. I point her out to Pat.

"God, how I hated wind sprints," she says.

"Not for the queen of cross-country, huh?"

She laughs softly. "Hell no."

Pat falls silent, so I do as well.

Brittany runs over as soon as practice ends. I get the first hug;

Pat gets the longer one before Brittany backs off. "This is a nice surprise. I knew the old guy was coming, but I wasn't expecting to see you here." Then Brittany gives her unexpected guest a bemused look as she reaches up to touch Pat's shades. "What's with the mysterious movie-star-recluse look on a cloudy day?"

Pat musters a sad semblance of a smile. "Just being mysterious."

Brittany's face falls. "Something's wrong, isn't it?"

"My mother passed away yesterday."

Tears spring to Brittany's eyes. "Oh no."

"Your father says I can hang out with you guys for dinner and a bit afterward."

"Of course," Brittany says, stepping close to give Pat a longer hug.

I'm not sure who's comforting who at this point. I suppose it doesn't really matter. A good hug is restorative for everyone involved.

On the way home, we decide on a dinner of pizza delivered from Lou Malnati's. Brittany calls ahead with our order, which arrives within minutes of our return home. No strangers to sudden death ourselves, we let Pat set the terms of our dinner conversation. Pat talks wistfully about her mother, a cathartic exercise that helps the bereaved deal with grief. Even the dogs are subdued—not that they stray from the table while we eat; spills still need to be managed immediately.

After eating, we relocate to the living room—me in Papa's La-Z-Boy, Brittany in Mama's recliner, and Pat on the sofa. Her old pal Deano snuggles close with his head in her lap, sad eyes seemingly in tune with Pat's mood. She once nursed Deano back to health, and he seems ready to reciprocate. Dolly lies at my feet with her face resting on my foot, her sad eyes watching Pat. I should be so reliably in tune with the moods and needs of others.

We're startled when the doorbell rings at seven o'clock. Brittany's eyes widen as she looks to me.

"Oh my God. Band rehearsal tonight. I forgot all about it."

"We both did," I admit, hoisting myself to my feet. "Stay put. I'll shoo them away. Everyone will understand."

"Shoo who away?" Pat asks.

Brittany can't mask a proud smile. "The rest of our band."

Pat's bemused eyes turn to me. "A band?"

I nod as I reach the front hallway.

"Let them in," she says.

I pause with my hand on the doorknob. "You're sure? It could get noisy."

"A distraction might be just what the doctor ordered."

I open the door and find Sara and Ashley Williams on the step along with Brittany's friend, Jocelyn.

"We on?" Sara asks.

I nod.

The girls troop back out to Ashley's Ford Explorer, bequeathed to her by her father after her mother died last year. When they return, Sara is lugging an oversized guitar case and Jocelyn is steering a wheeled trunk holding an electric piano. Our bassist and keyboard players have arrived. Ashley pronounces herself our backup singer. Who knew we needed one? All that's missing is our drummer. While I help the girls unload a pair of amplifiers, the deep rumble of a muscle car announces his arrival. Retired Chicago cop Max Maxwell parks his Carousel Red 1969 Pontiac GTO Judge at the curb and climbs out.

I walk down to meet him and we shake hands. Max may be twenty-some years older than me, but he still has the grip of a grizzly bear. He's also built like one.

"How's life treating you, Max?"

He pops the trunk and scowls heavenward. "Can't complain, aside from the damned weather."

"I was surprised when Jake told me you were a drummer."

Max pauses with a grin on his face after he hauls a bass drum out of the trunk. "What? You don't think I'm cultured enough to play in your basement band?"

"You never struck me as a musical kind of guy."

"A guy like me who likes to pound the hell outa things? Should have seen that one coming, my friend."

"Good point." We start lugging his gear inside. "Did you learn the songs Brittany sent?"

"Sure did."

"And?" He was a little skeptical about playing contemporary material such as Larkin Poe, Terra Lightfoot, and others.

"Good stuff," he replies. "Who knew? Tell you what, though."

"What's that?"

"You can tell those kids cut their teeth on the good stuff!"

Indeed.

"I should've stuck with a simple tambourine for percussion," he grumbles as we set the last of his gear down in the corner of our basement rehearsal space.

Max's eyes widen when Brittany and I haul out our guitars. In addition to her Fender Stratocaster, my Epiphone Casino, and the twelve-string Rickenbacker, Brittany has gotten her hands on a gorgeous, old, and ridiculously expensive Martin DB acoustic guitar, thanks to an equally ridiculous $5,000 birthday check from her mother.

"Jesus," he says. "I haven't seen a guitar collection like that since, I dunno, a guitar band concert way back in the day."

Brittany shoots him a wink. "We don't mess around with crappy gear."

I nod at Max's Ludwig drum kit. "You're no slouch gearwise."

"Very old-school, but very cool," Brittany agrees.

Everyone is set up, plugged in, and tuned up ten minutes later. Ashley and Pat settle on a sofa, Deano climbs up to snuggle with Pat while Dolly happily prances around us. She's turning out to be quite a little rock and roller.

"We have a groupie!" Max exclaims with a little vaudeville-era drum roll. *Bada- boom!*

Brittany, who has unofficially taken on the mantle of band leader, hits a chord. "Let's start with something for the old folks. Martha and the Vandellas, 'Nowhere to Run.'" Max beams as he and Sara lay down the original killer rhythm section groove. Jocelyn kicks in with her piano, and I add second guitar to the mix. Then Sara starts to belt out Martha Reeve's powerful, soulful lead vocal. The girl can sing.

Pat's face lights up. She grabs Ashley's hand, bounces up off the couch, and hurries over to stand in front of us, wiggling her butt and waving her arms. She and Ashley take up the Vandellas' backing vocals, punctuated with the patented Motown dance moves. We're sounding pretty good, or at least Dolly thinks so as she joins the fun. Her tail and body gyrate as her tongue lolls out the side of her mouth in an ecstatic doggy smile.

When we finish the song, our leader—having "given the old folks their due"—leads us into newer material. By the time things wind down a couple of hours later, Pat has declared herself our second backup singer. She was right; the distraction seems to have been good for her.

Brittany winks at Max as we pack up. "Almost ready for the big Independence Park benefit gig."

"The what?" Max asks.

"Yeah," I add.

Brittany shrugs nonchalantly. "You need money to get a swimming pool built. We've got ourselves a rocking little band here. Connect the dots, Pops."

Like hell.

After Max and the girls have packed up and the joy of

music has dissipated, Pat stands forlornly in the middle of the kitchen.

"Back to the real world," she says sadly, shoulders sagging under the weight of grief.

Words seem superfluous, so Brittany joins us in a group hug.

By the time the taillights of Pat's car disappear down Liberty Street, my thoughts are turning to tomorrow's meeting with Rana. Which is when I realize that I should have asked Max what he's doing this summer. He's a dogged investigator.

25

I'm thoroughly discouraged an hour into our meeting with Rana the next morning. Friday is Denzel's deadline for us to either show him a potential winning hand or negotiate a plea deal. We're making no headway. Penelope visited him in jail this morning to explain why we need more time, pointing out that a deal will likely remain on the table right up until the trial begins. It didn't sit well.

"A lot of good that's gonna do after some guy shivs me," Denzel retorted.

He has a point. While I'm not convinced Spike can get to Denzel in isolation at the jail, I may be wrong. Penelope and Becky have taken security precautions in the wake of Penelope being accosted at her car last week, and I'm being extra vigilant myself. Fortunately, I had the security at our home beefed up last year.

Penelope isn't sure what effect the supposed jailhouse snitch had on Denzel when she told him about it. His original reaction was indignant fury—"What a load of crap!" That passed quickly, digressing into a melancholic certainty that the fix was in. "May as well plead guilty and hope for leniency," he told Penelope as she was leaving.

Many, maybe most, criminal defense attorneys would be content with a plea deal and move on. But Brooks and Valenti isn't your typical law firm—especially when we have a client we believe to be innocent. I've come to like this kid. To my mind, he's what he claims to be—a fifteen-year-old who fell into a bad situation and wound up in the wrong place at the wrong time.

I recap my fruitless searches for Di and Spike, then turn to Rana. "Help!"

"I'm sorry, Tony, but you're going to have to chase those people down yourselves or find someone to give you a hand."

We may just do that. After clearing it with Penelope over our morning coffee, I called Max and left a voicemail asking if he'd be interested in doing a little investigating. I expect the old bloodhound to leap at the chance. I tell Rana about Max and ask if she has any issues with us bringing an old cop on board.

"Any and all competent assistance is cheerfully welcome."

Penelope grins. "Absolutely!"

I hand the jailhouse snitch statement to Rana. Her brow furrows as she reads. "This could be a serious problem. I'll dig up everything I can about Hernandez, but he'll be hard to impeach on the stand."

"Why?" Penelope asks in surprise.

"For reasons I've never understood, this stunt works at trial far too often."

"But he's obviously a lying scuzzball!"

"We see that easily, Penelope. Hell, the cops and state's attorney see it as well, yet prosecutors still serve it up as if it's the gospel truth. Snitches are always carefully coached and highly motivated by whatever deal the prosecution offers."

"They can't present perjured testimony!"

"The state does it all the time," I inform my naive partner.

Rana frowns. "You're right about Di and Spike, Tony.

Without one or both of them, your case is in trouble. I'm sorry I don't have time to do more than steal a few minutes here and there to dig into things. Keep me up to date on anything new."

I nod.

Then her eyes light up. "I have an idea that might help." She pulls out her cell phone, swipes a few times, then transcribes something onto a page of her notebook, rips out the page, and slides it across the table to me. "Someone I stumbled across a couple of years ago. A computer hacker. Good one, too. She has the chops to get into places we don't even know exist."

"A hacker?" Penelope asks skeptically. "How can we trust someone who makes a living stealing and selling people's information and who knows what all else?"

"She's a white-hat hacker," Rana replies.

"Whatever that means," I mutter. "A hacker's a hacker, no?"

"No, they're not. It's an unfortunate term, I suppose, dating back to old Wild West lore here in America where bad guys wore black hats and the good guys wore white hats. Remember that?"

I nod. "I saw my share of western movies as a kid. Which reminds me of my late girlfriend Trish's assessment of them: 'Like we need more of that thinking. We're still living that showdown-at-high-noon method of problem-solving in this country.'"

"Amen," Rana agrees.

A flicker of pain flares in Penelope's eyes at the mention of Trish. I seldom bring her up.

"Anyway," Rana says with a nod at the notebook page sitting by my hand, "do what you will with that. All I can tell you is that she's good—a magician, in fact. I've salvaged more than one case because of what she can do."

Salvaging a case is exactly what we need to do. I pick up the paper. "I just call this number? That hardly seems secure."

Rana grins. "I know, right? Whatever is hooked up to the other end of that number will automatically erase all evidence of your call. I had a tough time grasping her explanation of what happens. What I *do* know is that I check my phone company call records every time I reach out to her, and there's never a record of my outgoing call."

"Impressive."

"She is. Let her know I referred you. She won't take any work unless it's referred by a trusted source. Then she'll check you out."

"What's her name?"

"Who knows?" Rana says with a chuckle as she begins to pack up. "She'll let you know what to call her if she decides to take you on as a client. She gives every customer a unique name to refer to her as. Security measure, as I understand things."

We thank Rana for her time, then show her out.

"That was a little disappointing," Penelope says when we're alone in her office.

"That's one way of looking at it. We didn't accomplish anything constructive in our review of the evidence, but we may be growing our investigative team by two."

"But will it help?"

"In the immortal words of the Roman senator and philosopher Seneca"—how did that bit of trivia lodge in my brain?—"and countless others: time will tell."

"We don't have much of it, partner."

26

It's eleven o'clock when I arrive at work on Thursday morning, two days after our meeting with Rana. Pat's mother was buried yesterday afternoon. We all went to the service, so the mood is subdued. I stayed home with Brittany as long as I could this morning; she's utterly heartbroken for Pat and her family. After Penelope leaves to attend a deposition, I push papers around my desktop while I wait for my eleven-thirty appointment to arrive. It's the first of three I have today that relate to Denzel's case. We need all of them to go well.

The deep rumble of a muscle car outside my window announces Max's arrival. He called after dinner yesterday and apologized for taking two days to return my call. "I was fishing in Wisconsin, and I ignore the damned phone when I'm out there. Our whole family knows to call my wife to make plans—she runs our social calendar."

I wryly pointed out that I'm not family.

Max, drumsticks tucked into the back pocket of a pair of Levi's jeans, shakes my hand, then plops himself into one of my guest chairs. He pulls the drumsticks out as he does. "Don't want one of these up my ass."

"Certainly not."

He enthusiastically raps out a syncopated beat on my desktop. "Is Brittany for real about playing a gig in Independence Park?"

Is she? I shrug, then give him a quick overview of Denzel's case. "You interested in coming on board with this?"

He thinks for a minute, then nods. "The usual fee?"

"Sure."

He grimaces. "Figuring out how to keep tabs on this Wix character in the hood is gonna be tough."

Don't I know it. I spend a half-hour bringing Max up to speed on the case, have Joan make him copies of everything we've developed and received from discovery, and put him in touch with Rana Asadi. They'll work out their own logistics. Then I leave Max in Joan's capable hands to get him set up in our conference room. I grab my coat. Next stop: Tent Town.

Spring has certainly sprouted in Tent Town. Trees in full leaf, flower beds teeming with brightly colored flora, and rich green perennial shrubs recall Manzarek Park from days past. The population has swollen with the coming of warmer weather. Toe's tent is pitched in the same spot, but he isn't home. I smile a melancholy smile when I spy an oak seedling growing in the open space where Harry Hood's tent was pitched. Toe and the others haven't forgotten their old friend. A handful of daisies and marigolds ring the sapling. I decide to wait.

"Mr. Lawyer!" a familiar voice calls out fifteen minutes later. Toe wears a big smile as he approaches. The only indication that his foot might be short a digit or two is a minor hitch in his step.

"Good to see you, Toe. The place looks great!"

"Thanks to Mayor Smith's directive to Parks and Recreation to treat this place like any other village park. How's the legal world, my friend?"

"Tough sledding on this case, to be honest. Tell me you

had some luck tracking down Di and Horace, or at least gathering some information that will help us find them."

He frowns. "Let's walk. I worry about Horace, man."

I fall into step at his side as we begin strolling through the middle of the camp. "He never came back?"

"Nope. Just up and disappeared without a trace. Leaving Chicago for the winter wasn't a surprise, but he left his stuff behind. That's what worries me. We homeless folks may not have much, but every bit of it means something to us."

Instead of pushing him about Di, I keep quiet while he processes his thoughts and emotions. He'll get to Di when he's ready. I pull a Hershey's bar out of my pocket and offer it to him.

"You remembered, man! I'll save this for a cheerier moment." He drops it into his shirt pocket, then pulls a dog-eared little notebook from his threadbare cargo pants. "I asked around about Di for you. Learned a few things."

I gave Toe a list of items that might help us narrow down who Di really is: hometown, date of birth or at least her age, which schools she attended, where she grew up, places she's lived, any family information she might have shared, employers, career, and jobs.

I hand Toe my cell phone. "How about you read all that into a voice memo? I don't want to forget anything. Less chance of me misunderstanding as well."

"Sure. My memory ain't so hot anymore either." He sits down at the next bench we come to and begins reading his notes into it. I gather that Di's birthday is most likely October 13th and her birth year was probably 1986 based on her mentioning that she was born in the same year the teacher died on the space shuttle. Di and Harry first met in Florida when he was in the military.

"No hint of a last name?" I ask when he finishes. "Not even a guess based on some memory fragment?"

He shakes his head as he hands the phone back. "Sorry."

Pretty thin, but more than I expected. Maybe a computer genius can make something of it. How, I can't imagine, but hope springs eternal. I give Toe's shoulder a friendly chuck after I save the voice memo. "You did great, pal."

"It's a start. Di and Horace were pretty tight, so if he comes back…"

Neither of us expects Horace to resurface.

"A few summer regulars haven't returned," Toe says hopefully. "I'll ask around if any more of them show up."

"That would be great." I hold my phone up. "I appreciate what you've done, my friend. Could be a whole case of Hershey's bars coming your way."

Toe smiles, then we say good-bye.

My next stop is in the north Lakeview neighborhood. I have a tough time finding a parking spot anywhere near West Belmont when I arrive to meet with Rana's mysterious computer hacker. I eventually squeeze into a side street parking space being vacated by a Mini Cooper. After two minutes of incremental jockeying back and forth and a plethora of expletives, I finally put the car in park. I get out, look at the slivers of daylight between the cars in front of and behind my Porsche, and try not to think about how many dings my car might have by the time I return. Oh well, worries for later.

I walk back to Belmont. After a bus spews a lung-crushing cloud of diesel fumes in my face as it pulls away from the curb, my destination appears a couple of blocks away on the far side of the street. I glance at my watch. Right on time. I have to maneuver around several of Lakeview's geeky residents, who are gathered on the sidewalk around a storefront. I take a look as I inch around the gawkers. The window display announces that it's a collectibles store named KAPOW! No sign of Batman, however. I smile at the crowd before I look both ways and dart across Belmont.

I stop to admire my destination. Our Lady of Mount Carmel Catholic Church is a towering white stone edifice with twin bell towers flanking a trio of Gothic arches framing wooden doors. Stained-glass windows nestle within another set of arches above the entry. I climb five or six steps up from street level to enter though the middle door. The interior is spectacular. A towering ceiling arches high overhead and more stained-glass windows adorn the walls as they march away toward the front of the church. If the idea behind churches such as this one is to awe parishioners with the power of God, I imagine it works pretty well. The cynic in me pictures bishops in pointy hats salivating over the value of the church's real estate holdings while priests pass collection plates to parishioners of modest means.

A handful of people are scattered in the pews. None show any interest in me, so I make my way to the end of a rear pew that affords a good view of the entire church interior. I don't have a name or description, so Rana's hacker will have to find me. *I'll recognize you* 😊 her text had assured me. Assuming she's coming.

I've just glanced impatiently at my watch for a fifth or sixth time when a young woman shuffles in, looks around, and then heads straight for me. Her features are classic Native American: dark skin, round face, high cheekbones, almond-shaped eyes widely spaced, and shimmering jet-black hair cut short and spiky. She's dressed in black jeans, a red peasant blouse, and a pair of tan moccasins.

She grins when she sees me looking. "What, you were expecting Lisbeth Salander?"

Who?

When I stare back blankly, she chuckles. "The chick from the Stig Larsen books."

"The *Dragon Tattoo* girl?"

"There you go." She slings a backpack off her shoulder, spreads her hands wide, and looks herself over. "Aside from the black hair, no resemblance, right? I weigh at least two of her."

Her self-assessment leaves me slightly uncomfortable. What do I say to that?

She laughs. "No worries, Mr. V. I'm a real hacker, not a movie queen." She bounces her ample bosom in her hands. "*This* is what happens when you spend most of your life at a keyboard, surrounded by cupboards full of salty snacks and a fridge full of Grape Nehi."

I can't help but smile. "They still make Grape Nehi?"

"Sure, but Dr. Pepper or someone owns it now. Best soda ever."

"Good to know. I was always a fan. I'm a big salty-snack guy as well."

"Cool. Sorry I'm late," she says without a hint of remorse. "I got hung up at KAPOW! I always lose my sense of time in there."

"I noticed it on my way here. I have to admit, I expected to see a picture of Batman in the window."

She smiles. It's a great smile, almost impish, with a hint of devilry. "Maybe back in the Dark Ages when you were a kid."

First, the Mr. V thing reminds of how we Liberty Street kids used to refer to our friends' parents as Mr. and Mrs. L or whatever, and now the crack about the Dark Ages. What's next? Grandpa? Time to change the subject. "A church for a clandestine meeting?"

She looks around. "Privacy, anyone?"

"Should we use a confessional?"

"I don't have time to listen to all that!" she protests with a theatrical wide-eyed look of horror. "Let's just do a basic bio. Okay?"

"You go first."

"Good call. I already know all about you."

"I should hope so."

"So, I was born on the Kickapoo Reservation in Kansas.

We moved away when I was three. Dad is a professor at the Haskell Indigenous School at the University of Kansas in Lawrenceville."

"Small world. My partner is from around there."

"Yeah. Penelope Brooks. I got a kick out of that. She looks *so* Kansas!"

I nod and chuckle. "She *is* so Kansas!"

"Yeah. Anyway, we lived on campus. End of story."

"No, it isn't. That's just the end of what you're going to tell me."

She nods.

"What do I call you?"

She thinks on that for a beat. "You like chips, I like chips. Let's riff on my real name."

"Which is?"

She wags a finger. "I never use it for work." Then she opens a flap on her backpack and angles it toward me so I can see a bag of Fritos corn chips tucked inside. "You can call me Chippy."

"That's memorable. Schooling?"

"Me?"

I nod.

"Yes," she replies with a twinkle in her eye.

"Come on, I'm not going to hire you if you flunked out of grade two!"

"Studied computer science at UK. Dad was a little disappointed that I didn't enroll at Haskell. That was his big pipe dream."

"Why a pipe dream?"

"I've been hooked on computers since I first got my hands on a Nintendo DS while I was in diapers. Computer science was preordained."

"Ah. Why Chicago?"

"Why not? Tons more IT jobs and an endless supply of geeks to hang with."

"Hence Lakeview and KAPOW!"

She laughs and nods. "So now you know the tale of Chippy."

"I guess so. You know, I kind of hoped it wouldn't take you two days to check me out, what with you being a computer whiz and all."

This cracks her up. "Checking you out took all of two minutes, Mr. V. It took two days to get around to meeting you because I was busy with other stuff."

"I'm a shallow book, am I?"

She shakes her head and then gets serious. Like Penelope, Chippy has an earnest game face. Must be a Kansas thing. "Not shallow, just an open book. Now, tell me exactly what you hope I can do for you."

I give her an overview of Denzel's case, concluding with the brick wall we've run into when it comes to identifying Spike, Di, and Horace.

Her eyes glitter with interest. "That's all you have for names, one first name and a couple of nicknames?"

"I'm afraid so."

"I love it. A challenge! What else can you tell me about them?"

I do. It takes all of a minute or so.

She frowns. "Not much to go on for Spike and Horace. But okay. We've got a little to work with for Di. I'll want that voice memo. Good job recording it, by the way."

I nod.

She leans back and locks eyes with me. "Now tell me why you're defending a drug-dealing, murderous Black kid."

The question takes me aback, but she's watching intently as she awaits my response. I explain how the case came to us, walk her through my initial reservations about Denzel and detail the course the case has taken through juvie and now adult court. "As my partner said, quoting Harry Bosch, 'Everyone counts, or nobody counts.'"

"Love Bosch! And?"

"Penelope is right, of course. Somewhere along the way, I came to believe in Denzel."

"You think he's innocent?"

I nod, then smile. "This feels a little like being grilled in a job interview."

"It is! I can only learn so much online, right? I need to look you in the eye to take your true measure."

"To see if I measure up?"

She rolls her eyes. "Lame, Mr. V. *Lame*."

"Ouch! Other than the lame humor, how am I doing?"

She settles back on the pew and eyes me thoughtfully. "Heart in the right place. Check. Don't take yourself too seriously. Check. Good dad. Check."

"Good dad? How do you figure that?"

"Brittany is active on social media. She worships you. At age sixteen, no less. Nuff said."

I find myself grinning stupidly. Who knew? "And?"

"Some insecurities. That's a good sign, especially in an old white guy."

"Wow," I retort. "Old. White. Guy. You managed to label me with three *isms* in three words."

Chippy looks a little chagrined. "You know, it dawned on me recently that my tribe—millennial women and self-professed so-called progressives—are pretty bigoted, just like everyone else. I'm sorry I offended you."

I smile. "I've gotten used to it. Doesn't mean I like it, but we'll count it as progress if some of you are beginning to notice."

"Yeah, I guess all our little cliques are pretty tribal when it comes right down to it, aren't they? No pun intended, of course," she adds with a self-conscious smile.

I wink. "Your tribe would crucify you for that little slip of the tongue."

"Crucify? Now you've gone and offended Christians—right here in this beautiful church!"

"It is beautiful, isn't it?"

She nods.

"What else do you need to know about me before you decide if I've passed the screening process?" I ask.

"Oh, you passed. I liked what I saw online. I just wanted to see for myself, make sure it wasn't all PR spin from a dastardly business type."

"There you go, stereotyping me again."

"Sheesh," she groans. "Tough crowd!"

"Actually, I don't trust that type either."

She grins.

God, I like this woman. "Where have you been all my life?"

Chippy smiles and dips her chin so that she's looking up at me through her eyelashes with a sultry look. She spreads her arms wide and pivots from the waste up. "You like, mister?"

"I didn't mean it that way!"

"I know. I was just goofing off."

I don't miss a tiny flash of pain in her eyes, as if we've just surfaced some hurt from her past.

"Now, don't take this the wrong way, but you're plenty pretty. I just meant that…"

When I falter, worried I'm going to say something easily misconstrued, she laughs and touches my arm. "Admit it, you've always pined for a brilliant, witty computer hacker, haven't you?"

"Something like that," I murmur, hoping for a change of topic before I manage to work my entire leg into my mouth.

She surprises me by leaning in to plant a little peck on my cheek. "Thanks. You're a good guy, Mr. V."

I feel myself blush, which sends her into a spasm of laughter.

"I meant it, Chippy, or whatever the heck your name is. You *are* pretty."

She beams. "Thanks. It is kinda tough to have a serious heart-to-heart with someone named Chippy, isn't it?"

I laugh. "I was just thinking that." I'm visiting with people named Toe and Chippy. You can't make this shit up.

She looks at me for a long moment. "It's Chepi, Mr. V."

I look back at her blankly.

"My real name. Chepi, not all that different than Chippy. It's officially an Algonquin name that means fairy spirit." She places the fingertips of both hands on either side of my face. "Now you will forget my real name and never utter it aloud to another living being."

"What's this? Telepathy?"

"Vulcan mind meld."

"Star Trek? Mr. Spock?"

"You're a fan?"

I laugh. "I'm no Trekkie, but I watched."

She stands up abruptly and holds a hand out to me. "I'm gonna enjoy working with you, Mr. V."

I scramble to my feet and take her hand. "I think you're right. This could be fun."

She smiles, then digs a smartphone out of her backpack. "A Vulcan communication device. Use this to communicate with me. Nothing else, okay?"

"Got it," I say as I take the phone from her hand and study it carefully, turning it this way and that. "Who knew? This looks just like an iPhone."

She rolls her eyes. "Heavily modified, sir. That thing is encrypted to hell and back."

"If you say so."

"I do." She holds her hand out, palm up. "Give me your phone so I can send that voice memo to myself."

It takes her less than a minute to do so. She returns my phone and turns to go.

"One more thing."

She turns back. I explain who Darnel Wix is, my encounter with him, and that I have a sense he's worth keeping tabs on.

"Why?"

"To see who he runs with, who he talks to, hear what gets said."

"You think he's involved in this?"

"Probably not. I just have a feeling we might learn something from watching and listening to him. Maybe he knows Spike. Maybe that's how Denzel got mixed up with the guy."

Chippy looks skeptical. "His own kid?"

"Seems a stretch, doesn't it? But Darnel Wix isn't wired like you or me." I tell her about the neighborhood Wix lives in. "Tough place for white guys to sneak around in."

"Some white guy hanging around will stand out just a wee bit, huh?" she quips.

"To put it mildly."

"Plant a camera to watch the building. Use a directional microphone to monitor what is said."

"Same issue. Wix has eyes everywhere on that street. I don't see how we sneak into or out of the neighborhood."

She thinks on that for a beat. "Darnel Wix is his real name?"

"So far as I know."

"Any businesses on that block?"

I think back. "A convenience store down the street, maybe in the next block."

"Send me the address. Maybe I can do something. Don't get your hopes up."

27

After only two days on the job, Chippy calls early Saturday evening to tell me that she's set up surveillance on Darnel Wix. She hacked into the CCTV cameras at the convenience store and is using them to monitor the front entrance of Wix's place.

"Not an optimal set up but better than nothing," she says, then informs me she's still working the Spike and Di angles as well. She doesn't hold out much hope for locating Horace unless we can dig up at least a little more information than his first name. When I press for something of a detailed progress report, she laughs. "I'm on it, Mr. V. Patience."

Not a commodity I have in abundance these days. I end the call and finish whipping up a gourmet meal of hot dogs with a side of mac and cheese, ably assisted by my daughter, who is slicing hot dog buns. Pat is supervising. This is our first visit with Pat since her mother's funeral. She seems surprisingly upbeat; maybe we're a distraction from the family grief. We all spent the afternoon out and about, so we're eating a little later than normal. We discuss our outings, then sit down to eat. Brittany begins dinner conversation by informing me that she'll be delivering a guitar lesson after dinner.

"Who's the student?" I ask.

"You! We need to work on a few songs, Pops."

So.

Pat forks up some mac and cheese and turns to me. "Did you buy a swimming pool for us today?"

"No, but I did negotiate a couple of firm quotes. We can vote on them at next week's meeting."

"How much is it going to cost us?"

"Between sixty and seventy thousand dollars if we go fancy, closer to fifty if we go bare-bones."

"Didn't someone tell us not two weeks ago that we'd be looking at forty grand?" Pat asks.

"I might have been lowballed on price."

"Might have?"

"Yeah. I'll have a little egg on my face at the next meeting."

Brittany cocks her head and studies me. "Might be a good look on you, old-timer."

"Thanks for your support, smartass."

"Anytime, Pops!"

I polish off my first hot dog. "Looking on the bright side, our friendly neighborhood hardware retailer twisted some arms at their corporate office to get us another five thousand toward the pool decking and other finishing touches."

"Cool," Brittany says.

I nod. "Yes, it is."

"I broke fourteen seconds in the hundred meters," Brittany says proudly. She was at track practice this afternoon.

We do fist bumps all around, then Brittany tells us about practice while we finish our meals, liberally lacing gossip into the telling. She manages to put an amusing twist on much of it.

Pat slips the dogs little bits of mac and cheese, pretending not to notice us pretending not to notice this gross infraction of Valenti family dinner table rules. *What the hell?* I think as I flip each dog a tomato. Deano drops his and lets it roll away —apparently not impressed with a healthy snack when there's meat on the table. Dolly noses hers around for a minute before finally eating it.

"Better for you," I tell them.

Brittany laughs. "I never liked that line when I was a kid."

"Was?"

"*Was*," she retorts, shooting me the stink eye.

I toss my paper napkin on my empty plate and push back from the table. "I need some air. How about you two tidy up and do the dishes while I take the mutts for a walk?"

Brittany pops to her feet. "How about *I* take the dogs while you do the dishes?"

I laugh and shake my head no. "I cooked. You clean up."

Brittany gives Pat a pleading look.

"Uh-uh," I say while wiggling a warning finger at Pat, who promptly holds her hands up in a gesture of surrender.

"I never get in the middle of family squabbles," she says wisely, as if she hasn't joined Brittany to gang up on me plenty of times.

Darkness has fallen when I set out for Independence Park with Deano and Dolly.

"Hey, Tony!" a deep voice calls out to me from a monster pickup truck at the curb of Liberty Street where it dead-ends at the park. When the interior light pops on, I see Mountain Man smiling at me.

"Hey, Rick. How's things?"

"Good. You?"

"Pretty good."

He reaches through the open window and holds a hand down so Dolly can have a sniff. "Nice dogs."

"Thanks. What brings you out here at night?"

"Just looking things over a final time. Figuring out where to stage equipment next weekend."

"How did that sneak up on us so quickly? What time are we starting Saturday?"

"We'll be up and at it early. Shouldn't need the rest of you here until midmorning at the earliest. Anyway, I need to get my ass home for dinner. See you Saturday."

"Sure. See you then."

He roars away and I head into the park. I reverse our usual route to enter by the pool so I can have a look at what is shaping up to be a little larger of a money pit than anticipated. I try to envision one of the new pools I've seen in brochures replacing the sorry remains of the pool of my childhood. Imagining it finished and packed with families lifts my spirits. So what if it costs a little more than expected? The childhood memories I made here are priceless. The value of new memories made possible by our project will be every bit as enduring.

"We'll make it happen," I tell the dogs, who are walking to either side of me. As we turn away from the pool to continue following the well-worn dirt path around the perimeter of Independence Park, a solitary figure emerges out of a stand of trees thirty or forty feet ahead of us and heads the same way. By the time we reach the far end of the park, we've closed the distance to fifteen or twenty feet. I'm wondering if it's someone I know when the person stops and turns back. I slow as a deep rumble builds in Deano's chest. Dolly is instantly fully alert. I tighten my grip on their leashes, one in each hand, as whoever appears to be confronting us takes a few steps closer. My breath catches when light glints off the handgun he's pulling out of his hoodie.

"Keep them fuckin' dogs under control unless you wanna get them shot," comes a gravelly voice from within the folds of the hoodie. Something in the voice is off, as if he has a wad of gum in his mouth. Or maybe his nostrils are pinched closed.

This could get awkward. I'm being mugged while my wallet sits on the dresser in my bedroom. At least I have an expensive watch the jerk can have—one of the few remaining trinkets left from my days as a high-flying corporate lawyer. What the hell, cheap watches keep time.

Deano's rumbling escalates to a full-throated growl as the man steps closer, gun in hand. Dolly has fallen deathly quiet and strains against the leash. She's by far the greater threat to my unknown adversary, who keeps looking toward the larger, more outwardly threatening Deano. I'm tempted to turn Dolly loose but am afraid he'll shoot before she reaches him. My Glock is in a shoulder holster under my jacket. Getting to it quickly with dog leashes in hand isn't an option.

"Dolly, sit," I command. She does, but she's clearly ready to go in an instant. Deano doesn't sit when I tell him to, but he gives no more than a tentative pull on his leash. I turn back to the man. "What do you want? All I have on me is a watch, but it's a good one."

A harsh bark of laughter escapes the dark figure. "Don't give a shit what all you got. What the hell Denzel be telling you and the cops?"

The question takes me by surprise. "Denzel? That's what this is about?"

The gun steadies, aimed right at my chest. "Asked you a question."

Menace radiates off the man facing me down. Is this the elusive Spike?

"Answer," he demands.

"What would Denzel have to tell us?" I counter, angling my head this way and that to get a better look inside the shadows of the hoodie that conceals him. Nothing doing.

"You tell the boy that he be wantin' to keep his mouth

shut 'bout that night, leastways if he wants to see his next birthday. Y'hear?"

"Yeah, I hear. Thing is, you can't get to Denzel anyway, right? Bluster all you want, pal, but I don't see that you have much leverage here."

"That right?"

"Yeah."

"Cocky bastard, ain't you?"

"Just a realist. You can't reach Denzel, so you're trying to intimidate him. I'm not going to play along."

"Think I can't touch the boy? Know who I am, cracker?"

I'm not about to admit my suspicions. Doing so would reveal that Denzel had mentioned Spike, even if he didn't give up his identity. My worries about this guy's gun have all but evaporated. If he had come to shoot me, he would have pulled the trigger already. No, he's only here to deliver a message.

"Not a clue," I reply. Then my mouth runs away from me. "Just some sorry punk in a park, near as I can see."

He takes a step closer and thrusts the gun to within inches of my nose. "Ain't no one talks at me that way!"

My heart leaps into my throat. Time to shut up, deescalate, and send this clown on his way before someone gets hurt. I'm supposed to be done playing hero. Or cowboy. Or whatever it is I do when I challenge people I have no business confronting.

After a precarious moment when I think he just might pull the trigger, he backs off a step but keeps the gun aimed at my chest. "Last thing I'm gonna tell you, then you get this shit handled. Denzel be at risk, but he ain't the only one who is, understand? I know where you live. Where your partner be, too. And I know you got yourself a sweet little daughter."

The threat to Penelope angers me; the mention of Brittany infuriates me. My thoughts turn to my Glock. Dare I let this guy walk away? If I transfer both leashes to my left hand, I can go for my gun when he turns away.

"Make my problem go away," he adds, "or people in your world is gonna go away."

Or I'll make you go away, you SOB. I'll draw down on him when he turns his back, then call the cops to come haul away the trash.

"Turn around and go back the way you come in, motherfucker," he says, short-circuiting my clever plan.

I tug on the leashes and turn to walk away, dragging a mile-long trail of fear for my daughter and partner. I peek over my shoulder as I near the pool. No sign of the man. I dial 911, then stand beneath the nearest streetlight and wait for the cops.

28

An hour later I'm sitting at our kitchen table with a coffee, giving a statement to a Cedar Heights PD detective. After taking a look at my ID, one of the initial responding officers sent me home while they joined the manhunt to track down "a man in a dark hoodie and dark pants," which was as much as I could tell them about my assailant. Good luck with that. Pat and Brittany are in the basement with our neighborhood cop, Derek, who stopped by to check in as soon as he saw the police activity on Liberty Street. It's just as well if they don't hear every detail about my latest adventure—especially the not-so-veiled threat to my daughter.

We're almost done with the statement when I hear a familiar voice at the front door. My inquisitor's eyes cut to the kitchen entrance and lock on her boss, Cedar Heights chief of police Jake Plummer. Jake is dressed in jeans and a polo shirt. I feel bad that he's been dragged out of his home on a Saturday evening.

He grins at me and tells his detective, "Finish up, Shelly. I've had my fill of questioning this character over the years."

I flip him off as he steps into the kitchen, snags a handful of doggy treats, and saunters into the living room with the dogs in hot pursuit.

After a final five minutes of Q and A, the detective gathers up her things. She pauses at the door and turns back to me. "I'll pass this along to the detectives working the Harry Hood homicide. They'll probably want to talk with you." She lets herself out.

Jake follows, and they have a brief chat on our front porch before he comes back inside. He meets my gaze and shakes his head. "Jesus, Tony. Again?"

"What are you doing here?" I ask. "Surely you don't roll on every 911 call in Cedar Heights?"

"The watch commander noticed your name and gave me a shout. Is a year ever gonna go by without you getting yourself mixed up with the underbelly of society?"

"I'm fine, Jake. Thanks for asking."

"You always seem to land on your feet, my friend. How, I don't know."

I relate the supernatural sense of menace that Di attributed to Spike, whom I'm all but certain I met a little more than two hours ago. "That guy scares the crap out of me, Jake."

"You really think it was him?"

"If not, then a sidekick. Scary SOB either way."

Jake looks away thoughtfully for a long moment. "My guess is that you're right. If so, he really does exist."

"I never doubted it."

Jake's brow furrows in concern. "He mentioned Penelope and Brittany as well, huh?"

My hands ball into fists. "Yeah."

"What's the plan?"

"The plan?"

"With Brittany. What are you gonna do with her?"

"What do you mean, what's he going to do with me?" my daughter asks from the top of the basement steps. Her eyes are ablaze.

"Nothing," I reply.

"Oh, cut the crap, Dad. Why would I need to go anywhere?"

"I haven't had time to process all this, Britts. We'll talk about it later. Okay?"

"Not really," she grumbles. "We *will* discuss it, though. You're not going to decide 'what to do with me' without talking to me first."

"In all fairness, Brittany," Jake interjects, "those were *my* words, not Tony's."

Brittany gives him a sharp look, then sighs.

Pat and Derek followed Brittany up the stairs and have been listening.

"You're out of school in two weeks, then you're off to Brussels to visit your mother, right?" Pat asks.

"Not necessarily," Brittany replies, then looks at me. "I'm going sometime this summer. We haven't nailed down the dates yet."

"We'll discuss it more, but think about going sooner rather than later, okay?"

"Which means I'm in danger again, doesn't it?"

"Maybe."

Her eyes narrow. "I'm sick of being chased out of my home! I'm sick of my father being in danger all the time. What's wrong with this world?"

I cringe, then prepare for tears, which don't come. Instead, Brittany finishes her tirade by slamming an open palm on the countertop and turning angrily on Jake. "Isn't it *your* job to keep us safe?"

Jake's eyes widen in surprise; he and Brittany have a good relationship. When he senses me gearing up to intervene, he holds up a hand to wave me off. "You're right, Brittany. It *is* my job to keep the people of Cedar Heights safe, and to run scum like this guy out of town or put them behind bars—and we will."

Brittany snorts, then storms off to her room. We watch her go, then Pat and Derek come the rest of the way into the kitchen.

"Count me in on that, Chief," Derek says. "I live down the street. I'll keep an eye out as best I can."

Jake grins. "Hey Double D."

"Double D?" I ask with the hint of a smile, suspecting there's a story behind the nickname. Given the nature of cops, I suspect I'll get a chuckle out of the explanation.

Jake's eyes swing to me. "His last name is Donahue. He hasn't told you about this yet?"

Derek has a pained expression on his face as he waits for the story to play out.

"Have you met Derek's wife?" Jake asks me.

I nod.

"Maggie says her husband is just a big boob, so some joker at the station hung the title DD on him," Jake says through laughter. "Get it? Derek Donahue: DD. Boob size DD."

Pat nods with mild bemusement. I offer up a wan smile. I'm not sure I'll ever quite get cop humor. The DD thing is a bit of a laugh, but it sure isn't thigh-slapping funny. Whatever. Maybe I'm just grumpy from having a gun pointed in my face.

I turn to my neighbor. "Thanks for coming by, Derek."

"Any time, pal. Thanks for not perpetuating the locker-room humor."

Jake's eyes cut to Derek. "Does it bother you?"

"Not on the job, Chief, but I don't like to bring it home."

"Fair enough." Jake's eyes settle on me. "I hear you've gotten yourself a new gun?"

I nod.

"Good things to have. Not a reason to start hunting down bad guys, though. Right?"

I nod my understanding but don't commit to being sensible. The guy threatened Brittany.

Derek has wandered off to inspect the front door. He whistles as he turns back to me. “This is some impressive security. You keep a vault of gold somewhere in the house?”

I briefly consider explaining why I felt the need to fortify the house last year, but we’ve been working at moving on, so I just shrug. “Long story, Derek, but those days are over. Excitement at the Valenti household is a thing of the past.”

29

I collapse in my office chair late Monday morning, relieved to get off my feet after an hour in court arguing on behalf of a dipshit client trying to beat a red-light camera ticket. I mean, really? There are pictures! I get it—the guy drives a gravel truck for a living and is close to losing his license on demerits—but he might have thought of that *before* he floored the gas pedal in his Dodge Charger when a yellow light threatened to slow his progress toward a local watering hole at the end of the workday. I kick off my shoes and reach down to massage my foot.

That's not really why my feet ache today. I spent eight hours traipsing around a bingo hall yesterday afternoon and evening, fundraising for the Independence Park swimming pool. We made over two grand, so we're going to do it all over again in two weeks. Yeehaw!

I hear Penelope enter the outer office, where she chats with Joan for a minute, then passes my open office door, flashing a smile and a little wave as she does.

"Be in to chat in a minute," she calls out.

God bless her. I don't want to put my shoes back on to go even ten feet. I groan inwardly as I look ahead to band practice tonight and more time on my feet. Worse still, Brittany has invited everyone for a dinner of Tony Valenti's famous BBQ burgers beforehand. That means a long stint on my feet preparing the patties and tending the grill. Woo-hoo.

"When?" my partner shrieks from her office.

I start fishing with my toes to locate the shoes beneath my desk.

"Hurt how badly?" Penelope wails.

Given how upset she is, my thoughts turn immediately to Penelope's partner. Something must have happened to Becky. I finally manage to snag my loafers and cram my feet into them. Then I'm up and out of my office in a flash. Joan is already at my partner's open office door, staring aghast at Penelope. My partner is on her feet with her phone pressed tight against her ear, eyes wild with fear as she paces.

"Where did it happen?" she asks in a shaky voice as her eyes meet ours. Hers narrow as she listens to the reply. "Did they get the attacker?"

Attacker? Is this my fault for baiting the idiot in the park? We took the threats seriously. Penelope and Becky have security—apparently not enough. I should have done more. Shit. Shit. Shit.

"Which hospital?" Penelope listens to the answer, ends the call, and grabs her purse off the credenza. "That was Judy Edwards. Denzel was attacked this morning. They've taken him to Stroger."

"How bad?" I ask with a sick feeling in the pit of my stomach. Stroger is a Level I trauma center—a good one, thankfully. The fact they've taken Denzel there, however, isn't a good sign.

"No details. Just that it's bad."

We know no more an hour later as I pace around the emergency waiting room, beating up on myself. Nobody will tell us anything, least of all the two Cook County Jail guards loitering around. Neither seems overly upset that one of their charges is on an operating room table yards from where they stand—a fifteen-year-old kid they were charged with protecting. It's no surprise that they're avoiding us, given the tongue-lashing I delivered about allowing this to happen. "What part of isolation don't you clowns understand?" I shouted before Penelope dragged me away. Over-the-top? Sure, but it's what happens when someone is looking for others to blame for their own failings. My cocky assertion in the park that I didn't think Spike could get to Denzel has turned to ash in my mouth.

Thelma Payton hustles into the emergency room and makes a beeline for us. "How is he?"

We explain that the hospital staff won't tell us anything. "Family only," I conclude bitterly, as if the poor kid has much family.

Thelma marches straight to reception, where she enters an animated discussion with a young woman, who eventually summons a nurse to speak with Denzel's aunt. They move away from the window and lean their heads close while they speak quietly for a minute or two. Then Thelma walks back to us, clearly shaken by what she's been told. She dabs at her eyes with a tissue. "It's bad."

"How bad?" I ask anxiously. "Is he going to make it?"

"He's still in surgery. Denzel was stabbed a couple of times. Deep wounds that caused a lot of internal damage and bleeding. He was in shock from blood loss when he arrived. It's touch-and-go."

I sink into a chair. I'm startled to see Mike Williams stride in several minutes later and head straight to me.

"What are you doing here?" I ask as we shake hands.

"I hear you made a scene. Penelope's concerned you're going to get yourself in a pickle if you don't cool down."

My eyes cut to my partner, who has just walked up to us.

"You went off pretty good on those guards, Tony."

"No less than they deserved."

"They did," she agrees. "Someone at the jail does, anyway, but it isn't going to do anyone any good if you get yourself in trouble making the point."

My shoulders sag. She's right.

"How is Denzel?" Mike asks.

Penelope relates the news from Thelma.

Mike's jaw sets in anger as his eyes flash to the jail guards but he holds his tongue. He and I are fantasizing about meting out retribution when Penelope's phone beeps with an incoming text message.

She reads it, types a quick reply, then pokes my shoulder. "Our escort is here. Time to get to work."

"What?"

"We're not accomplishing anything constructive here. I want to know what happened, who's responsible, and then kick some tail. Let's get started."

"Okay."

Her eyes swing to Thelma. "You'll keep us up to date about Denzel?"

Thelma nods.

"What's this about an escort?" I ask Penelope as we turn to go.

"Becky doubled our personal security from one person covering each of us to two. My team is waiting outside."

I'm happy to hear that they've beefed up their security. But—

"What am I supposed to do with my car?"

"I'll ride with you, but I want these people around. They can follow us."

I glance sideways at my partner as we exit the hospital parking lot. "It's pretty sad that the only family to rush to the side of a fifteen-year-old kid fighting for his life is an aunt he barely knows."

Penelope frowns. "At least he has Thelma."

"He has a father. He should be here."

"I doubt he even knows."

He's about to find out.

After dropping off Penelope and her security people at Brooks and Valenti, I call up Darnel Wix's address on my car GPS, then peel out of the alley behind our office. On some level, I know this is a bad idea. There's nothing subtle about my arrival outside the building where I first encountered Wix four months ago. A new pair of kids is standing guard at the top of the steps.

"No time for your tough-guy act this afternoon," I tell them as I climb out of the car and brush my suit jacket back to give them a good look at my Glock. "One of you needs to get his tail inside to tell Mr. Wix that Tony Valenti is here to discuss his boy. Denzel's in the hospital. He might die."

The boys exchange startled looks. The largest shoots me a quick nod and disappears inside while the smaller boy eyes me suspiciously.

"Y'all don't wanna be coming around here sayin' what we ought to do, dude. Could be bad for your health. Know what I'm sayin'?"

"I'm in no mood to put up with crap from a child," I snap back.

His eyes smolder with resentment but he keeps his mouth shut.

"What the fuck you doin' here again?" Darnel Wix shouts as he bursts through the door. His eyes are ablaze and the cords on his neck are bulging.

I shoot a withering look at the kid standing at the top of the steps. "Junior here didn't tell you?"

"Somethin' about Denzel and a hospital?"

I explain, concluding with, "You should be at the hospital, Wix."

"Nothin' I can do about that. I ain't no doctor."

Seriously? "Whatever else you may be, Wix, you're that boy's father."

He shrugs. "Ain't nothing for it."

"You can be a parent! What kind of man brings a child into the world and then abandons him?"

Wix simmers but doesn't reply.

I take a step closer. "Denzel is in danger. Step up for once and *be a father!*"

"What the hell can I do?" he asks with a dismissive snort as he eases closer still. "I put up with enough of your shit now, mister. Time to get your cracker ass outa here while you still can."

I don't give an inch. "What you can do is lean on the punk who was with Denzel the night Harry Hood died. Talk to your lowlife gangsta buddies, get the word out that anyone who hurts Denzel is going to have to deal with you."

Something flickers in Wix's eyes. He's made a decision. I hope it's the right one. When he turns and starts to walk away, I try to nudge him in the right direction.

My eyes cut to the two kids standing sentry as I call out after Wix. "You don't give a damn about your own flesh and blood? You expect these children to have your back when you won't lift a finger to help your own son?"

He pauses on the top step to look back at me, then shoots a sideways glare at his little soldiers. "Count to thirty, men. If this prick ain't gone when you be finished, waste his white ass."

For some reason, I just don't feel welcome in this neighborhood. Whatever. I came to deliver a message. I did. Where things go from here is up to Wix. Perhaps that last little show of bravado about wasting me was for show—something to impress his kiddie soldiers.

But maybe it wasn't.

30

Three days later, Penelope and I are at the Sandwich Emporium for our weekly Thursday lunch meeting, chowing down on today's PB&J daily special—pork, beef, and jalapeño peppers. Penelope came straight from the hospital.

"Denzel's still pretty much out of it, but he may be plugged into one or two fewer tubes and lines than he was the last time I saw him," she tells me.

"I suppose that counts as good news." Denzel seems to be out of danger, but he lost his spleen in the attack and his intestine was perforated—more of a nick then a serious tear, thankfully.

"Judy told me that a guard figured out what was happening and rushed in to break up the attack. She figures that's the only thing that saved Denzel."

"Judy Edwards?"

Penelope nods. "She asked me to keep her up to date. I called her on my way here."

"So I guess not all the guards at Cook County Jail are complete assholes," I mutter. It's some small comfort when I think of Denzel being sent back. I offer Penelope a tight smile. "Maybe this good guy was from Kansas."

She smiles back. "Could be!"

It's May 19th, a little more than five weeks before the trial is set to begin on June 27th. "Any sense of whether or not Denzel will be ready for the trial?"

"No way to know at this point." Penelope takes a bite of her sandwich. "Let's assess where we're at. You start."

"Mary Ann should be working on the DNA this week." Mary Ann Higgins is the DNA expert we've come to rely on. "She should have a report for us a week or two after she finishes, so let's say first week in June or thereabouts. Oleg has reviewed the fingerprint evidence. He's baffled that the prosecution seems unconcerned that Denzel never touched the baggies with the drugs or the cash in his own pocket. He thinks we can attack that at trial to suggest the evidence was planted."

Penelope sets her sandwich down. "But the bat."

"I know. Oleg is bothered by how clean that print is—especially by the fact there's just one set."

"Why?"

"He expected to find lots of prints on a bat used to beat a man to death. Clean prints, smudged prints, indecipherable prints."

"But nobody beat Harry Hood to death, Tony. He was hit exactly once."

"And it killed him. A tough bit of luck," I say, echoing the conclusion of the retired coroner we hired to review the autopsy. Harry had a steel plate on his skull, the result of injuries suffered during an IED attack in Iraq. The bat landed at the margin of the plate, driving it into Harry's brain—something that wouldn't have happened "if the surgery was done properly," according to our medical examiner. "At any rate, Oleg probably can't rescue us."

She nods glumly. "Probably not."

"It could be a blessing in disguise if Denzel isn't medically fit by the trial date. Given the state of our case, a continuance wouldn't be the worst thing."

"It may come to that, partner, but we need to plan for a June twenty-seventh start."

I nod grimly as we get up to leave. It's a quiet walk back to the office.

"Let's hope your friend has some good news," Penelope says as we part outside the building. Her lips curl into a grin. "The church again, huh?"

I nod.

"Maybe this girl thinks you need a little religion."

The girl in question is my hacker friend, Chippy, and the church is the same one we met at a week ago.

I stare at Chippy when she slips into the pew alongside me thirty-five minutes later. Strands of purple hair peek out around the edges of a fedora-style white hat. She's wearing a flowery dress that hangs midcalf and a pair of sensible black pumps. "I barely recognize you."

"That's the idea, Mr. V. We don't want anyone getting curious as to why I'm frequenting the place."

Makes sense. "Any truth to the rumor that you're trying to turn me on to religion?"

"None, and hello to you too."

"Hi."

"Who's spreading rumors about me evangelizing on behalf of the Catholic Church?"

"My partner."

"Ah. She's not one of those Midwest Bible thumpers, is she?"

"Hardly, though she goes to church with her mother every Sunday."

"Of course she does!" Chippy says with a grin. "Totally Kansas."

"Totally. What have you got for me?"

"First off, ballsy move with Wix on Monday, Mr. V."

"You saw that?"

She laughs. "I saw that you showed up very pissed off. Nice wheels, by the way."

"Thanks."

"I couldn't hear it all, but it looked like you kicked some ass."

"Who are you, the NSA?"

"Hardly. Then I would have heard *every* word, not just the yelling."

"How did you hear anything?"

"I planted a little camera and microphone across the street, but there's some sort of interference that I can't figure out. If everyone there would shout like you and Wix did, then I'd hear everything."

"How did you get a camera and mic into that neighborhood?"

"Paid a guy I know to do it."

"A ghost?" I can't imagine any other way to slip in and out unnoticed.

"May as well have been, Mr. V. A Native guy. He just wandered into the neighborhood shambling along with a bottle of whiskey. Typical drunk Indian, y'know? Nobody pays no nevermind to a drunken Injun on the street carrying a mickey of booze. It pains me that so many people still buy into that caricature of us."

"But it worked in this instance."

She nods but doesn't look happy about it. "Yeah, it worked."

"Sorry you had to do something you're not comfortable with."

She waves it aside. "Oh piffle, Mr. V. You didn't make us do it. I'm not sure we're getting anything useful out of it anyway. I see people coming and going, but who are they? I programmed the audio to flag the word Spike, but nothing doing so far. I'm flagging anyone who fits the general description you gave me, but a lot of Black men fit that profile."

"What seems to be the problem?"

"Some sort of audio interference. I have a phone sniffer set up to monitor cell phone calls, but whatever interference they're using is screwing with that too. These people are pretty tech savvy."

"Isn't that kind of surprising in a neighborhood like that?"

"Yeah, it is. Maybe these folks are running a more sophisticated operation than you bargained for?"

"Could be," I reply uneasily. I hope she didn't bring me all the way here just to tell me she's struggling. "Any good news?"

"Sorta." She pulls a computer thumb drive out of her backpack. "This is why we needed to meet in person."

"I figured you just didn't want to risk being overheard on a phone call."

"Not likely. I'm the queen of encryption!"

I nod at the thumb drive. "What is it?"

"All in good time. Let me tell you about the hunt for Di. That's going better."

"It is?" Given the paltry amount of information I passed along, tracking down Di seemed like the longest of long shots.

"Sure, with the birthday clue and the mention of Florida, I started digging into the state databases. I ran searches of birth records with the name Di and its many permutations—Diane, Elizabeth, and so forth. No luck with that, but according to Harry Hood's military records, he was stationed in Tampa Bay. I ran searches of Florida driver licenses for the years he was stationed there, reasoning that Di might have had a Florida driving permit at the time."

"Clever," I say, impressed by the breadth of the reach she seems to have into cyberspace. I don't imagine state and military databases are the easiest to tap into. "That sounds like an awfully big haystack."

"No biggie. I filtered the driver's licence data according to what we had." She hands me the thumb drive. "This is what I found."

I study the piece of plastic in my hand. "And this is?"

"Close to a thousand Florida driver's licenses, complete with photos. Have your guy look through these and see if one of these folks is Di. You can take your computer into the jail, right—you being a lawyer and all?"

"I'll show these to Toe first, although I can ask Denzel to have a look when he's feeling up to it."

"He's sick?"

I shake my head and explain.

Chippy is mortified. "Sounds like we're up against some dangerous people, Mr. V. I better be sure to fly below the radar, huh?"

"Absolutely," I reply with a stab of guilt. I seem to have a knack for unwittingly placing good people in jeopardy.

Her eyes drift to the front of the church as she falls silent, perhaps worrying about what she's gotten mixed up in. What can I do to keep her safe? I felt confident in her ability to remain in the shadows—right up until a few minutes ago when she mused about the level of tech sophistication she's run up against at Wix's place.

"You can bail if you feel threatened. I don't want anything to happen to you."

She winks mischievously. "Nobody's gonna track me down. Heck, playing the cyber cat-and-mouse game is fun."

Until it isn't, I think, but I take some comfort from her confidence.

"So, back to Di," she says with a nod at the flash drive in my hand. "Every license record on there has a unique identifier beneath it, made up of numbers and letters. If this Toe guy—love the name, by the way—care to share how he came to be called Toe?"

I tell her the tale.

She frowns in distaste. "War is such bullshit."

"Can't argue with that."

"Anyway, if Di is in that pile of people, send me a text with the code I attached to each file."

"You mean the unique identifier number thing?"

She chuckles. "To use the technical term, yeah. It's probably overkill, but I added a crypto code to label each file. If anyone intercepts your text, they'll just see a bunch of gibberish. Even if they were able to sort out that they're driver's licenses, they'd have no way of knowing which record we're referencing. Heck, even if they had *this* file, they still wouldn't know."

"Clever."

She grins. "I am."

I pocket the thumb drive. "Anything else?"

"Nope." She stands and slings her backpack over a shoulder. "Talk to you soon, Mr. V. Be careful out there."

"You as well, Chippy. See you around, maybe at a church service sometime."

"Only if I want to be seen." She winks, makes the sign of the cross, and slips away.

31

I park at the edge of Manzarek Park early Saturday and walk into Tent Town. It's my third visit in forty-eight hours. I came straight from my meeting with Chippy on Thursday afternoon and returned last evening. Toe wasn't around either time. He still isn't here when I arrive at his tent.

"Looking for Toe?" a vaguely familiar woman of indeterminate age asks. She's dressed in a pair of pink flannel pajama bottoms and a clashing orange Syracuse University sweatshirt. A black bandanna is wrapped around a head of frizzy reddish hair.

I smile. "I am."

"Seen you around with Toe a few times."

"He's a friend."

"I'm May. And you are?"

"Tony."

"Well, Tony, Toe's away for a bit. Something to do with family. We don't know when to expect him back."

"Do you know how to reach him?"

She emits a hoarse smoker's laugh. "We're homeless, my friend. Don't keep tabs on folks, y'know? Toe will be back when he gets here."

"Do you have a phone?"

"Maybe," she replies with a guarded expression.

I pull out a business card and fold a twenty-dollar bill behind it. "Can you do me a favor and let me know when Toe gets back?"

May eyes the card and twenty with disdain. "You don't need to bribe me for a favor, mister."

Stupid move, Valenti. "Just trying to show my appreciation, May. Sorry if I offended you."

She turns the card over in her hand and studies it, then pockets the twenty. "I'll give this to Toe when I see him. He'll call you if he wants."

"Deal." I refrain from adding how desperately I need to speak with Toe or anything similarly whiny. May doesn't strike me as the type who has much time for whiny men in suits.

She holds up her fingers and waggles them as she turns to walk away.

"Thanks," I call after her.

"Uh-huh," I think I hear her murmur as she continues on her way. Or maybe she said, "Fuck you." Hard to say. Anyway, I have a swimming pool to bust up. I backtrack to my car and drive home, uttering a fervent prayer to a god I don't believe in for Toe's prompt return. We need Di. Badly.

Brittany and Pat are cleaning their dishes from a late breakfast when I get home. We have a quick cup of coffee before setting out for Independence Park, where Rick the Mountain Man and his crew are hard at work. A rail-thin Black man greets us effusively with an enormous smile as soon as he spots us.

"Reverend Jakes!" I exclaim happily as we shake hands. "What are you doing here?"

He winks at me after he hugs Pat and Brittany. "Pat mentioned this little party when she was out last week. Figured we could help out."

Pat points to a front-end loader, which is scooping up chunks of broken concrete as Rick's men dig them out of the pit that was once a swimming pool. A row of three dumpsters is positioned nearby for the loader to dump the refuse into. "Reverend Jakes brought some equipment to help Rick's crew."

"Meaning we won't have to haul it by hand?" I ask hopefully.

Jakes has a twinkle in his eye. "We'll leave you the little stuff. You know how the Lord disapproves of idle hands."

Rick climbs out of his big diggy thing, whatever it's called. It has a big shovel on the front, if that helps. He walks over. "Hey, folks."

We exchange hellos before Rick turns to Jakes. "Thanks for this, Reverend. Much appreciated. It's gonna save us some serious time."

"And seriously sore muscles," I add with a grateful smile.

Brittany touches Jakes's arm. "Thanks, Reverend. You've rescued me from a weekend of listening to the old man griping about aches and pains."

Rick laughs, then gives me a friendly slap on the back that almost propels me into a face-plant.

Pat catches me. "Pathetic, Valenti."

"Sorry," Rick says with a laugh before he turns and walks back to his equipment.

Reverend Jakes rests a hand on my arm as we set out to inspect the progress of the demolition. "Hold on, Tony."

I stop and let Pat and Brittany get ahead of us.

When we're alone, Jakes says, "I heard about what happened to Denzel Payton in jail. How is he?"

I flashback to the painful five minutes I spent with Denzel yesterday, the first time we'd spoken since the attack on Monday. "This is your fault!" he said bitterly. "I told you this would happen if you didn't settle the case." I don't blame him for being angry, but I didn't give the order to have someone stab him. Then again, he did warn us.

I bring myself back to the present and answer Jakes's question by detailing Denzel's injuries. "The doctors say he's out of danger but will be rehabbing for quite awhile."

"Until he goes back to that darn jail. They'll try again."

I go on a rant about Wix. "I wish the guy would do more for Denzel."

"Darnel Wix, you say? That's his old man?"

"Yeah. Well, maybe. Wix says it could be any one of five or six guys. He claims he stepped up to care for the boy."

"Don't know about that, Tony. Bad news, that man."

"You know him?"

"More like I know *of* him. We ran him out of Lawndale a few years back."

"Why?"

"Dealing drugs, though we could never prove it. A teenage street thug who never grew out of the life, y'know?"

"Stupid SOB."

"That ain't so, Tony. Wix is a sly fox, which makes him more dangerous than the average petty criminal. If you've crossed his path, watch your back, my friend."

The warning nags at me over the next two hours while we try to make ourselves useful at the demolition site. Pat's brother and sister are here with the faraway stares of the recently bereaved. I imagine they're lost in memories of happy times spent right here in Independence Park with their parents. I can relate. I once enjoyed family times here as well. Now the only surviving family member I have is Papa, who is an ocean away in Italy.

Being at loose ends affords me an opportunity to get to know some of my neighbors a little better. I have a good chat with Derek Donahue, who has been conspicuously visible lately, puttering in his front yard and driveway while keeping a wary eye on our house.

"Thanks for watching out for us."

"No problem." He looks past me and grins.

I follow his gaze, then smile myself. Derek's wife, Maggie, and their two children are rolling into the park with what appears to be a lemonade stand teetering on a Radio Flyer red wagon. Maggie is pulling a wheeled cooler with one hand and using the other to help balance the structure on the wagon. I wander over to have a look when they stop several feet away from the workers.

"Hey, Tony," Maggie says as Derek unloads the wagon. "We're here to audition for the concession stand gig."

Derek and his daughter tack a sign to the front of a kid-size folding table: *Lemonade and Cookies. 25¢.*

"What, no open bar?" Pat asks.

Maggie rolls her eyes and laughs. "This is a family event."

So it is. I accept a small plastic glass of lemonade and an enormous peanut butter cookie from an adorably solemn seven-year-old girl and hand her a quarter. "Thanks, sweetheart."

She frowns. "That's fifty cents, mister. They're twenty-five cents *each*."

"Oh! I'm sorry." I dig out another quarter and hand it over.

She drops my cash into an empty Planters mixed nuts tin. "That's okay, mister."

I meet Maggie's dancing eyes as she pats her daughter's head. "The Independence Park pool concession will be very lucrative with this gal on the job," she informs me.

"Indeed." My phone chirps with an incoming text message from Mike Williams.

I have something to tell you about.

I text back, explaining where I am and why.

Meet me at your place in 20 minutes?

Sure, I reply.

K.

I walk over to Brittany and Pat to tell them I'm going home to meet Mike.

"What's it about?" Brittany asks.

"I'm wondering the same thing."

I hope all is well with the Williams family as I walk home and start a pot of coffee. Dolly hurries to the front door several seconds before the doorbell chimes. Deano lifts his head an inch or two off his paws, then goes back to luxuriating in a sunbeam.

"Hey," Mike says when I open the door to let him in. He looks down at the new dog standing at my side. "Who is this?"

"Dolly," I reply, reaching down to give her an affectionate pat on the head. "This is a bad man, Dolly, Keep an eye on him."

Mike laughs, then looks me up and down. "You don't look like a man who's been working the dirt."

I explain about the unexpected help.

"Sounds like a good gig." He follows me into the kitchen and sits down.

"Beats lawyering."

"Amen, brother." His expression turns serious. "I heard something at work about your case."

"Denzel's case?"

He nods. "Seems that Marcie had a heated argument with Darnel Wix a few days before she was killed."

"You heard it?"

"I wasn't in the office when it took place. I just heard about it yesterday afternoon."

"Who was there?" I ask, thinking ahead to calling witnesses in the unlikely event this proves relevant.

"Guess it was loud enough that everyone in the office heard them going at it. Marcie was pissed that Wix wouldn't lift a finger to help the boy."

"Yeah, I've already been there with the guy. Anything useful in what you learned yesterday?"

He shakes his head. "Not really, just that the man seems to have one hell of a temper."

"I know." A light bulb goes off in my brain. "Do the folks in your office think Wix might have killed Marcie?"

"The timing gives you pause, doesn't it?"

"I suppose it does. Is that all they argued about, Wix not helping Denzel?"

"Marcie said something along the lines of, 'I better not find out that you know more about this man than you're telling me.'"

"Interesting. Maybe she shared my suspicion that Wix might know who Spike is. Peas in a pod. Mind you, Wix has had his own challenges to battle through."

Mike's nostrils flare. "I get tired of that woe-to-the-Black-man shit to explain away the behavior of lazy, selfish men like Wix. They don't care who they hurt. This guy is hurting his own kid."

"He isn't Denzel's biological father."

"Where did you hear that?"

"From Wix. I think he's telling the truth."

Mike looks surprised, then thinks it over for a second. "Father, stepfather, whatever—he put himself in the father role. Denzel's grandmother—Wix's own mama—stepped up to do what he should have done. That's family, man. Wix? Just a worthless street punk who quits when the going gets tough."

"Denzel's aunt is ready to step up if we can get him out of this."

"See?" Mike says. "That's family—willing to take in a boy she hardly knows. No, Wix ain't getting any sympathy from me. He shouldn't be getting any from you either, brother."

I don't reply.

"Lean on Wix," Mike suggests. "If he doesn't personally

know Spike, he can probably find out who the guy is—if he's willing to stick his neck out a bit to save his son."

"Doesn't seem the type."

"Keep hammering away at him, Tony. Marcie seemed to think there was something to that idea. Maybe Wix hooked Denzel up with Spike, something like that."

"The thought occurred to me, but I don't know how to get Wix talking."

"Give me five minutes with him in a dark alley."

Not the worst idea, given the grim set of Mike's jaw and the fire smoldering in his eyes. Heaven help Wix if he had a hand in Marcie's murder and Mike finds out. Marcie's killing nags at me now and then. Would solving it shed any light on our case? It's an interesting question, one I'd like the answer to. But I have a different murder case to tend to.

32

Late the following Thursday afternoon, a full week after Chippy handed me the thumb drive full of potential Dis, I find a text waiting for me when I turn my phone back on after leaving court. Toe is home. I immediately set out for Liberty Street to collect the thumb drive.

"Early dinner, old-timer," Brittany calls from the kitchen as I sweep into the house and head for my bedroom. "Don't forget!"

I already have, I realize as the dogs greet me. Brittany and her friend Jocelyn are going to a drama workshop tonight. I change into jeans and a powder-blue polo shirt, collect the thumb drive from my desk, pick up my laptop, and backtrack to the kitchen. I peer over Brittany's shoulder at the stir-fry she's cooking up. "Smells good!"

"Of course it does. *I'm* cooking it! We'll eat in about five minutes."

"Sorry, kiddo, but I can't stay. Something has come up."

She side-eyes me. "Something more important than a family dinner made by your loving daughter?"

"Afraid so."

"Off with you, then," she says, waving me away. "I'll eat and then call my therapist."

"Yeah, yeah." I lean in to plant a kiss on her cheek. "Have fun with Jocelyn."

"Have fun working, Pops! I'll leave a plate of this feast in the fridge for you despite how callously you treat me."

"Thanks. Love you."

"Love you too."

Deano gives me a curious look as I open the front door, as if to question my sanity. Who leaves the house when food is about to be served? Then he gives me a lopsided doggy smile that I swear says *More for me!*

The late-afternoon sun is slanting through the trees when I arrive at Tent Town, angling in under a wall of threatening gray-purple clouds that portend rain. I spot Toe sitting outside on his lawn chair.

He grins when he sees me coming. "Hey, Mr. Lawyer! I hear you've been looking for me."

We shake hands. "True story. I hope you had a nice visit, wherever you went."

"Ma's sick again."

I pull my foot out of my mouth. "Sorry to hear that."

"She's been sick for a few years now. I try to make it home for a visit every couple of months."

I think of Mama. She would have cupped Toe's cheek in her hand and told him he was a good boy. I smile and pass that along.

"She sounds like a peach."

"She was."

"Was? You lost her?"

"A couple of years ago."

"Sorry, man." He pauses for a moment. "How tough… well… is it?"

"I won't lie, Toe. It hurts. Always will, I imagine. But

you'll get through it. Call me if you ever need to talk about it."

He reaches over to squeeze my shoulder. "Thanks, man. I just might."

"Please do."

"So, what are you so anxious to talk to me about?"

I pull my computer out of its carrying case. "Di."

"You found her! Where is she? Is she okay?"

"We haven't found her yet, but we may be close to figuring out who she is."

"Oh." He looks at the computer. "What have you got there?"

I explain as I power up my laptop and insert the thumb drive. I navigate to the Florida driver's license photos and spin the laptop to face him. "Look through these and let me know if one of them is Di."

He leans in, squints hard, then sits back and throws his hands up in defeat. "My eyes aren't so good these days, buddy. Can't tell one picture from the next."

My shoulders slump.

"No vision benefits in Tent Town."

"How bad is your sight?" I ask as an idea forms.

"Haven't been able to read without glasses since high school. I broke the frames on my last pair a couple of years ago. Taped them back together, which worked well enough, but the lenses shattered a while back. Been blind as a bat ever since."

"Reading glasses?"

"Yeah, I don't see half-bad at a distance."

"Cool!"

"Cool?" he parrots in confusion.

"Cool. They sell readers at drugstores. Pack up and let's go before it rains. I'll even buy you dinner on the way. Somewhere dry," I add as the first fat raindrops begin to dot the ground around us.

He folds his chair and slips it inside his tent. "You don't have to buy me anything."

"No, I don't. I want to. Accept gracefully, Toe."

He zips the tent flap. "Okay. No need to offer me a free meal more than once."

I'm turning back toward the car when the rain starts to come hard, as if someone has turned on a spigot in the sky. Toe sprints past me with his jacket pulled over his head, laughing his fool head off as he splashes through a few instant puddles. I run behind him with the laptop cradled against my chest inside my jacket, my arms pinned awkwardly against my body.

"C'mon! Open up!" Toe shouts as he waits beside the passenger door of my Porsche. So he's noticed which car I come and go in.

I fumble in my pocket for the key fob and unlock the doors. Toe is already inside with the door closed by the time I catch up. He reaches across to pop the driver's side door open.

"Nice wheels," he says as I close my door. "Lawyering must pay pretty well."

"Not as well as you might think." I toss the laptop into the back seat.

"Bet it pays better than Tent Town."

Well.

The clerk at the CVS store we pull into eyes us warily when we walk in five minutes later, dripping all over their brightly waxed floor. Or perhaps the sight of Toe in all his homeless splendor puts her off.

"Screw her," Toe whispers once we're out of earshot.

I shoot him a conspiratorial wink. "Absolutely." I pluck a *Sports Illustrated* magazine off the rack as we pass by on our way to the eyeglasses rack, where we spend a few minutes sampling the wares. I pay for a pair of 2.5X magnification readers ten minutes later.

After a quick sprint back to the car, Toe points out a Chili's restaurant a couple of blocks away. "I like Chili's, if you don't mind chain joints."

"Nothing but chains in the suburbs, Toe. I kinda like Chili's."

"Well, there you go," he says happily as we drive out of the CVS lot. "I love their Oldtimer burgers. With cheese."

After we're seated in a booth, I pull out my laptop. Toe objects before I can boot it up. "Eat and then look," he suggests. "I don't get out much. It would be a shame to waste a nice hot meal by working through it."

Despite my eagerness to get on with the search, I nod in agreement, slide the laptop back into its case, and set it on the seat beside me. "Good point. I've had many a good meal spoiled by work."

A server arrives almost immediately. "What can I get you gentlemen to start?" Cute kid, maybe eighteen or so, doesn't give Toe's appearance a second glance. I see a big tip in her immediate future.

Toe shoots me a questioning look.

"Whatever you want, Toe."

He pops his readers on and glances at the server's name tag. "He's paying, Sadie. Bring us a bottle of your best champagne!"

"Champagne? I don't think we have any."

Toe winks at her. "Maybe just a beer, then. Whatcha got?"

Sadie recites an impressive list of beer, on tap and bottled, and does it all from memory.

"Corona with lime, please."

"Make it two," I say.

Sadie slides menus in front of us. "Be right back with your drinks."

Toe nods in approval as she walks away. "Textbook."

"Huh?"

"Sadie did that perfectly. I used to manage one of these joints back in the day."

"A Chili's?"

"Yup."

The guy is a bushelful of surprises. "When was this?"

"Long time ago. So what's up with you?"

We're not supposed to be working yet, so I steer clear of Denzel's case and tell him about our Independence Park project.

"Cool," he says when I finish.

Sadie returns with our beer and whips out a pad to take our orders. Good for her. Someone once told me that the HR and marketing types at corporate restaurant offices claim that customers feel more valued if their servers can remember their orders without writing them down. Maybe they do, at least until some poor, stressed, over-worked kid running their ass off between tables mixes up orders and delivers a nice, juicy red steak to a vegan. As a customer, I kinda like it when I get what I order.

After his chatter about liking the burgers here, Toe orders something called a Quesadilla Explosion.

Sadie frowns. "I'm sorry. That's no longer on the menu."

"You're kidding. It was the best thing on the menu back in the day."

Sadie apologizes again and offers a quesadilla alternative. Toe accepts.

I order the Oldtimer burger, and smile as I imagine Brittany wisecracking about the old-timer and his oldtime burger, or some such.

Toe is horrified. "What kind of a person orders a burger without cheese? Put cheese on his burger," he tells Sadie.

She shoots me a bemused look and cocks a questioning eyebrow.

"With cheese," I say.

"Am I right?" Toe asks Sadie.

She laughs and nods, then leaves to put in our order. We return to sipping our beers.

"You and your partner work for people without much dough, right?" Toe asks after a minute.

I nod.

"How did the Porsche come about?"

"I was once a hotshot corporate lawyer in Atlanta. That's where I raked in the big bucks. My next car will be a little more modest. A Yugo, or something like that."

He laughs. "They don't even make those crappy little things anymore."

"Well, whatever ill-fated crappy little car they happen to be churning out when the day comes." Then I change the topic. Explaining the Porsche in the face of cutting remarks about how a lawyer to little people can afford a Panamera has gotten old. "How about you, Toe? Where's the family from?"

"Upper Peninsula. They're all still there."

The only Upper Peninsula I know of is northern Michigan, but there could be others. Geography class is a distant memory. "Michigan?"

"Yup." He tells me the family history while we wait for our food: dad, a dentist; mom, a schoolteacher; brother, US Army, didn't return from Afghanistan; sister number one, another schoolteacher; sister number two, a nurse. "Churchgoers all, 4-H Club, Rotary. Small-town icons."

Sadie returns and slides our meals in front of us. "Here you go, gentlemen. One quesadilla, one hamburger, *with* cheese. Bon appétit!"

We chuckle, thank Sadie, and dig in.

My anxiousness to get down to our Di business grows as we work through the meal, so I have to stifle a groan when Sadie returns with dessert menus and Toe happily opens his with an enthusiastic "Yes!" We order chocolate brownies, smothered with fifty-five types of chocolate toppings, and a couple of coffees to wash it all down. Then we talk sports. Toe is a big Detroit Red Wings ice hockey fan.

"Football and baseball are for pussies," he says with a chuckle. "See how those guys fare trying to play on ice skates."

I cringe at the word *pussy*. I've heard it and its cruder linguistic cousin more than I ever care to again, mostly from the lips of my recently deceased older brother—most often directed at me. I let it go without comment. For an ex-soldier, Toe's language is pretty tame.

By the time I finish shoveling a pound or two of chocolate into my gullet, I'm thoroughly steeped in Red Wing lore.

"So," Toe says after he pushes his dessert plate aside, "Let's see if you found Di."

Finally! I sip my coffee patiently as Toe pages through the Florida driver's licenses with his brow furrowed in concentration.

"Can you see clearly?" I ask.

He nods without looking up. "Just taking my time. These pictures are kinda old, huh?"

"Sure are."

"I don't wanna miss her. Could be different color hair and style, y'know?"

"Good points. Just be thorough quickly."

He glances up and smiles. "Quick is the enemy of thorough, Mr. Lawyer."

I pull out my phone and scroll through the news while he bends back to his work. Toe will take as long as he needs to, no matter how impatient I may be for him to finish. I'm browsing through an article about a village controller being perp-walked out of his office to face embezzlement charges when Toe slaps the tabletop.

"Here she is!" he exclaims triumphantly, spinning the laptop around so I can see.

"Wow." Diane Lennstrom's driver's license photo displays

a woman who fits the mold of any number of corporate middle managers I've known, in both looks and bearing. How did she end up homeless? No matter. We know who she is!

"She looks mighty fine all dolled up," Toe says. "I mean, she's still a looker, but, well, now she's homeless, y'know?"

I do. No more shining hairdos that cost upwards of a hundred dollars, no dangling diamond earrings, no business suit, no high-end makeup. That said, I bet the intelligence in those sky-blue eyes is as sharp as ever. I hope so.

33

Summer has arrived with a vengeance. It's midafternoon on Saturday of Memorial Day weekend, almost two days since I texted Chippy with the news that Toe had identified Di. No news so far on her whereabouts, although I'm sure Chippy is working the problem hard. As seemingly impossible as it seemed to me that she would be able to help us to identify Di at all, locating her in a country of more than three hundred million people promises to be at least as challenging.

"Unless she's posting on social media," Chippy said.

Fat chance of that. Di doesn't seem to have a phone, or at least Toe doesn't recall her having one at Tent Town. I set the thought aside and snag a couple of beers from the fridge, then head back out into the blistering sunshine on the back patio. Dolly meets me hopefully.

"Alas, no doggy beer," I tell her, stealing a quick glance at the water bowls I set out for her and Deano. I detour to refill them from the hose. I'm dressed in a pair of shorts and a short-sleeved shirt that I've left open in the eighty-five-degree heat.

Pat sits up from the lounger she claimed on arrival two hours ago. She's wearing shorts and a crop top. Her face and eyes are shaded by an enormous floppy-brimmed hat. "Where's my beer, Valenti?"

I smile and walk over to deliver a frosty bottle of Amstel Light.

She tips the bottle to her lips. "About time."

"No gratuity for your server?"

"Not a penny. Maybe if you served me before the dogs."

It's like old times, Pat and me hanging out, relaxed in each other's company. There was a time when I thought we were inching toward being something more than friends, but Pat had slammed the breaks on that notion. When I reconnected with Trish Pangborne, any thought of Pat and me as a couple quickly receded into the rearview mirror. I sigh heavily as a wave of melancholy settles over me. I still miss Trish horribly, although the pain is subsiding in dribs and drabs as time passes. I miss my family acutely as my eyes pass over the roses Mama lovingly toiled over in her rock garden and the tomato plants Papa babied for years. Then my gaze settles on the mural my late sister, Amy, painted on a panel of the stucco fence that runs the length of the backyard.

"Trish thoughts?" Pat asks.

I turn my head and find her gaze on me. We had a lengthy talk about Trish earlier, the first time we've done so since she passed away last year.

"Some, but I'm mostly thinking about Mom and Amy. Even Papa."

"Is he ever coming back?"

"Good question. I'm beginning to doubt it."

"Still beating yourself up over Trish?"

I nod glumly.

"There was nothing you could do, Tony. Nothing." When I don't respond, she circles back to Papa. "Why do you think your dad is staying in Italy?"

"Apparently, everyone there understands him when he speaks."

Pat chuckles. Papa's broken English is, let's say, unique, even after living in the US for forty-plus years. We all came to understand it, but people who don't speak to my father regularly often struggle to decipher his speech.

"You still have Brittany," she says.

"True. And you."

Pat goes still, then lifts her sunglasses and looks me in the eye. "Yes, Tony, you do. Always will." She reaches across to squeeze my hand, which is resting on my bare stomach.

I turn my hand over and squeeze Pat's fingers, then look away in a confused jumble of emotions.

"Sorry."

"No." I interlace my fingers through hers and sit up to face her. "It's complicated."

"You and me, Valenti? Always has been."

"I didn't expect to hear that from you."

"That shouldn't surprise me."

"You know that I thought we were on that path a couple of years ago, right?"

She nods. "Then I screwed things up."

"Don't say that. You weren't in the right place for us at the time."

"And you're not now."

"Like I say, it's complicated."

She leans across to peck my cheek. "No worries. No hurry. I meant what I said. As things stand right now, I'll be ready and waiting, if and when you're ready."

"Pat—"

She puts a finger on my lips. "No need to say a thing. Let's just enjoy the day."

My phone rings. I pluck it off the table beside my lounger and shield my eyes from the sun. *Unknown caller*. For some reason, perhaps because Brittany is out, I feel a pull to answer.

"Britts?" Pat asks.

I shake my head. "Unknown caller."

"Argh."

With less than a month to the start of Denzel's trial, I can't afford not to answer a call. I press talk.

"This is Thelma Payton, Mr. Valenti. I think you should come to the hospital right away."

My heart leaps into my throat. "Is Denzel all right?"

Pat's eyes widen in alarm as my thoughts race through possibilities. Are they releasing him from Stroger? We've been hoping they'd keep him there, safe behind 24/7 security.

"No. He's fine, Tony. He has something to tell you."

I exhale a breath I didn't realize I was holding. I'm surprised he wants to speak to me at all; our last conversation was the acrimonious, "You let this happen to me!" blow up.

"What is it?" I ask.

"Just come. Please."

The possibility that this may be the long-awaited Spike reveal sends a jolt of excitement through me. I shoot a look of regret at Pat. "I can be there in thirty minutes."

"Thank you," Thelma says. Then she hangs up.

Pat is sitting up and reaching for her purse. "Is he okay?"

I wave her back onto her lounger. "He wants to tell me something. It shouldn't take long. Why don't you stick around and keep the mutts company? I'll grill the steaks when I get back."

She smiles. "Dogs, beer, and steak. Hmm. That doesn't sound half-bad. I'll stay."

I lean down and plant a kiss on her forehead, happy to know she'll be here when I get home.

I walk into Denzel's hospital room thirty-five minutes later. Thelma leans down to smooth Denzel's brow and kiss his cheek. "I could use a fresh cup of coffee. I'll leave you two to talk."

She pats my shoulder on her way out the door. Then it's just Denzel and me, staring at each other warily. I'm the adult, so I break the ice.

"How are you feeling?"

He pulls an exasperated face. "Still sore, but better. Are they really gonna send me back to jail this week?"

"Not if we can stop them."

We received word of the possibility on Friday from prosecutor Judy Edwards. She's against the plan, so I assume it's her boss, state's attorney Timothy Walker, who's anxious to put Denzel back in danger. Penelope is filing a motion with our trial judge as soon as court opens tomorrow, imploring him to intervene. We'll offer to pick up the bill to maintain security here, so the state can't whine about the costs of security while Denzel is in the hospital—which, in Walker's telling, would undoubtedly be positioned as a burden on long-suffering Cook County taxpayers. That's always a winning strategy in the slimy SOB's game of political flimflam.

"They'll kill me if I go back," Denzel says matter-of-factly.

I don't argue the point. "I hope you called to tell me who Spike is. He's the guy driving this. Take him off the playing field and I think you'll be safe, Denzel. It's also probably the only way we can win this case and keep you out of prison."

Denzel's jaw sets. "We've been over this how many times? It's not gonna happen."

I let it go. "Thelma says you have something to tell me."

"Maybe."

Nothing is easy with this kid. I switch gears. "Remember I told you about the woman who said you never went into the tent?"

"Yeah. She took off, right?"

"Would you recognize her again?"

"I won't be forgetting the look she gave me anytime soon. If ever. Why?"

I kick myself for not grabbing my laptop when I left home. We could have done this right now. "We figured out who she is."

His eyes light up. "Will she stand up for me?"

"We know who she is but not where she is. I think we'll find her, though. It's pretty hard to hide in this day and age."

His shoulders slump. "If you say so."

"People a lot smarter than me say so, Denzel."

The corner of his lip quivers, a tick that I've grown used to. It's almost a smile. "You ain't so dumb."

"Why thank you!" I say with a chuckle. "At any rate, I'll bring a picture of the woman, see if you recognize her."

"Sure."

We fall silent. Denzel is deep in thought, his eyes fixed on a point only he can see beyond the patch of ceiling he's staring at. "So, I had a dream, or a vision… or something."

"Okay," I say cautiously.

"Had it a couple of times. Thing is, I think it might be a memory from when I was real little. It's about my ma."

"I'm sorry you lost her."

Tears well up in his eyes. "Thanks. You still got your ma?"

"We lost Mama a couple of years ago. I miss her."

Something in the look he fixes on me suggests that we've finally bonded a bit. Sadly, it's taken the loss of our mothers to make it happen.

He takes a deep breath, then plunges ahead, his eyes again fixed on the ceiling. "Ma is on the floor in a kitchen. She's all bloody and kinda sitting, half laying down, with a hand raised up to protect herself. She's crying, begging. Then a man hits her, maybe even stabs her, it's hard to tell exactly. It happens a few times. Then she's still." Denzel's eyes fasten on mine. "So still."

"Go on," I whisper.

"Then my dad is in my face, all wide-eyed and crazy like. 'Whatcha doin' in here, boy? You didn't see nothing. Don't ever forget it. Y'hear?' Real threatening like. I'm not sure if that was at the same time, or if maybe it came later." He falls silent, his expression haunted.

"What do you think it means?"

"Dunno. I was told she walked out on us. But did she? Or did he kill her?"

I give him a chance to continue. When he doesn't, I say, "You think it's a memory, don't you?"

He nods slowly. "Y'know how you have these little bits of memory from when you were a kid?"

I nod.

"Like that. Little snippets of video."

"Yeah, I have some of those too. I didn't know what to make of them until my parents or brother or sister confirmed I was remembering things that really happened."

He frowns. "I've never really had anyone to ask about stuff like that 'cept Grams, and she didn't like to talk about my ma. I know she didn't like her much, but she didn't trash-talk her none either."

"Any idea if the police were involved?"

"Not that I remember."

I struggle to find words of comfort, but what do you say to a kid who may have just remembered seeing his father murder his mother? He needs a therapist to deal with this, but he's about to go on trial for murder. I don't see Cook County making a therapist available to him while he's in custody, not even at Stroger. What a mess. I may not be able to fill the role of therapist, but maybe I can at least get Denzel some answers.

I call Jake Plummer to get the ball rolling.

34

It's nearing ten o'clock in the morning on the first day of June. Spring is in full bloom. It's the month of weddings and other new beginnings. This June is also the month when Denzel Payton will stand trial for murder. Penelope and I are seated at the defense table in a courtroom at the Leighton Criminal Court Building for a pivotal pretrial hearing. The sheriff should be delivering Denzel from the hospital any time now. We'll soon be joined by the prosecutors and, finally, Judge Everett Wilke, who so far seems determined to continue bludgeoning us in the same spirit Judge Saunders embodied during Denzel's transfer hearing. As if the deck weren't already stacked high enough against us.

Today's will be one of a couple of evidentiary hearings during which Wilke will do his best to ensure that lawyerly squabbling is put to rest prior to trial. The last thing any judge wants during a trial is to have a jury cooling its heels while attorneys fight motions tooth and nail. We lawyers approach the hearings as an opportunity to get a leg up on the opposition.

Assistant state's attorney Judy Edwards enters the courtroom a few minutes after us, accompanied by a nattily dressed young man of Eastern ethnicity. He must be her second chair for the trial. His hair is dyed blond and slicked back with styling gel. After seeing the sneer on his face as they approach us, I wonder if maybe Edwards picked him up on a used car lot. He promises to be a royal pain in the behind. Not that I'm judgmental or anything.

Judy smiles and shakes hands with my partner. "Good weekend, Penelope?"

"Great one. You?"

"Also good." Judy holds out her hand to me. "Nice to see you again, Mr. Valenti."

"Likewise."

We're seconds away from breaking into a chorus of Kumbaya when Judy's pal ruins the budding Zen moment. He stands back, eyeballs us, then points at me.

"Valenti?"

I nod.

His finger swings to Penelope. "Which makes you Brooks."

Geez, the guy should have been a detective.

He taps his chest. "D. W. Seaver."

Penelope shoots him a look that could chill Hades, then looks back to Judy. "That must make you Edwards."

A smile plays on the corners of Judy's lips. They sit down, unload their briefcases on the prosecutors table, and get organized.

A pair of deputies marches Denzel into the courtroom. He's once again decked out in an orange Cook County Jail jumpsuit, hands attached to a chain belt that circles his waist and attaches to ankle shackles, causing him to walk in a clanking shuffle.

Penelope meets the eyes of Denzel's escort and points at the shackles. "Really? Is that necessary?"

The taller of the guards shrugs. "We're told it is, lady. Nothing we can do about it."

"It's ridiculous. We'll see what the judge says."

Good luck with that, partner.

Denzel maneuvers into the chair at the far right of our table, leaving Penelope seated between us. "How was your weekend?" he asks her politely.

Penelope launches into a recitation of her and Becky visiting the Shedd Aquarium, attending a country music festival at Millennium Park, and going to Milwaukee for dinner with friends. She's well into this story when it dawns on her that Denzel spent the long weekend confined to a hospital bed. She stops abruptly. "Sorry."

Denzel shrugs it off with a crooked grin. "Glad someone had fun."

When he asks about my weekend, I don a bored expression. "Didn't do much of anything."

A door opens and all five feet five inches and two hundred plus pounds of Judge Wilke waddles to the steps leading up to the bench. The thirty-six-inch climb seems to wind him—he's sweating by the time he sits down in a monstrous executive chair. The bench blocks my view, but I picture his feet sticking straight out from the seat. Was it Alice in Wonderland who found herself seated on a chair twenty times too large for her? Like that.

"Good morning," Wilke says with a glance that takes us all in before his eyes come to rest on D. W. Seaver, who receives a judicial smile.

"Good to see you this morning, Your Honor," the little turd says.

"And you, Mr. Seaver."

So.

"Our first order of business this morning is a defense motion to exclude the testimony of Jose Hernandez," Wilke announces. His eyes turn to the prosecutors. "Do the people wish to speak to this matter?"

"Thank you, Your Honor," Seaver says. "We do."

Penelope and I exchange a look. She, too, must be surprised that Edwards is allowing her second chair to argue the first motion of the day. The kid must have some juice downtown. Seaver gets to his feet, buttons his suit jacket, and girds for action. I decide that the initials D. W. will henceforth stand for Dickweed.

"Go ahead, Counselor," Wilke says.

"The defense motion to suppress the testimony of Mr. Hernandez isn't worth the paper it's printed on, Your Honor. Mr. Hernandez was a disinterested observer when the defendant uttered his admission of guilt. Mr. Hernandez had no reason or incentive to lie."

So long as you don't consider whatever enticement Walker offered him, I barely restrain myself from blurting.

Dickweed continues. "Mr. Hernandez was a reluctant witness, but he was concerned that a murderer might walk free if he didn't come forward. His testimony is relevant and credible. Excluding it would be a grave miscarriage of justice."

I'm tempted to check our seat backs for barf bags. Rana Asadi, our investigator from the office of the public defender, dug into the past of this Good Samaritan. He's a real choirboy.

Penelope rises when Wilke asks if we have a response to Seaver's beatification of his jailhouse snitch. She side-eyes Dickweed. "Would the fact that Hernandez faces an aggravated sexual assault charge have played into this attack of conscience?"

"Address the bench, Miss Brooks," Wilke snaps while Dickweed smirks.

Penelope glowers at Seaver a moment longer, then turns to the bench. "This is the third time Hernandez has come forward with a supposed jailhouse confession in a felony case, Your Honor. Always in cases in which the state's attorney's office is faced with evidential deficiencies to proving their version of a crime."

"Relevance?" Wilke asks disingenuously.

Penelope shoots the judge an "are you kidding me" look. "We find it suggestive that a case of aggravated sexual assault against Mr. Hernandez—coincidentally, his third—has been continued until after our trial is scheduled to conclude. Why might that be?"

"I have no idea," Wilke replies impatiently.

"Charges were dropped after each of his previous jailhouse snitch incidents, Your Honor. I hope you're as outraged as I am that the state's attorney keeps putting a serial rapist back on the streets. This pattern suggests a quid pro quo arrangement to entice Hernandez to come forward with this ridiculous story."

Wilke's lips tighten into a straight line as he glowers down at my partner. "That's an extremely serious allegation, Counselor. Do you have any evidence to back it up?"

"I imagine I could find another desperate criminal to contest his statement if I could dangle a Get Out of Jail Free card as an inducement, Your Honor."

Happy as I am to see Penelope finding her mojo in a courtroom, she's playing a dangerous game with a judge like Wilke. I touch her arm and whisper, "Cool down."

"So you have nothing, Miss Brooks?" Wilke asks sharply.

"Beyond common sense, no."

Wilke's eyes are blazing and the color is up in his cheeks. "Yet you come into my courtroom to insult the bench and slander the highest law enforcement official in this county! What do you say to that?"

"I'm attempting to represent my client under impossible circumstances."

"Impossible circumstances, you say?"

"I do."

"I do, *Your Honor*!" Wilke thunders.

I wondered how long it would take him to blow his stack over Penelope's lack of deference to the pompous little ass's exalted position.

Penelope doesn't reply.

"You will address the court with the appropriate respect, Miss Brooks. As it seems that you need a pointed reminder to do so, I'm holding you in contempt. We'll take that up at the conclusion of this hearing. Now, I suggest you permit your colleague to present your case from here on."

Penelope doesn't respond.

"Motion denied!" Wilke says curtly, shooting Penelope a self-satisfied smirk as he does.

The little king enjoyed that. Great. Little-man syndrome married to a judicial God complex. Penelope's lucky Wilke didn't just have her shot. Thankfully, I'll be arguing our next motion.

Judy Edwards stands when Judge Wilke introduces the next motion, which has been filed by the prosecution. Once again, it's a move to strike potential testimony.

"We received notice from the defense a week ago, Your Honor, claiming they have an eyewitness to the senseless slaying of Harry Hood."

Wilke lifts the corner of a sheaf of papers on the bench. "You have moved to exclude testimony from this witness, Counselor. Please explain the basis for your motion."

Edwards glances sideways at Penelope, almost as if she's telegraphing an apology in advance of what she's about to say. "Who is this woman? Where is she? The defense claims she was an eyewitness, yet the police know nothing about her. Why didn't she come forward that night, or even the next day? The police spoke with everyone in Tent Town in the hours following the crime, yet this mystery witness wasn't available. Or chose not to make herself available. Why?"

"Mr. Valenti?" Wilke asks.

"These are questions the state will be free to ask this witness when she testifies, Your Honor."

"If she takes the stand."

"Why wouldn't she, Your Honor?" I ask sharply. What judge would prevent someone claiming to be an eyewitness from testifying, especially when that same judge is perfectly happy to allow a jailhouse snitch to spin a steaming pile of crap?

Seaver speaks out of turn. "Really? A homeless druggie, I suppose, and you want to put her on the stand to try to bamboozle our jury? She probably avoided the police that night because she was stoned out of her mind, was in possession of drugs, or both."

I look to the judge, waiting for him to reprimand Dickweed for his outburst. When he doesn't, I turn to Seaver. "This coming from prosecutors who are willing to put a serial rapist back on the street in trade for perjured testimony."

"That's enough!" Wilke snaps at me.

"May I continue without another interruption from Mr. Seaver, Your Honor?" I ask.

He sighs and spins his hand in a *go on* gesture.

"We spoke with the witness several days after we took this case, Your Honor. Her testimony will corroborate Denzel's statement to the police."

"Why isn't that in discovery?" Seaver asks angrily.

"Judge?" I ask.

"Answer Mr. Seaver's question, Counselor."

Really? Is Dickweed running this hearing? He may as well be. "It isn't in discovery because we did not have the witness's full name at the time," I say. "She came forward very reluctantly, and only to tell us that Denzel did not commit this crime. She subsequently fled Tent Town when the man we think is the real killer reappeared."

"A fascinating tale," Wilke says. "You still haven't

explained why this individual's statement was not forwarded to the state as required by the rules of discovery."

"We could hardly send the prosecution a note informing them that we had an as yet unidentified witness, could we?"

Edwards ponders the answer for a moment. "I understand Mr. Valenti's decision—*at that point*. But now she suddenly appears on the defense witness list. How did that happen?"

I explain, offering no details about how we identified Di. "We're actively looking for her, Your Honor. Excluding her testimony before we are able to take a proper statement seems an awful lot like putting the cart ahead of the horse."

Wilke sighs, then looks down at his blotter for a long moment. When he lifts his head, he locks eyes with me. "I will hold this matter in abeyance until such time as you locate the witness and inform the court of her whereabouts. I will then inform Ms. Edwards so she can interrogate the witness and make a determination as to whether or not the testimony is credible. If so, I'll then rule on the motion. If the witness cannot be located, the matter is moot anyway."

Seriously? "My apologies, Your Honor, but is the court suggesting that it will allow the prosecution to vet a defense witness and then permit them to make a determination as to whether or not a *defense* witness will be permitted to testify?"

"Are you suggesting there may be some impropriety taking place in this court, Mr. Valenti?" Wilke asks in consternation.

You're damn right I am! "It's unusual, Your Honor. Out of the ordinary."

"I understand the meaning of unusual, Counselor." Wilke stares me down for a long moment before he sets the stack of papers aside and reaches for the next motion. "I've ruled, Mr. Valenti. Sit down."

After I reluctantly comply, he looks at the prosecutors. "Let's move on to our third and final matter for this morning."

This is also our motion, so Penelope rises to challenge the DNA evidence. Our DNA expert, Mary Ann Higgins, is disturbed by what the prosecution has provided. Wilke seems surprised that he hasn't yet cowed my partner into submission.

"DNA discovery was tardy, Your Honor," she says.

Seaver shrugs. "Backups at the lab. Same old story. It frustrates us too."

By this point, we realize there's no point in complaining about Dickweed hijacking proceedings whenever it suits him. I make a note to look into whatever connection the guy has to Wilke.

"The delay was the first issue, Your Honor," Penelope continues. "When the evidence finally did arrive, our expert was deeply concerned with what was provided. We would like confirmation that we are in receipt of *all* DNA evidence that the state intends to use at trial."

Wilke, who continues to look aggrieved to be dealing with Penelope again, turns to the prosecution team. "Your response?"

"We sent everything we had," Judy Edwards replies.

Penelope turns to her. "I was afraid you might say that. Our expert doesn't believe that to be the case."

Edwards shoots a look at her co-counsel. "We did send everything, right?"

Dickweed doesn't appear to be the least bit concerned. "Sure."

Edwards seems troubled. Why? Because she's worried that something fishy is going on? That she's somehow out of the loop? Both?

Penelope looks back to the judge. "It appears that the prosecution is prepared to present incomplete DNA testing as a match to Denzel Payton, Your Honor. As far as our expert is concerned, the DNA testing is, in fact, inconclusive."

"That's the nature of evidence, Miss Brooks," Wilke says dismissively. "Juries decide. Why are we discussing this?"

"We all know how DNA evidence is perceived by the general public, Your Honor. To introduce an inconclusive finding and claim that it proves Denzel was in that tent is disingenuous at best, criminally unethical at worst. To permit this to be presented at trial will be highly prejudicial, at the very least. You cannot permit this."

I'm relieved when she stops short of accusing Judge Wilke of misconduct. Not aloud, anyway. Her expression of disgust does it for her.

"Now you presume to tell this court what it can and cannot do, Miss Brooks?"

"I'm arguing law, Your Honor. That's my job."

"I'm beginning to understand why I haven't seen you in criminal court, Miss Brooks. The jury will decide how much weight to accord the evidence presented to them. This is how our criminal court system works, Counselor. I suggest you brush up on criminal law before you return to my courtroom."

My partner refuses to back down. "And it's up to us as officers of the court to present credible evidence to the jury, Your Honor. Misleading a jury with evidence we know to be tainted is improper, unethical, and unfair. It's up to *you* to ensure that the evidence at trial is untainted."

"I know my responsibilities," he snaps back. Then he pauses to think. Perhaps suddenly concerned that this might come back to bite him on appeal, he softens his tone. "Are you suggesting that your expert claims the DNA evidence has been tampered with?"

"No, Your Honor," Penelope answers in something close to a civil tone. "The issue is that the prosecution apparently plans to present scientific evidence that doesn't support their preferred conclusion."

"As the judge says," Dickweed cuts in. "The jury will decide."

Wilke nods approvingly. "Mr. Seaver is correct, Miss Brooks, it all comes in. Anything else?"

Penelope looks at me in disbelief. I nod toward her chair in a suggestion to sit down. She does so, albeit reluctantly.

"No, Your Honor," she replies.

Wilke wraps things up and dismisses us.

Penelope and I depart the courtroom in silent dejection. We went zero for three this morning. We can't afford another drubbing like this, but we need more firepower if we hope to rally in the closing innings. A lot more firepower.

35

Two days after Judge Wilke hands us our tails, I'm in our conference room with Penelope. She's fresh off her second of three nights in jail, compliments of the good judge. We're surrounded by a mountain of files—everything we have for Denzel's case. You'd think there'd be at least a single helpful tidbit somewhere in this mass of information. You'd be wrong.

Penelope, as she is wont to do, does her best to find a ray of hope. "Chippy is on Di's tail, Tony. We just need a little luck there."

"It's a long shot and completely out of our control. Which leaves us with the Spike angle to work. How are we going to find him?"

"I don't know."

"We have to convince Denzel to tell us who the guy is. Simple as that."

She blows out an exasperated sigh. "We've been trying to do that since day one of this darned case, partner. I don't think it's going to happen."

"We just haven't pressed the right button. Yet."

"Yet?" she parrots with a bitter laugh. "I'm supposed to be

the one in this partnership who glimpses sunshine in the middle of a hurricane."

"Then it's about time for me to start delivering my share of cockeyed optimism in the face of disaster, isn't it?"

Penelope locks her hands behind her head and looks at me as a smile forms. "Which means I get to take a turn as the hard-boiled cynic?"

"Ha!" I scoff. "You don't have it in you."

"No?"

"No."

"How about this? We don't have a snowball's chance in Hades of winning this case."

I shake my head. "Nope. That's just defeatist. We don't do defeatist here at Brooks and Valenti, Tilting-at-Windmills Attorneys at Law."

"We'll never find Di or Spike."

"Same."

"Timothy Walker will try to screw us over?"

"That's a given, but better," I allow. "See? Being a hard-boiled cynic isn't as simple you Pollyanna types think, is it?"

"Point taken. You're the uncontested Gloomy Gus around here."

I do my best to look smug. "Hey, don't sweat it. Either you've got it or you don't. I've got it."

"In spades."

We smile at each other for a moment before the corners of her mouth turn down. "Thanks for the giggle, partner, but we're still behind the eight ball and time is short."

I make as if to flick a speck of lint off my shoulder. "The way forward is clear, partner. Denzel tells us who Spike is, we run with it, we win."

"I've been thinking, Tony. I want to take a harsher approach with Denzel to see if I can shake him up."

Penelope harsh? "Have at it."

"I'll need your help."

She explains what she wants to do. I'm surprised, but I'm mindful of how her last visit with Denzel went. Penelope had stopped by for a quick visit with him in the hospital the evening after the evidentiary hearing to commiserate with him about the beatdown we received in Judge Wilke's courtroom. She did so on her way to report for her first night in jail.

"He didn't seem all that upset about it," she told me the following morning. "Almost, I don't know, maybe resigned."

We need to put some fight back into our client.

After lunch and a pair of client meetings, we arrive at Stroger Hospital three hours later. We faced off with the attorney for the Cook County sheriff at a hearing late yesterday, during which they tried to have Denzel transferred back into their custody. Their attorney made a big show about how the standard of care in their infirmary for a patient in Denzel's condition is the equal of the hospital's. Yeah, right. Fortunately, their motion was heard in a different courtroom by a judge not connected to the case. A real judge as opposed to a prosecution lackey.

When we reach Denzel's room, we run into one of the doctors who testified at yesterday's hearing.

"That was fun!" she says with a chuckle while we rehash our victory.

"How's he doing, Doctor?" Penelope asks.

"No complications, thank goodness. He's young, relatively fit, healthy, and he's working well with our therapists. It's all good."

I'm happy to hear it but also concerned about Denzel doing so well that he'll be discharged and returned to prison before the trial.

"How long can you keep him here?" I ask.

"When is the trial?"

"June twenty-seventh."

"How long will it last?"

"A week or so."

She winks. "My best estimate is that Denzel should be fit for release on July fourth, give or take a day or two."

"My goodness!" Penelope exclaims. "What a happy coincidence."

"Isn't it, though?" The doctor starts to open the door, then pauses. "He's a great kid. Good luck in court."

"Thanks," we reply in unison.

"If he's still here, will they allow him to come to court?" Penelope asks me after the doctor goes inside.

"I don't know. I can ask Mike Williams how it usually works."

"I hope he can stay. He's safe here."

"True," I agree. "But I'd really like to have him in court."

"I'm sure the jury will be sympathetic and won't hold it against him when they find out why he isn't there."

"Dollars to doughnuts the state will talk Wilke into keeping that little detail from the jury."

"Why?" Penelope asks in true Kansan *But that wouldn't be fair!* indignation. My partner is smart and learning fast, but she's still a little wet behind the ears when it comes to appreciating how cutthroat the world of criminal law can be.

"If Denzel's not in court, the state gets to paint their own portrait of him for the jury, and you can bet it won't be of a scared fifteen-year-old kid. On the other hand, if he's in court, that's exactly what the jury will see."

Penelope's jaw firms up. "Then we need him in court."

"Yeah, but we also want him alive."

The doctor leaves with a thumbs-up as she passes us. Time for our little dog-and-pony show.

"We're here to cheer you up," I announce as we take up positions on either side of Denzel's bed.

"Oh yeah? How you gonna do that?"

"Looks like you'll be staying here until the trial."

"I guess that's cool." He looks from me to Penelope and back again. "Time to do that plea deal thing."

Penelope and I exchange a startled glance. We thought this discussion was over with.

"Why do you say that?" she asks.

"We're screwed after what that judge did, right?"

My partner gamely casts aside her newfound cynicism. "Never give up hope, Denzel. I have something to discuss with you."

"Yeah?"

"You know we're still tracking down the witness who says you didn't do it, right?"

"So I keep hearing, but you still haven't found her, have you?"

Penelope holds her thumb and index finger a fraction of an inch apart. "Not yet, but we're this close."

Denzel's expression brightens for a millisecond before the gloom settles back over him. "We've only got a little more than three weeks, Miss Brooks."

She rests a hand on his foot. "That means we have more than twenty-one days, Denzel. We know who she is, we know where she was a couple weeks ago, and some really smart people are looking for her. Chin up."

"If you say so."

Penelope beams one of her thousand-watt smiles at him. "I *do* say so!"

Faced with that force of nature, Denzel can't help smiling back. I ease out of his line of sight. This is Penelope's show.

My partner pats his foot and winks, then dons a serious expression. "That's one avenue we're pursuing. Then there's Spike."

This prompts a pained expression. "We've been through this, Miss Brooks."

"Yes, we have. Time is growing short, Denzel. That's why you're talking about a plea deal again, isn't it?"

He nods.

"Did you kill Harry Hood?"

His eyes widen in surprise. "Now *you* don't believe me?"

"Answer the question," she shoots back.

"You know I didn't!" He sounds more hurt than angry. He's *so* fifteen years old in this moment.

"Yes, Denzel, I do know that."

A look of confusion washes over his face.

Penelope leans closer, eyes narrowed, voice sharp. "That doesn't help you one darned bit, Denzel. That's why I'm angry. The only person with the key to help your case is you, and you won't do it."

He shrinks back a little. This is a side of Penelope he's never seen. Neither have I, come to think of it.

She looks at him as if he's a bug under a microscope. "Look at you, carved up like a Thanksgiving turkey. It's a miracle you're still with us, Denzel. I doubt you'll be so lucky next time—and there *will* be a next time if you go to prison and leave Spike on the street. Man up, will you?"

As difficult as it is to watch Denzel wilting under Penelope's verbal assault, I suspect she's suffering even more. She moves close to the head of the bed, eyes fairly dripping with sympathy as she looks across at me. Then she squares her shoulders and leans back in.

"So, here's where things stand. The prosecution is going to throw everything they have at you: the drugs in your pocket, the cash with Harry Hood's fingerprints on it, your fingerprints on the bat, your DNA in the tent, and the jailhouse snitch testimony. Pretty grim, isn't it?"

He nods in dejection.

Penelope finally tosses him a lifeline, but it comes with a bare-knuckle challenge. "So, here's how we fight back, Denzel—unless you want to quit."

His eyes flash in response to the gauntlet she's thrown down. We males, so predictable.

"Go on," he mutters.

"You give us Spike, we find Di, and then maybe you testify if we have Di to back up your story. We have no way to contest the physical evidence—not unless you can explain it away with Di's support. Then we hold Spike out to the jury as an alternative suspect. Give us all that and we have a fighting chance. Take away any leg of that structure, and we're in tough. It all hinges on you finally mustering the guts to fight back."

Penelope steps back and falls silent. The next move is Denzel's.

He squeezes his eyes shut and settles back to think. His fingers twist the bedsheet while he wages what appears to be a fierce internal battle for a good minute or more. "I can't," he finally whispers in a tortured voice.

Penelope's shoulder slump. We have one card left to play, and it's mine. Penelope steps back as I lean in.

"We're going to subpoena Darnel Wix," I say. "We think he knows who Spike is. He probably knows where to find him as well. Maybe he'll tell the truth under oath."

Denzel's wild eyes swing to mine. "No! You can't do that!"

His objection is delivered with genuine, unfettered fear—and an equal dose of determination.

I level my eyes on his. "I'm not going to let you get yourself killed for a crime you didn't commit. Spike set you up to take the fall for what he did. I don't know what he promised you, if this is a case of misplaced loyalty, or if you're understandably scared to death of him, but it's you or him, Denzel. If you plead out, you'll be murdered in jail. If you're found guilty, same result."

His expression is oddly neutral; I hope it means we're getting through to him. "The only way out is by giving up Spike."

"The only way," Penelope echoes.

His eyes flicker to hers. Is he worried Spike will try to silence Wix if we call him as a witness?

I realize I'm holding my breath while we wait for Denzel to make the right decision. But he doesn't. He makes no decision.

"I need to sleep," he says, then closes his eyes.

36

I'm at Independence Park the next day for the weekly progress inspection. Brittany, Pat, and the dogs are with me. This is Brittany's final day at home before she leaves to visit her mother in Brussels. The discussion over how long she'll be in Europe is ongoing.

She looks at the pool taking shape. "I *will* be home for the grand opening, Pops."

I think on it for a moment. The big day is scheduled to kick off Independence Day weekend. Denzel's trial should be over by then, so I suspect that whatever threat Spike poses will also be at an end. "I'm good with that."

She hugs me. "Cool!"

Mountain Man Rick grins and waves up at us from the bottom of the pool's new deep end. Dolly edges up to the pool and peers down at Rick, her tail wagging. Maybe she thinks this is going to be a giant water dish. Rick and a couple of his guys are giving the pool contractor a hand, helping to speed things along and saving us a few bucks in the process. Speaking of money, I'm astounded by how much we've raised over the past few months. The final quote for the pool came in just under $50,000. We've raised that sum and are still going strong; the pool house may be within reach by spring. Who would have guessed? Not me.

Brittany lays her head against my shoulder. "Thanks for not working this weekend."

I plant a kiss on her forehead. "I have to give you a proper send-off, right?"

"Darned right you do! The zoo was a nice surprise this morning. Thanks."

The zoo has always been a special place for us. Taking time off to spend the day with Brittany is a welcome break from the grind of work. This is probably the last weekend Penelope and I will take off before Denzel's trial; we need a break before we enter the home stretch She and Becky are off with a bunch of cycling zealots on an eight-hour cross-country trek up into Wisconsin. I'm flabbergasted that otherwise sane people do such things to themselves. Just thinking about it exhausts me. Whatever turns your crank, I guess. I'm enjoying lazing around.

When the dogs pull at their leashes, I turn to find the Donahue children throwing themselves at the mutts for a little doggy love. Maggie and Derek are right behind them. I shake hands with Derek.

Maggie surprises me by delivering a big hug. "Thank you, thank you, thank you!" she exclaims as she takes in the rapidly developing swimming pool. "The kids are so excited. This is wonderful!"

"You're welcome. We'll see how excited the wee monsters are when their mother has them flipping burgers while their friends frolic in the pool."

"I second Maggie's thanks," Derek says. "You're a magician, Tony."

I smile at Pat. "Let's not forget the magician's assistant."

She smiles back. "Always nice to be recognized as second banana."

Brittany joins the kids at Doggyfest, leaving the adults to make small talk while we watch the pool workers.

Jake Plummer walks up to our little circle a few minutes later as we laugh at a crack of Derek's. "Is Double D regaling you folks with tales of his heroic policing derring-do?"

Maggie turns a look of wide-eyed surprise on her husband. "There are stories of derring-do in police work, honey? I thought it was all drudgery and crappy senior management?"

"There's probably some of that, Maggie," Jake says with a chuckle. Then he tugs at my sleeve. "Let's talk for a minute."

I hand the leashes to Pat and follow Jake until we're twenty or so feet away. The noise from the pool work affords us privacy.

"You asked me to look into Denzel's mother's death."

I nod.

"What Denzel described comports with what went down, Tony. You always know it's a bad one when detectives are still bothered by a case years later. Sometimes you know in your gut that someone is good for a crime and you can't prove it. Cases like that haunt a guy, I tell you. Sissy Payton was beaten black-and-blue and sliced up like a plate of cold cuts, then left on the kitchen floor with a kid in the house."

"Jesus, that's awful, Jake. How much do I tell Denzel?"

"Tough call. How do you tell the kid that his father probably murdered his mother?"

I have no answer to that. "Let's get back. I don't want to waste Brittany's last day at home thinking about Darnel Wix."

Jake cuts a surprised look at me. "She's off to Europe already?"

I nod.

"Glad to hear it. Last I heard, she didn't seem too keen on the idea."

I chuckle, recalling Jake falling on his sword the night I

was accosted right here in Independence Park. "I remember. Thanks for taking the heat on that, by the way."

He keeps pace with me when I start walking back. "Hey, it was my big mouth that got us into trouble."

"True."

"Everything okay?" Pat asks with a look that encompasses Jake and me when we walk up. She and Maggie are standing beside a swirling mass of dog hair, little limbs, and squeals of joy.

"Just a little update on one or two things," Jake replies. "No biggie."

Pat eyes me skeptically. "Uh-huh."

I push all thoughts of Darnel Wix out of my mind for the rest of the day. I even manage to mostly set aside trial thoughts until Brittany is winging her way to Brussels later that evening. Then my mind starts churning. Wix is soon at the forefront of my thoughts. The lousy SOB still won't lift a finger to help Denzel. It's time to force his hand.

37

I wake up Sunday morning eager to get on with my next play in Denzel's case, which Penelope refers to as a Hail Mary. But first, I have to finalize the settlement of a dispute between a local Ethiopian food restaurant we represent and a clown who sued it for $500,000 over a food poisoning claim. Yes, it is Sunday morning, but the other lawyer is on his way out of town for a couple of weeks and wants to put the matter to bed. I suspect he's as anxious to see the backside of his client as I am. The private investigator course I took last year pays off now and again. It certainly did in this case.

The judge took our side at a hearing last week after I presented evidence that this is the sixth food poisoning lawsuit this plaintiff has brought against ethnic restaurants. His evidence each time has been a statement from a dodgy doctor, who just happens to be his cousin.

The attorney—also a cousin—is waiting for me in his seedy little office. He quickly signs off on paying our costs and confirms that he'll file the paperwork to withdraw the suit tomorrow morning. As he shows me out, I suggest he could save us all a lot of trouble in the future if he counsels his cousin to be a little more discriminating about his eatery choices. "You might also be able to keep your law license," I add as a final warning to make sure he files the promised paperwork. Ambulance-chasing lawyers are the epitome of ethical when compared to guys like this.

The victory, minor as it is, gives me a little confidence boost as I gird myself for the confrontation to come. A stop at a coffee shop for a brew and doughnut gives me time to organize my thoughts. As I gather up my things to leave the coffee shop, I say a little prayer to the legal gods. I'm sailing into action on a wing and a prayer, so I'm happy to appeal to any deity that might blow a little wind into my sails.

My first stop is to pick up my backup for the upcoming row, which has every possibility of escalating into something dangerous. My GPS guides me to a tidy little bungalow on a well-treed street of them—not unlike our home on Liberty Street. I pull into the driveway and honk the horn. Max Maxwell emerges within seconds, wearing jeans and a red polo shirt with a conspicuous Chicago PD logo on the chest. He shrugs into a Chicago PD windbreaker, which he leaves unzipped so that the gun in his shoulder holster is visible—and easily accessible if needed. His presence puffs up my courage. I wouldn't mess with this guy.

He hops in, says, "Good Morning," then makes a big show of ogling and rubbing the supple leather interior of my Porsche. When he looks across at me, there's a twinkle in his eye. "Lawyers to little people, huh? Makes a guy wonder what the hoity-toity lawyers drive."

"They don't. They get chauffeured around in block-long limos."

He chuckles, then rubs his hands together. "This is gonna be fun."

"I'm not sure if we're going to have fun, Max. Things could get exciting."

"Like I say. Fun."

We chat about Denzel's case on the drive. Max laments the

lack of progress in his search for Spike. Then, as we near our destination, we turn our attention to how we intend to play the next few minutes.

"This is it, huh?" Max says with an amused snort as I coast to a stop at the curb in front of the walk-up apartment block that serves as HQ for whatever enterprises Darnel Wix is involved in. As always, two kids stand guard at the top of the worn concrete steps leading to the front entry.

Max hooks a thumb at the slouching sentries and smirks. "This is his muscle?"

My initial reaction to Wix's first line of defense was the same, but after taking note of a few recent news stories about kids involved in lethal shootings, I realized that even youngsters have trigger fingers—and they may be even more indiscriminate about how and when to use them. I share the thought with Max as we step out of the car.

"Point taken," he says as our eyes meet over the car roof. His game face slides into place when he joins me at the bottom of the steps. "Seen enough of that shit out on the street when I was on the job."

"Get that thing outa here," one of the kids orders us with a sneer. He was the number two guard during my first visit. Recognition dawns on his face. "The hell you doin' here again?"

"Same as last time. Here to see Wix."

"Mr. Wix be a busy man. Crackers don't just come 'round here thinkin' he gonna have time for 'em."

"Tell *Mr.* Wix that he'd be wise to make time to speak with us," I shoot back.

"Now," Max adds menacingly. He's looking plenty badass.

The kid pulls himself to his full height of maybe five feet six and squares his scrawny shoulders. "Like I say—"

"Tell him to get his ass out here now," Max growls. He adds, "Get moving!" when the kid hesitates.

The kids exchange a flustered look before the shorter of the two disappears inside.

Wix struts out the door a minute later and glowers down at me. "Whatcha doin' here again?"

"Looking out for your son. Again."

He comes halfway down the steps, crosses his arms across his chest, gives Max a long look, then turns back to me. "Let's hear it."

"We have some good news, if you're interested."

"What's that?"

"We tracked down a witness who was there that night."

His eyes widen a little. With interest? Or fear?

"She says Denzel didn't do it," I continue. "Says he never entered Harry Hood's tent. Claims there was an older man with Denzel. Says that's who went into the tent."

"She get a look at this guy?" Wix asks. I watch the wheels turning in his head.

"Good enough to ID if she sees him again."

"She gonna testify?"

"Of course. We need to ID Spike and track him down."

"And you're gonna help us do that," Max adds.

Wix cuts his eyes to Max. "Just like that, huh? How I gonna do that?"

"By telling us what you know," I reply. "You know who Spike is—no doubt in my mind. You can protect him or save Denzel. What's it going to be?"

He doesn't reply, but he's thinking.

"Do the right thing for your boy," I say.

Wix surprises me by changing gears. "Where she be at now?"

"Who?" I ask.

"This fuckin' witness."

The question unnerves me. There's only one reason I can think of for him to ask. "None of your business. You'll see her in court."

"I ain't gonna be in no courtroom."

"You're wrong about that," I tell him as I pull a folded sheaf of papers out of my pocket and slap them into his hand. "Have a look at this."

He unfolds it. "The fuck?"

"It's a subpoena, Wix. You'll be testifying right before her. Same day. You can wave to her on your way out."

Wix's smoldering eyes rise to mine. "Ain't no fuckin' way I be doin' that."

"Oh, but you will. You've been served with a lawful subpoena to appear as a witness in Denzel's trial. If you don't appear, the cops will come looking for you."

"And drag your ass into court," Max says. "This ain't optional, pal."

"We'll see about that," Wix retorts. "I got me some lawyers too."

"That's good," I say. "They'll confirm what I just told you. You might want to rethink how far you're willing to go to protect Spike."

Which is, of course, what this subpoena gambit is really about. I give Wix a half-assed salute before I turn back to the car. Max follows. Wix is frozen in place on the steps, glaring at us as we pull away.

"I sense the net closing in on Mr. Spike," Max says with evident satisfaction.

I'm not so sure. Wix seems to be afraid of Spike; that much is clear. Should we be afraid, as well? "Which might make him desperate," I caution Max.

"Desperate crooks do dumb shit."

"Dumb shit like trying to silence witnesses."

He shoots me a sideways glance. "True."

Or maybe a lawyer or two?

38

Meet Tony Valenti, animal lover and zoo-goer extraordinaire. For the second time in three days, I'm at the zoo. It was Lincoln Park Zoo with Brittany on Saturday, and now Brookfield Zoo—Chicago's other zoo—on Monday afternoon. But whereas Saturday was all about fun, this afternoon is business. Mind you, the person I'm meeting today usually brings a healthy dose of fun with her.

My phone rings as I pull into the parking lot. It's Jake Plummer.

"Got a call from the Chicago PD detective I talked to about the Sissy Payton murder," he says. "He talked it over with his boss this morning and they'd like to speak with Denzel."

"Why?"

"No statute of limitations on murder, Tony. They want to confirm that Denzel's memories line up with how they figure the killing went down."

"I thought they already told you they do?"

"In general terms, yes. They want to hear it for themselves."

"They're reopening the case?" I ask, circling in search of a parking spot that isn't a mile from the entrance.

"An unsolved murder case is never closed. They're taking another look at it."

"Based on the fragmented memories of a kid who was three at the time?"

"Long shot, for sure. Like I said, though, this case stuck in the craw of the detective. He'd love to nail Wix's ass. If there's even a small chance he can, he'll run with it."

I'd also like to see Darnel Wix suffer, just on general principal. "What do you want from me, Jake?"

"Chicago PD has no history with Denzel. They hope you'll pitch the idea of an interview to him, maybe smooth their way."

I hit the gas to dart into a parking spot that has just opened up. "We're three weeks from trial, Jake. I need Denzel to keep things together, and I don't know what this might do to him. I mean, his dad killing his mom right in front of him? Finding out that his memory is true would be some kick in the teeth, right?"

"Absolutely."

I shift the car into park. "He might be pissed with me simply for having passed it along to you. We can't afford to be at loggerheads about anything that isn't trial related."

"Understandable. Maybe after the trial?"

"If we lose, I doubt he'll be talking to me at all."

After a beat, Jake says, "They don't need anyone's permission, you know. It's still an active murder investigation."

"I get that, Jake. I do. I'll be happy to bring it to Denzel after the trial. Before? I'm not so sure. Leave it with me for a day or two?"

"Sure. The case has been open for over a decade. Another couple of weeks ain't gonna hurt. Just think on it."

"I will."

"Thanks. What's up today?"

"I just arrived at Brookfield Zoo."

"Again? Didn't you just go?"

"I took Brittany to Lincoln Park on Saturday."

"That's right. Zoos are a thing with you two, aren't they?"

"True story. Anything else?"

"Nah. Go play in the lion cage."

"Bye, Jake."

I smile as I slide the phone back into my pocket, hop out of the car, and hurry over to the entrance.

"Bless you, sir," a familiar voice says from behind my shoulder.

I turn to find Chippy smiling up at me from beneath a stylish hat with a droopy brim that hides half of her face. She's dressed in a flowing, sunshine-yellow dress with billowing half-length sleeves. Victorian? Who knows? I'm not one for fashion trends; not one for history either, come to think of it. "Hi, Chippy."

"I assume you went to church yesterday, so I thought we'd commune with nature today," she says.

"I wondered why we didn't go to church today. How are you?"

"Good, Mr. V. Thanks."

She takes my arm and steers me across the parking lot. We enter the south gate, pay, and set off in the direction of the towering Roosevelt Fountain.

I look at Chippy as we bear left toward Tropic World. "What skullduggery have you been up to?"

"You'd be shocked."

"I probably would be."

"Your partner survived her bicycle ride over the weekend?"

My eyes narrow. "Why are you keeping tabs on Penelope?"

"I worry about you and yours, Mr. V. You're mixed up with some bad people."

We fall silent for a moment. I break the silence. "I was surprised to hear from you this morning."

"Why?"

"It's only been ten days or so since Toe identified Di. I didn't think I'd hear from you for quite a while yet."

"You'd be surprised by what I can do in ten days."

"Try me."

"I found Di. How's that?"

I stop. "Really?"

She pulls an indignant face.

"Okay, dumb question. It's one I seem to ask quite a bit at inopportune moments. Note to self: stop asking dumbass questions. Better?"

She laughs. "You might want to write that on your palm until it sinks in, but maybe that wasn't such a dumb question after all. I lost track of Di again. I was a few weeks behind her."

Damn.

"She was in Tampa. That's where she and Harry Hood first crossed paths. Maybe she felt a pull there after she lost him."

"Makes sense."

"Don't they feed these darned things?" she asks as we approach the racket of the monkey exhibit. The cacophony reaches new heights with our arrival.

"Apparently not." I put a foot up on a bench, rest an elbow on my knee, and watch the monkeys' antics while I remember being grossed out by the sight of monkey butts when I was a kid. Still am. "Are there uglier butts in nature?"

"No."

"How did you find Di?"

She gives me a blank look. "I'm sorry, I didn't catch that. Let's get away from these things."

We move on.

"I asked how you tracked down Di," I say when we can hear ourselves think.

"She was working at a supermarket, stocking shelves at

night. Rented a little apartment. She up and left both three weeks ago. No idea why."

"Not a sniff since?"

"I'm looking. If she does anything that leaves an electronic trace, I should see it."

We continue along, each with our own thoughts.

"Coyotes," Chippy says as we approach a woodlands enclosure. "Keep your foxes; *these* are crafty, sneaky little buggers."

My eyes track to the display sign. Regenstein Wolf Woods. "These are Mexican gray wolves."

She looks again. "That's gotta be a baby, then. It's not big enough to be real wolf."

As long as we're on the topic of coyotes. "The coyote didn't seem so bright in the Road Runner cartoons."

She laughs. "God, I loved those cartoons. You're right, though. Old Wile E. wasn't the brightest bulb in the coyote litter."

I chuckle as the little guy scampers over to a bigger wolf, which edges out of the trees to eyeball us. Mom?

"Now there's a stalker," Chippy says with a sense of wonder and admiration. "Relentless. I'd never want a pack of wolves tracking my butt, but I wish I had a couple to track Di."

The wolves disappear back into the bushes. We leave the Wolf Woods behind.

"Spike?" I ask hopefully.

"Nada. My surveillance isn't working worth crap, Mr. V. I don't think we're going to find Spike by watching Wix."

A bear is staring at me as if I'm a potential meal.

"I'd sure like to know what gear Wix is running that's keeping my toys in check," Chippy mutters. "I'm tempted to go down there to investigate."

I take her arm and slow to a stop beside the bear. "No."

She stares back at me.

"No," I repeat firmly. "The whole idea of monitoring Wix is to get a peek at Spike. That's a dangerous bunch down there. I won't have you put yourself at risk to satisfy your curiosity."

Her eyes flash, then it's gone, replaced by the hint of a smile. "I don't like people telling me what to do."

"Yeah, well, my motives are pure."

Her eyes stray to the grizzly, which is now standing on its hind legs. "Which is why I haven't thrown you over the fence to play with that nice bear."

"Ha!"

She tugs my sleeve and starts walking toward the bison enclosure, then tells me a few childhood stories as we pass it. I tell a few of my own. The stories continue as we stroll by the African Savannah and the pachyderms.

Chippy casts a disapproving look at the monkeys as we pass by at a distance. "So, given the sophistication of the electronic countermeasures Wix and his pals are running, I was naturally curious to know more about him, right?"

"And when you're curious…"

She grins. "I dig. Wix is not a nice man."

"That's one way to put it."

"You should see his criminal record."

"I have."

We pass the fountain again and a marker informs us that we're heading into big cat territory.

"So you know about Wix's wife," she says.

How does this woman get so deep into supposedly secure records? "I heard about that."

"I know."

"What? You better not be monitoring me," I say with a sideways glance at the tigers. "Those guys look hungry."

"Touché."

I wink. "And unlike you threatening to feed me to the bear, I'm big enough to actually throw you over the fence."

She strikes a muscleman pose. "Never underestimate me."

I pull up short when we find ourselves uncomfortably close to an enormous Amur leopard. A pair of intense blue-green eyes study me. "Now, there's a scary beast."

She nods. "Beautiful, though."

"These guys scare me a lot more than wolves and bears. Maybe because I'm a dog person? I don't know. Panthers, though, they're the worst. They've given me nightmares ever since I was a kid. I imagine one of them silently appearing out of the darkness without me hearing it coming; then it strikes. No warning."

"No warning, huh? Whatever happened to panther chivalry?"

I laugh. "Now couple that with the wiliness of a coyote and the relentless stalking of a wolf, and we're getting a picture of Spike."

The big cat curls a lip and sneers, sending a shiver down my spine. I turn and walk away, hurrying to put some distance between us.

"Wix seems like a coward," Chippy says.

Whatever turned her thoughts to cowards?

"What makes you say that?" I ask.

"You've seen the kids he keeps around, right?"

I smile. "The adolescent muscle."

She doesn't return my smile. "He's corrupting those kids, leading them into the same life of petty crime—and worse—that he's wallowed in all his life. He puts them out front, probably to take the first bullets if someone comes after him. I see him leading them off most nights to who knows where to do God knows what to other people. They're usually out until well into the night."

Yeah," I say as something nibbles at the margins of my thoughts. I try to tease it out but can't before we near the south gate.

Chippy pulls a face. "Looks like Brittany ran into some fine weather in Belgium."

"Oh? I thought you weren't monitoring us?"

She laughs. "You. No. Brittany? She's fun on social media."

I glance around in search of large, hungry animals. All I see are people streaming in and out of the gate we're approaching. Chippy is safe for the moment.

"Brittany didn't send you any pictures?" Chippy asks.

"Nope, and I don't follow her on social media."

She pulls out her iPhone. "Not curious?"

"Of course, but we have an understanding about me intruding into her business."

"You really trust her, don't you?"

I nod.

"Good on you, Mr. V." She swipes a finger across her screen a few times, then turns it toward me.

"Yikes!" I exclaim, confronted with images of a city apparently in the midst of a rainstorm of biblical proportions. "Brussels?"

"Sure is."

I look up at the cloudless sky above us. "Not a good trade, was it?"

"No, it wasn't," she says with a laugh. "The important thing is that she's safe."

True. But is Chippy safe?

As we prepare to part ways outside the zoo gates, I rest my hands on her shoulders and stare into her eyes. "Keep your distance from Darnel Wix, Chepi."

"I will if you promise not to call me by my real name in public ever again."

"I'm serious."

"I know, and I appreciate it, Mr. V. I just don't do serious concern well, you know? Character quirk, I guess. But yes, I'll be careful. Always am."

39

Penelope and I are finishing our weekly lunch meeting at the Sandwich Emporium three days later when her cell phone buzzes on the table.

"Text from Pat," she says after glancing down at it. Then she looks up and gives me a long look. "We haven't talked about the shooting at Brittany's school."

No, we haven't. Two students were gunned down yesterday in a drive-by shooting on an athletic field at Hyde Park College Preparatory School—perhaps the very field I walk across every time I go to watch track practices and meets.

"Thank God she's in Brussels," I murmur.

"Do you know much about what happened?"

"Just what's been on the news. Jocelyn's mother called last night to let me know that Jocelyn wasn't involved. She didn't know anything more."

Penelope's eyes drop to her phone as she scrolls. "They've publicly identified the girls. Pat wanted you to see the pictures before they're plastered all over."

"Why send them to you?"

She turns the phone so I can see. "To make sure someone's with you in case you know these girls."

I barely hear her as I stare at headshots of the dead girls. One looks vaguely familiar. The other looks a little like my daughter. "Jesus, those poor parents."

"A gangster-style drive-by shooting as the girls were leaving track practice," Penelope says sadly. "No one at the school can imagine either girl being involved with a gang."

Track practice? Maybe that's why the girls look familiar. I sigh heavily. "Brittany probably knows these girls."

Penelope nods, then continues to look at me expectantly.

"Am I missing something?" I ask.

"Look at the second girl again, partner. Remind you of anyone?"

"She looks a little like Brittany."

"Exactly. Whose father is mixed up in an investigation in which he's been hounding someone with gang connections."

Screw lightbulbs; a searchlight snaps on inside my head. Was someone—Wix perhaps—targeting my daughter yesterday? "Did *I* get those girls killed?"

Penelope covers my hand with hers and squeezes. "Don't go there, Tony. *If* that's what happened, it's not your fault."

"The hell it isn't. If I'd just left Wix alone…"

"See? This is why Pat sent the pictures to me, partner. She knew you'd find a way to blame yourself. Not everything in the world is your fault."

"Looks like this might be." I push the last bites of my sandwich aside. "Let's get out of here. I need some air."

Penelope nods and gets up, then gathers up our trash. She deposits it in a waste bin on our way to the door.

"Thank you, Miss Brooks!" Maiko calls out.

Penelope lifts a hand to wave. "You're welcome, Maiko. Bye."

"Goodbye, Miss Brooks. You too, Tony-*san*."

I'm sullen and silent on the walk back to the office. Nothing changes when I sit at my desk upon our return. I gather up a few Denzel case files, stuff them into my briefcase, and walk to Penelope's office door. "I'm going to take some work home and hang out with the dogs. I need time alone to process this."

Penelope comes around her desk to give me a hug. "Call if you need anything, partner—even if it's only to talk."

I nod miserably and walk out. Maybe there's another explanation for the shootings—there probably is—but the possibility that it points back to me haunts me nonetheless. It also nudges my paranoia into high gear. I've had the sense of being watched a few times of late. It's a sense I've experienced before. It can be prescient. So when I glance in my rearview mirror in the homestretch of the trip home and see a big, black SUV with tinted windows for the second time in five minutes, I take note. I pass by the turn onto Liberty Street —Brittany may not be home, but the dogs are. I add a little gas for a few blocks. The SUV hangs with me, so I take a quick right, then another. The tail stays with me. My mouth goes dry as a box of soda powder. My heart starts thumping against my ribs. I hit the gas hard as I round a corner that leads out of the residential area I've been cruising through. A satisfying g-force pushes me back in my seat as the Porsche's twenty-inch tires bite into the pavement. *Eat my dust!* I think with satisfaction as I rocket forward, opening the distance between my sleek sports car and the lumbering SUV. To my amazement, the red and blue flashing lights of a police vehicle flash in my mirror from the front grill of the SUV. What is this? I ease off the gas as the cops—I hope they're cops!—close up on my rear bumper. As I coast to a stop in the curb lane, a hand emerges from the driver's side window of the SUV, waving me onto a side street.

No, we don't want to block traffic after baiting me into breaking several traffic laws, do we? I think bitterly. Or, am I being lured onto a side street because whoever is in the SUV doesn't want witnesses to the next act of this little drama? After a moment's hesitation, I gun the Porsche and whip around the corner, slip my Glock under my thigh, and pull to the curb. I keep the car in gear, my foot hovering over the gas and my hand on the shifter.

The SUV, emergency lights now off, coasts around the corner and slides in behind me. I nervously watch my mirror as the passenger door opens and a woman steps out. She's a stocky Black woman in a dark suit. Her frizzy hair is pulled back in a knot. She pauses to look up and down the block—scanning for witnesses?—then saunters up to my driver's side window without drawing a gun. She leans down and taps the glass. What kind of cop does that?

Calista Fontenot of the FBI, that's who.

I stab the window-down switch. It slides open.

"Mr. Tony Valenti," she says in a Louisiana-tinged accent. "We meet again."

"Calista," I say uncertainly.

"Spooked you, did we?"

"A bit."

Dimples form in her cheeks when she grins. "I'd say a lot. Who did you think we were?"

"Maybe the same people who murdered those two schoolgirls yesterday."

All traces of humor drop from her face. "Come again?"

"My daughter goes to that school."

"Connect the dots for me, Tony—the shooting and you scared of being followed."

"Long story."

"I have one for you as well. I was planning to follow you home to have a chat without drawing attention."

"Oh."

"You thwarted our plan," she adds with a trace of humor. "Now you've gone and made a spectacle of being chased and stopped by the police."

"You know where I live. Why not just call and stop by?"

"Part of that long story. Let's get out of here. Go home, and we'll be along in about five minutes."

My head is spinning as I drive home, let the dogs out, then start a pot of coffee. Agent Fontenot and I crossed paths several months ago. The case had gotten her a gold star or whatever the FBI hands out for good behavior. She was also promoted to the FBI Chicago field office.

The coffee pot is just getting a good gurgle going when the doorbell rings. Dolly turns and heads straight for the front door. Deano streaks past her. Just kidding. The old fart looks up at me as if to say, *Can't a dog get a little peace and quiet around his own home?* In his defense, he's been a little mopey since Brittany left for Europe. He's even spending time in her room, perhaps commiserating with Puckerface.

I look down at Deano as I follow in Dolly's wake. "The cops have finally come to haul your lazy butt away for loitering."

Fontenot and a defensive lineman in a business suit are waiting on the front step when I open the door.

"This is Buck," she says as I stand aside to let them enter.

Of course it is. I consider suggesting "Tank" as an alternate name, then abandon that thought when a hand the size of a horse crushes mine in a handshake—and I don't think he was even trying to turn my hand into a folded napkin.

"Calista was just telling me about your adventure together, Mr. Valenti. Well done. It's always a pleasure to meet folks who will put it on the line for others."

I nod, happy to be on the right side of this guy. "Nice to meet you, Buck."

"I smell coffee," Fontenot says as she walks in. "You're making enough for company?"

"Sure am." I lead the way to the kitchen. The FBI agents follow, Dolly happily bounding along beside them, shooting adoring looks up at Calista. What is it with dogs and cops?

Deano, on the other hand, gives them a quick once-over, paying particular attention to their hands. Seeing nothing edible, he drops his chin back on his paws to watch the action.

We fill the time waiting for coffee by making small talk. Buck is from Iowa, of course, where they apparently grow big burly boys to toss bales of hay and cows around. Calista has rented a condo in trendy Wrigleyville. After we're settled at the table with coffees in hand, she leans back in her chair and fixes her dark eyes on mine.

"Why don't you tell us what's going on with you, then we'll see if our stories intersect?"

"Fair enough. You want to know why I ran when you started following me, right?"

She gives me a sardonic smile. "How about we start with when you noticed us? We followed you all the way from your office."

"You did?"

She smirks and nods.

Good thing there weren't any bad guys on my tail. They probably would have shot me before I realized anything was amiss.

Fontenot pauses while lifting her coffee mug to her lips. "Tell us why you thought you might be in danger and who you were afraid of."

"I mentioned the school shooting."

She nods. "I had a look at the pictures of the girls on the way here. I had a tough moment before I read the names. One looked an awful lot like your daughter."

I swallow hard. "The thought crossed my mind that maybe Brittany was the intended target."

"Why would you think that?"

I explain about Denzel, Darnel Wix, and the subpoena. "If Brittany had been at school, she would have been at track practice."

"Where is she?"

"Visiting her mother in Brussels."

"Got it. So, you're thinking this poor girl was shot because someone thought she was Brittany?"

"Exactly."

"Tell us why someone would target your daughter."

"And why you think you might be next," Buck adds.

"I'm working a murder case involving a fifteen-year-old boy."

"Denzel Payton," Calista says. "I read up on it after you popped up on our radar."

"Right, so—" I stop as her response registers. "Your radar? What's your interest?"

"No direct interest," Fontenot replies. "Go on."

"No direct interest," I parrot. Cops have the art of the nonanswer down to a science. The agents still haven't explained why they're here, other than that I 'popped up' on their radar. They probably won't. "I think our client is innocent. There was an adult with him that night. The guy set Denzel up to take the fall."

Fontenot nods. "We spoke with Chief Plummer, so we've heard your client's story. Between you, us, and the gatepost, he seems to have doubts about their case."

"We're all in on trying to identify and then find this Spike character," I say.

"Your client isn't saying?"

"Right."

"Why not?" Buck asks.

"You know he was attacked in jail?"

The agents nod.

"Denzel is afraid Spike will kill him if he says anything."

Calista sets her coffee mug down. "No change of heart after he was attacked?"

"Nope."

Buck snorts. "What's your defense if Denzel keeps quiet?"

"Really? You expect me to answer that?"

"We're not interested in a local murder case," Calista says. "Buck's just considering different angles."

I think on that for a moment and decide it makes sense. "We have an eyewitness."

The news surprises Calista. "You have her on ice?"

"I wish. We don't know where she is."

Calista looks into her coffee mug for a long minute. "This is good coffee. What brand is it?"

"We're talking about murder and you're fixated on coffee brands?" I ask.

"This stuff is good. Wouldn't mind picking some up myself."

I get up, walk to the fridge to pull out a bag of coffee beans, and toss them to her. "Brittany gets it somewhere. Make a note of it."

She pulls out her phone to snap a photo of the bag. Then she throws it back to me with a grin. "It's the twenty-first century, you know. We don't make notes anymore."

"I never think of using the camera," I admit.

"That's right. You're a bit of a Luddite, aren't you?"

"I'm not a Luddite. Just a little technologically challenged."

She shrugs. "So this witness of yours is also scared of this Spike dude?"

"Apparently so. She disappeared when he started hanging around again."

"Probably the smart thing to do," Calista mutters. "What else have you got?"

"We're grasping at straws."

"Such as?"

"Denzel's father is a guy named Darnel Wix." The agents exchange a look. Why? I take a gulp of coffee and swirl it around in my mouth to stall while I consider their reaction. "You know who Wix is, don't you?"

"Finish, Tony," Calista says without answering my question. "Then we'll explain."

"I think Wix knows Spike, or at least knows who he is. Both criminals. Both with a connection to Denzel."

"Hence your visits to Wix and your surveillance attempts," Calista says. "You're hoping Wix will lead you to Spike."

"Makes sense," Buck adds. "Decent play."

Calista nods. "Okay, so—"

"Hold on," I cut in sharply. "Explain your surveillance comment."

Calista drains her coffee and holds out the mug.

"Refill?" I ask.

She smiles. "Have you ever considered police work? You never miss a clue."

"Top me up too," Buck says.

"You ever think of being a lawyer?" I ask Calista as I retrieve the coffeepot. "You're slippery enough when asked a question."

She looks aghast at the idea—theatrically so. "Perish the thought!"

I fill her mug anyway. After I return the carafe to the coffee maker and start a fresh pot, I sit down and lock eyes with Calista. "So. Answer my surveillance question."

"This is where our stories intersect."

I settle back to listen.

"Darnel Wix is, as we like to say, a person of interest in an FBI investigation."

"Not a word of this to anyone," Buck interjects.

Calista and I shoot him annoyed looks.

He holds his hands up and shrugs. "It needed saying."

It didn't, but I let it go. Calista doesn't.

"That's understood," she says in a tone that leaves no doubt about who's the senior agent. To Buck's credit, he displays no resentment over the reprimand. He simply nods and turns his eyes to mine. "Sorry, Mr. Valenti."

I wave it off. "Go ahead, Calista."

"We were naturally curious when we realized that someone else was trying to keep tabs on Wix."

"Did you figure out who it is?"

"As a matter of fact, no." Her expression suggests that she's impressed they couldn't. "But you know, don't you?"

Good on Chippy. "No idea."

Calista chuckles. "Sure you don't. We deployed some countermeasures that are, hopefully, making things difficult for this unknown person."

Well, that explains who Chippy is up against. "What put me on your radar?"

"Your name came up in a report I was reading a few days ago. You've paid the delightful Mr. Wix a visit or two lately."

I nod. "Trying to get the miserable SOB to take an interest in the welfare of his boy."

"At least you didn't shoot him," Calista says.

"Of course I didn't!" Sheesh. Pop a couple of guys and people think you make a habit of it.

"I might have," she says with a grin.

Time to get the conversation back on track. "So I landed on your radar."

"Right. Our people started checking you out, wondering if you were in on Wix's action."

"Me? I'm an officer of the court."

She winks. "You're a criminal defense lawyer, Tony. Not a favorite breed of we law enforcement types."

I ponder what I've just been told, and then—what with me being a lawyer and all—I parse the conversation for an angle I can turn to my advantage. I retrieve the coffeepot and refill their mugs. "Sounds like we're on the same team here."

"Beware of defense lawyers bearing gifts," Calista says to

Buck, then turns back to me. "What's on that lawyer's mind of yours?"

"My eyewitness. We tracked her as far as Florida, but we were a few weeks behind and didn't quite catch up to her."

"Chief Plummer told me you only had a first name for someone from Tent Town, and even that wasn't certain. Is that who we're talking about?"

"Our investigator tracked her down."

"From a first name?" Buck asks, as if he hasn't heard correctly.

I nod.

"This wouldn't happen to be the same person trying to keep tabs on Wix, would it?" Calista asks.

"Maybe."

"Right. Whoever this is sounds pretty good."

"Maybe," I repeat.

Calista smiles. "You're admirably tight lipped. Do me a favor?"

"Maybe," I say for a third time.

"Let this person know that the FBI has been known to hire people with computer smarts. If they want to learn more, you have my contact info."

I can't imagine Chippy in a buttoned-down outfit like the FBI, but I'll pass along the offer.

Calista takes a slug of coffee. "Back to your witness."

"Right. Any chance you can help track her down if I give you what we have on her?"

"Not our case," Buck replies.

"Let's not be hasty," Calista says. "Wix has a tenuous connection to Tony's case. Maybe we can justify utilizing a few Bureau resources."

Buck looks skeptical. "On what basis?"

"I'll think of something."

She turns to me. "When is your trial?"

"June twenty-seventh."

She whistles. "Cutting it close with this witness."

"We're cutting it close with everything. Realistically, what can you do?"

She holds up a finger while she works the problem in her head. We wait until her eyes settle on mine. "You believe she's in danger from Spike, correct?"

I nod.

"And *she* thinks she's in danger?"

"I can't say for sure, but she took off at the first sight of him."

She goes back into processing mode for a minute before her lips curl into a smile. "We take her into protective custody as a material witness in a federal investigation."

"How the hell do you plan to sell that?" Buck asks.

She waves a hand as if she's shooing away a fly. "I'll work something out." Then she turns to me. "Of course, if we locate her and she's under a lawful subpoena to appear, the FBI will duly deliver her to court to testify."

How cool would that be?

Calista slaps her palms down on the table and gets to her feet. "Okay, so that's settled. Work for you, Tony?"

I'm shell-shocked. "Assuming we find her, yeah. That would be great."

Calista winks, waves Buck after her, and walks to the front door. "Send me everything you have, Tony. You have my card."

I feel more hope than I've experienced in weeks. With Chippy and the FBI on the job, perhaps we *can* make this happen. I text Chippy as soon as the FBI agents leave the house: *Call me when you get this. We need to talk ASAP.*

Jake Plummer calls. "Got a minute to talk about the Sissy Payton murder case?"

I had a change of heart about bringing Chicago PD's request to our client, and Denzel surprised us by agreeing to speak with them. It seems that his dream may have broken down his resistance to speaking about his old man. I imagine Jake wants to follow up.

"I'd like to get out of the house. Meet me for coffee?" I ask.

"Dunkin'?"

I reach the Dunkin' a couple of blocks from the Cedar Heights police station before Jake and score a couple of coffees. On a whim, I add a dozen doughnuts to the order. I've been known to comment on cops and doughnuts.

"For me, smartass?" he says when he arrives and finds them sitting on his side of the table.

"Of course."

He pulls a face but opens the box to pluck out a doughnut. "Thanks for helping set up Chicago PD's meeting with Denzel."

"Denzel wanted to do it."

"I guess killing a kid's mother can come back to bite you. Chicago PD is gonna run with this, Tony. Thought you should know. Tell Denzel if you think you should."

I tell Jake about my FBI visit while he eats three doughnuts. By the time I finish, I've grown vaguely uncomfortable with the assertion of power Calista is proposing. "I don't see how this doesn't violate Di's rights in any number of ways."

Jake snorts. "What rights? When the feds have you in their sights, you have none. I wish I had that kind of power in our little backwater village."

"I don't," I retort with a disarming smile. "Mind you, I'm kinda okay with the FBI having it in this one limited instance."

"This Di can make or break your case, can't she?"

"Yeah, I think so."

"Well then, go get her."

"We're on it." We shoot the breeze for another fifteen minutes, then head home.

ASAP for Chippy turns out to be an hour after I get home from meeting Jake.

"What's up?" she asks.

I bite back the urge to grouse about how long it's taken her to call back and simply tell her about my visit with the FBI. "What do you think?"

I can hear the smile in her voice when she says, "They couldn't find me, huh?"

"Nope. Even said you were pretty good."

She chortles happily, then bursts into laughter when I relay Calista's suggestion that Chippy call to discuss employment prosects. "That'll be the day! I'm for protecting people's rights, not for running roughshod over them."

This from a hacker? To be fair, however, I trust Chippy's ethical mores than I do the government's. How sad is that? I feel a little twinge of guilt that I'm happy enough to let the government trample on Di's rights if it serves my purposes. What does that say about *my* ethics in the face of expediency?

Chippy hauls me back from my uncharacteristic foray into things philosophical. "You think we should help the FBI, Mr. V?"

"If it helps find Di, why not?"

"How can they help us?"

Trying to sell the idea of basically arresting Di and holding her to testify would be a steep uphill climb—like to the top of Mount Everest and beyond—so I settle on a lie of omission. Fontenot did tell me to keep it under my hat, right? "The FBI doesn't explain itself, Chippy."

The line is silent for a long moment. "You trust this agent?"

"I do."

After another long pause, she sighs. "I guess it can't hurt to share what we know."

"I agree. I'll send what I have."

"No you won't! You'll send me Fontenot's contact info and I'll send what we have to her—encrypted to hell and back. She'll never know where it came from."

"She'll suspect me. They may be so impressed by my cyber sophistication that they offer me a job."

"Pshaw."

"Pshaw? Even we old folks don't use that expression anymore."

"That's what brings things back into style, Mr. V."

"Egads," I say lightly. "Speaking of out-of-date terminology."

"Ooh. I like that word. Are you sure it's out of favor?"

I groan. She laughs harder.

"Send me that contact information," she orders me before signing off.

I allow myself a single celebratory bourbon, cross my fingers that we may have turned a corner in this case, and go to bed with dreams of Di in FBI custody floating in my head. Then the images of two dead girls displace them. One could have been—perhaps was meant to be—Brittany. What kind of hornet's nest have I stirred up? Somehow or other, the nest needs to be neutralized.

40

Penelope wanders into my office after lunch the following day and leans against the doorframe. "Any weekend plans, partner?"

I slap a hand on top of a pile of case folders. We're down to our final two weeks of preparation for Denzel's trial. "A little light reading that we should discuss."

"Up to dinner with Becky and me?"

The invitation unexpectedly stings by bringing back a memory. Not long before Trish died, Penelope had been discussing having her and me over for dinner. When I don't immediately reply, Penelope walks over to drop into one of my guest chairs.

"What is it?" she asks.

I explain.

"Sorry, partner."

I wave the apology aside. "It just jumps up to bite me now and again. What's on the menu?"

"Lasagna."

My eyes light up. "Set the table for three."

"Four. Mom's coming. Dinner will be ready at six. Why don't you come by around five?"

"Will do."

Her eyes stray to the pile of files. "I suppose we can chat about this while we're at it."

"A working dinner. Good times. That will cost you a second helping of lasagna."

"Deal."

I fall silent for a long moment.

Penelope settles back in the chair and crosses her legs. "Something else is bothering you, partner. Spill it."

"I still can't wrap my head around those girls getting murdered at Britt's school."

"Are you still blaming yourself?"

"Some."

"Don't."

My thoughts stray back to a relatively recent pair of violent deaths I was party to. Door-to-door sales types have nothing on the gall of journalists who descend on a story like this, baying for quotes in the face of tragedy and, of course, a byline for themselves. "Those poor parents. There's probably an army of media vultures camped out on their front lawns."

"Probably so."

Penelope was in court all morning, so this is the first chance we've had today to talk. I tell her about my visit with the FBI last evening.

"The FBI, huh? Won't it be sweet if they come through?"

"It sure would."

She slaps her hands on her thighs and stands. "Lots of work to do, partner. Let's get to it."

Not all of it has to do with Denzel, so I decide to clear my desk of as much of the mundane case work as I can before delving back into the murder case. I settle in with the transcript of a phone interview with a client accused of shoplifting. I can't help but laugh at her effort to convince the cops and us that she has "a weak metabolism that makes it a challenge to regulate my body temperature. I always layer my clothing. I get too hot or cold otherwise." Right. She was busted leaving an upscale clothing store wearing a mix of six shirts and sweaters, five of which had price tags affixed. On a May afternoon with the temperature in the mideighties, no less. As for the price tags, she claimed she never removes price tags from her clothing in case she has to return an item. My phone rings.

"FBI for you," Joan announces. "An Agent Fontenot."

"Put her through."

Fontenot gets right to the point. "I received an anonymous file of information about your potential witness."

"Anonymous?" I parrot with a smile.

"Near as I can tell. Our technical people will try to track down the sender."

"Good luck to them," I say, hoping they have no luck at all. "Seems like a waste of resources to me. The FBI has nothing better to do?"

"I think so, but the cyber testosterone is running. You wouldn't happen to have something of Di's that we could use to grab a DNA sample, would you?"

"Not a thing," I reply, wondering why she's asking.

"How about the homeless camp?"

"Why?"

"I tasked a junior agent with going through a database of unidentified bodies in Florida. She's flagging anyone that might bear a passing resemblance to Di."

My spirits plummet at the implications. "Do you know something I don't?"

"No, Tony. Just covering all the bases. The Tampa police need a sample to rule her in or out."

"What did your agent find?"

"She found four unidentified bodies in the Tampa Bay/St. Petersburg region that fit the general profile of Di."

"As I understand it, Di took everything she owned with

her when she left Tent Town, but I'll touch base with my contact at the camp."

"Worth a shot."

"Actually," I say as a spark of inspiration strikes, "she spent time with Harry Hood. Maybe she shed a hair or two in Harry's tent."

"Who has the tent?"

"Cedar Heights PD, I imagine. The murder took place in their jurisdiction."

"You're pals with Chief Plummer, aren't you?"

"Yup."

"Ask if they collected a longish blond hair."

"I will."

"Does your hacker friend have contact information for Di's family? Address? Phone number?"

"I'm not sure. Maybe."

"Find out, will you?"

"Why?"

"If so does, we'll approach them for a DNA sample."

"What good will that do?"

"Familial DNA, Tony. We share a lot of genetic traits with our family members. Think of it like a car serial number. Specific models share a lot of commonalities, but you need the entire VIN to positively identify a specific car, right?"

"I'm with you. Sorta."

"Let's say that the first six digits of a VIN identify a vehicle as a Ford F-150. If that's the case, any VIN that doesn't start with those six numbers isn't a Ford F-150."

"I'm not equating this with DNA, Calista."

"Familial DNA can serve a similar purpose. To stick with the VIN analogy, let's say that all members of a particular family shared those first digits of the VIN."

The low-wattage bulb that is my brain finally flickers to life. "A DNA sample that doesn't have those first six digits can safely be ruled out. A sample from a member of Di's family provides a basis to exclude."

"Exactly."

Interesting. "Got it. I'll call Jake."

"Don't forget the contact info."

"Right. I'll call Chi—" I catch myself just short of blurting Chippy's name, then cleverly continue, "Er, my investigator. I'll call him."

"So it's a he."

"Busted," I mutter. "I'll have him send you the contact info directly, assuming he has it."

"Him, he," Fontenot says with amusement. "Have *her* do that ASAP."

This is why I don't play poker with FBI agents. Or pretty much anyone else, come to think of it.

I say goodbye and call Chippy.

41

I spent an hour last evening toiling over a few of the songs Brittany has charged me with mastering while she's in Brussels, then collapsed into bed for a surprisingly sound sleep. I wake up early the next morning, a Saturday, brew coffee, rustle up breakfast for one, and feed the dogs. It's time for the weekly ordeal of changing the water in the goldfish bowl, which challenges both my limited marine biology expertise and my equally deficient plumbing talents. I'm never quite sure I get it right, and goldfish seem to die all too easily. Nonetheless, Puckerface survives yet again—at least for now. Being too lazy to research the name of the Catholic Patron Saint of Goldfish, I toss off a quick prayer to Poseidon, hoping his realm includes little fishies. Time to get on with the day.

I do a quick email check—messages from Jake Plummer and Chippy. Jake's evidence techs recovered several blond hairs from Harry Hood's tent, including a couple on a hairbrush with their roots intact. *Good enough for DNA samples,* he writes. A sample will be provided to the FBI. Chippy has sent Fontenot the contact information for Di's parents: address, home phone, email addresses, and cell phone numbers. How does she do it?

Dogs in tow, I set out for my weekly Independence Park inspection tour at eleven o'clock. It's apparently children-and-parents day in the park, which is overrun with little demons while their parents hang out chatting and sipping coffee. It's nice to see the park coming back to life. The pool is in the ground and looks great. It's a nice aquamarine blue. I find Rick and a couple of his workers running pipe for electricity and plumbing and whatever else a pool needs to operate. A cinder-block building to house the machinery is under construction.

I've been talking with Rick for a couple of minutes when I spy the Donahue family strolling across the park. Maggie and Derek are holding the hands of their youngest, swinging him in the air between them as they walk. The kids spy us and break away from their parents. I'm not sure who's more excited at this turn of events, the kids or Dolly. By the time Maggie and Derek catch up, the roiling mass of little limbs and dog fur is in full swing.

Maggie looks into the pool after we exchange greetings. "Looks good."

As I nod, their son, Bobby, runs up to me with Dolly hot on his heels. "Are you it sure ain't Jimmy Henricks, mister?"

Derek and Maggie supress chuckles when I glance up at them for an explanation. Derek lifts a shoulder in a shrug. "We passed by the house a couple of times last week and heard you playing guitar in the basement. Bobby asked who it was."

"He asked who was making the noise," Maggie clarifies with a wide smile.

I shoot her a look of mock indignation after I put the pieces together. "And you told Bobby, 'It sure ain't Jimi Hendrix'?"

"Well," she says. "Not hardly, right?"

"Not that just anyone can sound like Hendrix," Derek says in an effort to assuage my bruised feelings.

I bend down and wink at Bobby. "I *am* that guy, Bobby. I'm practicing to get better, though. My other name is Tony. You can call me that. Okay?"

Bobby gives me an uncertain smile, then wraps his arms around Dolly's neck and gets back to something he understands.

Maggie nods at the ongoing work. "Are we on track for July fourth?"

"Last I heard. Rick is filling in as project manager until Penelope and I finish a big trial we have coming up."

"That's the Harry Hood murder?" Derek asks.

"It is."

"Good luck," Maggie says.

Derek shoots her a surprised look. How dare she root against the police!

"Thanks, Maggie." I cast an amused glance at Derek, then sneak a peek at my watch. "I should be running along. Company coming for lunch."

Separating the kids from the Dolly is a chore, as it always is, complete with histrionics and tears, but I eventually get home in time. My guest arrives five minutes later. Apparently exhausted by Dolly frolicking with the neighborhood children, Deano is already collapsed on his bed, sound asleep.

Pat sits down and looks at him. "What's with Deano?"

"Tough morning."

"Is he okay?"

"Just lazy," I reply, although her concern reminds me yet again that he's getting on in years. The old guy is slowing noticeably with each trip around the sun.

Dolly, who appears to be none the worse for wear, happily dances around Pat.

Pat shoots the slumbering Deano a reproving glance. "At

least one of the dogs around here knows how to welcome a girl."

Five minutes later, the coffee is brewed, Dolly has settled down, and I've served a couple of grocery store sub sandwiches for lunch.

Pat takes a bite out of the dill pickle spear that came with her sub. "Did you spend all morning making the sandwiches?"

"Not *all* morning."

She catches me up on O'Toole family news while we eat. Having her parents' house sitting empty concerns her and her siblings. After procrastinating over the decision for a few weeks—"none of us can bear the thought of parting with the family home," Pat says—they are putting the house up for sale next month. "I'm a little jealous of you," she concludes.

"Because?"

"You still have this place."

"Why don't you buy out your brother and sister and move in?"

"I thought about it. I never imagined I'd see the day when we'd disagree about something like this, but my sister—prodded by her husband, I think—put up a fuss about the idea."

"Why? You get an appraisal and go from there."

"I know, right? She's convinced we can get more than the appraised value, maybe as much as ten percent above asking price. Even if she's right, it will net each of us all of five grand or so."

"Families."

She gives me a long look. "I guess it could be worse."

Indeed. She could have had my brother for a sibling. I catch her up on the Brittany news, such as it is. The kid has never been very good at keeping Dad informed about the details of her adventures in Europe.

Pat laughs about the lack of email. There's a long, sordid

history of Brittany failing to send regular updates to Pat. "I've given up on the little twit ever sending me an email," she says.

We spend the next few minutes polishing off our subs while we discuss the Independence Park project. Pat is lining up all the inspections, permits, and whatnot we need to have in hand to open on July 4th.

We finish lunch and move to the back patio, where we settle side-by-side on a handcrafted swing for two under a hawthorne tree.

"How are things coming along with the Hood trial?" she asks.

"Very slowly."

She tucks a foot under herself. "You'll do fine."

"I wish I had your confidence. We're in tough, Pat."

"You *always* do fine, Valenti. I'm sure this trial will turn out well, just like all the others."

I don't bother to argue the point. This time *isn't* like all the others.

Her brow furrows. "Does Britts know about the school shooting?"

"Oh yeah. That was a tough phone call. She knew both girls."

Pat fishes her cell phone out of her back pocket. "Did you see the kids the cops are looking for?"

"What kids?"

She turns her phone screen toward me. It's open to a *Tribune* story. "They suspect these two of being the shooters."

My eyes lock on the screen in disbelief.

"They're children!" Pat exclaims. "I bet they're barely in high school, if that. What's the world coming to?"

I'm fixated on a familiar face. I pinch the photo larger. "I'll be damned."

"What?"

"Last time I saw this kid was on the front step of Darnel

Wix's place, back in January or whatever." I tell her about the child sentries Wix uses.

"I remember you mentioning something about teenagers. These are *children*!"

I hand the phone back to Pat. Does this mean Wix is behind the school shooting? Spike? Are they working together?

"You need to take this to the police, Tony."

I call Jake Plummer and bring him up to speed.

"Do you have a name for the kid?"

"It was in January," I reply. "If I heard a name, I don't remember it now."

"Think on it."

"I will."

"I'll call Chicago PD with this," Jake says. "They might have a line on the kid if he's been in trouble. Cross your fingers."

I tell him about the FBI's sudden interest in our case. "I'm glad for the help, Jake, but I can't help wondering why Fontenot is in on this."

"Why do you think?"

"I'm not sure, but I've learned to never look a gift horse in the mouth and all that."

Jake pauses for a beat. "I'll say this, Tony. The FBI doesn't do anything that isn't in their own interest."

"Is that a warning?"

"I suppose it is. Never bank on the feds to help you. Anytime they do, it's because their interests align with yours at a point in time. As soon as they have what they want, it's sayonara. I've been left holding a big, steaming bag of shit for a case more than once after they took what they were after and left the locals high and dry."

I file that away, then ask Jake if he has any thoughts about why Wix or Spike would target Brittany.

"You pushed Wix pretty hard, right?"

"I did."

"Someone's sending you a message to back off."

"Yeah? I'll send them a fucking message."

"Sit tight, Tony. Let Chicago PD deal with it. This is no time for another one of your vigilante episodes."

Pat stays another fifteen minutes before she leaves to cover some city political event or other. It's just as well—my mind is elsewhere.

An hour later, I'm ensconced in our backyard hammock, idly watching a fat caterpillar inch its way along the edge of the canvas fabric above my head. We're having an infestation of the things this year, defoliating giant trees in a matter of days. This one is like a little machine, its tiny feet marching in a push forward. I never realized this about caterpillars, that it's a push rather than a pull that propels them. The critter hitches its rear end forward a fraction of an inch before each pair of feet move forward in turn from that impetus. Its mouth relentlessly searches for food every step of the way. There's something awe-inspiring in the singular purpose of the caterpillar as it goes about its business, all day, every day—perfectly adapted to the quest for sustenance. Maybe people would be better off if we spent more of our energy foraging for our next meal and had less time to cheat and kill one another.

My thoughts turn back to Darnel Wix. Did he send someone to kill my daughter? Did he do so in cahoots with Spike? I have a mind to go ask. Probably a bad idea. I refocus on the caterpillar while an idea flickers at the edge of my consciousness. It's been there on and off all day—something to do with what Calista Fontenot said about familial DNA. I try to empty my mind of all extraneous thought as I resume watching the caterpillar's march forward. Push, push, push. It's exactly what I need to do, keep pushing forward. Relentlessly, and with a singular focus. Why is Di's familial DNA nagging at me? I picture myself turning the problem this way and that, searching for the angle that will reveal the heart of the matter hiding within. I'm still at it in bed several hours later when the crux of the mystery finally seems to reveal itself.

Holy crap!

42

I've been awake since four o'clock this morning, too jazzed by last night's epiphany to do more than doze in scattered snippets. Google is getting a workout. I sent an early-morning email to our DNA consultant, Mary Ann Higgins, asking her to call as soon as she can. Of course, it's Sunday morning, so that may not be until she begins her workweek tomorrow. If I don't hear from her by noon today, I'll try calling again. I'm not sure if the phone number I have is for her office or her cell, so best not to get my hopes up. In the meantime, I've been poring over her report on the DNA recovered from Harry Hood's tent, cross-referencing the technical terms on Google in a bid to unravel their meaning and put it all in context. Perhaps I should have paid more attention in biology class, or chemistry, or whatever science relates to this. Then again, maybe DNA wasn't yet a thing back in my school days.

I'm finishing a second pot of coffee when I realize the sun is up. The dogs are hanging around the back door, looking highly aggrieved by my neglect. The coming of daylight signals that it's time for their morning constitutional, followed by kibble. I start a third pot of coffee, throw on some old sweats and a T-shirt, retrieve the leashes from the front hall, and off we go. We're rounding the far end of Independence Park when my phone rings.

Jake Plummer greets me with a question. "Do you ever sleep?"

I left Jake a post-epiphany message last night. "Now and then. Thanks for calling."

"What else does a police chief have to occupy himself with at the crack of dawn on his only day off this week? You have a DNA question?"

"A boatload of them, but only one or two for you."

"Well, ask away," he mutters gruffly.

I chuckle. "If you're trying to make me feel bad for calling, you're wasting your time."

"What's this DNA bug you've got up your ass?"

"Law enforcement collects a DNA sample from all criminals these days, right?"

"Generally speaking, only for felony convictions and when we book someone on suspicion of same."

"The DNA from Harry Hood's tent needs to be looked at again."

"Why? It's Denzel's."

"Not necessarily."

"What, you're a DNA expert now? C'mon, Tony. The state had it tested. You can try to muddy that up with the jury, but don't waste my time with defense lawyer bullshit. Hell, even Timothy Walker himself deigned to weigh in on it. It's a done deal."

I bite back the angry reply that comes to mind. The mention of the state's attorney's involvement is instructive. So far as I'm concerned, anything that Walker touches immediately becomes suspect. I have the battle scars to prove it. "Humor me, Jake. Assume the DNA isn't necessarily a slam dunk. Maybe it's familial DNA."

The line is silent for a long moment. "Go on."

"In a second," I say as I scoop up a pile of dog poop.

"Breakfast is waiting," Jake grumbles impatiently.

"Isn't there a village bylaw about cleaning up dog crap?"

"Is that what you're doing?"

"Yup."

"Fun shit," he says with a chuckle.

He's a riot. The dogs and I resume our walk. "Paternal DNA, Jake. The DNA from Harry Hood's tent might be from Denzel's biological father. What if that's Spike?"

"Whoa," Jake says, then falls silent.

I imagine he's turning this over in his detective mind. I wait him out.

"How convenient for your client," he finally mutters with a note of sarcasm.

"Convenient?" I snap back.

"Classic SODDI bullshit, Tony."

"Your attitude kinda pisses me off, Jake. I'm not looking to muddy the DNA results. Our DNA expert has concerns. What if the DNA isn't Denzel's? What if it *is* from his father?"

"Game changer," he allows after a moment.

"Exactly. Are you done insulting me?"

"For the moment."

I smile in spite of myself. "I assume you ran that DNA sample against whatever database exists?"

"Not personally, but that's standard procedure."

"Can you check?"

"Jesus Christ, Tony. You want me to second-guess my own people?"

I don't respond.

"You going on a fishing expedition with this?"

I blow out an exasperated breath. "What's it going to hurt, Jake? Don't *you* want to be sure you have the right suspect behind bars?"

"Of course I do!"

"A wise old homicide detective once told me to keep digging deep on a case until it gives up its secrets."

This gets a chuckle. Jake once told me exactly that.

"Anything else on that devious mind of yours?" he asks.

"Such as?"

"Are you looking at any alternative suspects besides Spike?"

"To be honest, Jake, I'm throwing a dart and hoping it smacks Denzel's biological father right in the ass."

"Long shot."

"It's the best shot I've got."

"We done talking about this?" he asks.

"I guess."

"I have an update from Chicago PD about the suspect in the school shooting."

"The kid in the picture?"

"Yeah. He's popped up on their radar a time or two regarding some penny ante shit, but they don't have a name for him—at least not one they're confident is his real name. He dropped out of sight a couple of months ago. That picture is the first they've seen of him since."

"They'll keep looking for him?"

"Dead white girls with connected parents, Tony. Bank on it."

We say our goodbyes as I arrive home to throw together a breakfast of Raisin Bran and precooked bacon. Throwing a plate or two a day into the dishwasher seems a waste of time now that Brittany is away, so I wash and dry the dishes by hand. It reminds of doing the same with Mama back in the day.

Mary Ann Higgins calls while I'm drying. "What's up, Tony?"

"Thanks for calling, Mary Ann. How sure are you that the DNA in Denzel's case isn't a definitive match to him?"

"Reasonably. The report from the prosecution is sloppy. I think we can argue that the work the state did was inconclusive."

"Sloppy how?"

"It's not complete, at least not to the standard I would expect from a state lab. There's just enough there to implicate Denzel, not enough to reasonably exclude other possibilities."

"You mentioned familial DNA."

"I did."

"Do you know if the state ran the DNA sample against any databases?"

She's silent for a long moment. "That isn't information I usually receive. They should have. Why do you ask?"

"But we don't know for sure, at least so far as you know."

"Correct."

"And Timothy Walker is involved. That's enough to raise doubt in my mind."

"Maybe so, but that won't raise doubt in the minds of a jury."

"I know. How confident are you that Denzel didn't leave that DNA in Harry Hood's tent?"

"As I said, I can raise questions."

"I'm not asking what you're comfortable testifying to, Mary Ann. What does your gut tell you? Denzel or not?"

She hesitates.

"I'm playing a hunch here, Mary Ann. What's your best guess as to whether or not that DNA might belong to Denzel's biological father?"

"It's possible, Tony, but you'll need DNA from the father to play that card."

"That's all I needed, Mary Ann. Thank you. Now, get back to your *New York Times* crossword puzzle or whatever it is you do on Sunday morning."

"How did you know?" she asks with a laugh.

"Isn't that what all you smart New Yorkers do instead of going to church?"

She laughs again, then we say goodbye.

I glance at the time after ending the call. If I wake anyone at my next stop, it won't bother me in the least. I consider calling Max to come with me to what promises to be an extremely unpleasant confrontation, but he and his wife *do* go to church every Sunday. I change into jeans and a polo shirt, slip my Glock into its shoulder holster, and stuff my phone into a back pocket. I don't need GPS to find my destination. I've been there before.

The street is quiet and empty when I coast to a stop outside Darnel Wix's front door. A lone sentry slouches at the top of the steps. The kid is sound asleep, propped up by the railing. I lean on the horn, keeping it blaring even after he startles awake and looks around in momentary panic. Then he glares at my car. I give the horn another triple blast. I want Wix's butt out here on the double. When he storms out the door a minute later, I climb out of the car, meet his fiery eyes, and walk around until I'm at the bottom of the steps.

"Gettin' *real* tired of seeing your white ass 'round here," he bellows before he comes down to within two feet of me. His fists are clenched at his sides.

I stand my ground, every bit as incensed as he seems to be, if not more so. I lean a few inches into his personal space. "I saw the picture of your little soldier on the news last night, Wix. The cops are looking for him as a suspect in the shooting of those girls at my daughter's school last week. What do you know about that?"

"Don't know nothin' 'bout it."

"Did you send that little bastard to deliver a message to me by murdering my daughter?"

His eyes widen.

I lean closer. "Because if you did, or your pal Spike did so with or without your knowledge, I'm here to deliver a message of my own. If anyone ever lays a finger on my daughter, I'll be back for you, Wix. You won't be the first man I've killed. If you doubt it, do a little reading up on me." *If you can read at all, you miserable SOB.* I lean closer, forcing him to look up to maintain eye contact. *Yes, I'm a big SOB, Wix. Big and angry.* "Understood?"

"Ain't no one come to my crib to threaten me," Wix shouts in my face, but there's a measure of unease lurking in his eyes as he blusters through the tough guy response.

"I just did."

"Done wit your bullshit?"

"As a matter of fact, I'm not." I lower my voice so only he can hear. "I've delivered a message that I hope you heard loud and clear. You've done the obligatory hardass routine for the kids. Now, let's talk about Denzel."

He glares at me wordlessly as I step back.

"There's a connection between you, Spike, and Denzel. I *know* it. You're leaning hard on Denzel to keep his mouth shut about it to protect Spike."

He doesn't deny it. Doesn't confirm it either.

"You need to stop," I continue. "Denzel's a scared fifteen-year-old kid. I get where he's coming from. But you? You're supposed to be a badass. You're supposedly committed to being a father to the boy, yet you're putting him in danger. What gives?"

"Why you hassling me, dude? I probably ain't really the kid's daddy. Sissy was a whore, man. She be fuckin' every guy in the ghetto."

Yeah, yeah. "Did you hear that they found DNA in Harry Hood's tent?"

"I hear it be Denzel's."

"Maybe not."

"The hell you say."

"There's a good chance it belongs to Denzel's biological father. Any chance that Spike is our man?" The statement pulls Wix up short. It also seems to frighten him. "Did Spike run with your crowd when Sissy got pregnant with Denzel?" I ask.

Wix takes a step back and looks away. "Long time ago, dude."

I have him thinking. Good.

"This DNA shit," he eventually says. "Y'all think this can help Denzel?"

"Only if we can match the DNA sample with DNA from his biological father."

"How ya gonna do that?"

"You tell me who the biological father candidates are. I'll take it from there."

"How?"

"Not to offend you or anything, Wix, but my guess is that most of the guys you run with have probably been in trouble with the law at some point. Right?"

"Might be so. What about it?"

"You give me the names. The cops see if they have DNA samples on file. If they do, the sample is tested against the DNA from Harry's tent."

"Say they don't get no hits. Then you don't know no more'n you do now."

"Pretty much."

"Cops can't force no one to give blood?"

"They can ask, but they can't compel anyone. Not unless the person is a bona fide suspect and the cops can convince a judge to issue a warrant."

"'Bout that subpoena bullshit?"

"What about it?"

"Why you wanna drag me into fuckin' court, man?"

"Why not? You won't voluntarily tell us what you know about Spike. Maybe you'll reconsider under oath."

"I don't know shit, man. I'm not the big dog 'round here, y'know? If Denzel got hisself mixed up in some bad shit, ain't got nothin' to do wit me. I just be another yeah man 'round here. I get a little divvy on the action, that be all."

I pause to interpret the answers. As if I know what a "yeah man" is. A "yes-man," maybe? "Divvy" must mean a share. I need an urban dictionary to talk with this guy. But he *is* talking. That's promising. "You *act* like you're the big dog around here. These kids treat you like you are. If not you, then who?"

"Like I gonna tell you," he says with a grim chuckle. "That be sumthin' for you and the man to figure, ain't it?"

I stare into his eyes for a long moment. "And we will. That's why we subpoenaed you, Wix. To find out."

"I ain't no dumb nigger, Valenti. Ain't gonna be no dead nigger for tellin' you what y'all wanna hear."

"You can make this whole business go away by giving me Spike."

"Don't know nuthin' 'bout that."

"You have nothing for me about who could be Denzel's father?"

"Lemme think on it."

Is that a promise of cooperation? Have I, at long last, finally gotten through this man's hard exterior to touch his beating father's heart?

43

I'm on my way to work the following Thursday when Calista Fontenot of the FBI calls. I take it hands-free.

"Good news," she announces after greetings have been dispensed with. "None of the bodies in Florida is Di."

It's the first positive news we've heard in days. "Good to know. I don't suppose you've figured out where she is?"

"You want the whole loaf, don't you?"

"Sorry. We're down to eleven days until trial."

"Lots of pressure. I get it."

"Afraid so."

"Chin up," she says. "Keep at it. You never know when something might break your way. You've pulled a rabbit out of a hat at the last minute before."

The encouragement is welcome. I could use more. "Are you at the office?"

"Yes. Why?"

"Got a few minutes?"

She hesitates. "About?"

"Wix."

"Now?"

"Yup," I reply. Then I tell a little white lie while wheeling into a U-turn. "I'm in the neighborhood."

"I suppose I could use a coffee."

"Good. Where?"

"Here, if you don't mind Bureau java."

"It has to be better than the swill they serve at Cedar Heights PD."

She laughs. "Probably so. I'll tell security to expect you. How long?"

"Ten, fifteen minutes."

"In the neighborhood, huh?"

"More or less."

"Right. Did you just lie to an FBI agent, Mr. Valenti?"

I don't answer.

"That's a felony offense," she says with a smile in her voice.

"I'll see you in a few minutes."

"He says, effectively taking the fifth."

"Have the cuffs ready."

It turns out that FBI brew is great, much better than what Joan cooks up at the law offices of Brooks and Valenti, attorneys to Maxwell House and Folgers coffee hounds everywhere. I hold up my shiny new FBI coffee mug. "Not bad."

"The Bureau thanks you," she says sonorously. "Now, aside from saving a couple of bucks on coffee, why did you want to see me?"

The fact that I'm after an emotional lift in addition to my caffeine pickup is pathetic, so I take a sip of coffee.

"You mentioned Wix," she prompts as I drink.

"Right."

"I hear you had another shouting match with him the other day."

I nod. "Then we talked a bit. I confronted him about the school shooting last week. One of the possible shooters they're looking for was working for Wix the first time I visited him."

Her eyes go wide with an expression I can't read. Not shock. Surprise, mixed with some measure of excitement. Odd. "We didn't know any of this. You took it to Chicago PD, right?"

"I did."

"And?"

"Crickets. Jake Plummer tells me the kid is somewhat known to Chicago PD, but they don't even have his proper name. They're looking for him. I hope they are, anyway."

"Oh, they are, Tony. Couple of rich white girls shot down at a private school? Yeah, they're all over that."

"So Jake says. Pretty sad commentary."

She nods. "It is. Most of us give equal weight to every victim, but the folks at the top call the shots."

"Seems to be the way of the world."

"Back to Wix. You think he went after Brittany?"

"Wix or Spike."

"Hence your visit to Wix and the shouting match."

I nod.

Her eyes narrow. "You went by yourself."

"Yup."

"That wasn't the best decision. What did he have to say?"

"Denies it, of course, but I served notice that he'd regret it if anything happens to my daughter. Then we actually had a constructive chat about DNA."

Her lip curls in a bemused smile. "You 'chatted' about DNA. Who does that?"

"A guy defending a kid in a murder case in which the DNA evidence points to the suspect's biological father."

Fontenot gives her head a shake. "Come again?"

I explain. "Wix insists he isn't Denzel's biological father."

We sit for a minute, sipping coffee and thinking. Then I

give myself a mental kick in the pants for wasting valuable face time with the FBI. Fontenot seems to be interested in the potential Wix connection to the murder of Brittany's schoolmates. Actually, she's clearly interested in all things Wix. Can I use it?

"Wix seems to be a bit of a small fry for the FBI to be sniffing around, Calista. At best, he's a bit player in a bigger picture. That's my guess, anyway." Fontenot doesn't reply, so I carry on. "I mean, you're the feds. You chase the big fish. So why Wix?"

"I can't get into the details, but you're not wrong."

"The school murders aren't an FBI case, yet you're interested in the possibility of a Wix connection. You're interested in Harry Hood's murder, another local case. Aside from the prosecutors, almost nobody else is. If the media had played up the angle that Harry was the son of a sitting congressman, maybe the cops and prosecutors wouldn't be satisfied with railroading a fifteen-year-old—"

"Come again?" Calista blurts. "Hood's father is in Congress?"

"They apparently hadn't spoken in years, but yeah."

"You seem pretty sure that Wix and Spike are connected."

"And I'm sure Denzel can explain that relationship. He *knows* who Spike is. He must!"

"Yet he won't tell you."

"Exactly."

"Even after Spike tried to have him killed in jail."

"We don't know that for sure, but Spike sent a man to warn Denzel to keep quiet a few days before he was attacked."

"We're missing something here," she says thoughtfully.

"We're missing a boatload of stuff. I thought Denzel might come around after the attack and the dream about Wix killing his mother."

"What dream?"

I explain.

She shakes her head. "We looked at Chicago PD's case file on that. This is a new spin on it. Does Denzel really believe Wix killed Sissy Payton?"

"I think he does. It really shook him up. Maybe it's a snippet of memory from a traumatic event. He was just a toddler at the time."

"Or a repressed childhood memory." She drains her coffee mug and stands.

Time for me to leave. "Thanks for letting me bend your ear," I say as she rides down the elevator with me. No civilians wander free in FBI facilities.

Calista doesn't exit the car when the elevator doors open. She holds them open with her left elbow as she shakes my hand. "Thanks for stopping by, Tony. It's been instructive—plenty of new revelations for me to chew on."

We say goodbye. It's time for a chat wit Denzel. I call Penelope, relay the Di news, and ask her to meet me at the hospital. Then I dial Chippy.

She answers on the second ring. "Hey, Mr. V!"

"Hey yourself, Chippy. Di lives!"

"Cool! The hunt continues."

"Yes it does."

"I'm glad you called," she says. "I picked up Di's trail. She went to Mobile when she split Tampa Bay. I have her checking into a motel and starting a waitressing job three days later."

"Excellent!"

"It's a start. I haven't found a thing since that first week, though, which I suppose shouldn't be a surprise. She never leaves much of an electronic trail."

I sigh.

"I know, right?" she says. "Someone in Mobile should

follow up with the motel and job to find out if she's still there, Mr. V. Can you get the cops to do it?"

"I'll try. If not, I'll go myself."

"Super. I'll send the job and motel details. Be careful if you go."

"I will," I assure her. Then I call Calista Fontenot, who also answers on the second ring. I'm on a roll.

"You again?" she asks lightly.

I tell her about Di in Mobile, providing the details from an email that Chippy just sent.

"This gal of yours is good."

"You mean my guy?"

She snorts. "Yeah, her. I'll contact our Mobile office and ask them to get the local police on this right away."

"Perfect."

"I'm not sure how long it will take, Tony. It probably won't be high on the locals' priority list."

"Understood." I'll give it three days, then I'll go myself. We have eleven days to trial, so there's no time to waste. As Fontenot put it, we need to pull a rabbit out of hat, and we need to do it soon.

Penelope meets me at Stroger. Denzel is up and around, sitting in a chair watching TV. He's noticeably thinner, and he wasn't exactly buff before the attack. Penelope delivers the latest Di news, which seems to perk him up a little.

"I spoke with your—with Darnel Wix the other day," I say. "He might be coming around a little in terms of cooperating."

Denzel appears openly skeptical. I guess it's to be expected.

I lean in closer. "Tough question for you, Denzel. Is Spike your father?"

"Of course not!"

"You know Wix isn't your biological father, right?"

The corners of his eyes tighten in pain as his mouth falls open. He didn't know. "Why would you say that?"

"Wix told me. A few times now."

"But—" he says before his eyes squeeze shut and his chin drops to his chest. He draws into himself. After a full minute, he looks up. "I want to be alone."

"We need to talk," Penelope says softly.

He shakes his head. "Go."

"Heckuva thing to spring on the poor kid," Penelope says as we walk down the hallway on our way out of the hospital.

"Yeah," I mutter, still haunted by the hurt in Denzel's eyes. "Why didn't someone tell him the truth?"

It's still eating at me when I call Thelma Payton to let her know what happened. I don't want her to be blindsided when she next visits Denzel.

"Denzel *was* told the truth about his lowlife father," she retorts.

"Wix told me it wasn't him." I relate Wix's story about Sissy having a revolving cast of bedmates. "So, as he puts it, Denzel's biological father could be any one of six or seven men."

"That man! Now you listen to me, Mr. Valenti. Whatever else Sissy may have been, she was a one-man woman. 'Course," she adds with a little laugh, "she went through a lot of fellas, but all one at a time."

I don't know how to reply. Am I hearing a sanitized account of Sissy's sexual proclivities? A sister's effort to protect the memory of a beloved sibling? The truth?

"So I ain't buying whatever nonsense story Darnel Wix is selling," Thelma says. "Best I recall, it was Sissy and him for quite some time before young Denzel came along."

"It's like being in a house of mirrors, Thelma. No wonder Denzel took the news hard."

The line is silent for a long moment. "You told that jive story to that poor child? Tell me you didn't do that, Mr. Valenti!"

"I did," I reply in a voice that reminds me of a child caught with his hand in the cookie jar.

Thelma hangs up. Chagrined, angry, and confused, I go to bed reconsidering everything I thought I knew about Darnel Wix, which is admittedly very little. What game is he playing? *If* he's playing a game. Maybe he's the only one giving me the straight goods. How ironic would that be?

44

It's the tail end of the worst Father's Day ever, about an hour after I've polished off not one, but two frozen beef stroganoff dinners—enough to give Deano and Dolly a couple of bites each. I've just dished Puckerface a few flakes of fish food. With my fatherly duties done for the day—I called Papa in Italy this morning—all that's left is to keep wading through the trial preparation materials I've fruitlessly plowed through for the past two days. Denzel's trial begins a week from tomorrow and we're still clutching at straws. I have a ticket to fly to Mobile, Alabama, in the morning to follow up on Chippy's leads. Will I come face-to-face with Diane Lennstrom? If so, will she agree to help? Will the FBI pick her up if she doesn't? What will she say at trial? I try not to allow my hopes to rise, but surely we're due for a break.

The phone rings. Belgium. Brussels. Brittany.

"Hey, Pops!"

"Hey, Britts. How are things on the continent?"

She laughs. "You sound like Pat. Happy Father's Day!"

"Thanks."

"What excitement have you been up to?"

I recite the exciting details of my day, being careful not to sound as glum as I feel.

"Sounds like fun. Making any progress on that case of yours?"

"Maybe."

"How about the guitar, old man? Building them chops?"

I relate the "not Jimi Hendrix episode."

When she finally stops laughing, Brittany says, "Maybe you better get downstairs when I hang up, huh?"

Maybe I should. "The Donahue kids may not think so, but I'm making a little progress, kiddo."

"About time."

"Having a good time?"

"Same old, same old." She goes on a little rant about her mother working until all hours, leaving Brittany to fend for herself most days and evenings.

I give her an update on the progress at Independence Park, which lifts both our spirits.

"I'm thinking I might go visit Papa for a few days," she announces out of the blue.

"What does your mother think?"

She giggles. "Think she'd notice if I did?"

I feel a surge of anger. My ex-wife, Michelle Rice, has made a big issue about custody arrangements a few times now, angling for more time with our daughter. For this? Neglect? It's just a typical Rice family power play, all about the Rices' massive egos and thirst for one-upmanship—Brittany's well-being and happiness be damned. And never mind that Michelle was the one who walked out on us two years ago for a career move to Europe.

"Go see Papa if you want to, Britts. If your mother won't foot the bill, call and I'll take care of it."

"I'm tempted."

"Then do it. Maybe it will prompt her to start being a mother to you when you visit."

"I miss Papa."

I think for a moment. What the hell. "I assume you have your computer at hand?"

"Sure. Phone too."

I talk her through logging into a travel site I use, then we search flights out of Brussels that will get her close to Penne, the village in Italy's Abruzzo province where Papa is on an extended visit with his sister's family.

"You sure about this?" I ask as my mouse hovers over the purchase button for an airline ticket on Ryanair that will get her to Pescala, which is about a half-hour drive from her destination. I'll try to get her cousin Beppe to pick her up at the airport. If not, she can cab it. The itinerary is up on both our screens.

Her trepidation about her mother's reaction gives way to a sense of adventure and her longing to see Papa. "Sure. Why not?"

"Shitstorm coming," I warn her.

"Bring it on, Pops!"

I laugh and complete the booking. "If things get too heated, just call and we'll fly you home from Italy."

"Cool. Thanks, Pops! You're the best father!"

I chuckle. "She says when she gets her way."

The line is silent for a beat before she responds. "No, she says that because it's true. I couldn't ask for more in a father, Dad. Love you."

A lump forms in my throat. "I love you too, Britts."

"So," she says lightly, after a moment. "Can I charge an English-Italian dictionary to the credit card?"

"Why? Papa can translate for you."

She laughs. "I haven't seen him for a bit, Dad. I was thinking I might need it to talk to him!"

"Ah," I say with a chuckle. "Go for it."

"Thanks, Pops."

"You're welcome. And now I guess you better go tell your mother about your plans."

"Maybe I'll wait until the morning."

"But you're flying tomorrow afternoon. Isn't that leaving it a little late?"

"I'm thinking that if I tell her when she's leaving for work, she won't want to hang around to argue."

Sadly, it probably isn't a bad strategy. I don't envy Brittany her predicament. "Whatever you think, kiddo. Good luck. Call me from Penne."

"Will do, Pops. Now, go see if you can't figure out how to sound a little more like Hendrix."

We say goodbye, then I decide on a single glass of bourbon to cap off Father's Day. The chat with Brittany did me a world of good. Heading to the basement to do a little practicing isn't a half-bad suggestion. Beats sitting around the kitchen moping and wearing myself out looking for things that aren't in the case files. I spend an hour fumbling my way through a few tunes, and then head upstairs to take the dogs for a quick stroll before packing a carry-on bag for the morning. My flight to Mobile leaves at six thirty.

I've moved Dolly's bed into my room while Brittany is away, so I have a dog sleeping on either side of the bed. They plop down and go to sleep while I brush my teeth. I've just settled into bed with a Kurt Vonnegut novel—a loaner from Pat in her never-ending quest to civilize me—when my phone rings. My ex-wife already? I reluctantly peek at the screen. Nope. FBI.

"Bad news, Tony," Calista Fontenot says without preamble. "The Tampa police entered the DNA sample from Di's mother into the national missing persons database. They got a hit on a Jane Doe in Alabama."

"Mobile?" I ask with a sense of foreboding.

"I'm afraid so."

"Di."

"Hard to imagine it being anyone else."

I climb out of bed and head for the kitchen. "Did the cops there ever get off the stick to look for her?"

"I don't know."

"Not that it matters now," I grumble.

"I'll speak with Chief Plummer in the morning and put him in touch with the folks in Mobile. They can compare DNA from the Jane Doe with the sample Cedar Heights took off the hairbrush in Harry Hood's tent."

"I think we already know how that turns out."

She sighs. "Yeah, I think that's a safe assumption."

Another door closed. I pull a beer out of the fridge, twist off the cap, and plop into a chair at the kitchen table without turning on a light. "So that's that. Do you have any good news for me, Calista?"

"Maybe," she replies cautiously. "We'd like to speak with you and Penelope at our office Tuesday morning."

"About?"

"Your client. You gave me a few things to think about the other day. We'd like to discuss one of them."

"Tell me now."

"No. In person. With your partner."

I slam my palm down on the table in frustration. "Nothing but bad news and uncooperative cops!"

"Hey! I'm just the messenger—*and* I'm trying to help."

I palm my cheek and slump in my seat. "Oh hell, I'm sorry, Calista. I'm just tired of having doors slammed in my face."

"I get it," she says after a beat. "My mother used to have a saying."

I recall how Mama spun little pearls of wisdom to shine a little light in the darkness. "Don't they all."

"Yours too, huh?"

"Oh yeah," I reply with a resigned chuckle.

"One of Mom's was that every time a door closes, a window opens."

"If I had a dime…"

"You heard that one too?"

"Plenty."

"Well, I may be able to crack a window open for you Tuesday morning, Tony."

"Wix?"

She pauses. "Sorta."

Jake's warning about the FBI comes to mind. "What case are you working on, Calista? Ours? Yours?"

I tilt the bottle back and drain the first third before Fontenot replies. "The big fish in criminal enterprises insulate themselves well, Tony, so we cast as wide a net as we can. Sometimes one of the little fish we scoop up lures a bigger catch into the waters we're fishing. Sometimes we set that up, sometimes we just get lucky."

"Sounds like what I was trying to do at Wix's place in hopes of stumbling across Spike."

"Something like that."

"Wix is a little fish to the FBI."

"He is, and that's all I can say."

"We don't have time to help you with your case," I say curtly. "Maybe after Denzel's trial."

She's talking when I hang up. Jake was right about the FBI. Everything is about moving their own cases forward. We have a trial coming up in a week. I don't appreciate being asked to burn any of our limited time and resources helping the FBI do their own work.

I sit at the table for another minute to polish off the beer, then walk to my office and fire up the computer to cancel my flight to Mobile. With my calendar for tomorrow now cleared, there's no hurry to get to sleep. My thoughts turn to Di. I can't help feeling a little guilty. My reaction to her death has been colored by the impact it will have on Denzel's chances in court—which is both shallow and coarse of me. A life has been cut short. I'll have to tell Toe, of course. The news will gut him. Should I tell him tomorrow or wait until the DNA results are official?

I spend a few minutes musing about the twin tragedies of Harry Hood and Diana Lennstrom, two people just trying to get by in the world whose lives were cut short because they crossed paths with the wrong people. There's no doubt in my mind that Spike was responsible for both deaths. The SOB needs to be taken down, for more reasons than simply exonerating Denzel. He's killed enough; he'll surely kill again.

"What are you going to do about it?" I ask myself. Dolly sets her snout in my lap and gazes up at me. I gently rub the crown of her head with my knuckles, then stand and walk back to the kitchen to give her a Milk Bone. I eyeball the fridge, where more beer awaits, then the cabinet above the fridge, where the bourbon lurks.

"Nope," I tell Dolly, who is sitting attentively at my knee, probably waiting for Milk Bone number two. Then again, she may simply be hanging out to be supportive—I imagine I'm giving off plenty of negative vibes.

My thoughts drift back to Denzel. What is motivating him to shield Spike? He knows what this is likely to cost him. Why is he willing to sacrifice his own life to save a man who has betrayed him so completely? It has to be more than fear of being harmed. I'm missing something in the psychology at play here. If I could only get into Denzel's head. Damn. I should have had a professional speak with him! I can't believe I didn't think of this sooner instead of simply assuming that fear was the only motivator in play.

I turn to Google for insights on grossly dysfunctional father-child relationships. Perhaps the dynamics between Denzel, Wix, and Spike hold the key to prying the truth out of Denzel. I'm deep into a bag of Vitner's chips when I come across a YouTube clip of a motherless rapper on a late-night talk show, talking about his conflicted emotions toward a largely absent and neglectful father—the man who killed his mother. Despite it all, the son laments his inability to let go of his old man. Sounds familiar, doesn't it?

"Sometimes I think the problem must be me," he says to his interviewer. "I mean, am I so worthless that he doesn't have time for me?"

The rapper then gets up to sing a song he wrote about it. I don't listen to rap, which Brittany has told me is my loss: "You have to listen to the words, Pops." Yeah, well, I prefer guitars, but I listen closely this time:

I still gotta protect the devil,
Cause that be my job, being spawn of the devil,
Ain't no heaven in this world, ain't no hell,
But that devil, he be right here, the demon who took my mama away,
And he all I got left to cling to,
He tells me that lettin' go be the death of me,
That I ain't never gonna be free.

There's a message in there for me. I play the song clip back two or three times until the pieces seem to fall into place. What if Thelma is right? What if Wix *is* Denzel's biological father? What if the DNA from Harry Hood's tent *is* from Denzel's real father? If so, Wix is Spike. That's a lot of supposition, but it would explain so much. I pop out of my chair, startling Dolly, who was dozing at my feet.

I lean down to comfort her. "We need a sample of Wix's DNA to prove my theory right or wrong."

But how?

45

Judge Wilke isn't pleased to be here with us late Tuesday morning. We filed an emergency motion yesterday to exclude the DNA evidence, basing it on a grab bag of reasoning, Mary Ann Higgins's assertion that she received incomplete results foremost among them. As much as anything else, I'm hoping to buy time to finagle a DNA sample from Wix that we can test against the sample from Harry's tent. It's a plan. Sort of.

Judge Wilke glares down at me after I make my points about Mary Ann's reservations. "Didn't we already litigate this, Counselor? I don't see anything new in this motion. I don't *hear* anything new in your argument. You are wasting the time of this court!"

Sleep-deprived, frustrated, and with my nerves stretched taut, I go rigid with anger. Penelope steps in to rescue me before I rip into Wilke.

"But there *is* something new here, Your Honor," she says while nudging me back into my seat.

Wilke glares at me a moment longer before he reluctantly turns his attention to my partner. "And what might that be, Counselor?"

"We raised the issue of incomplete data at our last hearing, Your Honor. The state offered assurances that we would be given any additional data we had yet to receive."

"And you didn't receive it?"

"We did not, Judge."

Dickweed Seaver snorts. "Because there wasn't anything missing in discovery, Your Honor. We checked. They have everything we have."

"The data is incomplete," Penelope says.

"So says your so-called expert," Seaver retorts.

Wilke piles on. "Maybe your expert is the problem, Miss Brooks. At any rate, I think we're done here this morning."

"There were other concerns, Your Honor."

"From the same source?"

"Yes, Your Honor. Dr. Higgins is an eminent scholar in DNA science. She is considered—"

"She wouldn't be the first hired gun I've had in my court who isn't reliable," Wilke interrupts. "We're done here, people. See you in court on Monday morning."

"Can we appeal *before* the trial?" I ask Penelope as we walk down the hallway after leaving the courtroom.

"I'm afraid not, partner. If ever there were a time when it was justified, though."

"What's going on in there? This is outrageous."

She nods. "It is, and I can't explain it. Looking on the bright side, I can't imagine this is going to sit well with an appellate court."

"One problem with that."

Penelope shoots me a sideways glance. "Which is?"

"Denzel will be dead in jail by the time an appeal runs its course."

We came in Penelope's Audi, so at least I'm not behind the wheel in my current state. I rant a little more on the way back to the office. Penelope does her best to calm me down. It doesn't work. As we walk through reception at the office, I toss my briefcase through the open door of my office, then march straight to the coffeepot.

Penelope follows and plants her fists on her hips. "Think you need to be a little more caffeinated, partner?"

"What's that supposed to mean?" I retort, though I know exactly what she means: I'm being an ass.

"It means no more coffee for you until you cool off."

I sigh. "Maybe I should just go home."

Penelope eyeballs me a moment longer, perhaps trying to decide if I'm being petulant or if I'm really as stressed as my behavior suggests. I guess she settles on the latter. She hugs me. "We're all stressed, Tony. Losing Di is a blow, I know, but we still have the Spike angle to play."

"If we can figure out a way to play it." I haven't yet mentioned my Wix-is-Spike epiphany from Sunday night. As certain as I felt about it two nights ago, I'm starting to wonder if I'm not just reaching for something that isn't there. I'll chew on it a bit longer before I set us all off on a wild-goose chase.

"We can't afford to have you lose hope, Tony. Maybe something good will come out of this afternoon's meeting."

Penelope told me first thing this morning that we have a meeting scheduled for one o'clock but wouldn't discuss details. I was bemused at the time. Now I'm irritated.

I step back to meet her gaze. "What's with this meeting, Penelope? Why all the secrecy?"

"I'm hungry partner. Let's go to the Sandwich Emporium. I'll explain over lunch."

"Give me five minutes," I say before walking into my office and closing the door. I call Cedar Heights PD and ask to speak with the man at the top.

"I've only got a minute or two," Jake says after we exchange greetings.

"I only need one. Darnel Wix hasn't been in jail for years, right?"

"I don't think so. Why?"

"Can you check to see if he has a DNA sample on file?"

"What's this about, Tony?"

"Suspected murder."

"Sissy Payton?"

"Harry Hood."

"With Wix as the killer?" he asks with a note of disbelief.

"I don't know, Jake. We're grasping at straws."

"I thought this Spike character was your SODDI?"

"I'm playing a hunch."

"And you need Darnel Wix's DNA to play it?"

"Right."

"You're hoping Cedar Heights PD can get a sample for you?"

"Exactly."

Jake is silent for a long moment, then sighs. "I'd need a reason to do so, Tony. Wix isn't in jail, and he isn't a suspect in a crime we're investigating. I can't just go to a judge asking for DNA samples anytime I want one. I need something concrete to sell to a judge to get a warrant."

"Can you at least check the DNA database?"

"If you're hoping for a match to Harry Hood's murder, forget it, Tony. We ran that sample against the databases months ago. Nothing."

I feel myself deflating, then have another idea. "Arrest him, Jake. Then you can take a DNA sample, right?"

"If there was a reason to suspect him, Tony. There isn't."

"What about the school shooting?"

"Not my case."

"But that kid from Wix's place."

"Jesus, Tony. You saw him there months ago. Unless Chicago PD finds him *and* the kid points a finger at Wix, there's nothing there. And, I repeat, it's not our case."

So it's all going to come down to me trying to break Wix on the witness stand? God help us. "But—" I begin.

Jake cuts me off. "The answer is no. I have to go."

Penelope gives me a quizzical look when I storm out of my office and start down the stairs to street level. She follows. "Everything okay?"

I vent about Jake, Judge Wilke, and about the fact that we're a week away from a trial we're not ready for.

"You really asked Plummer to arrest Wix to get a DNA sample?"

I don't reply.

We walk a block in silence, then she stops and claps her hands together. "You think Wix is Spike!"

"No, I wonder if maybe he is."

"That would answer a lot of questions."

I nod.

"But there are alternative explanations."

"Yeah."

"Let's kick that around over lunch, partner," she says as we start down the final block of our walk.

We talk it through while we eat. By the time we finish, Penelope is excited about the possibility. I still don't know who we're meeting when we get back to the office, so I ask Penelope about it yet again. This time she answers. I think back to Sunday evening and prepare to eat a little crow.

46

Calista Fontenot is waiting when we arrive back at the office. Penelope glances at her watch as she steps over to shake hands with the FBI agent. "You're early."

"Quick lunch."

Penelope waves Fontenot toward the conference room. "Sorry we made you wait."

"Hold on a sec," I interject, then redirect the agent toward my office. "A minute alone, please?"

Fontenot appears annoyed, but she nods and steps inside the office.

I follow and close the door. "I apologize for hanging up on you Sunday night. I was out of line."

"To put it mildly, Mr. Valenti."

"I'm sorry."

She doesn't accept my apology. "I was trying to help. Both of us."

"So you went around me and called Penelope."

"I'm not about to let you get in my way. That's not a good place to be, Mr. Valenti."

I step aside and open the door. "Let's hear what you have to say."

Seeing as how my effort to make peace with Fontenot has fallen flat, I decide it's probably best to let my partner handle this meeting. I don't want the agent's anger with me to undermine it. Joan delivers coffees to Fontenot and me, and Earl Grey tea for Penelope.

"We'd like to interview Denzel Payton," Fontenot announces once we're seated in our conference room.

"About?" Penelope asks.

"Darnel Wix. We agree that there's probably a connection between him and Spike."

"Denzel won't tell you a thing about it."

"We'll see. The attack on Denzel may have an indirect connection to a federal case. We're trying to connect the dots. Denzel may be able to help."

My instinct is to argue—those lawyerly instincts again—but I bite my tongue. It turns out that Penelope is on my wavelength anyway.

"If you think we're going to allow you to interrogate our client about a case we know nothing about, you're dreaming."

The agent eyes Penelope in surprise. She clearly wasn't expecting a sharp pushback from my partner.

"You're going to have to develop your own evidence regarding whatever you think Denzel may be involved in," Penelope adds.

Fontenot is annoyed. "We don't think Denzel is a player in what we're investigating. We think he may have information that will help us. The FBI would be willing to deal if he does."

"Deal what?" I ask. "What can the feds possibly offer our client, who is days away from going to trial in a state murder case you have no jurisdiction over?"

"There may be an opportunity for interagency cooperation."

"Interagency? You mean between you and the Cook County state's attorney, don't you?"

"Of course."

I snort. "Tim Walker is *not* going to cut a deal, Agent Fontenot—not in a case I'm involved with."

She gives me a skeptical look. "You think it's personal?"

"Yeah. I do."

"I highly doubt that."

That's because she's a sharp, ethical cop and expects the same from others in law enforcement. "You don't know Walker very well yet, do you?"

She gives me an inscrutable look. "I've dealt with him once or twice."

"Then you know."

Fontenot turns to Penelope. "I don't really need to be here. I've come as a courtesy, hoping to speak with your client with you present. Can we arrange an interview with Denzel through you, or do I need to get a subpoena?"

Penelope's eyes narrow. "When you put it that way, we don't really have a choice, do we?"

"Of course you do. You can make this easy, or you can make it hard on yourselves and your client. Your choice."

An hour later, Fontenot meets me in a park across the street from the FBI building.

"I was surprised to hear from you," she says by way of greeting. "What's up?"

"It's been a rough few days. I'm sorry I've been disagreeable."

"You already tried apologizing once today."

"And it obviously didn't work, so I thought I'd try again."

"That's why we're here?"

"Not entirely, but I think we need to settle that first."

She leans back against a light post and studies me for a long moment. "You want to be friends again."

I nod.

"Which means you want something from me."

"What I have in mind benefits Denzel, and I think it will benefit you."

"Interesting that you position it as something that will benefit Denzel."

"He's our client."

"This isn't just defense lawyer BS, is it? You really believe this boy is innocent."

"I do. *We* do."

She gives me a half smile, which I suppose is something, so I proceed to explain a plan that has been hatching in my mind all morning. As always, Fontenot plays her cards close to the vest. She gives nothing away as she grills me on details, motivations, and execution. Then she tells me what she can do and what's expected of me. "Not a word of this to anybody. Not even Penelope Brooks."

"She's my partner! This is her case too."

"This isn't up for discussion. I trust you. I don't know her."

"I do."

"Maybe I'll come to trust her at some point, but she's not in the loop on this."

"I think that's a mistake."

"So noted. Do we have a deal or not?"

I nod. "We're friends again?"

"I won't beat you up, if that's what you mean," she says with the hint of a smile. "That was touch-and-go a few minutes ago. How's that?"

"Better than the alternative."

"And maybe I'll stop wondering if I did the right thing by not just standing aside and letting you get shot last year."

"We're pals?"

"Don't get carried away."

I hold my hands up in surrender.

"I mean it," she says. "Not a word about this."

"Understood. When will I know?"

"When it's done, *if* it gets done."

"When should I expect to hear from you?"

"When you do," she replies with a hint of impatience.

I sigh. "I don't see another way out for Denzel—not with this judge. You wouldn't believe some of the evidentiary rulings he's made."

She doesn't ask for details, just nods. "Wilke, huh?"

"So you know what we're dealing with."

"Sure. I've been getting up to speed with the local judges. Wilke seems to be what we law-and-order types refer to as a hanging judge."

"You say that with a certain smug look of approval."

She smiles. "I'm a cop. Our kind of judge."

"Even if he's corrupt?"

Her smile vanishes as her eyes narrow. "Not then. Never. Is there something I need to know about him?"

"It's wrong for a judge to steer a trial in the direction he wants it to go. It's corrupt."

"Hmm." She appears ready to say more, then changes her mind. "Anyway, I should get back inside. I'll be in touch."

47

The next morning, Penelope and I are with Fontenot and her partner, Buck, at the FBI Chicago field office on Roosevelt. We're waiting for the sheriff's office to deliver Denzel from Stroger Hospital so the FBI can have their chat with him.

"I'd appreciate it if you two would keep out of this," Fontenot tells us.

Penelope turns an indignant look on her. "I've never had a law enforcement officer tell me what I can and cannot advocate for on behalf of a client."

"Denzel is not coming here as a suspect, Miss Brooks. He's here for the sole purpose of an informational interview."

Penelope shoots Fontenot a warning glance. "The second you cross the line from informational interview to conducting an interrogation, this ends."

The agent gives Penelope a look not unlike the ones I suffered through yesterday when I was in her doghouse. "You can trust me to know where that line is."

"My grandfather, who was a judge, told me that I should never, *ever* trust the reassurances of a federal law enforcement officer," Penelope retorts. "From all I've seen and heard over the years, it was sound advice. I don't intend to ignore it now."

I've been wishing I hadn't agreed to keep my partner in the dark about my chat with Fontenot yesterday, never more than now. Things would be easier if Penelope knew the whole story.

Fontenot's eyes meet mine. I wonder if she's also regretting not involving my partner. She turns back to Penelope. "What assurances do you want from me?"

"None, Agent Fontenot, but don't ever again tell me what I can and cannot do when I'm representing a client. We'll get along just fine if you remember that."

"I think I can manage that."

"You'd better be good to your word, or I'll haul Denzel out of here faster than poop shoots through a goose."

I stifle a chuckle. A snort escapes Buck. Even Fontenot's scowl eases a smidgen.

"As they say in Kansas," I quip.

Penelope's eyes twinkle, which breaks the tension. She's made her point.

As the clock ticks past the nine o'clock start time for our interview, we make small talk about sports and anything else deemed to be a safe topic—anything but the reason we're here. The rain pelting against the outside windows adds to my sense of doom and gloom. The sheriff delivers Denzel twenty-five minutes late because, of course. I suppose someone down there relishes this type of petty crap, all to show that they think of themselves as very-important-bureaucrats-not-to-be-trifled-with. Personally, I enjoy trifling with them.

We meet the new arrivals in the hallway outside the interview room. Denzel is clad in the orange rompers of the Cook County Jail. They must have made him change in his hospital room. He's also manacled again, hands cuffed to a waist chain, which is in turn shackled to leg irons.

Fontenot isn't impressed as she flicks a thumb at the restraints. "Whose idea is this?"

"Orders," a cocky young deputy retorts with evident satisfaction to be sticking it to defense lawyers *and* the feds. He's a gym rat, no doubt supplemented by steroids and HGH. The shaved head and goatee go with the bulging muscles. A true bullethead, as I've come to refer to the type.

"Take them off," Fontenot orders him.

"No can do. We'll be staying with the prisoner during the interview."

"More orders?" Fontenot asks icily.

Bullethead straightens his shoulders and squares up to her. "That's how it's gonna be."

Fontenot isn't impressed with his he-man routine. She takes a step closer. "I don't suppose you happened to read the big sign on the building when you came in? The one that says *F-B-I?*"

I stifle a grin. This boy is in for an ass-whupping.

Buck pushes off the wall. "Assuming he can read."

The deputy's eyes go cold. He taps the Cook County Sheriff insignia on his uniform. "You see this, lady? We're in charge of this prisoner."

I meet Denzel's eye. He looks more than a little frightened. I shoot him a quick wink and mouth, *It's all good.*

"Unshackle Mr. Payton, Officer," Fontenot says in a voice barely above a whisper. Funny how scary people manage to fill a whisper with menace.

"No can do."

"I mentioned the sign on the building to make a point," Fontenot says. "You're in a federal building—a federal law enforcement facility—in which I have complete jurisdiction. You're a visitor here, and not a particularly welcome one at the moment."

"I have my or—"

Fontenot cuts Bullethead off by stabbing a finger within an

inch of his barrel chest. "Take the cuffs and leg irons off Mr. Payton right now, or we'll do it for you."

He almost smirks as he looks down on the agent. "We have the keys."

Fontenot smirks back. "Yes, you do. Now do as I say or we'll relieve you of the keys and release Mr. Payton ourselves."

The idiot rests his hand on the butt of his service revolver, which proves to be about as dumb as it gets. Buck has squared off with the second deputy. As the tension escalates, I feel the first stirrings of fear. Poor Denzel, stuck in the middle of all this law enforcement bonhomie, looks terrified.

Fontenot glances at Bullethead and almost smiles, but it's anything but a pleasant expression. "Not that I need them to deal with a punk like you, but this building is full of armed FBI agents who would be happy to teach you some manners, jackass. Hand me those damned keys *now*!"

The deputy's eyes cut to his partner, who shrugs.

"The keys are Sheriff's Department property," Bullethead says with a malevolent glare at Fontenot.

"Then I suspect someone there showed you how to use them. You have about five seconds to get started, pal. Then I'll take them and do it myself."

I don't doubt for a second that she will, or that she'll succeed. Bullethead seems to come to the same conclusion. He unclips the keys from his utility belt and unshackles Denzel. Then he insolently tosses the restraints on a chair.

"Thank you," Fontenot says curtly as she looks at the cuffs. "I was going to suggest that you could wait in those chairs while we speak with Mr. Payton, but I'm tired of looking at you. Someone will escort you downstairs. You can wait outside."

"We will not—"

"Shut up," Fontenot snaps, then gestures to a couple of

wide-eyed young agents who have stopped to watch the show. "Please escort these men out of the building."

The Cook County good old boys are shell-shocked into silence. Bullethead recovers first. "We're not leaving without our prisoner."

Fontenot hands him a business card. "Have your boss call to register a complaint if he's so inclined."

"Oh, you'll hear from us."

Fontenot rolls her eyes, then shifts her gaze to the waiting agents. "Get them out of here. Get a number we can reach them at when it's time for them to come back to collect Mr. Payton." Then she turns her back on the deputies and waves us toward the interview room.

Buck collects the manacles and tosses them at Bullethead. "Take that shit out with you, boys. Enjoy the weather." He stands between the deputies and us as we follow Fontenot. I see them retreating with their escorts as I step inside.

Fontenot has a hand on Denzel's shoulder as she guides him to a chair. "Sorry about that."

"No problem, ma'am. Thanks for taking care of them."

She winks. "My pleasure."

I'm pretty sure it was. I enjoyed it as well. As I watch Denzel looking at Fontenot with unabashed admiration, it occurs to me that she may have taken advantage of the confrontation Bullethead started to position herself as Denzel's friend and guardian. Judging by the look of near reverence on Denzel's face, it was well played. She sinks the hook in deeper by dispatching Buck to fetch a Dr. Pepper and a bag of Cheetos from somewhere. Penelope and I are directed to help ourselves from a coffeepot in the corner.

Once we're all seated at the conference table, Fontenot meets Denzel's eyes as he stuffs a handful of Cheetos into his mouth. "Bet it's tough to get a good snack at Stroger, huh?"

He nods as he chews.

"Not even a Dr. Pepper?"

He swallows and grins. "Aunt Thelma sneaks stuff in when she visits."

Fontenot smiles. "Good for Aunt Thelma!"

"You should have mentioned it," Penelope tells Denzel. "I'm a pretty good smuggler myself. Next visit, okay?"

He nods.

I wonder how many more Stroger visits remain. The trial starts in five days.

Fontenot sits forward with her elbows on the table, folds her hands in front of herself, and levels her eyes on Denzel's. Game on. "Do you know what the FBI does, Denzel?"

"Sure. Me and Grams used to watch an old TV show about you folks."

Fontenot's smile is one of genuine delight. "You mean the really old one, *The F.B.I.*, with Efrem Zimbalist?"

"Yeah, that one. You watched it too?"

"Sure did. Loved it. My earliest FBI agent training."

"That's pretty cool."

"That's a really old show for you to have watched."

"Yeah, well, Grams was pretty old," he says with a wistful smile.

Fontenot allows Denzel a moment of reflection.

I should be taking notes. If anyone is ever going to get Denzel to talk about Spike, my money is on Calista Fontenot today. She has him eating out of her hand. A little glimmer of hope stirs in my cynic's soul, but I'd still want pretty long odds to place that bet.

"I'm working a case—an important case—that seems to intersect with yours," Fontenot eventually says. "I hope you might be willing to help me out."

"Sure," he replies. "What can I do?"

"We believe that the man you know as Spike is hurting a lot of people, Denzel. We'd like to stop him before more people are hurt."

A guarded look drops over Denzel's face. He doesn't respond, but he's still listening.

"We're sure that Darnel Wix has a connection to Spike. I think you know about it."

Denzel's eyes go wide as he realizes why he's here.

Fontenot gives him a sympathetic look. "The idea of talking about it scares you, doesn't it?"

He replies with a whispered, "Yes."

"As it should." She reaches out and touches his sleeve. "I know about the attack at the jail. I hear that you're doing well in recovery, working really hard at rehab. That's smart."

His eyes fill with gratitude. "Yeah, I'm doing pretty well."

Fontenot leans in and winks. "Therapists are monsters, aren't they?"

"Sure are," he answers with a grin. "Good folks, though."

"For monsters."

"Right."

She leans back and gives him a long look. "Given what happened at the jail, I'd be scared too. Spike has convinced you that you're a dead man if you tell anyone the truth, right?"

Denzel nods.

Fontenot eases forward just enough to reinforce the level of intimacy she's established. "Here's the thing, though, Denzel. Spike will keep coming after you, no matter how the trial turns out. He won't take the risk that you might decide to talk somewhere down the line."

Denzel swallows with a haunted look I've seen before.

"It's not just Spike you need to worry about," the agent continues. "He doesn't work alone. There are even worse people than him in his orbit. Even if Penelope and Tony win in court next week, Spike will still come for you. If you lose in court and go to prison, he'll get to you there. Do you understand?"

"I'm not safe anywhere."

"Not while Spike roams free. You'll be safer when he's behind bars."

"Maybe so, but the threat won't go away even then, will it?"

"Absolutely not, but if you can help me put Spike away, we may have a few ideas about how to keep you safe."

Denzel looks a little disillusioned. "But I have to help first."

Fontenot delivers a rueful *what can I say, I'm just a worker bee* shrug. "That's the deal."

I'm almost surprised that the agent doesn't finish with one of those smarmy "if it were up to me" mea culpas. Fontenot has been masterful this morning. To have her stoop that low now would be a big letdown.

"I don't think I can do it," Denzel replies after a lengthy pause.

Fontenot takes the reply in stride. "I can see that you're not sure, Denzel. Tell you what."

"What?"

"Think about it for a day or two. No hurry, no pressure. I'll be in touch. Okay?"

"Will I have to come back here?"

The question seems to catch Fontenot by surprise. Then she grins. "You mean, will you have to come back with the goons who brought you today?"

His lips curl into an answering grin as he nods.

She winks. "Nope. I can come visit you at Stroger. As a matter of fact, the FBI has a basement garage full of those big, shiny black Chevy Suburban SUVs you see on TV all the time. How would you like a ride back to the hospital in one of those?"

Denzel's eyes light up. "That would be cool!"

Fontenot's eyes flicker to us. "Anything else, Counselors?"

"No," we reply in unison.

The agent stands and smiles at Denzel. "Let's get you back to Stroger, young man."

"*You'll* drive me?"

"Darned right. In the biggest, baddest SUV we have in the garage!"

"Cool."

I can't help laughing at the look of astonished delight on the face of our client. Then he frowns. "What about the sheriff guys? Won't they be pissed off?"

Fontenot grins. "Who cares? They have their own wheels."

Penelope shoots me a look of concern as we get back into her car five minutes later. "Fun as that was, I can't help thinking the sheriff will take his revenge on Denzel."

That would be in character. Then again. "What will they do, Penelope? Throw him into jail on a trumped-up murder charge?"

"Ha ha, partner, but I'm not laughing. He's vulnerable as long as those thugs can get their hands on him."

"True."

48

I'm in a surly mood when Pat calls me on Saturday morning three days later. We're seventy-two hours closer to Denzel's trial—three days during which we've developed nothing new to help shore up his defense.

"I'll be by at eleven thirty, Valenti. Be ready to go for a walk."

"In this weather?" Dante's little bonfire had nothing on the heat in Chicago this weekend.

"Yes, in this weather. Wear your Speedo if you want."

"I don't own a Speedo."

"I know," she says with a chuckle. "We couldn't be friends if you did."

"Where are we walking to?"

"It's a surprise. Not far."

"The only surprise I want today is something to set Denzel Payton free."

"Don't be a killjoy, Valenti. A little distraction may be just what Dr. O'Toole prescribes for a grumpy old fart like you."

"A little distraction, huh?" My spirits, defying all laws of curmudgeonly gravity, lift just a teeny, tiny bit.

"See you in an hour," she says.

"Okay. Lunch?"

"Don't get greedy."

"Meany."

She laughs. "I gotta go. Remember, no Speedo!"

And with that, she disconnects, thus ensuring she has the final word. I've wandered over to the kitchen window while we've been talking and am mortified when I look out to see Mama's roses wilting in the heat. When did I last water them?

Get your head in the game, Valenti, I admonish myself as I head for my room, where I shower, shave, and toss on a pair of cargo shorts and a ratty old Marquette University T-shirt. Then it's off to the yard, dogs at my heels, their curiosity aroused at the sudden burst of activity.

After soaking the rose garden, I head to the front yard and begin watering everything there. Mama and Papa would be appalled to see the plants in such bad shape. I wave to Derek and Maggie Donahue, who seem to be checking me out every few minutes. Perhaps they're also aghast at the condition of our yard.

A yelp from Dolly grabs my attention. When I spin to see what she's worked up about, I see Pat's Hyundai stopped at the curb. Dolly's tail goes into hyperdrive when the driver's side door swings open and Pat steps out, dressed in her standard summer wear of cutoff jeans and a crop top.

She meets my gaze. "Is it safe to approach?"

I release the handle of the water gun to cut the flow. "The dogs don't bite."

"I'm not worried about the dogs, Valenti. Are you still Mr. Grumpy?"

"If you keep talking smack, I might be."

Dolly, trained to the nth degree as she is, remains on the porch, doing a little happy dance of greeting as Pat walks up the sidewalk. Deano, who knows Pat will reach the porch soon enough, waits patiently with a few tail wags.

Pat gives me a peck on the cheek, then glances at her watch. "You about done here?"

"We're in a hurry?"

"We're meeting someone."

"Who?"

"Get your rear in gear if you want to find out."

I give the flowerpot at the foot of the steps a final soak, then wind the hose up and turn off the tap." "Where to?"

"Just down to the park."

I notice that Derek and Maggie are watching again, unsuccessfully trying not to be obvious about it. What's with them today?

Pat grabs my arm and tugs until I fall into step beside her.

"Gotta water more in this heat," she says with a disapproving glance at the plants.

"I've been a little distracted with the trial and all."

"Put that out of your mind for a little while," she says as we approach Maggie and Derek's house. When I slow, Pat takes my hand and drags me along. I shrug at Derek and give Maggie a little wave as we pass by.

"What's this about, O'Toole?"

"Progress report," she replies as we reach the end of Liberty Street and enter Independence Park.

I immediately spot Rick's pickup in the parking lot. He's leaning his butt against the front grill, arms crossed as he waits for us with an enormous grin.

I walk up to him and shake hands. "Hey, Mountain Man. You're in on this little mystery?"

"I am." He unrolls a set of building plans and spreads them on the hood of the truck. "Got a little something to show you."

"What's this?"

"Drawings of a pool house."

I cut my eyes to Pat. "Whose idea is this?"

"One of Rick's architectural buddies drew them up gratis."

"Gives us a baseline to work from," Rick adds.

I study the plans. There's a fairly standard pool house, for sure, but there's another wing tacked on to one end. I point at it. "What's this?"

Pat flips to an end view of the plan. "A concession stand with a little kitchen, complete with a covered seating area."

"Big enough for two or three picnic tables," Rick says.

They've been busy. "It looks great, but I thought this was a future add-on. The plan is still to build the pool house first, right?"

"Fundraising is going well," Pat replies.

"It's just a plan," Rick adds. "Might be feasible sooner than we thought, though."

"How soon?"

"This season," Pat replies.

"Cool," I say, excited about the possibility of having this built before the snow flies. I look at Pat and smile. "You were right. This is a welcome diversion from moping."

"You should listen to me more often, Valenti." She takes my hand and leads me around the truck. "One more surprise."

I look ahead at a large gazebo. A familiar couple wait inside. I tear up as we approach the parents of my late girlfriend, Trish. What are they doing in Independence Park?

Mrs. Pangborne steps forward to take my shoulders and plant a kiss on my cheek. "Hello, Tony."

Her husband shakes my hand. "Hey, Tony."

I pull him close to deliver a bro hug and pat him on the back, barely trusting myself to speak. I release him while my eyes roam around the structure we're in. "What do we have here?"

Mrs. Pangborne leads me to the back wall, where a bronze plaque reads: *The Trish Pangborne Pavilion*. "Trish had some life insurance. We were the beneficiaries and, frankly, didn't know what to do with the money. Then we remembered you mentioning the park project here. Trish would have been a part of this."

"So now she is," Mr. Pangborne adds.

"It's beautiful," I manage to croak before I break down. They're exactly right: Trish would have enthusiastically pitched in.

Pat and Mrs. Pangborne reach for me together, then laugh and make it a group hug.

I pull myself together after a minute or two, wipe away the tears, and look from Mrs. Pangborne to her husband. "Thank you so much."

"You're welcome," the Pangbornes say in unison.

Mr. Pangborne nods at his wife. "She was a little concerned that you might not approve of this. Pat and I talked her through it."

Mrs. Pangborne lifts a shoulder and meets my eyes in a gesture she passed along to her daughter. "Well, you might not have liked it, or found it a painful reminder, and here it is, a done deal."

I rest a hand on her arm and smile. "I see where her compassion and consideration came from. I'll always remember Trish." Then I touch a finger to my heart. "Right here. Yes, it's still painful to do so, and I imagine it always will be, but there are so many happy memories as well. This is a wonderful tribute to her."

Tears well up in Mrs. Pangborne's eyes. She covers my hand with hers. "Thank you, Tony. I'm so happy you like it."

"I love it."

Pat steps over to an electrical box I hadn't noticed on the back wall of the gazebo. "We have enough power to plug in a ton of lights for Christmas and whatnot—even enough to set up for live music."

"This is great!" I turn back to the Pangbornes, who seem

to be pleased with my reaction. I hook a thumb at Pat. "How did you get mixed up with this character?"

Mrs. Pangborne laughs. "You told us you were working with Pat—Trish adored her, by the way. We know how busy you are with this trial, so we called Pat."

"Where did you get her number?"

Mr. Pangborne shoots me the exact same look Papa used to when I asked a truly moronic question. "We get the *Trib*."

"We deliver it complete with a telephone number," Pat adds with a smirk.

Duh.

I turn to Pat. "You're full of surprises today. Any more?"

She holds her thumb and index finger an inch apart. "Just a wee one."

"I can't imagine what. Is the pool open?"

"Next week."

Pat's final surprise is waiting at home. The Pangbornes walk back with us. Pat leads us around the side of the house and into the backyard, where Maggie and Derek await with a few neighbors. A pair of folding tables are heaped high with food: potato and pasta salad, sandwiches, cheese and cold cuts, fried chicken, and a couple of pies. So Maggie and Derek had me under surveillance earlier so they could swing by to set everything up as soon as I left with Pat.

"Wow!" I exclaim as Dolly runs over to greet us and check out Mr. and Mrs. Pangborne, who are new to her. You can guess where Deano is.

Mrs. Pangborne stops to fuss over Dolly for a moment, then walks over to Deano. "And you must be Deano. Trish loved you to bits!"

Deano shrugs her off impatiently and refocuses on the food table, paying particular attention to Maggie and Derek's kids. Children can always be counted on at mealtime.

Mrs. Pangborne looks over at me and smiles. "He certainly *is* food motivated."

"Just a little."

We fill our plates, snag beverages, and spend the next half hour enjoying the good company and delicious food. The kids and Dolly romp around the yard. I wink at Pat and mouth a *thank you.* She smiles. It's all good for a few minutes.

Then Chippy calls.

"Wix has disappeared," she announces without so much as a hello.

When several sets of eyes lock on me with concern, I make an effort at a nonchalant *it's nothing* wave as I hurry toward the house. "What do you mean, 'disappeared?'"

"I haven't seen him for three days," Chippy replies as I step inside the back door. "That's never happened before."

"When did you last see him?"

"Wednesday. I looked back through everything when I realized I hadn't seen him for awhile. He's never been gone more than a day, and that only happened once. I'm sorry it took me so long to notice, Mr. V. I have a lot going on."

It would have been nice to know this a day or even two days ago, but there's nothing for it now. "Nothing to apologize for. Just keep an eye out and let me know if he shows up."

"I will. This is bad, isn't it?"

"It's not good, but we'll roll with it."

"Oh, good. I was worried that I'd ruined everything."

I let it go. Worried doesn't been begin to describe how gutted I am. This seems to confirm that I was totally off base about Wix being Spike, and now Wix is gone. I call Max as soon as we end the call, give him the news, and ask if he has any ideas.

"Not a one. I'll think on it."

"Think hard," I say before signing off.

My next call is to Jake Plummer.

"Hmm," he murmurs in response to the news.

"We need him, Jake. He's been subpoenaed."

"I heard that. Can I ask why?"

Jake may be a friend, but he's still working the wrong side of this case. "Sorry, but no."

He chuckles. "Worth asking. You never know. Anyway, we'll keep an eye out for him."

I thank him and hang up. The exchange is a sharp reminder of the need to keep my guard up around everyone —particularly people like Jake and Calista Fontenot. That may sound ruthless, I suppose, but I wouldn't be above using anything one of them told me if it would help my client.

My final call is to Penelope, who tries and fails to find a positive spin to put on the news.

"I guess it doesn't matter," I finally say. "The subpoena was essentially a cudgel to get Denzel to talk. Hell I thought Wix *was* Spike. Guess not."

"We don't that for sure, Tony."

I'm thoroughly dejected. I share a disturbing thought with Penelope. "Did I just get Darnel Wix killed by subpoenaing him? Maybe Spike silenced him before he could testify."

The line is quiet for a long moment. "Don't beat yourself up about it, Tony. Wix probably just took a runner."

"I hope that's it."

49

Denzel's trial starts in the morning. I should probably be in bed. Instead, I'm sitting on the back patio with a glass of bourbon in hand and a dog on either side, staring up at the moonless sky. I was hoping the booze would make me sleepy. It's not working; I'm too amped up about getting started tomorrow. Not that I like our chances. Fontenot was wrong about a window opening. Di is dead. Wix is gone. If I was right about him being Spike, that door is closed. If I was wrong, Spike has undoubtedly done away with him. Denzel's only hope—and it's a slender one indeed—is that Penelope and I can do some truly inspired lawyering to foster doubt in the mind of at least one juror. If so, it will probably come from the prosecution making an error that we can pounce on and exploit. It's not much of a trial strategy, but it's what we have.

It's a beautiful evening. The dogs are restless, probably taking their cue from me, so I decide to burn off some of our restless energy by taking them for a walk. I down the last of the bourbon and head inside with Deano and Dolly at my heels. After rinsing the glass and setting it in the sink, I pull on a windbreaker. We're out the front door within a minute.

Independence Park is dark under a star-filled sky. The

Trish Pangborne Pavilion sits quietly in the night. Seeing it gives my spirits a needed lift. We go inside and sit quietly for several minutes as my mind ping-pongs between memories of Trish, thoughts of Pat, and worry about what tomorrow will bring. Deano and Dolly nose around, reveling in the smell of new wood and whatever scents animals have left behind.

It's time to move on. We set out on the walking path that circles the park. We've gone about a hundred yards when a figure walks out of the woods ahead of us. Judging by the build and gait, I peg the person for a teenage boy, someone about Denzel's age and size. I look for a companion; the stand of trees he emerged from is a popular makeout spot. *Always has been,* I think with a smile. No fun for this guy tonight, though. He's alone. Maybe there's a bottle tucked in the waistband of his jeans. Or maybe he's a doper. I wonder if I should mention it to Jake, then give my head a shake. Hypocrite. Whatever the kid is up to isn't anything we didn't do back in the day. I turn my attention back to the path and continue our walk.

Dolly uncharacteristically tugs at the end of her leash, straining in the direction of the kid, who is headed straight for us. Maybe something is wrong and he needs help. I slow to a stop and wait. The first hint that all is not well is the dogs going on point.

"Yo, Valenti," a young voice calls out when the kid is within twenty feet of us. Something about the voice is familiar.

A deep rumbling stirs in Deano's chest. Dolly has fallen deathly silent. We're in pretty much the exact same spot and it's about the same time that I was accosted here several weeks ago. Surely it's not happening again?

"Y'all keep them fuckin' things right where they are." The kid has a gun in his hand. Great.

I transfer Dolly's leash to my left hand so that my right

hand is free. My Glock is in a shoulder holster beneath my left armpit, hidden beneath my windbreaker. The kid looks around nervously. I imagine he's scoping things out, making sure there are no witnesses to whatever he has planned. I slip the Glock out of its holster and jam it into the waistband at the back of my jeans while his attention is elsewhere. He just missed the thing he should be most worried about.

He takes a few steps closer. "Didja hear me, man?"

"I heard you. What do you want?"

"You gonna tell me what the cops be having on Mr. Wix."

So this is one of Wix's little soldiers. "Wix is gone, kid. You might ask your pal Spike where he is."

The kid takes a step closer, waving his gun in my direction. "Don't fuck wit me, asshole!"

Whoever sent this kid is a cold SOB. "Spike sent you here all by yourself?"

The kid holds the gun out for me to see and snorts. "This be all I need to deal wit you, cracker."

Good to know. It's just the kid and me. Let's see if I can rattle him. "So the answer is yes—he sent you by yourself."

"Nah, my candy-ass homey split. He be like a scared little shit."

"Maybe like a *smart* little shit."

"What you say?"

"I don't repeat myself to punks with guns."

He takes another step closer as his eyes dart around. Good. I'm getting under his skin. He's getting nervous. Hopefully that doesn't mean he's about to pull the trigger. Not yet anyway. I don't think I'm meant to walk out of Independence Park tonight, but he wants something from me first. I'll stall for time and hope to get the drop on him.

"You call me dumb?"

"No," I lie. "Where's Wix?"

"I don't be here to answer questions, asshole." He points

the gun at my chest. "I be here to ask the questions. Now shut up and answer me!"

"Shut up *and* answer? How am I going to talk if I shut up?"

"You be pissin' me off, dude."

"Then we're both pissed off, kid."

I see teeth gleam within the folds of the hoodie. "Maybe so, but I got this." He lifts the gun high, as if he's going to pump a round into the sky.

I let the dog leashes fall from my fingers, shout, "*Fass,*" and lunge forward, reaching for the arm with the gun. Dolly, for whom the German word *fass* means attack, gets there first, leaping into the air and sinking her teeth into the kid's forearm. The kid screams and pulls the trigger, holding it tight as it pumps a stream of bullets into the sky. The idiot has the gun on full automatic, emptying the magazine in seconds. I wrap my hands around his arm above and below Dolly's grip and start to force his arm down after the magazine clicks on empty. The kid manages to twist away and break my grip, but Dolly hangs on.

"Fuck!" he screams in anguish as I wrap my arm around his neck. Then he's pounding on my stomach with his free hand. The kid is surprisingly strong—probably juiced on drugs as well as adrenaline.

A deep menacing growl announces Deano's late arrival to the party. All eighty pounds of him slams into the kid's chest, rocking him backward. Dolly gets her feet on the grass and tries to pull him the rest of the way down. I pile on, slamming him into the ground with a sickening crack of bone. The gun falls out of his hand as he screeches in pain. I toss it aside, then climb on top and pin him with my knees on his shoulders and my butt on his hips. He tries to buck me off. Not happening. He may be amped up, but he isn't going anywhere. I'm six five and outweigh him by a hundred pounds or thereabouts.

I rip the hoodie away from his face and stare at him in shock. It's the kid from Wix's front porch, the one the cops are looking for in the shooting at Brittany's school.

"Fuckin' hurts," he mutters with spittle flying from his lips.

"Who sent you here?"

"My arm," the kid groans. Dolly still has it in a death grip. It's cocked at an awkward angle just above her grip.

"That looks like it hurts," I say without an ounce of compassion.

"Get the fuckin' dog off," he pleads.

"Who sent you here? Wix?"

"Don't know where Mr. Wix be."

I'm tempted to pull the Glock out of my waistband. A gun barrel up the nostrils might loosen his tongue. The kid's eyes grow wider when Deano leans closer, his chest rumbling like a massive piece of machinery. I grab the kid's chin and give it a harsh shake "Who?"

"The dogs, man."

"Talk first."

"Guy Mr. Wix does work for. Russian dude, I think. Don't know his name."

Now I know who the target of the FBI's investigation is. I glare down a moment longer, then glance at Dolly. Her eyes are on mine. Her jowls glisten with blood. I reluctantly give her the command to stand down. She releases the arm but stays right beside me, watching the kid like a hawk. The comment about a Russian dude has solved the mystery of what Fontenot is up to, but I have another question, one that strikes close to home. "The girls at the school. Why did you kill them?"

He almost manages a smile. "Mistake. Supposed to be your bitch girl."

I fold my fists into my armpits to keep from pummeling the little son of a bitch.

His grin is fixed in place. "No worries, dude. We get her next time."

My Glock is in my hand without conscious thought. The punk's eyes widen in terror as I set the nuzzle into the hollow between his eyes, then lean into it. "There won't be a next time, you little piece of shit."

I can eliminate this threat to Brittany right now and deliver justice for killing her friends. The Glock's trigger needs very little pressure to fire a round. So little stands between this kid and oblivion, and I'm pumped full of adrenaline and hate.

"Mister," the kid whines.

"You were playing soldier the first time we met. Remember what I told you?"

His eyes move. Maybe a yes, maybe a no. Whatever.

"I told you that I know how to use this gun, and that I've used it." I press the gun even harder into his face and hold it there for several seconds. He's crying. "You wouldn't be the first person I killed."

But he would be my first execution.

His eyes are wide, pleading. Tears stream across his cheeks and into his ears.

I tuck the Glock back into my waistband. "You're not worth it." I'm pulling out my cell phone to call 911 when a voice I recognize cuts through the night.

"Police! Freeze!"

Footsteps pound toward us. The heavy breathing of a man exerting himself follows.

"It's me, Derek," I call out. "Tony Valenti. Everything's under control."

Derek Donahue is suddenly standing over us, flashlight in hand. He looks down in disbelief. "What's going on, Tony?"

"Someone picked the wrong guy to screw with tonight."

"Who is he? What happened?"

"Someone sent him to take me out." I point to where his

weapon sits in the grass several feet away. "That's his gun there."

Derek shines the light over it, then squats and looks at the kid's broken, bloody arm. "Jesus."

"Dolly still knows her stuff," I say with a tight smile.

Derek nods at the phone in my hand. "You calling 911?"

"I was about to."

He waves that off and pulls out his own phone, slipping a pistol I hadn't noticed into a shoulder holster. He scrolls for a second, then hits a number. "Constable Donahue here. I'm ten-twenty-three on the scene of the shots-fired report at Independence Park. The scene is secure. No GSW, but dispatch an ambulance for a severe dog bite and a broken arm. The wounded individual is the suspect in an armed assault."

He pauses while whoever is on the other end of the call talks. "Copy that. Ten-four to the request for backup. A single unit is good."

Derek puts the phone in his pocket. He leans over the kid and shines the flashlight into his face. Wix's little enforcer screws his eyes shut. Derek hovers a finger over the angry red indentation in the skin between the kid's eyes, then turns a questioning look on me. He knows what made the impression.

"Recognize the little bastard?" I ask coldly.

Derek gives the kid a longer look. "Should I?"

"He killed the wrong girls when he tried to murder my daughter last week."

50

I spent hours with the cops last night before I was finally allowed to go to bed. I slept little, and that fitfully. I'm physically and emotionally exhausted, mortified at the knowledge that someone tried to kill my daughter. How close I came to executing that kid haunts me; it could have gone either way. Yes, he threatened to kill my daughter—had even tried to, so there was an element of protective-father at play—but it bothers me that I wanted so badly to end a life, a life I suspect isn't all that different from the one lived by the kid we're here to defend this morning. Perhaps we're all a little more instinctually primitive than we'd like to believe. Thoughts for another day. We have work to do.

If I've ever felt less optimistic and more emotionally wrung out on the opening day of a trial, I don't recall it. Penelope and I spent much of yesterday at the office preparing for this morning. It felt like an exercise in futility. How do you prepare a compelling opening statement when you have nothing much in the way of evidence to preview? It appears as if state's attorney Timothy Walker is finally going to halt his losing streak against me in court. Sure, we have a few arrows in our quiver—Mary Ann Higgins to hopefully cast at least a little doubt on the DNA evidence, Oleg Volkov to raise issues about the fingerprint evidence, Rana Asadi's revelations about jailhouse snitch Jose Hernandez that will allow us to throw a little shade on him. If we grow desperate, we'll put Denzel on the witness stand. Having a defendant testify is generally the last thing a defense team wants to do, but desperate circumstances sometimes require desperate measures. I haven't said a word about my little dust-up last night. Penelope needs to focus on the trial, not be freaked out about my adventures. I also need to set that aside; the cops have the kid in custody. That's good enough for now. I'll speak with Derek and Jake for an update after court adjourns for the day.

Chippy and Max are doing all they can to locate Wix, but it's as if an alien spaceship swooped down and whisked him away. No activity on his credit cards or bank accounts, crickets on social media—Chippy says he hasn't logged into a single account, including email. It's out of character and weakens my belief that he's Spike. If he is, why go dark? I suspect I was wrong, which means we have Spike to thank for Wix's disappearance.

There's a sparse collection of interested parties in the bland, institutional courtroom. None of Harry Hood's relatives are here, and only Thelma Payton is sitting in the seats behind the defense table to support Denzel. A handful of courtroom hangers on dot the back row of seats. A few more will likely wander in when the action picks up after lunch. Judge Wilke has made it known that he wants this trial over with in a hurry, starting by selecting and seating our jury by noon.

The prosecutors at the table across the aisle to our left are a study in contrasts. Judy Edwards appears strangely subdued, as if maybe her heart isn't fully in the battle ahead. D. W. Seaver is bouncing a knee and tapping a pen on the edge of their table, which is the one nearest the jury box.

Dickweed is apparently raring to go, a little bantamweight boxer chomping at the bit to be unleashed on his opponent. Edwards finally plucks the pen from his fingers and sets it down. Good thing—Penelope looked about ready to do the same thing. Me as well, though I would have stuck the pen somewhere else.

I lean my head close to Penelope's. "Maybe he needs a dose of Ritalin?"

She laughs softly as the back door to the courtroom opens. We turn as a bailiff marches a group of people in and steers them into the seats behind the prosecutors. This is the initial batch of our prospective jury pool. Curious as I am to take their measure, I avoid an overt display of curiosity, lest I appear overly eager to ingratiate myself with them—regardless of how desperate I may be to do just that. My partner can't resist taking a longer look, which probably isn't a bad thing. Penelope is about as wholesome and approachable as we lawyers get. She's dressed in a cream business suit—skirt and jacket—and brown pumps. Our Kansan looks like an earnest Midwesterner on her way to church. I smile as I catch a couple of prospective jurors making eye contact with her. They both smile. That's simply what folks do when they encounter Penelope. Jurors ought to love her. It's a little ray of hope, anyway.

At five minutes to nine, we begin to get anxious because Denzel still hasn't arrived. The sheriff was supposed to deliver him to the courthouse no later than eight thirty so we could get him dressed. We also planned to give him a final pep talk about the decorum he needs to exhibit in front of the jury, no matter how difficult things get.

Penelope summons a bailiff for the third time. "Where's our client?"

The woman shrugs.

"Can't you call someone?"

"They're on the way," she replies. "Maybe they're stuck in

traffic. If the prisoner was in jail where he belongs, traffic wouldn't be an issue."

And there's our explanation. This is a little payback, compliments of the Cook County sheriff. Keep our guy in the hospital? Embarrass us in court? Let the FBI make fools of our people? Well, we'll show you!

When Judge Wilke enters the courtroom at nine o'clock sharp, he casts a disapproving eye at the empty seat at our table. Court is called to order, the preliminaries are dispensed with, and then Judy Edwards confirms her and Dickweed's appearance on behalf of the state. I stand and do the same for Penelope and me as counsel for Denzel.

"Where *is* the defendant?" Wilke asks crossly.

"The sheriff hasn't yet delivered him to court, Your Honor."

"It's your responsibility to ensure that the defense is prepared to proceed when court is scheduled, Mr. Valenti." The judge turns to our potential jurors. "The court apologizes for this inexcusable delay, ladies and gentlemen."

I bite down hard to keep from responding. We're thirty seconds into proceedings and Wilke is already casting aspersions on us.

When I don't respond, Penelope rises. "With all due respect, Your Honor, the Cook County sheriff is charged with transporting prisoners to court. They were to do so this morning no later than eight thirty. Perhaps one of their representatives would care to explain *their* inexcusable tardiness in doing so?"

Wilke glares down at her, then reluctantly turns to the head bailiff. "What seems to be the problem?"

"Traffic, we assume, Your Honor. Defense has made unusual arrangements for the defendant, such that he isn't kept in the jail next door, *as is customary* for criminal defendants."

And, of course, Wilke has ruled that no mention of the

attempted murder of Denzel or his injuries is to be made at any point in the trial, "lest it foster sympathy in the heart of a single juror." Heaven forbid.

Five minutes later, the bailiff informs the judge that Denzel has arrived.

I rise. "We need ten minutes to consult with our client and to permit him to change his clothing, Your Honor."

Wilke bats my request aside with an impatient flick of his hand. After a glance at the jury pool, he turns an aggrieved look on me. "We will not keep these good people waiting any longer. Your client can appear as he is." Then he turns to the bailiff. "Have the prisoner brought in."

Denzel is marched in wearing his orange prison overalls, complete with cuffs and leg irons all shackled together.

I'm on my feet almost before the smirking sheriff deputies get Denzel all the way into the courtroom. "This is highly improper, Your Honor!" I exclaim in a voice just this side of an angry bellow.

"Sit down, Counselor!" Wilke retorts.

"At least unshackle him," I say to the deputies, who ignore me.

I glance across at the prosecutors. Edwards appears to be appalled. Dickweed is grinning like the fool he is.

Edwards meets my eyes as she gets to her feet. "Your Honor, the state has no objection to the request by defense counsel to consult with Mr. Payton, and certainly not to having the defendant unshackled."

D. W. casts a look of disgust on his partner. The judge is also looking down on her with evident disapproval; she's made him look like the petty judicial tyrant he is. I note that the jurors appear to be confused, but a few nod in approval when Edwards finishes speaking and sits down. To my surprise, Calista Fontenot's FBI partner, Buck, slips into court and sits in the back row just inside the door.

"I'll permit the restraints to be removed from the prisoner," Wilke announces, as if this is a magnanimous gesture not generally afforded to defendants. He casts a stern gaze at Penelope and me while Denzel is unshackled. "The court will hold defense counsel responsible for the conduct of the prisoner while he is unrestrained in the courtroom."

"Is this guy for real?" I whisper to Penelope, who has had enough. She pops to her feet.

"With all due respect, Your Honor, Mr. Payton is the defendant in this matter, not 'the prisoner.' We object to the prejudicial characterization of him in this courtroom."

Wilke ignores her and locks eyes with me. "Mr. Valenti, do you understand what I just said?"

Oh, I understand just fine. He wants me to offer him cover by responding as if this crap is standard courtroom procedure. I stare back at the SOB for a beat while Denzel is finally deposited at our table in the seat beside Penelope. He appears shell-shocked. Understandably so.

"I understand," I reply to Wilke, further risking his wrath by failing to append Your Honor to my response. Screw him. He couldn't be treating us or the law with less respect. I'll show him equal deference.

Apparently feeling as if he's made good on his effort to fool the potential jurors into thinking all this is business as usual and that we've done something wrong, Wilke lets it go. He immediately launches into his spiel to the jury pool: they're here this morning on a sacred duty to the United States of America's jurisprudence; he'll keep things moving along so as not to "use up any more of your precious time than is absolutely necessary, so we can get you back to your families and loved ones." Blah, blah, blah. It's a pompous, nauseating performance. This is what we get for electing judges.

When Willke finally finishes, Thelma Payton eases up to the bar behind us. "Isn't there something you can do to have that repulsive little man removed from the case?"

"We wish," I mutter.

Penelope frowns. "I'm afraid we're stuck with him."

"But this won't be a fair trial with him on the bench," Thelma protests. She shoots a poisonous scowl at the judge.

"Welcome to American justice," I mutter. "This is our justice system in the twenty-first century."

The first prospective juror was seated in the jury box while we were griping. The circus continues, with Judy Edwards and me taking up arms for the next three hours of largely pointless questions, questionable answers, and the games lawyers play in an effort to seat the jurors they think will be most receptive to their side's version of events. Does it matter? A boatload of money is spent on jury consultants every year, people who claim to possess the secret sauce for selecting the "right" jurors for clients willing to pony up tens of thousands of dollars for their services. I have my doubts that they're any more effective than a gaggle of kids might be at playing pin the tail on the donkey with the jury pool.

When Wilke calls the lunch recess at five minutes past noon, we've seated a jury of twelve, plus alternates. They're a cross section of people with nothing better to do than to while away a few days in court for pocket money, a trio who seem to be upright citizens taking their civic responsibility seriously—one of whom seems to be taking it very seriously indeed—and an unfortunate few who were unable to convince Judge Wilke that they should be excused from serving due to various family and professional commitments. In my experience, this is about par for the course.

We think a couple of the jurors may be sympathetic to what passes for our defense strategy. We'll see; juries have an endless capacity to befuddle lawyers of all stripes. Suffice to say that *every* jury is a crapshoot.

We're finally able to get Denzel into the suit Thelma brought for him this morning. He tells us that the sheriff deputies who brought him to court dawdled at Stroger, and then took their sweet time on a very slow drive to court. It confirms my suspicions about why he was late. We can probably expect more of the same tomorrow, and the day after that, and every day of the trial. So, fully cognizant of the fool's errand I'm on, I call the Cook County sheriff's executive offices to voice a complaint. I beseech the disinterested man I finally reach to please, please deliver Denzel to court in a timely manner, "as a matter of fairness."

The flunky grunts a few times as I make my case, then informs me, "if your client was in jail where he belongs, we wouldn't have any difficulty getting him to court on time. As it stands, you're making this hard on everyone. We have limited resources."

"If Denzel had been kept in isolation as the court ordered, he wouldn't have been almost murdered in your jail," I shoot back. "If he's sent back, he probably won't be so lucky next time."

"I don't appreciate your tone."

Oh, boo-hoo. "I don't appreciate your Mickey Mouse schoolyard bullshit."

I'm seething when I hang up, annoyed with myself as much as I am with the clown on the other end of the line. We'll probably be lucky to see Denzel in court before noon tomorrow. Having wasted ten minutes of our valuable one-hour lunch recess, I hurry down to wolf down a sandwich with Penelope and Denzel. He seems surprisingly together—more together than I am, at any rate. Unfortunately, I'm the one who is going to get up in front of the jury to deliver our opening statement sometime over the next hour or two.

A couple of jurors seem to be surprised to see Denzel cleaned up when court resumes. I'm pleased with how he looks—exactly fifteen years old and about as nonthreatening as can be. Which image of him will jurors carry with them when it comes time to deliberate—this morning's manacled menace to society, or the composed, clean-cut young man sitting before them this afternoon? I glance back to make eye contact with Thelma Payton before Judge Wilke returns and see Calista Fontenot sitting in the seat nearest the door that Buck occupied this morning. Why?

A bailiff calls court to order. "The Right Honorable Judge Mealy-Mouth Wilke is on the bench."

I may have been projecting a little: the bailiff probably didn't say anything about Wilke being mealy-mouthed, even if he is. At any rate, everyone settles into place.

Wilke looks down at Judy Edwards. "Are the people prepared to deliver their opening statement?"

To our surprise, D. W. Seaver stands. "The people are ready, Your Honor."

My eyes drop from Dickweed to Edwards, whose downcast eyes are fixed on the table in front of her. I imagine she's miffed and/or angry to have been pushed aside so that her second chair can deliver what may be the most critical element of the prosecution case. The kid must really be connected.

He begins with a beneficent smile for the jury. "Good afternoon, ladies and gentlemen. Let me begin by thanking you for being here. There is no more sacred duty than to participate in the administration of justice on behalf of your fellow citizens in this great state and country of ours."

Puh-lease.

"We're here today to avenge the senseless death of Harry Hood, a down-on-his-luck US Army veteran who was wounded in combat while serving in Iraq. On the evening of October twentieth last year, Harry was at home in his tent." Seaver pauses to level an accusing finger at Denzel. "Then this man arrived out of the darkness to beat Harry to death with a baseball bat."

Dickweed pauses, allowing that accusation to hang in the air while he walks back to the prosecution table. He makes a show of consulting his notes while the jury considers the horror of Harry being beaten to death with a baseball bat. I imagine they're probably wondering why. Seaver waits a moment longer, priming their curiosity before he answers the question.

"The defendant bludgeoned Harry to death so he could steal a few electronic trinkets, a little marijuana and a few hundred dollars Harry's recently deceased grandmother bequeathed him."

Seaver pauses to shake his head in bewilderment, then thrusts that accusing finger back at Denzel. "But that wasn't enough. No, this… this animal then stole the clothes off the still-warm back of the man he had just murdered. He even took the shoes off Harry's feet!"

Dickweed screws his face into a mask of pain at the very thought of such evil. He's correct, of course. Only a monster would do such a thing. The problem, of course, is that the monster who actually did those things isn't in the courtroom with us.

"But, as criminals tend to do, the defendant left a trail of evidence behind, a trail that led the police directly to him," Seaver continues. "The cash found in his pocket when he was arrested had Harry Hood's fingerprints all over it. Denzel Payton's fingerprints were found on the handle of the baseball bat that was used to crush Harry's skull. The defendant left his DNA in the tent when he left Harry to die."

Another pause while Seaver recovers from the horror of his story. When he speaks again, his voice is earnest. "That's right, ladies and gentlemen, the defendant's DNA was found in the tent. Now, we can expect the defense lawyers to make spurious claims to try to confuse you about the DNA evidence, but we all know the truth, don't we? DNA doesn't lie, ladies and gentlemen. The DNA in this case points to Denzel Payton, and *only* to him."

Seaver pauses for a sip of water, then strolls over to stand in front of the jury box.

"We will show you forensic evidence proving that the defendant committed this heinous crime. You'll also hear from a witness to whom the defendant bragged about this crime. *Bragged,* ladies and gentlemen! The evidence we present will prove that this defendant is guilty, with malice aforethought, of mercilessly beating to death a defenseless, disabled veteran of our military. He did so for no other reason than to steal Harry's meager belongings. For this contemptible crime, we will ask you to mete out the justice this despicable man deserves."

Dickweed shoots a final contemptuous glance at Denzel before he tugs down his shirt-sleeve cuffs, as if he's just delivered a final verdict of guilty. Then he sits down.

The people in the courtroom—including a distressing number of jurors—seem to let out a collective sigh of disgust as their eyes settle on Denzel. I glance over at Seaver, who seems pleased with himself—as he should be. The little SOB was good. Very good. If the jury were asked to render a verdict right now, Denzel would be going down. No question about it. This is a moment when a defense attorney truly has to shine, because immediately after my ten minutes are over with, the prosecution will come right back with the evidence of guilt Seaver just promised to deliver. Unless I can persuade the jurors that there is a credible alternate story and deliver evidence to support it, the case is already over.

Unfortunately, I don't have anything much to offer. Sure, we can tell them about Spike, but we can't produce a scintilla of evidence to prove he even exists. Denzel seems to sense that we're already in trouble as he turns his head to give me a long, searching look. I push my seat back and shoot him a look that I hope conveys confidence that we're neither surprised nor overly concerned by Dickweed's opening statement.

I begin by thanking the jury for their service without pronouncing them all saints and soldiers in the cause of American jurisprudence. Who laps that crap up, anyway? Then I stroll over to stand in front of the jury box, making a point to meet every set of eyes. "Mr. Seaver just delivered a powerful opening statement, which is his job. Of course, he's only offered you one side of the case. I have no doubt that you will listen to *all* the evidence in this case, ladies and gentlemen, some of which you won't see until we present our case after the prosecution rests its case. I ask that you reserve judgment on the veracity of his insinuations until we have the opportunity to argue our case."

Insinuation is a great word. Dropped into the conversation here, it effectively suggests that Seaver is up to something underhanded to trick the jury, a suggestion they won't like at all.

"If you keep an open mind, you'll come to understand the weakness of the prosecution's claims against Denzel. We will explain why so much of the state's so-called irrefutable evidence is anything *but* conclusive."

Seaver stands. "Objection, Your Honor!"

The moment startles those of us familiar with courtroom decorum and tradition. It's exceedingly rare for an attorney to make an objection during an opening statement.

"Grounds?" Wilke asks.

"Argumentative, Your Honor."

"Sustained."

I'm shocked. While it's technically correct that an opening statement isn't intended to be a time for attorneys to argue their case—that's why closings are called arguments, after all—the reality is that it's done all the time. Seaver just finished inching into argument several times during his opening.

Well, so be it. I'll toe the line. "There is an alternative theory about who really murdered Harry Hood, ladies and gentlemen," I begin.

"Hold it right there!" Wilke says. He crooks a finger at me to approach the bench.

What the hell is he up to? I wonder as I walk over with Seaver hot on my heels. Penelope and Judy Edwards are right behind him.

Wilke locks eyes with me. "Sounds to me as if you're about to slip in something about your Lennstrom woman, Counselor."

I stare back in disbelief. Wilke has ruled Di off limits. He won't allow anything she said to be introduced, not even what she told Toe and me. "As a party to this lawsuit, Mr. Valenti, you may not testify, which renders Mr. Toe's prospective testimony hearsay." And that was that. The ruling still sticks in my craw, but I had no intention of going there. My temper frays a little more every second that Wilke sits and stares down on me.

"Perhaps we should recess so you can preview my statement, Your Honor? Then you can let me know what I can and cannot say in defense of my client without the jury present to draw inferences from this circus?"

Wilke's eyes narrow and his cheeks flush. "That's going to cost you a thousand dollars and two nights in jail. Mr. Valenti."

I say nothing.

"You are *not* to mention Miss Lennstrom again."

"*Again?*" I shoot back in disbelief. "Her name never passed my lips, and I had no intention of mentioning her. Perhaps you're hearing things?"

His eyes pop wide and his breathing quickens. Good. Maybe the sanctimonious little bastard is working himself up to a heart attack. "Two thousand dollars and four nights in jail, Counselor!"

Penelope tugs my sleeve before I can explode. I turn and meet her eyes, which convey an unmistakable plea to back off.

"Thank you, Your Honor," I mutter with every ounce of

contempt I can muster. "May I continue my opening statement?"

"If you think you can do so without breaking any more rules, get on with it. We don't have all day."

He's baiting me. Why? After taking a minute for a drink of water while I struggle to rein in my temper, I stroll back to stand in front of the jury. "We will present a highly regarded expert who will explain that the DNA evidence does not point directly to Denzel."

Seaver is back on his feet, looking thoroughly scandalized. "Objection, Your Honor! Mr. Valenti is testifying on behalf of a witness."

The hell I am. I'm foreshadowing her testimony, just as Seaver did with his jailhouse snitch.

"Sustained," Wilke snaps impatiently. "I will not tolerate any more shenanigans, Mr. Valenti!"

I can sense the jury's skepticism about me. Unbelievable. Wilkes has surely already given us grounds for an appeal? I decide to cut my losses before the tag team of Wilke and Seaver succeeds in making me look any more underhanded. Seaver turns in his seat just enough to present his back to the jury while he shoots a savvy smirk at me as I walk back to our table. I intend to have a quick word with Penelope to ensure that she's on board with my decision. When I lean in to ask, my eyes stray to the gallery, where Buck has joined Fontenot. Four other agents—what is it about the feds that makes them so readily identifiable?—stand just inside the doors.

"Time to stop the bleeding, partner," I whisper to Penelope.

She nods reluctantly.

"I need a good closing sentence. Any ideas?"

Her blank expression is answer enough.

I'm searching for the right words to wind down with, words that suggest a confidence I don't feel, when I'm startled to hear the latch leading through the bar click open. I spin around to see Agent Fontenot step through the open gate.

She holds up her badge as she looks up at the bench. "Agent Fontenot, FBI, Your Honor. If I may have a moment to approach the bench?"

"This is highly improper, Agent Fontenot," Wilke says curtly. "As you can see, we're attempting to hold a murder trial here. If you wish to speak with me, make an appointment through my office."

Fontenot's eyes and voice turn steely at the summary dismissal. "We're here to carry out a directive of the Federal District Court, Judge, and we intend to do so. I'm offering you the courtesy of an explanation. Now may I approach to explain?"

Penelope and I exchange a look.

Wilke is incensed, but because Fontenot has cited federal jurisdiction, he'll be on the losing end of any power struggle he initiates. He emits a theatrical sigh and turns to the jury. "I'm sorry for the interruption, ladies and gentlemen. I'm going to have to ask you to step out for a few minutes while I deal with this."

"What's going on?" Penelope whispers.

I think I may know but can't say, so I shrug.

After the jury is escorted out, Wilke peers down at Fontenot and crooks a finger to summon her. "Let's get this out of the way. You as well," he says to we lawyers.

Fontenot shakes her head. "With all due respect, Your Honor, this isn't related to your trial. These lawyers have no standing in the matter." She holds up a sheaf of paperwork. "This is for your eyes only."

"Chambers," he snaps.

"No need, Your Honor. If you'll read these papers, we can be on our way in a couple of minutes."

Wilke's eyes narrow at this affront to his authority. How

dare a mere FBI agent refuse a direct order from the bench? "If it will get rid of you that quickly, approach."

Fontenot walks to the bench and hands the paperwork to the judge. His face reddens in anger as he reads. Then he slams the papers down and summons Fontenot closer. Even so, we can hear his furious whisper.

"What is the meaning of this? You expect this court to grant a continuance to accommodate your business?"

"A federal judge expects you to, Your Honor."

Fontenot clearly has the upper hand, and that isn't sitting well with the little judge. That, in and of itself, is enough to make the drama playing out at the bench enjoyable.

After a final hurried exchange, Fontenot turns and nods at the other agents, then walks straight to the defense table. There's the mere hint of a smile on her face when she meets my eyes. She leans close to our client. "You're coming with us, Denzel."

"Why?" Penelope asks.

"The FBI is taking Denzel into protective custody as a material witness in the matter of a federal investigation."

"Like we talked about?" Denzel asks Fontenot.

"That's right," she replies. "You'll be safe with us."

"What are you talking about?" Penelope asks furiously "You can't speak with our client out of our presence!"

Fontenot leans closer to me. "I'll call you in a little while. Then we can all sit down to talk."

"With Denzel?" Penelope asks sharply.

"With Denzel," Fontenot replies. And with that, she and the other agents form a protective ring around Denzel and march out of the courtroom.

Wilke calls a fifteen-minute recess, then storms off to his chambers.

"What just happened?" Thelma Payton asks. "Why did the FBI arrest Denzel?"

"They didn't," I reply. "He's in protective custody."

"What does that mean?"

"Ultimately, I don't know, but he's definitely safe as long as the FBI has him."

Penelope eyes me suspiciously. "He's going to testify for them, isn't he?"

I'm going to pay for not letting her in on my and Fontenot's little secret. We arrive at the FBI field office two hours later and are shown into a conference room where Fontenot waits alone with Denzel. She comes around the table to shake hands—first with me and then with Penelope, whose hand she hangs onto a little longer.

"First off, Penelope, I swore Tony to secrecy on everything to do with this, so don't be angry with him for not tipping you off to what was coming."

Penelope's eyes cut to mine. Yup, there's going to be hell to pay over this.

"Not that I knew exactly what was going to happen," I say in my own defense.

"That's true." Fontenot says. She waves us into chairs, sits, and folds her hands in front of herself. "The FBI took Darnel Wix into custody a few days ago on suspicion of murdering Harry Hood."

Now we know where Wix disappeared to last week. I make a mental note to let Chippy know, then wonder what else Fontenot hasn't told me.

Penelope's eyes cut to mine as understanding dawns. "You guessed right about Wix being Spike, didn't you?"

"Seems I did."

"*He* killed Harry," Penelope adds.

I nod. "Which means Denzel was an eyewitness to the crime and can identify the killer, which allows the FBI to get involved with his protection."

"Mr. Valenti's instincts were right again," Fontenot says.

Penelope shakes her head in wonder and turns to Denzel. "Your own father was going to send you to jail for a crime he committed—heck, he was willing to kill you, Denzel. Yet you protected him?"

He nods sheepishly.

Penelope's brow furrows as she turns back to Fontenot. "Harry Hood's murder isn't a federal crime."

The agent shoots me a smile. "It is if the victim is a family member of a sitting congressperson."

"Only if the murder is somehow related to the congressperson's official duties," I counter. "I'm a little fuzzy on how you intend to argue that."

She grins. "Oh, it's a little thin, but we'll make it stick."

"How could you be sure enough to arrest Wix?" I ask Fontenot.

"Your DNA suggestion. We took a sample swipe when we picked him up last week, then subpoenaed a sample of the DNA found in Harry Hood's tent from Cedar Heights PD. We sent both to the FBI lab. Bingo."

"I'm impressed that you pulled it all together," Penelope tells Fontenot.

The agent hooks a thumb at me. "Your partner did most of it. He couldn't get the DNA tested, though. We could. End of story."

Penelope smiles at me. "So partner, you pulled another rabbit out of a hat."

"Keep this up and you'll become a legend in more than just your own mind," Fontenot adds with a wink.

"You didn't get involved in Harry Hood's case to help us out, Calista," I say. "There's more to the story, isn't there?"

"True. Saving Denzel is a nice bonus, though."

Penelope leans over to hug our client. "We did it, Denzel!"

"We may be getting a little ahead of ourselves," I say cautiously. "The murder charge against Denzel still stands"

Fontenot nods. "True."

"They can't possibly proceed!" Penelope protests.

Fontenot cuts her eyes to my partner. "You're probably right."

"Don't bet on it," I say. "Timothy Walker."

Matching eye rolls signal that Penelope and Fontenot have heard enough from me about Walker. Denzel shoots me a bemused glance after I'm silenced.

"I still don't understand how Denzel fits into your case," Penelope asks the agent.

"He's an eyewitness to Harry Hood's murder. The murder charge gives us leverage over Wix. We can use that in the case that first brought him to our attention."

"Where Wix is a bit player," I add. "You'll trade the murder charge for Wix's cooperation. Then you can go after the bigger fish you're gunning for."

Fontenot doesn't deny my speculation. In my books, that's confirmation.

"Wix will walk on Harry Hood's murder?" Penelope asks indignantly.

"No," Fontenot says. "He won't skate on it, but we may deal on sentencing if he'll cough up information about other matters of interest."

"That sucks," Denzel says, reminding us that he's still in the room.

Fontenot shrugs. "It's the way of the world, Denzel."

"The old *we have to break a few eggs to make an omelette* crap we hear about to explain away questionable government behavior," I mutter.

Fontenot looks guilty and uncomfortable. So she should.

Penelope glares at her. "And then you're going to abandon Denzel after you get what you want?"

"No, we won't," the agent says curtly, then looks at our client. "Right, Denzel?"

"I'm going into..." He looks to Fontenot. "What did you say the protection thing is called?"

"The Witness Protection Program."

I had only one concern when I first pitched this entire scenario idea to Fontenot last Tuesday. I voice it now. "How do you feel about leaving everything and everybody you know behind, Denzel?"

He shrugs. "Leaving what behind, Mr. Valenti?"

"Your Aunt Thelma, for one."

He frowns. "Yeah, there's that, but she's never been a big part of my life. I mean, I like her a lot and all, but I'm being offered a fresh start in life. I'll go to a new school and get a chance to make my way in the world without all the baggage I have here."

Penelope rests a hand on his arm. "There's a lot to be said for that, Denzel." Then my partner's eyes drift to Fontenot's. "I judged you harshly, Calista. I'm sorry."

The agent smiles and waves it aside. "If I had really been operating as callously as you thought, I would have deserved every word of that. Denzel's lucky to have a pair of advocates like you and Tony."

"Thank you," Penelope says.

Fontenot grins. "As for the murder charge against Denzel, even if Walker strings it along, there won't be a defendant. Walker will never know where he went."

I chuckle at the prospect of Walker flailing about, then settle my gaze on Denzel. "So a fresh start for you, sir. Might be just what the doctor ordered."

He looks me in the eye. "And I owe it all to you and Miss Brooks for believing in me."

I shake my head. "I think we all owe something to Agent Fontenot as well. Maybe I'm wrong—in fact, I hope I am—but I suspect an awful lot of FBI agents would have left you twisting in the wind after they'd wrung everything they needed out of you. Calista didn't, and I think we all owe her a big thank you for that."

She smiles at me. "That would be the same Agent Fontenot who wouldn't be involved in any of this if Tony hadn't put it all together and brought it to me. Speaking of which, have you ever considered a career in law enforcement? You'd make one hell of a detective."

I laugh. She doesn't.

Penelope scooches closer to me and wraps her hand possessively around my arm. "He already has a job, Agent Fontenot. We're going to keep him."

Dear Reader,

Thank you for spending a few hours reading *Scared Silent*, the fifth novel in the Tony Valenti Thriller series. I hope you enjoyed it.

If so, please take a moment to leave a review at your book retailer and—if you would be so kind—at BookBub **here**. Reviews are invaluable to authors, particularly those of us who publish independently. A brief line or two about why you enjoyed the book is sufficient. A final tip about reviews: Please be careful not to include spoilers that may detract from future readers' enjoyment. Thank you!

Do you wish to be among the first to hear about upcoming releases, giveaways, and contests? If so, please join my exclusive Reader's Club on my website at **neilturnerbooks.com**. Your email address will not be shared or used for any other purpose. I promise! While you're on the website, feel free to poke around a bit to learn a little more about the books.

My sincerest thanks again!

Take care, be well, and happy reading,

Neil

THE END

BOOK ONE - A HOUSE ON LIBERTY STREET

TONY VALENTI THRILLERS BOOK ONE

BUY IT HERE (click on cover)

When Tony Valenti's sixty-nine-year-old father inexplicably shoots a sheriff's deputy on their front porch, Tony is thrust into a life and death struggle to discover why his father shot a cop. He enlists the help of a public defender and a local newspaper reporter in a rush to unravel the truth about the night of the shooting, only to become a target himself. His initial bewilderment turns to rage and fuels a gritty determination to get to the bottom of what really happened—regardless of the risks. Can he save his father? The family home? Himself?

BOOK TWO - PLANE IN THE LAKE

BUY IT HERE (click on cover)

When the well-heeled owners of a crashed tour plane seek to pin the blame on the two-man team that does their maintenance, Tony is called to defend the outgunned partners. He's up against one of Chicago's preeminent law firms, a win-at-all-costs behemoth with resources that dwarf those of Tony's mom and pop firm. Only the truth can save his clients, yet Tony's search for facts is thwarted at every turn by adversaries who will stop at nothing to win. Suddenly, Tony is not only fighting to win a lawsuit… he's in a race to save the most precious people in his life.

BOOK THREE - A CASE OF BETRAYAL

TONY VALENTI THRILLERS BOOK THREE

BUY IT HERE (click on cover)

A woman is brutally slain and suspicion immediately falls upon her ex-husband. But should it? The suspect turns to Tony Valenti for help. The case is a bewildering maze with a mountain of contradictory evidence that points both to *and* away from Tony's client. What *is* the truth? Even Tony isn't sure of his client's innocence in a case where nothing is as it seems. Then a lethal terror from Tony's past surfaces to shake his faith in himself… and to threaten those dearest to him. Is Tony being pulled in too many directions to save anyone?

BOOK FOUR - A TIME FOR RECKONING

TONY VALENTI THRILLERS BOOK FOUR

BUY IT HERE! (Click on Image)

Tony Valenti and Penelope Brooks are enlisted to come to the aid of a young woman when her marriage turns sour in a remote corner of Wyoming. They don't practice law in Wyoming, but representing vulnerable clients battling impossible odds is what they do. They are quickly embroiled in a fight that may literally be to the death, with danger coming at Tony from several directions. Ill-equipped to face the battles he's forced to wage, he must rely on his guile and the help of unexpected allies to survive long enough to rescue his client… and himself.

FREE - LAST EXIT ON THE ROAD TO NOWHERE

FREE READER'S CLUB SERIES PREQUEL NOVELLA

CLICK COVER IMAGE TO CLAIM YOUR FREE COPY

Last Exit on the Road to Nowhere is a prequel novella about the high-stakes dramas at work and home that precipitated Tony Valenti's move to Cedar Heights. These are the events that propel Tony and Brittany into the opening chapter of *A House on Liberty Street,* and will continue to reverberate through Tony's world in the novels that follow. What will ultimately become of Tony's family? His career? His life? It all begins here. Become a Reader's Club member and find out!

ACKNOWLEDGMENTS

Thank you to the people who took time from their busy lives to read and comment on early drafts of *Scared Silent*. As always, you've helped make this a better book. A special shout out to Susan Turner—love you! Thanks also to Rachel Keith for editing and kudos to designer David Prendergast for another excellent cover. Thank you all. My gratitude also goes out to my fellow writers. In many ways big and small, your support helps me keep going. Credit is also due to the kind and generous folks who answer my many questions—including the dumb ones—about the many topics about which I'm not an expert. The errors, as always, are mine.

Most of all, I offer a heartfelt thank you to everyone who reads my novels. It's very gratifying to receive your comments, emails, and reviews. Knowing that you've enjoyed one or more of my books truly lifts me up. Thank you so very, very much for your continuing encouragement and support.

ABOUT THE AUTHOR

Neil discovered the thrill of losing himself in the pages of a book as a five- or six-year-old when Beatrix Potter and Thornton Burgess immersed him in the worlds of Jerry Muskrat, Peter Rabbit, and their furry friends. His mother and father had the good grace to indulge his excitement about being able to read *them* stories, which he thought was pretty darned cool. He's been reading and writing one thing or another ever since, but it was many years before the audacious idea of *writing a book* wormed its way into his head. He's lived throughout Canada, spent three years in Europe, and lived in Chicago and Arizona, somehow managing to squeeze a career in banking and finance into his travels. After doing an apprenticeship reading, reading, reading, taking courses, attending seminars and conferences, and churning out some truly atrocious manuscripts, After doing an apprenticeship reading, reading, reading, taking courses, attending seminars and conferences, and churning out some truly atrocious manuscripts, he began writing and stockpiling the Tony Valenti series of thrillers. The series will total four published novels by the end of 2021, plus a free prequel novella for members of my exclusive Reader's Club. There will be more titles to come in 2022 and beyond, probably at the rate of two or three per year . Stay tuned!

Neil lives in Ottawa, Ontario, Canada.